**The moon had risen and its
reflection shone upon the quiet water
that was just beneath them.**

"You know what Easterners call Texas?" Gabe asked.

"What?"

"The land of milk and honey."

Josie's gentle laugh rippled through the night air. "Do they know that it's necessary to milk the cows and gather the honey? It's a hard life out here."

Josie felt Gabe staring at her, deeply, intensely, and it was as if his eyes were burning into her.

"Would you ever leave here?"

"Where would I go?"

"You could always come with me."

He moved toward Josie, and she knew he was going to kiss her. She should get up and run back toward the square, or at least she should turn her head, but she didn't do either. She welcomed what was coming—her very first kiss.

His lips were as gentle as the breeze around them. He put his arms around her and drew her into an embrace, his mouth covering hers now with an urgency that Josie instinctively recognized as desire. . . .

ALSO BY SARA LUCK

Susanna's Choice

Available from Pocket Books

CLAIMING THE HEART

SARA LUCK

Pocket Books

New York London Toronto Sydney New Delhi

Pocket Books
A Division of Simon & Schuster, Inc.
1230 Avenue of the Americas
New York, NY 10020

This book is a work of fiction. Names, characters, places, and incidents either are products of the author's imagination or are used fictitiously. Any resemblance to actual events or locales or persons, living or dead, is entirely coincidental.

First Pocket Books paperback edition May 2012

POCKET and colophon are registered trademarks of Simon & Schuster, Inc.

For information about special discounts for bulk purchases, please contact Simon & Schuster Special Sales at 1-866-506-1949 or business@simonandschuster.com.

The Simon & Schuster Speakers Bureau can bring authors to your live event. For more information or to book an event contact the Simon & Schuster Speakers Bureau at 1-866-248-3049 or visit our website at www.simonspeakers.com.

Manufactured in the United States of America

10 9 8 7 6 5 4 3 2 1

ISBN 978-1-4516-5224-6
ISBN 978-1-4516-5225-3 (ebook)

CLAIMING THE HEART

PROLOGUE

St. Louis, Missouri—June 1851

Push, chile, push!" the midwife said.

Mary had never felt such pain, but with one final effort the baby was born. She fell back in total exhaustion, relieved that the pain was over.

She heard a cry; then, a moment later, a smiling black face beamed down at her.

"It's a little girl. Lord help us, you are nothin' but a baby yourself."

"I want to see her," Mary said.

"You wait, honey, till I clean the chile; then I'll put her in your arms."

A moment later the baby was handed to the young mother, and she hugged it to her.

"What are you goin' to name her?"

"I—I'm not going to give her a name."

"What? Why not?"

"Because I'm not going to keep her. Doaney, you haven't told Mama or Daddy, have you?"

"No, chile, you asked me to keep it a secret and I have. You ain't showed that much, and I've made clothes to cover it up. Now, what are you going to do with the baby?"

"I don't know. I just know I can't keep her. Oh, Doaney, help me. Please help me."

Doaney Waters reached down to brush away Mary's tears.

"Don't you worry, honey. I'll help you. But this chile is goin' to need milk, and we don't have a new mama except for you on all of White Haven."

"I'll come feed her. Mama thinks you're teaching me to sew. She won't think anything about it."

"You're not goin' to make milk till tomorrow, but the baby's got to start suckin' right now. You may as well get started."

Mary bared a breast and the baby instinctively took the nipple and started sucking.

"Oh, Doaney, oh, how I wish I could keep her."

One month later—July 14, 1851

"Honey, we can't be keepin' a white baby here in the slaves' quarters without gettin' found out. We're goin' to have to find some place for the baby to go."

"But where?"

"I know someone that will give the baby a good home. The only thing is, we can't let him know, 'cause if we do, then he'll find out who your mama and daddy are and that won't be good."

"Who is it?"

"His name is Henri Laclede. He owns the grocery store where I get the groceries for the house."

"Yes, I know Mr. Laclede. But, didn't Mrs. Laclede just die?"

"That's right."

"Then, he won't do. She's got to have a mama."

"She's got a mama, honey. An' that mama is you. Mr. Laclede, he is a good man. A real good man, and he will give the baby a good home. And there won't be anybody ever take your place as the baby's mama, even though the baby won't ever see you."

"Oh, Doaney, I can't let her go, I just can't."

"Then, we're goin' to have to tell your mama and daddy, 'cause, honey, the baby can't stay here. I wish she could, she's a beautiful baby and a good baby. But you know she can't stay here."

"I know. All right, when do we do it?"

"I heard Mr. Laclede say he was goin' to the bank at three o'clock today. We'll go down there and wait. When he goes inside, we'll put the baby in his carriage."

When Mary returned to Doaney's cabin, she was carrying a bag. She pulled something from it and showed it to Doaney. "I want to have the baby christened."

"That's your family christenin' dress."

"I know. But she's part of the family. At least for now."

"All right, we'll stop at the Holy Salvation Church and let the parson baptize her. It's a church for people like me, but it's the same Jesus and the same God."

"And when we leave her with Mr. Laclede, I want her to be in this dress."

"Honey, there's already been three generations christened in that dress. There will more chil'run born, and their mamas and daddies are goin' to want to use that dress."

"I know." Mary wiped the tears from her eyes. "But I want her to have something of me, something that will connect us always."

Two hours later, Doaney and Mary were standing in the shrubbery near the Boatman's Bank when they saw Henri Laclede drive up in his carriage. They watched as Henri tied off his team in the shade of some trees, then went into the bank.

"If you're goin' to do this, chile, now's the time," Doaney said, reaching for the baby.

Mary raised the baby to her lips and kissed her, then, blinded by tears, held her out toward Doaney. Doaney put the baby in a basket, then moved quickly over to Henri's carriage. Looking around to make certain that no one saw her, she kissed the baby, then placed the basket on the floor between the two seats.

Doaney went back to stand with Mary, and she put her arms around her and pulled her closer. They watched until Laclede and another man came out of the bank.

"Henri, it's good doing business with you. You always pay your notes as agreed. Any time you need anything, you just come see me."

"Thank you, Mr. Budd," Henri replied.

"Please, it's George, not Mr. Budd."

Henri chuckled. "Thank you, George."

With a final wave, George Budd went back into the bank, and Henri Laclede walked over to his carriage, where he untied his team, then started to climb in. That was when he saw a wicker basket on the floor between the two seats.

"Hello, what is this?" he asked as he looked inside.

He pulled a light blanket aside, then jerked back with a shock.

It was a baby!

"What? What are you doing here?"

Quickly, Henri looked around, hoping to see someone whom he could connect with the baby, but nobody was in sight.

The infant, who could not have been more than a couple of months old, was dressed in what looked to be an heirloom christening gown. It had delicate stitching across the chest that flowed into a long skirt banded by a five-inch lace hem at the bottom of the dress. The design of the lace seemed to be elaborate repeating crests of some sort.

Henri reached down to touch the tiny, outstretched hand, and the baby's lips curled in a smile.

"Who are you, little angel, and what are you doing in my carriage?"

That was when he saw the note. Opening it

quickly, he read it, hoping it would shed some light on this mystery.

> *Mr. Henri Laclede,*
> *I am leaving my baby with you because I know you are the kind of man who will take good care of her and give her a fine home. I wish I could raise her myself, but I cannot. Please do not try to find me. It will be better for the baby if she never learns who I am.*

Instead of shedding any light on the situation, the note just deepened the mystery. It did tell him, though, that this leaving of her in his carriage was not an accident.

"So," Henri said to the baby. "You are a little girl, huh? I don't know much about little girls, but you just coming into the world don't know much about being a little girl yet either, do you? I guess we'll just learn together."

After looking around one more time just to make certain nobody was lurking about, watching, Henri climbed into the driver's seat, then clucked at his team.

Mary watched them drive away as tears streamed down her cheeks. She turned toward Doaney, who wrapped her arms around the girl and pulled her into her ample bosom.

"Don't be ridiculous, Henri, you can't keep her," Henri's sister, Desiree Bellefontaine, said.

"Why not? You know that Bridgette and I always wanted a child, but it never happened. Bridgette is dead now, and this child has just dropped into my life. I don't believe it was an accident."

"Of course it wasn't an accident. The note says that the baby's mother had been watching you."

"I don't mean that. I mean, I don't think it was an accident that God led her to me."

"You have no business keeping this child, Henri."

"Give me one good reason why not."

"For one thing, you are forty-two years old. You aren't that young a man, certainly not young enough to just be starting a family, with no wife. How are you going to care for her? Have you thought of that?"

"What is there to taking care of a baby? Feed her, keep her warm in the winter, what else is there?"

"Well, for a start, how are you going to feed her?"

"I don't know yet."

"She's going to need someone who can be both a nanny and a wet nurse, and I think I know just the person. I'll make the arrangements."

"Desiree?"

"Yes?"

"Thank you for accepting this."

Desiree smiled at the baby, who returned her smile. "She is a pretty little thing. What is her name, do you know?"

"Of course I know her name. Today is Bastille Day."

"Bastille Day? What does that have to do with it?"

"It just gave me the idea, is all. Desiree Bellefontaine, meet your niece, Empress Josephine Laclede."

Ida Scott was an eighteen-year-old black slave whose baby had just died after having lived only two days. Desiree went to see her owner, and it was agreed that Henri would buy Ida to be the baby's wet nurse and nanny. Henri found out the name of the father of Ida's baby; he agreed to buy him also. When Willie Lane came to live with Henri, he gave both Ida and Willie their freedom, and they were married immediately. Willie was then hired to be Henri's carpenter and all-around handyman.

With the Lanes' help, Henri quickly settled into life as a family man and couldn't have loved Josephine more if he had been her father by blood.

ONE

Fort Worth, Texas

After the storm of the Civil War had passed, Henri saw opportunities in Texas. He sold out in St. Louis, and when Josie was sixteen years old, they and the Lanes, along with the Lanes' two-year-old son, Julius, moved to Fort Worth, where Henri started the Laclede Grocery and Dry Goods store. They had been in Fort Worth for five years when seven-year-old Julius, who was sweeping the boardwalk in front of the grocery store, looked up to see the stagecoach arriving.

Dropping his broom, Julius ran inside to give the news.

"Miss Josie, the stagecoach is comin' in! The horses are runnin' fast!"

Empress Josephine Laclede brushed aside an errant fall of blond hair and walked to the front of the store to look out onto the street. A cloud of dust assailed her nostrils.

"Dooley, why do you have to do this? We know you're coming," Josie said aloud to no one in particular. She stepped out of the store, watching the other shopkeepers up and down Main Street hurry to meet the stage.

Dooley Simmons liked to make a grand entry, so the coach rolled down the street with the six horses at a trot far more rapid than their normal rate on the open road. Dust flew from the horses' hooves and roiled up from the wheels, leaving a long haze hanging in the air behind it.

"Heyah! Heyah!" Dooley shouted to his team, snapping the reins. Children, black and white, ran down the street, keeping abreast of the coach, until it reached Andrew's Tavern. There, the coach stopped, but the dust did not, and the cloud rolled over it so that when the passengers, three men and two women, stepped down, dust was on their clothes, in their hair, and hanging on their eyebrows. The women were coughing.

"How was your trip, Dooley?" someone called up to the driver as he was setting the brake and tying off the reins.

"No problem, but I've got news," Dooley said as he threw down the mailbag to the postmaster.

"What news is that?"

"The railroad is a'comin' to Fort Worth."

"What?"

"I heard it with my own ears," Dooley said.

"There's some fellers from the Texas and Pacific that's on their way to Californey. They's scoutin' the route for the railroad, and I heard tell they's comin' to Fort Worth."

"You don't say. When do you think they'll get here?"

"I can't say for sure, but they'll be pullin' into Dallas more'n likely by the end of the week."

"The railroad is a'comin', the railroad is a'comin'!" several of the children began to shout.

As Josie looked toward the coach, she wondered what had caused all the excitement.

"Good morning, Josie," John Jennings said, touching the brim of his hat. "Do you know if Paddock is upstairs?"

Paddock was Buckley Paddock, publisher and editor of the *Fort Worth Democrat*, the town's only newspaper. Paddock's office was on the second floor over Laclede's grocery store.

"I'm sure he is, Mr. Jennings," Josie said. "I haven't seen him this morning, but I've heard him moving around up there. What's going on? What's all the excitement?"

"The most wonderful news you can imagine. The railroad is coming to town."

"The railroad?"

"Yes, ma'am, the Texas and Pacific. I'm sure you know that a lot of town folks have been trying to get this; now it looks like it's actually going to happen. You and your pa better get ready for a lot more business. This town is going to start growing like a weed."

Shreveport, Louisiana—July 1872

Gabriel Corrigan stood on the platform waiting for the incoming train that would bring Colonel Thomas Scott to Shreveport. Colonel Scott, his immediate superior, was coming to congratulate Gabe on a successful business endeavor that had brought the bankrupt Southern Pacific Railroad under the name of the Texas and Pacific Railway. Gabe had been in Shreveport for the past several weeks, enlisting the help of Loomis Galloway, a former Confederate general. Galloway had helped him find those bankers and investors who would relinquish their rights to the Southern Pacific.

Marthalee Galloway, the general's daughter, approached Gabe then.

"Captain Corrigan," she said in a soft Southern drawl, as she pinned a flower to the lapel of his jacket. "When you welcome Colonel Scott to Shreveport, Father"—in her sultry accent the word sounded like *fawthuh*—"wants you to inform the colonel that he stands ready to provide any help you might need in building your railroad."

"I'll tell him that, Marthalee."

He had met the general's daughter on the first day he arrived in Shreveport. With long red hair and green eyes, she was a lovely and effervescent woman. Gabe had never met anyone more vivacious, or more beautiful, and she had done much to make his stay in Shreveport pleasant.

But lately, he was beginning to have an uneasy feeling about their relationship. She seemed to be getting more and more possessive. If he had to describe it, he would say that it was cloying.

"Oh, Gabe, darling. Isn't it exciting? Standing on the platform of your very own railroad?"

"I'm afraid Colonel Scott may find a little fault with you assigning this railroad to me, when he is the one who paid the receivers one hundred and fifty thousand dollars of his own money."

"You're just being modest. We both know he wouldn't own this railroad if it had not been for you and my father." Marthalee took his arm and began clutching it to her chest, rubbing her barely covered breasts against it. With embarrassment, Gabe glanced toward General Galloway, who was just coming toward them.

"My boy, you've got to get used to these Southern belles. They'll sing your praises, even if you won't do it for yourself," General Galloway said, removing an unlit cigar from his mouth.

Then the oncoming train blew a whistle announcing its approach. Gabe disentangled himself from Marthalee and stepped toward the arriving train as it roared into the station, gushing steam and spilling glowing cinders from the firebox. The driver wheels were three-quarters as high as Gabe was tall, and the train was so heavy that it shook the very ground.

Shortly after it came to a stop and sat there wreathed in escaping steam, the passengers started detraining. A man stepped down to be greeted by a woman, apparently his wife, who ran across the platform to take him in her arms. An older couple stepped off the train and stood there for a moment as if confused over what they should do next. Then a striking gentleman, whom Gabe knew to be twenty years older than his own twenty-nine years, disembarked. Gabe smiled, for that was Colonel Thomas Scott.

"Welcome to Shreveport," Gabe said as he extended his hand to Colonel Scott.

"A job well done," Colonel Scott said, shaking Gabe's hand and clasping his shoulder. "And who, pray tell, is this beautiful lady?"

"You, of course, know General Galloway," Gabe said, indicating the general. "This is Miss Galloway. Marthalee, this is Colonel Scott."

"I am charmed, sir," Marthalee said as she curtsied to the colonel.

"Tom. Call me Tom."

"Why, thank you. I'm sure you and I will become very fast friends, and I will be honored to address you, my future husband's superior, by your first name."

"Really! Well, now, Gabe, I didn't know congratulations were in order. I can see that you have chosen a beautiful woman to be your wife, and that is a business asset that cannot be overlooked. Isn't that right, General Galloway?"

"When Marthalee told me of this young man's plans for her, I was a little apprehensive, but I've decided he can be a damn Yankee if he's a rich damn Yankee," General Galloway said with a chuckle. "I've even decided to make him the junior senator from the state of Louisiana if he plays his cards right."

"But, but . . ." Gabe was speechless. What was happening to him? He had no intention of even living in Louisiana, let alone being the state's senator. And marry this woman? What was that about? Gabe had to admit he had enjoyed Marthalee's company, and he had taken more liberties with her than perhaps was considered proper, but he could testify that this dalliance had not been her first.

"Gabe, darling, isn't it exciting? We can be married while Colonel Scott—Tom—is here in Shreveport."

"Oh my dear, has Gabe not told you why I am here? He and I are taking the maiden run to Longview on the newly christened Texas and Pacific Railway. Governor Throckmorton is going to join us there for a cross-country trip that will take us all the way to San Diego. I want to see exactly where this railroad of mine is going to go."

"Yes, that's right," Gabe said. "I'm sorry. I won't be able to marry—"

"That's nonsense, my boy. Why, while you're gone, Marthalee can plan the biggest wedding Caddo Parish has ever seen. We'll invite everybody who is anybody in the whole state of Louisiana, and, hell, we'll throw in politicians from Arkansas and Texas to boot. They may as well get to know you if you're going to be a politician, son. You'll be here, won't you, Colonel?"

"I wouldn't miss it," Colonel Scott said. He looked back toward the train. "Oh, here's John."

"John?" Gabe said.

"John Forney, editor of the *Philadelphia Chronicle*. I invited him to make the trip with us." Colonel Scott smiled broadly. "We need people to know that there is more to Texas than the Gulf Coast, and I figure a few good articles can prime the pump. There's no money to be made from a railroad if there are no people to serve."

The Texas and Pacific Railway train, appropriately pulled by a 4-4-0 locomotive named *Scott*, would make the trip from Shreveport to Longview in a little less than three and one-half hours. Gabe stared through the window as he thought about Marthalee Galloway and her determination that they get married.

This trip to the Pacific Coast and back would take over two months, and maybe a little longer. Three months of cooling off. He was sure that in that time a woman such as Marthalee, impetuous, aggressive, and free-spirited, would forget all about him. He made a silent vow to write not one letter to her in the whole time of his absence. Out of sight, out of mind. He smiled. There was nothing to be worried about. He was certain that

Marthalee was not the kind of woman who could be kept waiting.

"Why are you smiling?" Colonel Scott asked.

"Because I am here, part of the beginning of history in the making," Gabe replied, not wanting to even mention Marthalee's name.

When they reached Longview, the three men left the train. The engine in the background was still but not quiet, emitting loud sighs as the pressure-relief valves made rhythmic releases of steam, almost as if it were a living creature breathing hard from its recent exertion. Overheated bearings and journals popped and snapped as they cooled.

A man stepped down to be greeted by a little girl who ran across the platform, her arms wide, calling, "Daddy!"

"Gabe!" called a distinguished-looking gentleman with chin whiskers and a pinched face as he stepped away from the small group of townspeople who met the train.

"Governor Throckmorton, it's good of you to meet us."

James Throckmorton had been brought on board the Texas and Pacific venture at Gabe's suggestion. The former Texas governor still had tremendous political influence among the state legislators and enjoyed a lot of support from the citizens. Gabe thought if the T&P needed it, the governor's popularity could sway public opinion in their favor.

Gabe had telegraphed ahead to make arrangements for a private stagecoach to meet them at the depot in Longview. It would be at least a three-day trip to Dallas, then another day on to Fort Worth, the only two towns of any size that the group would encounter as they made their way across West Texas and on to San Diego.

Colonel Scott's ambition was to construct another transcontinental railroad, this one across the South, where his main selling point was the advantage of better weather year-round.

"I thought you arranged a coach for us, Gabe. What happened to it?" Colonel Scott asked as he and John Forney joined Gabe and Governor Throckmorton.

At that moment a coach, pulled by six horses, came driving up. The coach was painted red, and on its side, in big gold letters, were the words TEXAS AND PACIFIC RAILWAY.

"I believe that is it," Gabe said.

Scott and the others laughed. "I should never doubt you, Captain Corrigan. I would stake my life on you getting done whatever it is I ask of you. I like it."

"I thought you would. We may as well let people know who we are."

"Tell me, Mr. Corrigan, if you ever tire of working for this moneygrubbing railroad tycoon, would you consider coming to work for me at the *Chronicle*? I could use a good advertising man," John Forney said. "This is a good idea. No, it's a great idea!"

"Stay away from my main man, Forney, or I'll send you right back to Philadelphia before we even start this trip," Tom said.

"You can't do that, because we both know you need my articles to sell this crackbrained idea of yours."

It had taken quite an effort on Gabe's part to get the coach, but he prided himself on his resourcefulness and his persuasiveness. He had made arrangements with Wells Fargo to provide replacement teams, replacement drivers, food, and some sort of lodging—even if it meant pitching a tent—for the entire fifteen-hundred-mile trip to California.

As the coach got under way, the men returned to conversation. "Disabuse yourself, Governor, of the notion that you are the only politician aboard. Captain Corrigan here could be the next senator from Louisiana," Colonel Scott said.

"Really? You didn't mention that, Gabe," Governor Throckmorton replied.

"I think Colonel Scott is putting the cart before the horse," Gabe said.

"Not too far before it. As soon as you marry Marthalee, I've no doubt you'll be made a Louisiana senator." Then, to Throckmorton, Scott explained, "Gabe's fiancée is the daughter of General Loomis Galloway."

"Ah, yes," Throckmorton said. "I know the general quite well. And I know what political influence he has in the Louisiana legislature." He stuck his hand out. "I know that congratulations are pre-mature, my boy. But if you marry the general's daughter—"

"Who is one of the most beautiful women I have ever seen," Scott interrupted.

"—then you are truly to be congratulated," Throckmorton continued.

Gabe smiled at the governor, not wanting to give credence to this scenario by refuting the suggestion or accepting it.

"I'm all for it. With all the stink of Crédit Mobilier, we are going to need all the influence and goodwill we can muster in Congress. Right now, it's the devil's own task to get any railroad money from them," Colonel Scott said, making known his own reason for promoting the marriage.

As the coach continued on its journey, Gabe stared out the window, oblivious to the conversation going on among the other three. He had only met Marthalee a few months earlier when the T&P had acquired the Southern Pacific Railroad, which ran between Shreveport and Longview. He had gone to Shreveport to inventory the stock and supervise the takeover. Why hadn't he just tended to business?

Fort Worth, Texas—July 1872

Fort Worth was known as a cow town, not because it had so many cows of its own, but because it was the last town of any consequence where cow-boys driving cattle could reprovision and raise a little hell before entering Indian Territory. The cows trailed through Fort Worth, entering through the south end of town, where the Chisholm Trail became Rusk Street, following the street through town, then crossing the Trinity River just east of the Courthouse Bluff.

Once the cows were across the river, the drovers would rest their herds for a few days, during which time they would return to Fort Worth. Not only would they stock up on supplies—coffee, flour, beans, dried fruit, and bacon, among other items they would need before crossing the Nations—they would enjoy whatever pleasures the town had to offer.

Being a focal point on the cattle drives was a two-edged sword for Fort Worth. Everyone depended on the business the cattle herds brought, not just the saloons and brothels. Grocery stores such as the one owned by Henri Laclede, leather and boot shops, gunsmiths, all commercial enterprises were enriched by the money brought in by the cowboys and cattlemen. On the other hand, when the cattle came through town, they had the absolute right of way. All horses, carriages, and pedestrians had to be off Rusk Street for up to an hour as up to fifteen hundred cows passed through. Mounted cowboys herded the cattle, and if nothing spooked them, all went well.

"Won't they ever get through?" Buckley Paddock said, the tone of his voice showing his irritation as he watched a herd of cattle ambling down the street raising a cloud of dust. "Let's hope the railroad people aren't trying to get here right now."

"Be of good cheer, Buck," Henri Laclede said. "You know that without the cows, there'd be no reason for Fort Worth to be here and no reason to even get a railroad. And if there was no Fort Worth, where would your newspaper be?"

Outside, the sound of the passing herd and the whistles and shouts of the cowboys continued to fill the streets.

"Where are we going to hold the meeting?" Paddock asked.

"We're going to hold it right here, in my store," Henri said. "Khleber Van Zandt, Ephraim Daggett, J. J. Jennings, Judge Hendricks, John Peter Smith—all of them know to come here."

"Assuming the cows get out of the way," Paddock said.

When the leading businessmen of the city began to gather, the noise had diminished somewhat because the herd was now considerably farther up Rusk Street, though the bawling, snorting, and whistles could still be heard.

"Are we sure they're coming?" Judge Hendricks asked. "Our only confirmation is what the stagecoach hearsay tells us, and we all know how Dooley likes to spin yarns."

"It's real," Paddock said. "My newspapers from Austin and Galveston came on today's stage, and both say there's a T&P delegation coming. And then there's the Waco paper. Those folks are still bellyaching because they think the road should pass through McLennan County."

"Do we know just who it is that's supposed to be coming?" Khleber Van Zandt asked.

"Well, you can't get any higher up than the president of the company. They say Colonel Thomas Scott is coming and he's bringing someone named Gabriel Corrigan. He's supposed to be an 'executive administrator,' but I'll just bet he's some horse-holding flunky for the colonel." Buck Paddock paused for a moment. "And John Wien Forney is coming, too."

"And what do we know about him?" Henri coaxed.

"Well, I hate to admit it, but he's probably one of the best newspaper columnists in the country."

"Don't sell yourself short, Buck. Since you took over the *Democrat*, we've got a fine newspaper the whole town can be proud of," Van Zandt said.

"Thank you, sir," Paddock said. "I've saved the best for last. All of us will be happy to see our old friend Governor Throckmorton."

"Good." Jennings said. "If you agree with the man or not, and most of us didn't when he voted against secession, everybody knows the former governor stands on principle, and he'll do what he thinks is best for Texas. I guess it can't hurt that Fort Worth named a street after him."

"We should have a gala reception and invite the whole town. Maybe even have a dance."

The men as one turned toward the unexpected source of the comment.

"Josie, this is a meeting for men only, and it is most inappropriate for you to be caught eavesdropping. Gentlemen, I apologize for my daughter's interruption," Henri said. "Don't you have business to attend to at the counter?"

Josie lowered her head. "I'm sorry, Papa." She turned toward the front of the store.

"Josie, no, don't go, let's hear what you have to say," Major Van Zandt said with a chuckle. "After all, gentlemen, didn't we read just last week that the Equal Rights Party has chosen a woman to run for president? So we all better get used to listening to the women whether we want to or not."

"A woman? For president of the United States?" Daggett asked. "I've not heard that."

"Khleber is right," Paddock said. "Victoria Woodhull is running for president."

"Oh, that woman. I'll bet ole Grant is shaking in his boots over her entering the race," Jennings said.

Josie had read about Victoria Woodhull and her sister. Newspapers called them "the lady brokers of No. 44 Broad Street" when they were being nice, and "prostitutes" when they were being nasty. Josie blushed in embarrassment at the thought of being compared to such women.

"Just a minute, Josie, I'm serious," Van Zandt called out. "The reception and dance seems like a good idea. What do you have in mind?"

Josie looked at her father before she answered, and with a smile, he nodded.

"I would say that we clean the first floor of the courthouse, decorate it with bunting, and paint a few signs that say WELCOME TEXAS AND PACIFIC. I'm sure we can get the band to play, and we can have a square dance. We'll get the word out to Birdville and Johnson's Station for sure and maybe even as far away as Grapevine, so we'll have a big crowd. With that many people here, the railroad folks will see that Fort Worth and the whole area really are interested in having the line come through our town. And more important to them, it will show that we have a big enough population so that if they do decide on us, they'll know they can make the road profitable."

"You've been hiding this young woman in plain sight, Henri. She makes a lot more sense than many of us do, and with the head for business she seems to have, why, who knows?" Van Zandt said.

"And," Jennings suggested, getting into the spirit of the event, "we could charge a fee and use the money for a special fund to be used by the town in preparing for the railroad."

"No, no fee. That might leave some people out. I think everyone should be welcome," Josie said.

"Josie is right," Van Zandt said. "If we put you in charge, will you get some ladies to help decorate the courthouse?"

"I can do that."

"How long do you think it will take you to get it ready?"

"If we start right away and work in the morning, we could have it done by noon tomorrow."

"That sounds good, because we want to be ready anytime they get here. And, Josie, if you need to buy anything, come see me."

"Thank you, Mr. Van Zandt."

Late that afternoon Josie and four other women—Jenny Welch and her daughter, Hannah, Mary Daggett, and Mattie Van Zandt—were working on the first floor of the unfinished courthouse. The hard-packed dirt floor had been swept and the windows washed until they sparkled. The women hung swags of red, white, and blue bunting.

"The only thing left to do is hang the banner, and that has to be a job for you youngsters," Mrs. Daggett said.

"I guess that means us, Josie," Hannah said. "Some people think that an unmarried woman of twenty-one is a spinster, but these ladies call us youngsters."

"Speak for yourself, I'm not twenty-one yet," Josie said, and she smiled broadly.

"Until tomorrow, that is."

"Girls, girls, let's get this done," Mrs. Van Zandt said, unfurling a large banner that read FORT WORTH WELCOMES THE TEXAS AND PACIFIC RAILROAD. MAY IT BRING PROSPERITY TO ALL

"I'm sure Ephraim will furnish a steer, if we

can get someone to cook it," Mrs. Daggett said.

"If the steer is butchered and prepared, Uncle Willie will cook it," Josie said. "He'll spit it over a fire. He does a wonderful job."

"Will he cook it out behind the store?" Hannah asked.

"I suppose he will. Why do you ask?"

"Because the smell makes me so hungry."

"Willie Lane does make the best barbecue in Fort Worth," Mrs. Van Zandt said.

The women worked out the menu, each of them taking on the responsibility of preparing a dish and then finding others to help. Hannah and her mother would fix German potato salad; Mrs. Van Zandt, boiled eggs; Mrs. Daggett, a big pot of beans cooked with bacon and molasses; and Josie would bring Ida Lane's fried peach pies.

"I'll have someone deliver the steer today," Mrs. Daggett promised.

"Thank you," Josie said.

"Oh," Hannah said, after her mother and the other two women left. "This is going to be so much fun!"

"Yes, it is," Josie agreed.

"Have you ever ridden on a train?" Hannah asked.

"Yes, I have."

"Is it frightening? I mean, don't they go so very fast?"

"It isn't frightening at all. Why, when you're sit-ting inside the cars, it's almost as if you are sitting in your very own parlor. The only difference is you get to see the countryside just passing by the window."

"Oh! How wonderful that sounds!"

Josie and her father lived in quarters behind the grocery store. It was nearly dark when Josie walked out into the alley behind the building. Willie and another man had built a huge fire that had now burned down to glowing coals. Four huge quarters of beef were spitted over the coals, and Willie was carefully rotating one of the quarters.

"This seems like an awful lot of meat. How long will it take to cook?" Josie asked.

"It should be done by about noon tomorrow," Willie answered.

"You mean you'll have to be out here all night?"

"Yes, ma'am, but don't you be worryin' none about that, Miss Josie. Sam is here with me, and we brought us a bedroll. We'll take turns cookin' and sleepin' all night long. Tomorrow, when the folks bite down into this, why, they are goin' to say this is the best thing they've ever tasted."

Josie laughed. "I don't doubt it, Uncle Willie."

Once, during the night, Josie got out of bed and pulled the curtain aside to look out through the back window. She saw someone basting the meat, which now was glistening in the light of the fire. As she crawled back into bed, she wondered if the people who would be enjoying the beef tomorrow would fully understand what had gone into preparing it for them.

TWO

The next day Josie and Hannah were on their way back to the courthouse.

"Well, how's the birthday girl this morning?" Hannah asked.

"Starved to death. Did you smell Uncle Willie's meat cooking all night long? This morning I went out and he pulled off a piece of the outer crust for me. It is *so* good."

"I could smell it, too, and I'll bet half the people in town could. That's the best advertisement there is to get people in here tonight." Hannah lived with her family in a small house behind her father's tinshop. It was the closest building to the Laclede Grocery, and Hannah was the best friend Josie had in Fort Worth.

"I wonder if Oscar Manning smelled it. Do you think he'll be here tonight? We should have had you ask him to play his flute tonight, or maybe his violin, or his horn."

"Oh, Hannah, leave that alone," Josie said as she playfully swatted at her friend.

"He's sweet on you, and you know it. You're an older woman now, and you should think about getting married. Maybe tonight he will give you a birthday kiss and ask your father if he can court you. Wouldn't that be just wonderful?"

Josie shook her head, just looking at her friend.

"He's a schoolteacher, he's smart, he's always clean . . ." Hannah continued.

"Don't forget, he's got good teeth and he's right regular with his daily toilet." Josie was laughing now. "Oscar Manning is not the man for me. Now, let's get in here and get the benches ready so the wallflowers who won't dance have a place to sit and gossip."

"About you," Hannah said, getting in one last quip.

Josie and Hannah were separating the few chairs that were in the courthouse and lining them up against the walls. Then they laid fresh-sawn boards between them, making extra seating for the expected crowd.

Josie glanced through the front door. "Where did Julius go? I thought he was supposed to be pulling weeds for me."

"I saw him a few minutes ago."

Josie walked to the front door and looked out. She had given the boy, who she sometimes thought was her shadow, a nickel to pull some of the weeds from around the entryway of the courthouse. But now he was sitting beside the step, picking up handfuls of dirt and letting the dirt trickle through his fingers as the breeze scattered it. Clearly not working, he was doing that over and over.

"Julius Lane, stop that right now before you have to sweep the steps for me. I thought you were pulling weeds."

"Miss Josie, I don't have to pull no weeds. I'm not a slave anymore."

Josie laughed. "Baby, you never were a slave. Besides, I hired you. I gave you a nickel, didn't I?"

"Yes'm, you did. Maybe if I had somebody to help me, I could do better. This is too much work for me to do all by myself."

"Oh, it is, is it?"

"Yes'm. But, maybe if I got Troy to come help me, I could get it done faster."

"You think so?"

"Yes'm, I'm just real sure about that. If I got Troy to come help, would you give him a nickel, too?"

"I suppose."

"Thank you! You'll see! We'll work real good for you!" Julius jumped up to his feet and ran out into the middle of Rusk.

At that moment, two things happened. A bright red coach pulled by six horses came barreling onto Rusk Street just as a herd of cattle were heading north. Immediately, the drovers lost control of the cattle, and the unmistakable thunder of a stampede was heard and felt by all in the vicinity. Over twelve hundred disoriented cows were running everywhere throughout the town.

A couple of cowboys, lashing their horses to top speed and bending low over the necks of their mounts, raced ahead of the herd to give the alarm.

"Heah! Heah! Make way! Make way! You! Get that coach out of here!"

The driver of the coach, forewarned by the cowboys and now seeing the stampeding herd, hurried his team out of the way to avoid the oncoming cattle.

While all of this was happening, Julius Lane was standing in the middle of the street, staring in terror at the oncoming stampede.

"Julius! Run! Get out of the way!" Josie yelled.

Josie realized that Julius was too frightened to move. Without giving a thought to her own safety, she started into the street to rescue him.

A man leaped down from the coach and dashed out into the street, running toward Julius.

"Get back, miss! I'll get him!" the man shouted. He grabbed Julius, stuffed him under his arm as if he were a bag of oats, and ran back toward the line of stores opposite the courthouse square.

Gabe's intention was to dart into one of the buildings before the rampant cattle with their six- to eight-feet-long horns gored and trampled both him and the child. Then, as luck would have it, he saw a watering trough directly in front of him. Just a few more steps, if he could make it. He dove in, the child going underwater.

"Little man, are you all right?" Gabe asked as he brought a coughing and sputtering child's head above the water.

The child's eyes were wide with fear as he shook uncontrollably. The ground was shaking as cattle, wild-eyed and snorting, their hooves churning up the street, their horns banging against one another's, thundered by on both sides of the trough. The dust was so thick that soon both faces were covered in mud, the child's being cleansed by rivulets of tears. *Poor little fellow, he's scared to death,* Gabe thought as he gathered him into his arms, holding him tight against his body. The boy buried his face between Gabe's neck and shoulder, and Gabe had to smile when he saw the child's eyes squeezed tight to shut out the terror. Gabe held him reassuringly and gently rocked back and forth as the two sat in the cool water.

Finally the last cow passed, but the boy was still shaking.

"It's all right now," Gabe said. "They're gone."

At that moment Gabe saw the young woman who had started out for the boy running down the street from the courthouse.

"Julius!"

"Miss Josie!" Julius jumped out of the trough and ran to meet her.

Gabe watched as the attractive blond-haired woman scooped the child up in her arms and began smothering him with kisses.

"You scared me to death, you little rascal. I

don't know what I would have done if something had happened to you."

"Where's my baby? Julius, what do you mean running out into the street like that?" A large woman came rumbling toward the two people.

"Mama! I want my mama." The little boy began to sob uncontrollably as Josie handed him to his mother, and the two hurried off.

"Is this a pretty common occurrence? I mean, cattle stampeding down the middle of the main street?" Gabe asked as he splashed water onto his head and face, washing off the accumulated dirt.

"Oh, I'm so sorry, sir. I am most remiss in not thanking you for averting what would surely have been a disaster." Josie turned her attention toward the man in the trough. "Thank you, sir, from the bottom of my heart. Julius is very special to me."

"I can see that, ma'am."

That was not all that Gabe could see. The woman standing before him was tall for a woman, at least five feet eight inches, maybe taller. She had on a blue chambray dress with white eyelet trim around the high neck. Strands of her long blond hair escaped from her topknot as she stood looking down at him sitting in the trough. But what attracted his attention most was what the water from Julius's rescue had done to the well-worn cloth of her dress. The hardened nipples of her well-formed breasts stood in stark relief against the cloth, and Gabe could not keep his eyes off her chest.

"Did you hear me?" the woman was saying, but Gabe had no idea what she had said.

"Uh, no," Gabe said, hoping that was an appropriate response.

"I said that stampedes do happen during the season, but not that often. I'm afraid a coach approaching from the north didn't know to get off the street when a herd is coming through town. If I find that driver, I'll give him a piece of my mind."

"What about the passengers? Will you be upset with them, too?"

"Oh, that's right. I saw you run from the coach. You were one of the passengers, weren't you?"

"Yes, I was, and I am glad there was no harm done to the boy."

Just then the offending coach approached the watering trough. Josie read the words TEXAS AND PACIFIC RAILWAY across the side.

"Oh, no! The railroad people."

"You don't want us?" Gabe asked.

"It isn't that. It's just that everyone was planning to be in their best clothes. The men have their suits ready to put on and the women were going to be dressed in their Sunday best. Here I am in the oldest dress I have." Josie looked down, and then she saw the clear image of her breasts shining through the near threadbare cloth. To add to her mortification, she had left off her camisole this morning because she knew she would be working in the summer heat.

Josie crossed her arms over her chest and, with

her head down, ran toward the grocery store, not wanting to encounter anyone who was now getting out of the coach.

"Gabe, you've found a novel way to beat the Texas heat," Governor Throckmorton said. "Do you plan on joining us for a meeting, or are you just going to sit there?"

"I may just cool off a bit."

"Well, when you're ready, come on down to Andrew's Tavern. It's just ahead and it's about the best place in town to overnight." The governor got back into the coach, and it moved on down the street.

Just cool off a bit. Did he ever mean that! What was going on with him? Here he was sitting in a horse trough on one of the main streets of Fort Worth, Texas, waiting for his arousal to subside. And what had caused it? A country girl most modestly dressed showing protruding nipples through wet cloth.

Just short of a week ago, he had stood on a platform in Shreveport with one of the most beautiful women he had ever seen, her bosom barely contained in her low-cut dress. That woman had consciously rubbed her breasts against his arm, yet he found this chance meeting more titillating.

Once more Henri Laclede's store was the site for a town meeting with more than a dozen businessmen in attendance. These were no ordinary men. They had come west to find a better life, but when they were called, some had volunteered to serve in either the Mexican War or the Civil War. Most were still called by their respective ranks—captains, majors, colonels, and an occasional general—all without regard to the side for which they had fought. They were now Texans, and as Texas prospered, so would they all.

Major Khleber Van Zandt rose to speak.

"My fellow citizens, we are gathered here today to welcome our honored guests, Colonel Thomas Scott, Colonel John Forney, Captain Gabriel Corrigan, and our very own Governor James Throckmorton. They are here, gentlemen, to ensure the survival of Fort Worth, not only to put our fair city on the map, but to create an environment that will greatly enrich the lives of every man, woman, and child residing in this city—and for that matter, all of Northwest Texas."

Van Zandt's words were greeted with applause.

"Colonel Scott, as president of the Texas and Pacific Railway, perhaps you would like to say a few words?" Van Zandt invited.

Colonel Scott stood and, for a long moment, just looked out into the faces of everyone present. Gabe had been with Scott for many of his presentations, and he knew that this was his habit, to first make eye contact with everyone. It was as if during those brief few seconds, he was making a personal connection with each man in the audience, so that when he spoke, it was almost as if there were only the two of them, sharing a cup of coffee.

"Gentlemen, first let me thank you for this warm welcome," Colonel Scott began. "I must admit that we were a bit surprised by your welcoming committee, but as some of you may have witnessed, my executive administrator found a most unique method of cooling off." Colonel Scott looked toward Gabe as the men responded with a nervous titter, not knowing if the stampeding cattle would cause their guests to look unfavorably upon the community.

"Let me assure you that this transcontinental railroad is going to reach California, and it is going to be built in the South."

The room erupted in boisterous shouts and generous applause by most of the men in attendance. Gabe was observing the group and made a mental note to personally speak to those few who did not seem to be too enthusiastic about the prospect of the railroad.

While observing the room, he saw her. Standing at the front of the store, she was unpacking a crate of tinned fruit. He watched as she strained to place the cans on one of the higher shelves behind the counter. The action caused her pink gingham dress to pull taut against her breasts, and while he could not see anything untoward, the memory of his earlier encounter with her caused a stir in his trousers.

With a quick jerk of his head, he turned his gaze away from the woman and focused on Colonel Scott.

"As many of you know, the Texas and Pacific Act was the last bill passed before Congress that allowed federal land grants for the building of railroads across this great country. But we have friends in high places." Colonel Scott nodded toward Governor Throckmorton. "And we have powerful friends in Washington. You all know of Congressman James G. Blaine. A while back he and I had a mutual interest in an Arkansas railroad, and lo and behold, last month, thanks to Speaker Blaine's sponsorship, our federal contribution to right-of-way construction for the Texas and Pacific was raised to forty thousand dollars per mile. Now the good governor here has worked that same kind of magic with your legislators in Austin."

"I've done my part," Governor Throckmorton said. "Texas has set aside public lands that equal the whole state of New York for any and all companies that will build a railroad and open up the West. They're offering sixteen sections of land for every completed mile of track. Now, if I do say so myself, that's some kind of incentive to get the job done."

The group of men responded with oohs and aahs at this news.

"And we thank you, Governor," Colonel Scott continued. "Now, as some of you may know, the initial survey was to take this railroad south of Fort Worth. And the good folks of Waco are still lobbying for that to happen. I must say that this trip across Texas is an exploratory one, because I can promise you the final stakes for the survey have not yet been set."

"Colonel Scott, what is it you want from us? What can we do that will guarantee the stakes are set in Fort Worth?" Henri asked as he rose to his feet.

"Are you a businessman, sir?"

"I am. You are right now standing in my store," Henri stated proudly.

"This man understands the art of the deal. He wants to be the merchant prince of Northwest Texas, and this railroad can do just that for him and for all of you," Colonel Scott said.

"He's already got an empress; he doesn't need to be a prince," someone yelled from the group of men, whereupon several turned and waved to Josie, who was standing in the front of the store.

She hesitantly returned the wave as she tried to avoid the attention. She did not want to cause her father any embarrassment if she was caught eavesdropping again, but she was interested in what the men had to say.

This was the perfect opening for Gabe to again look at the woman. Why did she respond to the word *empress*? Surely that wasn't her name. It must be a nickname. He would find out. He smiled when he saw that she was now removing the cans from the shelf and putting them back into the crate, and he sympathized with her. She was obviously trying to look busy.

How many times had he been put in that position, when Colonel Scott had insisted that he be present when the colonel was making deals—no, demands—on unsuspecting partners? Gabe idolized and respected the colonel, but that was one aspect of his job he would rather not have to do.

"I want three hundred twenty acres of land south of town running from the West Fork to the Clear Fork of the Trinity River. In consideration of this, I will proceed as rapidly as possible to build the Texas and Pacific Railroad to your town. If you cannot see fit to do this, tomorrow the red coach will drop south to visit Waco." With those abrupt words Colonel Scott sat down.

For a moment no one said a word, everyone absorbing what had just been said to them. Slowly, Major Van Zandt rose to his feet and began to speak.

"Thank you, Colonel, for your enlightenment. I, for one, appreciate a plainspoken man. I do not believe you will meet a more civic-minded group of citizens in all of Texas, and you will find our people are up to the task. I believe you made the statement that this railroad is going to be built, and that it is going to be built in the South. Well, I am just as adamant that it is going to be built in Fort Worth. You will have a commitment this very evening."

To a man, everyone stood and gave a rousing cheer.

"Hooray for the T&P!"

"And now, gentlemen, as soon as I check with our hostess, I would like to invite you to a barbecue with all the fixin's and a good old Texas hoedown. Josie, is everything ready?" Major Van Zandt asked.

"It is, sir. The eating will start as soon as the sun drops behind the courthouse and we have a little more shade. Everybody is welcome."

"Thank you, Josie. This meeting is adjourned for everyone who doesn't want to put a quid in the pot. For those of you who are willing to ante up some land, labor, or cash, the meeting continues."

Josie watched as several of the townspeople began to file out of the meeting, leaving only Ephraim Daggett, Major Van Zandt, John Jennings, Judge Hendricks, her father, and a small handful of additional men to decide the fate of the whole community. She was proud of Henri Laclede. He always stepped forward to carry his part of the load.

Then she saw the T&P representatives rise and start to leave. Colonel Scott looked to be self-assured, used to getting what he wanted, no matter what it took. Josie thought that perhaps the trait was necessary to amass the great wealth the Eastern financiers such as Jay Gould, Cornelius Vanderbilt, and Jay Cooke, among others, were purported to have. She knew Colonel Thomas Scott belonged to that small fraternity.

Governor Throckmorton and the other two men followed the colonel. She had missed the introductions, so she didn't know which name went with each man. One was middle-aged, with a mustache and graying hair; the other was tall, younger, with dark hair and a muscular body. Then he turned around. With dark eyes that seemed to penetrate, he stared directly at Josie while his face spread into a smile of recognition.

The man. The man who had rescued Julius. With a reaction she would have given anything to have avoided, she instinctively crossed her arms over her chest. He responded by chuckling at her obvious discomfort. He raised his hand in a modified salute as he and the others left the store.

Josie and Hannah were pulling a wagon loaded with their food contributions for the barbecue while Julius rode. His charge was to keep the food from falling as the wagon rolled along.

"The potato salad smells wonderful," Josie said.

"How many fried pies did Ida make for tonight?"

"About a hundred and fifty, I think. I hope we have that many people," Josie said.

"They sure is good," Julius chimed in.

"Julius! You're not supposed to be eating the dessert," Josie said. "How many have you eaten?"

"I don't know Miss Josie. I lost count."

"Maybe I don't want so many people to come tonight. We won't have enough food."

"You worry too much," Hannah said. "The star of this dinner is going to be the meat. Probably nobody will have any room left for dessert, but anyway Mama made one, too, so we'll be fine."

"I don't know. Look at the wagon yard. It's full, and teams and buckboards are everywhere. We said we were going to invite the surrounding towns and it looks like they all came."

"That will just show the folks from the Texas and Pacific how serious we all are about getting them to build the road through Fort Worth. They did say that was going to happen, didn't they?" Hannah asked.

"Yes and no. Colonel Scott wants a commitment from the town, and Major Van Zandt seems to think we can accommodate him. The major and several others were still meeting when I left the store."

THREE

Gabe Corrigan arrived at the courthouse before the crowd and was asked to help several of the women set up bucksaw frames and planks to serve as makeshift tables for the barbecue. He helped the ladies cover the boards with oilcloth, the prints depending upon the store where they had been bought. He wondered which of the prints had come from the Laclede Grocery—which one Josie, as he had heard Major Van Zandt call her, had picked out. He decided it must be the one with roses growing on a fence.

At that very moment she rounded the corner of the courthouse pulling a wagon laden with food.

"There you are. I've been waiting for you," Gabe said, rushing to greet her.

"I beg your pardon, sir. I don't believe we have met," Josie said.

Gabe's eyebrows rose mischievously as a devastating grin crossed his face.

"Miss Josie, this is the man who dunked me in the horse trough. You know him," Julius said excitedly.

"What I meant was we haven't met officially," Josie said.

"That is true, but we have seen each other," Gabe said, coming down hard on the word *seen*.

Josie glared at the man as she rose to her full height. "I do not think I care to meet you, sir, because you are no gentleman. That was an accident and you know it. Come, Julius, we have to put the food on the tables."

Josie jerked the wagon so hard that Julius, along with a tray of fried pies, slipped off the wagon. Gabe grabbed the tray in midair, allowing only a few pies to fall to the ground.

"I've saved you again, Little Man. I'll bet you would be in big trouble if you let all these pies fall to the ground." Gabe placed the tray back onto the wagon.

"What do you think we should do with the ones that fell off, mister?" Julius asked.

"I think we should eat them, don't you?"

"I'd like that."

As Josie pulled the wagon off, she looked back to see the man and Julius sitting on the ground comfortably knocking the grit off fried pies and eating them. She couldn't help but smile.

"Can you tell me what that was all about?" Hannah asked when they had moved out of earshot. "I must have missed something, because that wasn't your usual reaction to a total stranger, especially one as handsome as that man is."

"It's nothing. It's absolutely nothing."

"Well, who is he?"

"He's one of the T&P people, and he will be gone tomorrow. That's all I'm going to say about it."

"If you say so, but there's more to this than what you're telling me."

Josie and Hannah began setting the potato salad on the tables next to the kettles of beans and plates of sliced ripe tomatoes and cucumbers.

"Oh, goody," Hannah said, "someone brought watermelon."

"Let me do that for you," Oscar Manning said as he stepped toward the two women. Even though the temperature had to be in the nineties, Oscar was dressed in a black suit with a string tie. His muttonchops seemed to be bushier than ever, Josie noticed.

"Good evening, Oscar," Josie said, as Hannah deserted her. "I am glad that you could come this evening."

"Most of my music students were absent their lessons today. There is no discipline among our young people."

As if on cue, Julius came running toward Josie, hiding in front of her while his friend Troy weaved in and out between the tables.

"This is exactly what I mean," Oscar said. "You should make it a point to teach that boy to know his place. You think you are befriending him by allowing him to accompany you wherever you go, but what will he do when he has to make his own way? Why do you let him be in our midst anyway?"

"He came with me, and he will stay with me, if that is what Julius wants to do. May I remind you that a war was fought, and whether you like the outcome or not, Julius and his people are free."

Oscar clucked his tongue. "Ma'am, you will be sorry." He walked away without another word.

"Now there's a real jerk," Gabe said as he walked up to Josie.

"Look who's calling the kettle black," Josie said.

"I want to apologize for my behavior. It was rude, and you were right to say I have not behaved in a gentlemanlike manner. May I say, I am sorry if I have offended you?"

"I will accept your apology."

"Let's pretend that this is our first meeting," Gabe said, extending his hand to her. "My name is Gabriel Corrigan, and I am enjoying the hospitality afforded me by the fine citizens of Fort Worth."

"I may have liked you better the other way. That tone seems to me like it would fit better at Queen Victoria's court. Look around you. You are at a barbecue in the yard of a courthouse that was built twelve years ago and still has a dirt floor."

Gabe threw back his head and laughed.

"All right, let's cut right to the nub. What's your name? I want to know."

"I'm Josie Laclede."

"Well, why did you wave when those men called you Empress at the meeting?"

"Are you ready for this? My full name is Empress Josephine Laclede."

"I am impressed. I wish my name was Napoleon, instead of just plain Gabe."

Josie's eyes searched his face: the dark eyes, the straight nose, the chiseled jaw, the sensuous lips. She took a deep breath and let out a long sigh. "Gabe is just fine."

He took her hand in his and squeezed it. This simple gesture caused a reaction in Josie that she did not anticipate. Her heart felt as if it were in her throat and her breath was short. She withdrew her hand more abruptly than she intended.

"I think we need to get some food before it's all gone. We wanted a big crowd tonight, but there are far more people here than what we prepared for. Let's see if Uncle Willie's barbecue is all gone. Did you bring a plate?"

"No, I didn't think about it."

Reaching into a basket, Josie retrieved two plates. Gabe smiled when he saw the pattern on the plates—a bouquet of roses, in the center. He couldn't tell if they had been red or not because they were now faded, but they were definitely roses. He just knew she would like flowers.

"This is Papa's plate, but since he is still at the meeting, you may use it."

"Good evenin', Miss Josie. I was thinkin' you were gonna miss my barbecue, so I saved a piece of the crusty part just for you," Willie said as he took an overturned crock off some meat he had placed to the side.

"Nobody takes better care of me than you do, Uncle Willie. Is there enough for Mr. Corrigan, too?"

"Lordy, missy, if you can eat all of this, I daresay you'll bust wide-open. There's plenty for you and your young man."

Josie smiled at Willie. "Mr. Corrigan is with the Texas and Pacific. He will be on his way tomorrow."

"Well, if he gets a taste of my barbecue I can guarantee he'll be back. Mark my words."

Gabe took a bite of the succulent meat. "Mmm, this is good, Uncle Willie. You may be right about my coming back."

Josie and Gabe walked on around the now almost depleted table, picking what food they could find.

"Does everyone call him Uncle Willie?" Gabe asked.

"No, just me."

"So why do you do it?"

"Because he is a part of my family. I guess in a cruel turn of fate, I could say he was bought and paid for."

"What do you mean by that?" Gabe questioned.

"Ida was a slave that Papa bought because he needed a wet nurse for me. She had just had a baby that died. Willie was the baby's father, but they couldn't be married because he was owned by someone else. So Papa bought Willie, too. Then Papa emancipated both of them and they were married. They have worked for Papa ever since."

"Did your mother die?"

Josie looked at Gabe for a long moment. She had told him more about herself than she had told a lot of people in Fort Worth. She wasn't prepared to tell him her story.

"I don't know," she said, dismissing the question.

Gabe knew from the way she had responded that this was an uncomfortable topic. He did not press her.

Just then Major Van Zandt, Henri, and the other men who had stayed to thrash out the proposal Colonel Scott had placed before the meeting came into the crowd.

"Ladies and gentlemen," the major said. "I have a very important announcement to make. Colonel Scott has accepted our pledge for three hundred twenty acres of land with a clear title in hand. This land is to be donated to the Texas and Pacific Railway, where they will construct a depot and stock holding pens just as soon as the first train rolls into the community.

"I don't have to tell any of you what the railroad

will mean for this town. We have an estimated population of approximately five hundred souls at the moment, and another five thousand people in all of Tarrant County. Within a year the population will double. In the first ten years of the railroad coming to Fort Worth and proceeding on westward to the Pacific, I believe the population will increase tenfold.

"I can see this city in fifty years equaling such metropolises as Cincinnati, St. Louis, Denver, and San Francisco. And it all begins here, today, with us."

A cheer erupted as all rose to their feet. Spontaneously, Josie threw her arms around Gabe.

"Thank you, thank you, thank you!" she said exuberantly. Then she kissed him. It was an innocent kiss, much as she would kiss Julius. Immediately, she realized what she had done, and her face flushed with color. "I am so sorry, Mr. Corrigan. That was most forward of me and I had no right to do that." Then she became aware of his arms around her, holding her close to him.

"I rather enjoyed it," Gabe said as a smile began to curl the corners of his mouth.

Josie tried to pull away from him but he continued to hold her.

"Please, sir, I beg of you."

"I will let you go, but I've been listening to the tuning of fiddles. Does that mean there is to be a dance?"

"Yes."

"Then, I would like you to save your last dance for me."

Josie stepped away from Gabe without answering.

Major Van Zandt signaled to the crowd that he had something more to say. "Ladies and gentlemen, before we step into the courthouse, we have one more item of business to dispatch, and for that I will call on Jenny Welch to speak."

Hannah's mother stood. "Thank you all for coming to this glorious celebration for Fort Worth and all of Tarrant County. I am sorry that some of you didn't get here in time to partake of the food, but we have another celebration to recognize." Jenny went to the table just as Hannah and Mary Daggett were carrying in a long board that contained many individual squares of cake. "I know no one is getting married tonight, but my wedding-cake recipe is the only thing I know of that will feed this crowd of people."

"How much brandy did you put in it, Jenny? Ain't that what makes your cakes last twenty years?" someone called out.

"Well, it does have a bit."

Everyone laughed because Jenny's wedding cakes were known for the brandy and the twenty-five pounds of raisins, citron, and currants that she used.

"Josie? Where is Josie Laclede? Will you come up here?" Josie stepped forward and Jenny continued, "You may not know that this celebration and all the organizing was due to this young woman, but if the truth be known, she did it all to guarantee that she would have the biggest birthday party ever. It's her twenty-first birthday, so let's all wish her well."

Shouts of "Happy birthday" rang out and Josie smiled radiantly as she graciously accepted the well-wishes of all.

"Jenny, did you make the wedding cake just 'cause it makes a big cake, or are you tryin' to tell Josie somethin'? After all, she's gettin' a little long in the tooth," someone else called out.

Josie just shook her head. "Get a bite of cake, and then everyone is invited to stay for the dance."

Gabe watched as Josie interacted with the crowd. She accepted the greetings from all without regard to their appearance. They could be wearing a dress or shirt whose cloth was so crisp that it might have come that very day from the seamstress or tailor, or they could be wearing clothing that had been boiled so many times that no color was left and the hems and sleeves were frayed beyond repair. She seemed to know everyone—the young and the old, the rich and the poor. She even graciously greeted women who Gabe surmised were working ladies of the evening, and men who were obviously passing cowboys.

Josie fascinated Gabe. There was something

about her. She was pretty, yes, with blond hair, pale blue eyes, high cheekbones, and lips that were slightly full. But it wasn't just her looks. If he was honest with himself, as far as pure beauty was concerned, Marthalee Galloway was prettier. Marthalee had a classic, elegant beauty, of a kind to equal that of the mythical Helen.

But he couldn't help but compare the way Josie interacted with people and the way Marthalee did. Both were beautiful women who attracted attention because of their looks, but there, the similarity ended. Marthalee seemed to take over a room, becoming a brightly glowing lantern around which moths gathered, the absolute center of attention. Josie, on the other hand, became a part of the room, accepting the attention paid to her not as if it were her due, but as if unaware of the effect she had on others.

"Folks, come inside for the dance," one of the fiddlers shouted, and everyone started toward the door of the courthouse. Gabe followed the crowd in and saw one of the young men of the town approach Josie. He couldn't hear what the young man said, but from Josie's gracious reaction, he knew she had just accepted an invitation to dance. Gabe stood to one side and watched as the couples moved out onto the floor and formed their squares as the dance began.

The high, keening skirl of fiddles kicked off the first dance, and John Hanna, a lawyer and himself a musician, began calling the dance.

Swing the man that stole the sheep,
Now the one that hauled it home,
Now the one that ate the meat,
Now the one that gnawed the bones.

Although Josie was enjoying the dance and had accepted the invitations of all who asked her, she found herself looking around the room for Gabe Corrigan. He had not danced with one person that she had observed. Finally, after the fifth dance, she saw him coming toward her.

"Miss Josie?" young Isaac Van Zandt said.

"Thank you, Isaac, but this dance has been promised," Josie replied.

Isaac turned quickly to one of the other single young ladies.

"Does this mean the dance is over?" Gabe said, taking her hand in his.

"Oh, no, it's just getting started, and you haven't danced at all."

Gabe smiled, pleased that she had noticed him.

"I was just waiting for my opportunity to dance with the belle of the ball."

"You flatter me, Mr. Corrigan. It's just that everyone is being nice to me because it's my birthday."

"Form your squares!" John Hanna shouted.

Josie took her place in the dance and Gabe followed. He wasn't sure he could follow the dance, but even though the calls were different, he had observed that many of the moves were familiar.

Hark, ye partners.
Right's the same.

Josie bowed, as did the others.

Then the dance started and Josie was seized by Gabe, swung, and passed to the next, then to the next, until finally she returned to the starting point.

For a moment she found herself in the center of a circle formed by Gabe and the second couple in the square. She exchanged places with Gabe at the call.

With the last call the dance ended as everyone dissolved in laughter.

"Would you have a glass of punch with me?" Gabe invited as he took out a handkerchief and wiped the perspiration off his forehead.

"Oh, I don't know," Josie replied. "I'm not sure I want to drink from that bowl. I saw Mr. Boaz pouring something into the punch, and if I know William, it's probably some of his stock of pisco that he brought up from Galveston."

"Ahh, pisco punch. They say that is San Francisco's secret weapon, you know."

"Well, they can keep all the grape brandy they want in California. We don't really need more spirits in Fort Worth, because our visitors"—Josie nodded toward a group of cowboys who were getting more and more boisterous—"do very well with what we have."

"I see what you mean. It's just that it has gotten a little warm in here, and I thought a glass of punch might cool us off. Would you like to step outside for a breath of fresh air?" Gabe invited.

Josie looked around the room as if trying to see if anyone was watching her. She found the idea of stepping outside, in the dark, with this man, intriguing but possibly scandalous. She had met this man for the first time this very day, and at that embarrassing meeting he had seen more of her than any other man in Fort Worth.

"The fresh air might feel good."

Once outside, Gabe took Josie's hand in his. It felt like the most natural thing she had ever done as they walked away from the courthouse. The sounds from inside the building began to recede. From across the Trinity they could hear the lowing of cattle and the call of a whip-poor-will.

"It's funny," Josie said.

"What?"

"The cattle sound so peaceful now. It's strange when you think that these are the same cows that were stampeding through town this morning."

"I'm glad I was there."

Overhead, the dark vault of night was filled with stars. They ranged from the brightest of the first magnitude and grew progressively smaller and dimmer until they could no longer be seen as individual stars, but only as a pale blue dusting.

A cat on its nightly prowl screeched.

From down the street a baby cried.

From a nearby stable, a mule brayed.

"This whole place is so peaceful," Gabe said.

"Yes, it is."

"Are you sure you want all this to change? Because it will, you know, when the railroad comes to town. People will start coming—some for legitimate business, others just as flimflams and hucksters."

"I suppose it's the price of progress," Josie said with a resigned sigh. "Fort Worth needs so much."

"Fort Worth has exactly what it needs, and that is a public spirit and enterprise that is seldom seen in a community of so few people. Someone will build more houses, more stores, more law offices, more saloons, and, I might say, I hope someone will build a hotel. Andrew's Tavern may be a great place to drink and play cards, but it lacks as a place to sleep."

"A hotel," Josie said. "I should suggest that to Papa. I'll bet it would be more profitable than the grocery store."

"Both businesses would do well. It just depends on what he wants to do."

Gabe and Josie talked comfortably as they got farther away from the courthouse square and its surrounding buildings. When they reached the bluff that flanked the Trinity, Josie found a large rock that overlooked the river. She sat down, recognizing that in so doing, she was giving Gabe permission to join her.

By now the moon had risen and its reflection shone upon the quiet water that was just beneath them.

"You know what Easterners call Texas?" Gabe asked.

"What?"

"The land of milk and honey."

Josie's gentle laugh rippled through the night air. "Do they know that it's necessary to milk the cows and gather the honey? It's a hard life out here."

Josie felt Gabe staring at her, deeply, intensely, as if his eyes were burning into her.

"Would you ever leave here?"

"Where would I go?"

"You could always come with me."

He moved toward Josie, and she knew he was going to kiss her. She should get up and run back toward the square, or at least she should turn her head, but she didn't do either. She welcomed what was coming—her very first kiss.

His lips upon hers were as gentle as the breeze around them. He put his arms around her and drew her into an embrace, his mouth continuing to cover her lips, now with an urgency that Josie instinctively recognized as desire. Her only reaction was to return the passion; then he withdrew from her. He began to plant small kisses on her chin, then down her neck and on toward her ear. Josie was shocked by her own response to his kisses. She took his head in her hands and brought his lips back to hers, and this time she was the initiator.

Then she felt Gabe pull back.

Josie looked at him with a questioning expression. Why had he stopped?

"We'd better get back to the others." His voice was a husky whisper.

"Is there something wrong?"

"No, my dear, there is nothing wrong. It's just the opposite. Everything is too right." He kissed her one more time, this time barely brushing her lips. "Happy birthday, Josie."

Confused by her own reaction to what had just happened, Josie rose from the rock and hurried back to the courthouse. She didn't say anything to Gabe as she left.

Gabe sat alone for a long time. What was it about this woman that made him go crazy? He would be on the Texas and Pacific coach tomorrow morning on his way to California. He had work to do, work that was important to his own welfare and to that of all the other towns that would benefit from the coming of the railroad.

What had ever possessed him to ask Josie to come with him? What if she had agreed? How would he have handled that? Thank goodness Josie had had the sense not to respond to his invitation. It was barely a week since he had escaped the clutches of a cloying woman in Shreveport. It would be good to be away from all women for the next couple of months, because he had to get his priorities back in order.

FOUR

After charting the proposed route of the Texas and Pacific across West Texas and the New Mexico and Arizona Territories, Colonel Scott and Gabe boarded a ship in San Diego. With little effort, they could have connected with the Union Pacific Railroad, allowing them to reach Philadelphia in less than two weeks, but Colonel Scott was still annoyed with Cornelius Vanderbilt's ousting of him as president of the UP, and he would not ride on his railroad. Therefore they took a ship to the Isthmus of Panama, traveled overland by pack mules, then boarded a ship bound for Galveston. There they caught a train that would take them to Pennsylvania.

"We'll be going through Shreveport," Colonel Scott said. "Shall we stop and see your lady friend?"

"What lady friend? If you mean Marthalee Galloway, I would sooner call her a vampire," Gabe said.

Colonel Scott laughed uproariously. "It didn't look like you minded her attention when we were last there. Anyway, you will see her because I telegraphed General Galloway to say we will be there tomorrow. I can't afford to give up even one vote in the Congress, or the money will not be appropriated for this project. The Marshall–Texarkana line depends on the Southern senators, and the general has enough influence that he can bring them all on board. My boy, this business is all about politics, and you will enjoy Miss Galloway's company. Do you understand?"

"Yes, sir."

Colonel Scott took out some papers and began reading and making notes, dismissing Gabe entirely.

For many miles, Gabe seethed with anger. The colonel was not his superior officer, and he resented being treated as if he were still in the military.

But his flare of anger subsided. He had to admit that Tom Scott was one of the most brilliant men he had ever known. His relationship with Scott had proven to be a tremendous boon for his own career. At twenty-nine years of age, Gabe Corrigan had a position that many men envied, a position that would help to shape the expansion into the great Southwest, and in the interim, when the Texas and Pacific was completed, his own wealth would be multiplied many times over. By the time they reached Shreveport, he knew he would stand with the colonel.

Shreveport, Louisiana—September 1872

Gabe had decided he would find some way to keep himself busy enough to avoid any contact with Marthalee at all. But that wasn't to be. To his chagrin, when he stepped off the train, there she was, standing under a big parasol, with a long feather boa draped around her neck. Gabe thought the boa might have been an attempt to cover her oversize breasts, which once again seemed to be straining to stay put in the low-cut dress she was wearing.

"Gabriel!" she squealed as she rushed to meet him. She threw her arms around his neck and kissed him full on the lips, a wet kiss that almost made Gabe shudder.

"I have missed you so much. I know that you were not in a position to write to me because you were in such dreadful places," Marthalee said as she furrowed her brow in an affected effort to look upset. "But, darling, I was a little put out when we got Colonel Scott's telegram and no word from you. Why, we hardly had time to notify everyone."

"Notify everyone? For what?"

"You naughty boy. You know what I'm talking about. Our wedding."

"Our wedding?" Gabe gasped in disbelief.

A sardonic smile crossed Marthalee's face. "Surely you haven't forgotten? You are familiar with the term *breach of promise*, are you not? You either marry me or we can just wait and see what happens in a Louisiana court where every judge has been bought and paid for by my father."

Just then General Galloway broke away from his conversation with Colonel Scott and turned his attention to his daughter and Gabe. He slapped Gabe on the back so hard that Gabe almost swallowed his tongue. As he coughed and sputtered, tears came to Gabe's eyes.

"My boy, stop with your caterwauling. Not on the last night you're a free man. I want to see just how much whiskey you can drink, because that's the mark of a real man, right, Colonel Scott?"

"If you say so." Colonel Scott's expression told Gabe that he could not expect the colonel to help get him out of this predicament.

The evening with the general was one of the most bizarre experiences of Gabe's life. He was accompanied by the governor of the state of Louisiana and both of its senators, a senator from Arkansas, and both senators from Mississippi. In addition, there were at least seven or eight congressmen from the three states, as well as some of the most important businessmen from both Texas and Louisiana. They went to every bar in Shreveport, and at each bar, Gabe was introduced as the general's son-in-law. And with each toast, yet another lie was told about his background. The last one he remembered was that he owned the T&P railroad. That was just before he was taken to a brothel, where his future father-in-law left him "to have a good time."

That was where he woke up the next morning with a pounding head. He could not recall anything about the evening before, but he saw a rather large woman sitting in a chair, a calico cat curled up on her lap, as she stared absently out the window. When she heard Gabe stirring, she turned to him.

"Hi, honey, do you want to have some fun this morning?"

Just then he knew he was going to throw up, and he rushed to the washbasin.

The woman laughed. "That bad, huh? The general said I was to make you a man before you took ahold of his baby. Are you ready now?"

Gabe looked down and was thankful to see he was still dressed. His head was whirling as he headed for the door. The last sound he heard was a cackle from the hag. The calico cat streaked out of the room just ahead of Gabe, almost causing him to fall headlong down the stairs.

It was too bad he didn't fall. A broken leg, a couple of broken arms, maybe even a fractured skull, would have been preferable to the fate that awaited him.

Gabe returned to the Inn Hotel and found Colonel Scott sitting in the front parlor.

"Let's get the hell out of this place before it's too late," Gabe said.

Colonel Scott took a deep breath. "I'm afraid it's too late already. Loomis Galloway is a very powerful man, and he has chosen you to be the man to marry his daughter. In this part of the country, his word is gospel, and nobody challenges him."

"Well, he hasn't had to deal with Captain Gabriel Corrigan yet. I will be the first to defy him, because I will not marry that woman."

"Gabe, there will be brash consequences if you do not go through with this—not only for your own life, but also think of the thousands of people who will be affected if the railroad cannot be built."

"Sir, forgive me for asking this question, but is the railroad the only thing of any value to you? Does nothing else matter?"

Colonel Scott stared at Gabe for a long moment before speaking. "I believe the general has left a new suit of clothes for you. See to it that you are presentable and down here within the hour."

Gabe climbed the stairs and entered his room. A new suit was on the bed, a gray suit, the same color as a rebel uniform. The ultimate irony.

Gabe thought back to the battle that had changed his life: Antietam.

Supplied with ammunition and powder, the Union Army was positioned to meet the invading Southerners. Gabe remembered seeing the glint of thousands of Confederate bayonets concealed in the cornfield. He had a bad feeling about the battle—not fear as much as resignation—and the idea that he was caught up in something over which he had no control. The cornfield exploded into absolute pandemonium as thousands of men in gray charged the men in blue. They fired at each other at point-blank range, and when they were too close to reload their rifles, they used their bayonets, or used the rifles as clubs.

By the end of that single day, over twenty-three thousand men lay dead or severely wounded—most of whom would later die from blood loss or sepsis. Gabe had survived, though it had always seemed to him more a matter of luck than of anything he had done to preserve his life.

Although this certainly wasn't the same thing, he couldn't help but feel that he was being pulled into this wedding. He had no control over the situation. He was experiencing the same sense of loss and helplessness he had felt on September 17, 1862.

Then, with a start, he realized that today was also September 17. This wedding would be exactly ten years to the day after the Battle of Antietam. He hoped it wasn't significant.

Gabe Corrigan lay on the bed, his hands behind his head, looking up at the ceiling.

The wedding had taken place at the Gaiety Theater, a mocking name for the most depressing day in his life. Over 150 people had come to watch a wedding that was indeed like an opera. It had all the characters—the beautiful heroine, the overbearing father, and the tragic hero.

Could this tragedy have been prevented? Yes. Why hadn't he insisted that Josie Laclede run away with him the night he had asked her?

"Are you ready, my darling?" Marthalee entered the room dressed in a flowing nightdress, her flaming red hair making a stark contrast against the virginal white cloth. "I won't be needing this," she said as she removed the gown and walked toward the bed.

Philadelphia, Pennsylvania—August 1873

Gabe and Marthalee had been married for almost a year. They had returned to Philadelphia, where Gabe had thrown himself into his work, taking on more and more responsibility for the financing of the Texas and Pacific Railway, always working in tandem with Colonel Scott. Gabe seemed to be in New York more than he was in Pennsylvania, constantly meeting with brokers and bond dealers, always chasing one more dollar. The schedule was tiring, but it made his life with Marthalee bearable.

Marthalee had entered the social whirl of the city and quickly become one of the most sought-after guests at any function. She never objected when Gabe's schedule forced her to attend these events alone because she was always able to find a willing escort.

While Colonel Scott appreciated the dedication and enormous discipline that Gabe provided the company, the colonel also acknowledged his part in perpetrating the comedy of errors that Gabe's life had become.

Colonel Scott and Gabe were preparing for a major fund-raising trip to Great Britain. Englishmen had long been investors in the Texas cattle industry, and they were most receptive to a railroad that would make that business more profitable. When the colonel realized they would be gone on September 17, Gabe's first wedding anniversary, he insisted that both Marthalee and his own wife, Anna, accompany them.

"Gabe, don't get me wrong, but you really aren't trying to make this marriage work," Tom Scott said when Gabe voiced opposition to his plan. "I don't think you realize what a powerful asset Marthalee is to you. Her social connections are invaluable to the company."

"How can I make you understand? I don't care if this marriage fails. In fact, I pray that it does."

"Believe me, you do not want that. You have befriended that public woman in New York and you have begun to believe the rubbish that she spews."

"Victoria Woodhull is a broker with whom I do business. I have never read *Woodhull & Claflin's Weekly*, and I have never heard her speak. I cannot help it that her sister is rumored to be Vanderbilt's paramour and anything that has his name attached to it, no matter how remote the possibility that it is true, infuriates you. Anyway, I'd just as soon Marthalee not go on this trip."

"I'm sorry you feel that way, because I've already booked passage for her and for Anna, and you can't disappoint Anna."

The USS *Pennsylvania* had been in service for less than a year. Counting passengers and crew, just over a thousand souls were aboard. Forty-six of those passengers were enjoying first-class passage, and included in that number were Colonel Thomas Scott and his wife, Anna, as well as Gabriel and Marthalee Corrigan.

Gabe was sitting at a table in the first-class ballroom, watching the swirl of dancers on the floor. The women were in butterfly-bright dresses, with jewelry that sparkled around their necks and at their ears. The male passengers wore dark tailcoats and white ties, and the ship's officers were resplendent in their white dress uniforms.

One of the most sparkling of the women was Marthalee. Tall and willowy, her long, flowing red hair was set off by the green silk of her grenadine dress. She was dancing with one of the ship's officers, and as the dance ended, the officer escorted her back to Gabe's table.

"How lucky you are, sir, to be married to such a beautiful and delightful young lady," the officer said to Gabe.

"Yes, aren't I?" Gabe's response was more conversational in tone than enthusiastic.

"Oh, isn't this just the most wonderful evening?" Marthalee asked, fanning herself with a silk hand fan that matched her gown.

"Is there a ship's officer you haven't danced with?" Gabe asked.

"Darling, you are jealous," Marthalee said with a little chuckle. "How quaint. Besides, I haven't danced with the captain or the first officer."

"No doubt you will before the evening is over."

"I'm only dancing with the officers because none of them have their family with them. It has to get lonely for them, a long voyage like this. But if you would rather I not, I won't dance with anyone else. I'll just sit here with you like the dutiful wife."

Before Gabe could answer, another officer came to the table. "Mrs. Corrigan, I believe I have your name on my card for this dance."

"Do you mind, darling?" Marthalee looked at Gabe.

Gabe made no response, but picked up his glass and took a drink.

Marthalee stood and put her hand on the young officer's arm.

Anna Scott came over to Gabe's table, and he stood as she approached. "May I join you, Gabe?"

"Yes, please do."

"We both seemed to be abandoned at the moment. Tom has some potential investors he is talking to, and Marthalee is"—Anna paused—"having such a good time."

"Marthalee always has a good time."

"I think Marthalee is what is referred to in modern parlance as the *new woman*."

"Perhaps."

Anna put her hand on Gabe's and patted it much as a mother would comfort a grown son. "So, are you looking forward to London?"

"I suppose, but there is so much riding on this trip."

Anna laughed softly. "Oh, you would look at it just from the business point of view. You are just like Tom. But I am looking forward to revisiting some of the sights with Marthalee. She tells me this is her first trip to London, and with her exuberance for life, I know she will be a delight."

"Thank you for entertaining her. I do appreciate it, Anna."

"It is my pleasure. She is a delightful girl. Oh, I see Tom is not engaged at the moment so maybe he has time for me."

Gabe stood as Anna did; then, instead of sitting, he left the ballroom and walked outside, onto the starboard promenade. With his forearms resting on the railing and his hands clasped together, he stared down at the sea, listening to the sound of the water slipping past the hull. The night sky was filled with stars; the moon was big and bright, and it projected a long, silver swath from the horizon to the ship. A quarter-mile-long luminescent white wake rolled and frothed behind them.

The moonlight and the stars and the sound of

the water made him think of a rock on the bluff of the Trinity River. He closed his eyes and re-created that night: the barbecue, the dance, the kiss, the sweet innocence of Josie Laclede. He had heard that the town of Fort Worth was feverishly preparing for the arrival of the railroad, with many new businesses being built. When he had learned that a new hotel was being built—The Empress—he had imagined that it was hers. The railroad had to be in Fort Worth by New Year's Day. As soon as he returned to Philadelphia, he would schedule himself for a trip to the celebration that he would insist upon when the first train pulled into town.

Why was he doing this? It was pure torture to obsess about something that could never be.

Gabe stood so engaged in his thoughts that he did not hear Colonel Scott come up to stand beside him.

"I needed a bit of fresh air. Do you mind if I join you?"

"Did you abandon Anna?"

"She abandoned me. She's dancing with Jason Colfax. The Jason Colfax of Colfax Steel. It's part of my plan to get some money from him."

"Too bad the ship's officers aren't potential investors," Gabe said cynically.

Scott laughed at his comment. "Yes, isn't it?" He was quiet for a moment before speaking again. "I should have been a sailor. I've always liked the sea."

"The railroad business isn't all that different, is it? Big things that move?"

Scott chuckled. "If you put it that way."

Someone opened the door to the first-class ballroom, and for just a moment the orchestra could be heard. Then the door closed and the music was gone.

"It sounds as if the party is still in full swing," Gabe said.

"Yes, it is. People have been asking about you, wondering where you got off to."

"I'm sure they are getting along just fine without me."

"Marthalee does seem to be filling in quite nicely."

"I'm sure she is."

"She has unbridled enthusiasm and is as effervescent as anyone I've ever known. Consider this, Gabe. A beautiful wife is always an asset. Especially given the task that lies before us. Before we leave England, we must raise ten million dollars."

Gabe whistled. "Sometimes the task seems insurmountable. Ten million dollars. Do you really think we can raise that much money?"

"We can, and we will. You did your part; you managed to line up the right people to come to our meeting. Now it is up to me to convince them to part with their money."

"I don't envy you your job."

"Darling!" Marthalee called from the open door of the ballroom. The shining gasoliers created a bubble of golden light behind her. "You simply must come back in here. You are missing all the fun."

Gabe sighed, then started across the short stretch of deck toward the door. "I'm coming."

Fort Worth, Texas—September 1873

It was Josie who suggested to her father that they start a hotel. But not just any hotel. She insisted that it should be of the highest quality. After all, with the railroad coming, they were bound to get visitors to Fort Worth who were used to such accommodations.

Henri agreed, and with a loan arranged through the newly formed Tidball-Wilson banking house, he bought the corner of Fifth and Rusk Streets. There, he built a two-story frame hotel, naming it The Empress, to Josie's mixed embarrassment and delight. Behind it he built a separate kitchen and smokehouse combination, a laundry facility, a storeroom with an underground icehouse and a root cellar, and a cottage for the Lanes. Willie would take care of general maintenance, and Ida would supervise the kitchen and laundry. Eight-year-old Julius was named the official keeper of the stairs, charged with dusting them every day.

Josie took an active part in designing and furnishing the hotel. There were twenty guest rooms, fourteen on the upper floor and six on the ground floor. Some rooms were plastered and painted with milk paint in various shades of blue, green, rose, and yellow, while others had paper wall coverings in patterns of exotic birds or foliage or flowers. The pine floors had been shellacked to a shiny red-orange, and a small carpet runner would be placed on each side of the beds.

At the moment, Josie and Ida were cleaning windows. Josie was dipping her rag into a bucket of vinegar water, and Ida came along behind her, drying the panes with a piece of cheesecloth.

Josie stopped for a moment, leaning against the wall.

"Miss Josie, look at you, honey, you're plum tuckered out working so hard on this hotel," Ida Lane said. "You need to just sit a spell and let me do some of this cleanin' 'cause you've been pol-ishin' the woodwork and washin' these window lights since early this mornin'."

"Oh, Ida, I want it to be perfect when the freight wagons arrive with the furniture. I got a bill of lad-ing saying my shipment has reached Dallas, and as soon as Conrad Morgan can get enough wag-ons together, he's going to send his men to pick up my freight."

The front door opened and Julius and his friend Troy came running through.

"Julius, you and Troy just go back outside," Ida scolded. "Don't you be trackin' dirt in here after Miss Josie cleaned so hard."

"All right, Mama," Julius said, and he and Troy went back outside. Ida took a cloth over to where the two boys had come in and, getting down on her hands and knees, began to wipe up the dirt.

"I hope you're not going to be disappointed in the furniture, and all, it comin' from New Orleans," Ida said. "There ain't no tellin' what kind of sickness your people might get from sleepin' in them beds. I don't like it that they came from some whorehouse."

"I shouldn't have told you where I got the furniture, but the ad in the *Times Picayune* said it was a nice lot. If it makes you feel any better, I am having all new feather beds made."

"Who's makin' 'em? You didn't ask me."

"There's a new couple that's settled across the river, and they're trying to make a living by farming and raising chickens, so I asked Betty Courtright to make them for me."

"Miz Courtright. Ain't she the one that's married to that man they call Longhaired Jim?"

"Yes, he's the one, but they seem like good people."

Finished with the floor, Ida stood up and returned to the window to begin wiping the panes behind Josie.

"You can't say that about everybody. If you was to ask me, I'd say we got a whole passel of scallywags and good-for-nothin's movin' in here. I heard Mr. Paddock say we got mor'n three thousand people living right here in Fort Worth. That sure is a lot of people to have come in little more than a year. Have you seen all them tents down by the river?"

"Yes, I have, but they will all be building new houses soon enough. And they'll be starting new businesses, too. And when the railroad gets here, a lot more people will be coming in. It will be good for business, and it will enrich us all."

Josie entered her room in the Lacledes' quarters behind the grocery store. She was exhausted after a hard day's work, but she was pleased with how the hotel was coming together.

She had thought that she would go to sleep quickly once her head hit the pillow, but sleep didn't come.

Why? Why couldn't she sleep?

Then, as she lay there in the dark, she knew why sleep was so elusive. It had been she who had talked Henri into building the hotel. He had borrowed $4,500 from the newly formed banking house, from men who had only come to Fort Worth last spring. Were they honest businessmen or were they here to get the town folks' trust and then abscond with their money?

Josie had tried to be frugal, buying used furniture based solely on an advertisement she had read in the *Times Picayune*. The ad had described the furniture in glowing terms: "Turned walnut bedposts on oversize bedsteads, carved headboards with magnolia-blossom medallions, chests with marble tops and carved pulls, various tables and chairs suitable for the finest bedrooms."

The ad had also said that the furniture had

come from Madame Garneau's House of Pleasure. It had not specifically said that the House of Pleasure was a bawdy house, but with a name like that, what else could it be?

"Yeehah! Yeehah!"

"Whoop, whoop, whoop!"

The shouting came from the street, and she could hear the sound of hooves as horses galloped through the town. Then she heard gunshots, followed by raucous laughter, and she knew that someone had been shooting at the big coffeepot that hung in front of Enoch Welch's tinshop. It was the favorite target as the cowboys raced through the town on their way back to their camps after an evening spent in the saloons and cribs. By now, the coffeepot sported at least fifty bullet holes.

What had she done? She had talked her father into building the hotel, for which he had gone into debt. At the time, she was sure it was the right decision, but now she was having second thoughts.

From her bed, she watched the moon shadows from a cottonwood tree that were projected onto her wall. After about an hour of restless tossing about, she got up, walked over to the window, and looked outside. The rustling leaves of the tree caught the moonbeams and, answering the slight breeze, cast slivers of silver into the night.

Fort Worth did not have a business district, per se. Private homes were interspersed with stores and shops and saloons, and the house closest to the grocery store belonged to Matthew Clark and his wife, Louise. A dim light was shining through one of their windows, and Josie imagined herself walking the floors of the neighboring house. Maybe Louise was up nursing little Eva. Or Frankie had been awakened by a nightmare and his mama was comforting him. Maybe Matt and Louise were settling an argument. Or maybe they had just made love.

What was that, *to make love*? Josie wasn't sure. She was convinced that it was more important to men than it was to women, because otherwise, why would men pay to lie with women in cribs? What did women get from that except money? Surely they didn't enjoy it.

But maybe they did. Once in her life, she had enjoyed being in the company of a man. Gabe Corrigan.

Josie recalled the last time she had seen him. He had kissed her, and it was surprising and exhilarating. So exhilarating that she was frightened by what she had felt, and her reaction to the kiss had been anything but amenable.

She wondered if he remembered. Right before the kiss he had asked her to go with him, but she had pretended that she didn't hear. What if she had said yes? She would never know what might have happened.

She returned to her bed and pulled a light blanket up over her shoulders. "The Texas and Pacific has to be here by New Year's Day. I'll plan a celebration, and who better to come than the executive administrator of the railroad?" When she lay back down, she began mentally composing an invitation to Gabe—no, she would make it to everyone at the T&P headquarters. She would invite them all to The Empress Hotel, and if he possibly could, she just knew Gabe Corrigan would come. She drifted off to sleep with a smile on her face.

London, England—September 1873

Close to fifty of England's leading financiers were gathered in the dining room of the Alexandra Hotel. By arrangement, the dining room was closed to everyone except those people who held invitations to the presentation that Thomas Scott was about to give.

Gabe had erected several easels about the room, and on each easel he had placed an artist's rendering of some projected element of the future of the Texas and Pacific Railway. One picture showed a train pulling cars loaded with happy passengers through picturesque countryside. Another showed a freight train laden with produce of the land. One showed cattle being loaded onto stock cars, another had buffalo robes piled high. At least three depicted huge and elaborate depot buildings, none of which had yet been built. And one showed Indians, in full regalia, mounted on horses and watching in awe as a mighty fire-engine-red locomotive, smoke billowing from the diamond stack, roared by. Gold lettering on the tender said TEXAS AND PACIFIC.

"Excellent, Gabe, excellent," Colonel Scott had said after he examined the layout. "You have done a wonderful job in getting everything set up."

"Thank you."

Sir Nigel Lancaster, Earl of Stradfordshire, was wearing the uniform of his regiment, complete with a medal-bedecked red tunic showing the insignia of a lieutenant colonel. He had come to the meeting with the intention of investing in an American railroad, not as the result of any financial planning but because he thought part of an American railroad would be a wonderful enhancement for his portfolio.

But his being present had been an added bonus. The wife of one of the American presenters was one of the most beautiful women Sir Nigel had ever seen; her flowing red hair, milky-white skin, and voluptuous body aroused him as no one had before. He was determined to have her, and in a flirtatious repartee with her he found that she was not inhibited. No courtesan he had ever engaged was more receptive to his advances than Marthalee Corrigan.

Sir Nigel was known throughout the kingdom as a lothario, a libertine who had debauched many women, married and unmarried. This woman was married, but Sir Nigel enjoyed the quest even more when his object was unavailable. He was also a good judge of women, and he knew that she was a plum ripe for picking.

As he moved quickly down the hall, he saw Marthalee just outside the dining room, leaning against the wall in a way that brought her dress more tightly against her body, showing her figure in a way that maddened Sir Nigel's senses.

"Sir Nigel," she said, her voice low, husky, and dripping with the sweet-as-honey accent of the American South. "What are you doing out here? Shouldn't you be inside, listening to Colonel Scott's presentation?"

"There is no need for me to listen. I have already committed to a rather generous investment in his railroad."

"Oh, how wonderful! I am sure that both Colonel Scott and my"—she paused for a moment before she emphasized the next word—"husband will be pleased."

"You are concerned about whether your husband will be pleased with my investment?"

"Yes, of course."

"But he will be much less pleased about my interest in you, will he not?"

"Why, Sir Nigel, whatever are you talking about?"

"I think you know what I'm talking about. Marthalee Corrigan, you are the most ravishing woman I have ever seen."

Marthalee giggled girlishly. "And you are the most silver-tongued flatterer I have ever encountered. Why, a girl just doesn't know whether to believe anything you have to say or not."

"Then, believe this. I want you—more than I have ever wanted any woman."

"Sir Nigel! Really, sir, you have gone beyond the boundary of gentlemanly conversation. What sort of woman do you think I am?"

"It isn't what kind of woman I think you are. It is what kind of woman I *know* you are. I know you are a woman of spirit, courage, and adventure. I know you are the kind of woman who will not hide your true desires behind quaint customs. Tell me that you are not intrigued by the thought of sharing an hour of exquisite pleasure and delight with me."

"I'm—not."

"You are not intrigued by the thought? Or, you are not going to tell me that you aren't?"

Marthalee's breathing began to come in shallow gasps, and the pupils of her eyes grew larger.

"Tell me, my dear, how long will Colonel Scott be speaking?"

"I don't know," Marthalee replied, her words barely a whisper.

"It is true, is it not, that all the while Colonel Scott is speaking, your husband will be occupied?"

"Yes, that is true."

"Good. That will give us time to get to know each other better, won't it, my dear?"

"I—I have not agreed to this."

"Oh, but you have. Your heart has said yes, and your head will soon follow."

Sir Nigel held out his arm, and Marthalee, after

a quick glance into the dining room, where the guests were beginning to take their seats, looked back at him.

"Sir Nigel, what kind of woman do you think I am?" She wanted to sound challenging, resolute in refusing his offer, but her voice was strained with barely controlled desire.

"The most beautiful, the most sensuous woman in the world, who wants to enjoy life. She wants more than what the man she is married to will give her. Come with me, and let me show you what you are capable of feeling."

"I'm just a country girl from Louisiana. It could be said that you are taking advantage of me, sir."

"Somehow, I do not think that is true." Sir Nigel extended his arm.

Marthalee took another glance into the dining room, then with her most flirtatious smile put her hand on his arm. "We mustn't be too long. I would not want my husband to become concerned."

"I will have you back before you are missed."

As they walked away, Marthalee could hear Colonel Scott beginning his talk.

Anna Scott left her room in a hurry. She had told Tom she would be in the dining room for his presentation, but as she looked at the watch pinned to the lapel of her jacket, she saw that she was late. Making the turn in the corridor, she stopped. She saw the unmistakable flaming-red hair of Marthalee Corrigan and a man dressed in the red tunic of a British officer coming toward her. She quickly stepped back, rehearsing what she might say when she was directly confronted. But her fears were for naught.

She heard the unmistakable click of a key opening a door, and when she heard flirtatious laughter, Anna peered around the corner. She saw the officer loosen Marthalee's dress, slipping it off her shoulders and exposing her breasts even before they entered the room. Just before the door closed, Anna heard the officer say, "We must hurry, my love. I must get you back before Mr. Corrigan knows you are gone."

Anna's heart sank, and she returned to her room. She could not face Gabe, whom she cared for as much as one of her own children. She could not tell him what she had seen, and she could not choose to keep it from him. He would be devastated. Or did he already know?

Gabe stood at the back of the room, studying the faces of those who had accepted his invitation to attend this meeting. He had been up-front in his invitation, explaining that there would be a solicitation for investment in the Texas and Pacific Railway Company. That meant that all who had come, by their very presence, were receptive to Scott's prospectus.

He had heard Scott's spiel before, and he knew what parts of the proposal would elicit the greatest response.

"Gentlemen," Scott began, "although for years petroleum springs have been considered a nuisance because they foul the water, we are now entering an age when oil will become as valuable as gold. In Texas, served by the Texas and Pacific Railway, there is an area in Hardin County where petroleum springs occur over a space of about fifty square miles. Engineers tell us that it is probable that much larger supplies may be obtained simply by boring into the ground after them.

"Professor A. R. Rossier's mineral survey tells us that the iron deposits of northeastern Texas are of the most remarkable character, equaling in extent and richness those of Sweden, Missouri, New Jersey, and New York. In addition, gold, silver, and copper exist in inexhaustible quantities in West Texas and on to the Pacific. The manufacturing, agricultural, and ranching opportunities in Texas are limitless.

"Those rich deposits are going to attract travelers and settlers, all of whom will use the Texas and Pacific Railway as their means of reaching the area. Also there are natural advantages to the southern route because it is never closed in the winter.

"If this information is not enough to entice you to purchase bonds to finance the T&P, let me whet your appetite even more. As of this date, September eighteenth, rails have been laid as far as Forney, Texas. I will admit I had hoped that we would have reached Fort Worth by now, but I believe you are aware that an outbreak of yellow fever has ravaged the Southern states this past summer, and our track-laying crews were not immune to this disease.

"Right now we have fewer than fifty miles of track to build, but, gentlemen, we must reach Fort Worth by January first, 1874. At that time the State of Texas has pledged to give us sixteen sections of land for every mile we have completed. At a conservative price of two dollars per acre, that is over twenty thousand dollars per mile. Gentlemen, I ask you, can you afford not to invest in this guaranteed venture?"

Watching the reaction to Scott's words, Gabe felt exhilarated. They had come to England to raise $10 million, and Gabe believed, from the enthusiastic responses from the investors, they might come at least halfway to their goal in this, the very first, meeting. Four more were scheduled.

"Mr. Corrigan?"

Slightly irritated that someone would intrude on the meeting, Gabe turned toward the person who had spoken to him, the hotel concierge.

"Yes?"

"This was just delivered, sir. It is a cablegram from the United States, and it is marked urgent."

"Thank you."

Still listening to Scott's appeal, Gabe pulled the cablegram from the envelope and read.

JAY COOKE & COMPANY HAS COLLAPSED.
FEAR THAT MANY BANKS MAY FAIL. US STOCK
MARKET CLOSED. BONDS HELD FOR T&P
WITHDRAWN. RETURN HOME SOONEST.

"Maybe we don't need to tell anyone about this," Scott said after the meeting was over and he had read the cablegram.

"Colonel, the same cable that brought us this news more than likely delivered it to the London Stock Exchange, and to all the newspapers in England. Jay Cooke is the fiscal agent for the general US government. Just think how many bonds people all over the world hold that his firm negotiated. It will be impossible to keep this a secret."

They were sitting at one of the tables in the meeting room, and Scott drummed his fingers for a moment. "This is bad. This is very bad."

"We still have the land grants, though. Maybe we can sell them to raise the operating capital we need."

Scott shook his head. "We don't have that yet. Until that engine pulls into Fort Worth, all of the land still belongs to the State of Texas."

"What now?"

"I have some favors I can call in. When we get home, I'll call on everyone I know who has any money at all and see what I can borrow from them. But you know how much we needed to raise on this trip. Now, we won't get a penny from London."

"Then, the best thing is to leave for home as soon as possible."

"Yes, but," Scott continued, "that brings us to your position. I think I would like to put you in charge of the feeder lines that we've started, but that means you'll have to leave Philadelphia."

"All right," Gabe said, trying to comprehend exactly what Colonel Scott was telling him.

"You understand that after we expend the funds we have on hand right now, there will be no capital for anything, and that includes salaries for everybody, you included. Now you can quit, and I can understand that if you do, or you can stay on. I can compensate you in T&P stock—which I believe in my heart is going to be worth a lot of money one day—but I can't pay you. And of course, there is also the possibility that the stock will be worthless."

"I understand."

"So which is it, Gabe? Do you walk? Or do you become a gambler?"

Gabe smiled. "Will I have to wear a little string tie like the gamblers on the Mississippi River boats?"

Scott laughed. "If you do, I'll buy one for you."

Shreveport, Louisiana—December 1873

"We could have stayed in Philadelphia. I don't want to be back in this Podunk town where there's nothing to do. If you would let him, my father could make you a senator from Louisiana and we could be in Washington." Marthalee was pacing around

Gabe's office, a mere ten-foot square in the back of the T&P passenger depot. "If you think I'm going to stay here, living like some fishwife, suffering the awkward silences and cutting glances of my friends, you have another think coming."

"If your acquaintences treat you that way, they aren't what I would call friends," Gabe said.

"What do you know about it, anyway? My father's connections made you and this railroad, and he can break you."

Gabe took a deep breath before trying to explain to his wife one more time what the situation was.

"He doesn't have to break me. Don't you understand? There is no money! The Texas and Pacific is on the verge of bankruptcy. Colonel Scott asked me to get the railroad as far as possible on the money and supplies we had on hand, and we got it six miles beyond Dallas. I chose to locate us in Shreveport because I thought you would be happier here than in Dallas, or worse yet, Eagle Ford."

"Well, I'm not. And you—why won't you even consider becoming a senator? Daddy could make it happen right now, but you have to at least act like you want the appointment."

"I *don't* want it. I am a railroad man. That's what I know."

"We are living in two rooms at a boardinghouse. A boardinghouse, mind you! I deserve more than this, Gabe Corrigan. I was not born to live in such squalor, and if you had even one ounce of self-respect, you would realize it. I mean, just look at where you are working! The great vice president of a would-be railroad, with an office no bigger than the clothes closet I had when I was living at home." Marthalee looked around the tiny office. "I should have known better than to marry a Yankee. Yankees don't have the slightest concept of what it means to be a gentleman."

Marthalee stormed out of the room, leaving Gabe alone at his desk. He picked up the unopened mail. One particular letter caught his attention because it had no return address, but it bore a British post stamp.

The penmanship was clear and quite readable:

My dear Mr. Corrigan:

It pains me to write this, for I wish to be neither the gossip nor the purveyor of scandal. But you, sir, have been made the cuckold. On the day of the solicitation of investors in the American railroad Texas and Pacific, at the very hour of the presentation, your wife was seen to enter the room of Sir Nigel Lancaster, Earl of Stradfordshire, her clothing in some disarray. The pair occupied the room for thirty-six minutes before your wife and Sir Nigel emerged. I share this information with you, sir, because I think you should know, and also because you were decent enough to inform the investors of the collapse of Jay Cooke & Company before any more financial calamity could occur.

Gabe reread the letter, then folded it and put it in his breast pocket. He didn't know what he would do with it. Not yet.

Gabe threw himself into his work, staying away from home as much as possible. He made trips to Dallas and Texarkana, Galveston and Jackson, New Orleans and Houston, talking to anyone who might possibly be able to come up with money to fund the railroad.

In Gabe's absence, Marthalee moved her belongings back to her father's sprawling estate, which overlooked the Red River.

"Father, do you have any idea how I am living? Why, there isn't a maid in this entire parish who doesn't have nicer accommodations than I do. And Gabriel? His office is so tiny you can scarcely turn around."

"But this young man has such potential, Marthalee. He is going to be a very wealthy man someday," General Galloway said.

"No, he isn't. You forget, Father, I've been to Philadelphia with him, I've heard talk of the meetings he and Colonel Scott have had with their investors. Jay Gould, for example, is chomping at the bit to get his hands on the T&P. And when he does, there won't be a Texas and Pacific Railway, and when that happens, Gabe would lucky to get a job as a baggage handler."

"If you are correct, we can forget any thought of him ever being a senator," Galloway said.

"Oh, Daddy, I am so miserable," Marthalee wailed.

Galloway took her in his arms to comfort her. "What do you want to do, Marthalee?"

"I don't know."

"I've always done right by my little girl, haven't I? Just leave it to me. I'll take care of it."

Gabe was returning from a trip to Austin, where, thanks to the efforts of Governor Throckmorton, he had been able to convince a sympathetic legislature to allow the T&P an extension to get the tracks laid to Fort Worth. Upon his return to Shreveport, Gabe went to see a lawyer. He was going to sue for a bill of divorcement.

Gabe thought that the letter telling of Marthalee's conduct in London would be enough, and when he approached Randolph Cutler, attorney-at-law, he showed it to him.

"I'm sorry, Mr. Corrigan, but an anonymous letter will have absolutely no validity in a court of law."

"But she committed adultery. Isn't adultery enough justification for a divorce?"

"It would be if we had absolute proof."

"I know she did," Gabe said.

"How do you know?"

"I remember that oily little bastard that was hanging around her. I suspected it even then. I should have confronted her."

The lawyer folded the letter, then passed it

back across his desk. "Unless you can get whoever wrote this to testify what he or she saw, it doesn't help you. And I must tell you, General Galloway would never allow such an accusation to be lodged against his daughter. He is a powerful man, and he could make things very uncomfortable for you."

"I don't see how it could be any more uncomfortable than it is now," Gabe said.

"As I said, I am sorry. But the only way you will be able to get a divorce is if Mrs. Corrigan is a consenting litigant."

Returning to the boardinghouse after his visit with the lawyer, Gabe had just started up the steps when a young man approached him.

"Are you Mr. Corrigan?"

"I am."

"This is for you."

"Thank you." Gabe handed the young man a coin.

The envelope looked official, and he supposed it was from Colonel Scott with more bad news about the railroad. When he opened it, though, he saw that it was something entirely different.

CERTIFICATE OF ANNULMENT

Know Ye All by These Presents
That the marriage between Gabriel Michael Corrigan and Marthalee Elizabeth Galloway does not exist, and is deemed not

to have existed. This union was declared
void because there was no mutual consent
of the parties. This annulment is final and
uncontestable. Given this day, January 10,
1874, by my hand and seal.
   Vernon R. DuPont
   Judge, Caddo Parish, Louisiana

"Yes, there is a God in heaven!" Gabe shouted
as he took the stairs three at a time. For the first
time in over a year, he felt like a free man.

FIVE

We've enjoyed having you with us, Mr. Cornett," Josie said as the hotel guest stood in the lobby.

"Thank you." Raymond Cornett looked around the lobby. "You sure have a fine hotel here. It's a shame you don't have many guests. I felt I didn't deserve all the attention you gave me."

Josie smiled broadly. "Why should you feel bad? You were a wonderful guest and it was an absolute pleasure to serve you."

Julius came in through the front door. "Mr. Cornett, Pop has the buckboard out front. He'll take you down to the stage depot when you are ready." Julius picked up the guest's satchel.

"You sure you can handle that? It's almost as big as you are," Cornett said.

"I can handle it. I'm strong." To prove his point, Julius hefted the suitcase, then started toward the door.

Cornett followed Julius out the front door as Josie watched from the window. She saw Julius put the luggage in the back of the buckboard, then turn around and smile at Cornett. Cornett dug down into his pocket, then pulled out a coin and gave it to Julius. Julius looked at it, and a broad smile spread across his face. He came running back into the hotel.

"Miss Josie, Miss Josie! Mr. Cornett gave me a dime. He gave me a dime just for carrying out his satchel."

"Well, I'm sure that's because he saw what a fine young man you are." Josie peered out the window again, watching as Willie drove the buckboard down the street, headed for Andrew's Tavern, which also served as the depot for the Butterfield Overland Stage.

"I'm going to put this money in my sock," Julius said proudly, running through the lobby and out the back door.

Josie got the carpet sweeper out and started pushing it across the floor. She was hard at work when Henri came into the hotel.

"I just saw Willie taking Mr. Cornett down to the depot."

"Yes, I'm sorry to see him go."

"We'll all miss him. He was a fine guest," Henri said.

"He was our only guest. As of now, the hotel is totally empty."

"Don't worry, we'll have more people."

Josie stopped sweeping for a moment. "Oh, Papa, what have I gotten you into?"

"Why, whatever do you mean, child?"

"It was my idea to build this hotel. I talked you into it, remember?"

"Indeed I do remember. That's why I named it after you."

"We aren't going to be able to keep it open much longer. If we didn't have the store, we wouldn't have any food to eat or any money at all. I think we should just board this albatross up and move back to our old quarters."

"And where would poor Mr. Manning go now that he doesn't have any music students?" Henri asked. "I like that young man very much, and I think he would make a good and decent husband for you. And you know he's doing a good job taking care of the store for us. He's smart and he's clean. . . ."

"Papa, I don't want to hear that ever again. I know he is smart, and I know he is clean, and I know he polishes his shoes every day, but that is not enough to make me want to marry Oscar Manning."

"It may not be, but, honey, do I need to remind you that you are twenty-four years old now? Many would say you have entered spinsterhood. You're getting of the age when you should start thinking about getting married and settling down."

Josie laughed. "Settle down? Why must I settle down? Am I too wild?"

"No, no, I didn't mean it like that. I think you are the most wonderful daughter any man could ever have. It's just that, like all fathers, I want only the best for you. And that will only happen when you find someone you can share the rest of your life with."

"Papa, you wouldn't want me to marry a man I didn't love, would you?"

"I worry about you. I'm sixty-six years old; I'm not going to be around forever, you know. Who will take care of you when I am gone?"

Josie looked around at her beautiful surroundings, her very own creation, planned to the smallest detail by no one but herself. "The Empress will take care of Empress."

"If only that were a certainty, my dear. I know I just told you we would have more guests, but, Josie, we have to be realistic. The population of Fort Worth is down to under a thousand people. You see all the boarded-up buildings and the houses that are standing empty." Henri took Josie by the hand and led her to the window.

"Do you see that?" He pointed toward the street. "That's grass. Grass growing in the street. Why? Because there are no new people coming here, there is no business, and now even the cowboys take their herds to load on the trains at Eagle Ford. The railroad is not going to get here anytime soon, and without it, the whole town will die."

Josie couldn't listen to any more. She dropped her sweeper and ran out onto the street, which was covered with at least three inches of fine dust. She ran until she got to the bluff overlooking the tree-lined river. When she saw the rock, her rock, she kicked it, and she hurt her toe. As she was hobbling around on one foot, she was screaming.

"I hate you, Gabe Corrigan! I hate the railroad! Why did you ever tell us you were going to come here and then not come?" By now tears of anger and frustration were streaming down her cheeks as she plopped down on the rock. She sat there for several minutes sobbing uncontrollably until she finally had no more tears.

At last the flowing water from the Trinity began to work its magic and she began to calm herself. She thought back to that day more than three years ago when the town was exuberant with expectation—the railroad was coming. The town had held up its part of the bargain. Everything that the town had promised had been done. But nothing that the Texas and Pacific had promised had occurred.

But maybe she wasn't being fair. The Panic of '73, as it was called, was caused by the collapse of Jay Cooke, and that had affected the whole country, not just Fort Worth. It had hit the railroads particularly hard because all their financing was with bonds. And if everybody all over the country was losing money, who would invest in new railroads?

But look at what was happening in Dallas, and even Eagle Ford. They were not dying the way

Fort Worth was; in fact, many of the people who were leaving Fort Worth were moving to Dallas. The railroad had to come to Fort Worth someway, somehow.

Then Josie had an idea. "Yes!" she shouted. "We can do it!"

She turned and ran back to the hotel as fast as she could, taking off her shoes and hiking her skirt up like a schoolgirl to run in the soft dust.

"Papa, I have an idea that will not only save our hotel, but save all the businesses in town. And bring in new businesses besides!" Josie panted for breath after her run.

"Josie, what in heaven's name are you talking about?" Henri asked.

"I'm talking about bringing the railroad to Fort Worth."

"Yes, we're all waiting and hoping for that to happen."

"No, Papa, you don't understand. I'm not talking about waiting and hoping. When I say bring the railroad into town, that's what I mean, literally. We don't wait for the railroad to come to us—we go to the railroad."

"I'm still not following you."

"Then, I will explain it to you."

When Henri stepped into the newspaper office, Buckley Paddock looked up. "Henri! How are you doing, my friend? I miss you now that we are no longer in the same building."

"I'm not that far away, Buckley. Anytime you want to visit, feel free to come on down."

"Well, I wouldn't want to disturb any of your guests."

"What guests?"

Buckley chuckled, then quickly cut off his laughter, realizing that a hotel without guests was no laughing matter. "I'm sorry, I didn't mean to make light of it. It's just that the whole town is such gloom and doom that one looks for an occasion to laugh, even if the laughter is uncomfortable."

"Well, it could be that we have just come up with a plan that might reverse the fortunes for our fair town."

"What plan is that?"

"Oh, I don't want to talk about it yet. But we'll explain it at the meeting."

"Meeting? What meeting?"

"The town meeting you're going to advertise in your paper."

"All right, when and where is this meeting to be held?"

"In the dining room at The Empress Hotel. Tomorrow evening. Oh, and, Buckley . . ."

"Yes, sir?"

"This meeting is open to everyone in Fort Worth, men, women, and children. I want you to stress that."

"Women, too? Women at a business meeting?"

"Why not? They may have something valuable to add."

"I've never known a woman to add anything of any consequence to a business meeting."

"I'll tell you what. It will not only be a business meeting, it will be a potluck dinner as well. Put that in your newspaper, too."

The ad ran the next day.

TOWN MEETING TODAY
All Are Invited, Men, Women and Children
To Discuss Problems That Beset Our City

COME ONE—COME ALL
Bring Favorite Dish for Potluck
Supper at Six P.M.
Business Discussion to Follow
Dining Room at

THE EMPRESS HOTEL

The dining room had been built to accommodate more than a hundred people, but since the crash two years ago, it had seen little use, often serving as little more than a storage room for the hotel. A small anteroom had been more than adequate to serve the hotel's few guests.

The meeting today did have a bit of a festive air about it, given that women and children were present, but the potluck food was mainly comfort foods—ham and beans with turnip greens and corn bread, chicken and dumplings and yams, and Ida had made her fried fruit pies. The dining room, which for over a year had sat in silence, now rang with laughter and conversation. But the primary purpose of the gathering, as discussed in the published advertisement, was to conduct a business meeting.

"Ladies," Mrs. Van Zandt said to several of her neighbors, "I believe it is time we cleaned up and left the menfolk to their business."

"Please, Mrs. Van Zandt, no! Don't leave!" Henri begged.

Mrs. Van Zandt looked at Henri in surprise. "Do you mean you aren't going to have a business meeting?"

"Yes, we are going to have one, but as it affects every man, woman, and child in Fort Worth, I think it is only fitting that you be present during the discussion."

"Well, I never heard of such a thing," Mrs. Van Zandt said.

"That's because you've never read the articles and speeches written by Miss Susan B. Anthony," Josie said.

"People, people, people!" James Courtright shouted in a fine, deep voice. He held his arms up to get everyone's attention. Courtright, who was Marshal Redding's jailer and all-around janitor, waited until the room grew quiet before he spoke again. Then he turned to Buckley Paddock. "We're about to start now, and Mr. Paddock has been chosen to chair the meeting. Mr. Paddock, the floor is yours."

Paddock walked over to a podium on one side of the room. Behind the podium was an easel, but whatever was on the easel was covered by a piece of canvas so it couldn't be seen. Paddock stood for a moment looking out over the room. Easily more than a hundred people were present, and he was pleased with the turnout.

"First, I want to thank Henri Laclede for making this dining room available for the meeting, and I think we should all give him a hand." Paddock waited until the polite applause ended before he continued, "Ladies and gentlemen, I don't have to tell you the problem, we all know it. When we thought the railroad was coming to Fort Worth, professional men from all over the country left their homes and businesses to start anew.

"They, and we, believed that Fort Worth was destined to become the metropolis of Texas.

"But it didn't happen. The railroad came as far as Eagle Ford, and then it stopped. And what has been the result? New businesses, once with bright futures, have been closed. Homes have been abandoned. The cattlemen who once made Fort Worth their departure point for the drive north now give all their business to Eagle Ford. And the roads into Fort Worth, once crowded with people flocking to the city to start new businesses and enterprises, are now crowded with residents fleeing the city.

"Those of us who stay are struggling to hang on." Paddock made a sweep with his arm. "I invite you to look around, gentlemen, at this hotel. The

Empress Hotel is as fine a hotel as you will find between New Orleans and San Francisco. Yet every room is vacant, and the dining room is not even used.

"We cannot let this condition remain. We cannot give up. We must find a way to overcome this travail, and that, ladies and gentlemen, is the task we will set for ourselves at this meeting."

"Did you see the article in the *Dallas Herald*?" Daggett asked from the floor.

"What article was that?" Tidball asked.

"I brought it with me," Daggett said. "The article was written by Robert Cowart."

"Is he that lawyer who used to live here?" Henri asked. "If I remember, he was always complaining about something."

"That's the one," Daggett replied. "He skedaddled over to Dallas as fast as a rat leaves a rotting ship."

"Well, what did he have to say?" Courtright asked.

Daggett cleared his throat, then began to read: "'Fort Worth is rapidly becoming a town of so little consequence that one wonders how much longer it will maintain its charter. There are more unoccupied buildings in the town than there are those that are occupied. Like a hollowed-out pumpkin, it is collapsing in on itself, so lazy a town that recently a panther was seen to be sleeping, undisturbed, in the middle of Rusk Street.'"

"What?" Jennings shouted in anger. "The Dallas

newspaper actually said we had a panther sleeping in the middle of Rusk Street? Why, no such thing happened."

"It doesn't matter whether it actually happened or not." Daggett tapped the newspaper with his finger. "The thing is, it has been written, and this story will be believed. Soon, we will be the laughingstock of the entire country, and we'll be known as Pantherville."

"We may not like what he has said, but it is a pretty accurate description of what has happened in Fort Worth," Jim Courtright said.

"I think Cowart has gone overboard with his sense of the ridiculous. He knows the people in this town are used to taking the bull by the horns, and in a way he is goading us to do something," Henri said.

"Pantherville," Paddock said. "I like that."

"You like it?" Jennings asked.

"Think about it," Paddock replied. "Panthers are noble beasts. Quick, strong, intelligent. They are the hunters, not the hunted."

"Buckley is right," Tidball said. "Instead of being angered by what the Dallas paper intended as a slur, I think we should adopt it as if it were a great compliment. In fact, I think it is an accolade, whether or not Cowart realized that when he wrote it."

"I like it so much that I intend to put a panther on the masthead of my newspaper," Paddock said.

"All right, other than change the name of our

town to Pantherville, what else do we have in mind?" Jennings asked.

"We aren't changing the name to Pantherville—we are merely saying that Fort Worth is the Panther Town, like New Orleans is the Crescent City," Tidball responded.

"And this is how we are going to become that Panther Town," Paddock said as he stepped to the easel and pulled off the canvas that was covering it. Displaying a slate board, he put a large dot in the middle, then drew nine lines extending out from the dot. "Ladies and gentlemen, this is Fort Worth"—he pointed to the dot in the middle—"and these lines are railroads, starting with the Texas and Pacific.

"These railroads will connect us to San Antonio, Galveston, New Orleans, Memphis, St. Louis, Kansas City, Denver, San Francisco, and San Diego. In short, ladies and gentlemen, this is the future I see for Fort Worth. A dynamic city that is connected to the rest of the world. Here we are, in the middle of Texas, but once this comes to fruition, we would be but four weeks from London or Paris."

There was a murmur of excitement among those present.

"Buckley, that's very nice and all, but the only thing you have there is a bunch of squiggly lines. It looks like a tarantula."

"Tarantula, yes!" Paddock said enthusiastically. Picking up a piece of chalk, he wrote above his map TARANTULA MAP.

"You've got railroads running hither and yon—there's only one thing wrong with your map," Daggett said. "We don't have even one road coming into Fort Worth yet."

Paddock held up his finger. "Ah, yes, and that brings us to the purpose of this meeting. Major Van Zandt has some proposals he would like to advance. I think you will find them interesting."

Van Zandt nodded. "Thank you, Buckley. I've discussed this proposal with Mr. Laclede, Mr. Daggett, and Mr. Smith, and they have all given their approval. But whether or not we can actually implement the plan depends upon you. All of you. Because the proposal is of a nature that will require universal participation."

"Well, quit talking about it, Khleber, and tell us what it is," Jennings said, to the nervous laughter of the others present.

"If the railroad won't finish laying the track into our fair city, I propose that we do it for them."

"What?" shouted at least half a dozen of those in attendance. Others shouted their own questions.

"What do you mean?"

"How do you propose to do that?"

"We can't do that, can we?"

"I believe we can," Van Zandt replied. "The reason we have the women with us tonight is because this is a woman's idea, and who better to explain it to you than she who proposed it? Josie Laclede, will you come up here?"

Josie moved to the front of the room. When she

first began speaking her voice was shaky, but as she continued her voice became strong.

"I ask you, what is so special about the railroad crew that abandoned laying the track at Eagle Ford? Were they highly trained professionals who know how to pull stumps or cut trees any better than any one of our people?

"Can they lay ballast and put down crossties any better than we can? And is any man stronger than our own blacksmith, Bull Turner? He can drive spikes as well as anyone."

Josie was getting the crowd excited as they listened to what she was saying.

"Mr. Van Zandt has asked Walter Roche and his brother to head up a company that we want to call, appropriately, the Tarrant County Construction Company. We say Tarrant County and not just Fort Worth because we will have to call on everyone in the whole county to help out. No one can do this alone, but we can do it if we all work together. And that is where you all come in. No one will be paid for any labor, nor will you be paid for any supplies that you can provide, but everyone will help everyone. If you are a farmer and you need your crop put in, those who are not working on the railroad will do it for you. If you are a shopkeeper, someone, whether it be a man or a woman, will keep your store open. We will become a commune in the purest sense of the word, but when this railroad reaches Fort Worth, we will all benefit. We can do this, and no one will ever say, even in jest, that a panther roams our streets again!"

When Josie sat down, the crowd erupted in hoots and hollers. When everyone had settled down, Major Van Zandt again began to speak.

"Do you see why we all love our Josie? But there is one thing missing from her plan. We cannot manufacture rails."

"Are you telling me you have gotten us all excited again, only to say we can't do this?" Jennings asked.

"I'm not saying that, but I am saying we will need some help from the Texas and Pacific. I believe they can get the steel if we supply the labor. And they have now moved their vice president, Frank Bond, to Dallas. I believe he should be able to help us."

"Tell me, Khleber, do we need to vote on this proposal? Because if we do, I vote yes."

"I vote yes as well," Tidball said.

The issue was brought to the floor, and the proposal received unanimous approval.

"Then, it is done," Paddock said, resuming the chair of the meeting. "Major Van Zandt, when will you see Mr. Bond?"

"We leave on the morning stagecoach," Van Zandt replied. "I'm taking Henri and Josie with me because I believe if the lady speaks with the same passion you heard here tonight, how can Mr. Bond say no?"

Willie was put in charge of the hotel so that Henri and Josie could accompany Van Zandt to Dallas.

Willie, Ida, and Julius were all standing in the lobby as the two made ready to go.

"I've got the buckboard hitched up, Mr. Henri," Willie said. He picked up the luggage and started toward the door. "Soon as I get your luggage loaded, I'll drive you down there."

"Thank you, Willie."

"Miss Josie, will you bring me something from Dallas?" Julius asked.

"Julius!" Ida scolded.

"Of course I'll bring you something," Josie replied with a smile. "What kind of friend would I be if I went to Dallas and didn't bring anything back for one of my favorite people in the whole world?"

A broad smile spread across Julius's face and he looked up at his mother. "See, Mama? She said yes."

Josie hugged both Ida and Julius before she walked outside to be helped up into the buckboard. It had rained the night before, and the wagon made deep ruts in the mud as the horses plodded down Rusk.

The Butterfield stage, standing in front of Andrew's Tavern, was covered with a patina of raindrops. The door was open and they could see someone half in and half out of the coach. When they got closer, they saw that the man had a cloth in his hand and was wiping off the leather seats.

"Here you go, folks," he said. "I've got the inside

all dried out for you. We forgot to close the window curtains last night and it rained in."

"It looks like you did a fine job, Elmer," Van Zandt said.

"Dooley will have the team hitched up in a few minutes. In the meantime, there's coffee in there."

When Josie stepped inside the tavern, she saw Jim and Betty Courtright, along with Mary Ellen, their three-year-old daughter.

"Good morning, Josie," Betty said. "Jim told me what a wonderful speech you gave last night. I'm sorry I wasn't there to hear you."

"I'm sorry you missed it, too. For the first time in a long time, I am beginning to feel good about the chances of Fort Worth coming out of our funk. I just hope Mr. Bond doesn't think my idea is a bunch of hogwash."

"Ladies, it's time we loaded up," Dooley Simmons said as he entered the tavern.

"Oh, Betty, are you going on this coach, too?" Josie asked.

"Yes, Max Elser brought me a telegram last night from my brother in Little Rock. He says Mama was bucked off a horse and broke her leg and she needs my help. Thank goodness for Marshal Redding. He loaned me the money to make the trip, so here I am."

"That's good that the marshal is letting Jim go, too."

"I'm not going," Jim said as he gave his wife a

big hug, then lifted his daughter into the coach. "Here's your gun. Keep it handy."

"I can take care of myself," Betty said as she put the short-barreled revolver into her reticule. "You just make sure you stay out of trouble while I'm gone."

Henri and Major Van Zandt were already settled in the coach, and Mary Ellen snuggled up against Henri.

"Are you my grandpa?" the little girl asked.

"No, honey, but I'd like to be. I'd like to have a little girl to play with just like you," Henri said, all the while looking directly at Josie.

Josie rolled her eyes and shook her head. Henri was always dropping not-so-subtle hints her way that it was time she married, and he, personally, had selected Oscar Manning as the man she would wed. And maybe she should.

Oscar was a good man, but shouldn't there be some sort of spark between a man and a woman? She had read poems and stories about love, and there was always a sense of excitement, a suggestion that when they were apart, they were unfulfilled.

Oscar had kissed her four times in the last three years. Four times, and never, with any kiss, had she felt anything more than the brush of his lips against hers.

Josie smiled as she thought of his attributes: he was smart, he was clean, and he always polished his shoes. She tried to suppress a giggle. She could write an article for the *Democrat* entitled "Ten Things You Need in Choosing a Husband." Well-polished shoes would be at the top of the list.

"What has you tickled, my dear?" Henri asked.

"Oh, nothing," Josie said. "I was just thinking about having Betty along on this coach. If we were attacked by robbers, how surprised they would be when Betty drew her gun. They wouldn't know they had come up against a sharpshooter in a Wild West show."

"That was a while ago when Jim and I did that. We'd probably still be touring if it weren't for this little tyke," Betty said as she tousled her daughter's hair.

"Have you been to Little Rock?" Mary Ellen asked Josie.

"No, I haven't been there. I've only been to Saint Louis, but that was when I was a little girl just like you are now."

"Don't you want to go anyplace?"

"Honey, I would love to go all over this country, but right now I am just happy I get to go to Dallas."

Josie thought about what she had just said. It had been eight years since she and her father had moved to Fort Worth, and even though Dallas was just thirty miles away, this was only her third trip in all that time. The railroad would make such a difference to everyone. She just had to convince Mr. Bond to somehow come up with the money to buy the rails so that her idea would work.

She wondered what Mr. Bond would be like. A vice president of the Texas and Pacific Railway. He was probably old and stuffy, a big man with thick whiskers and a bull neck. She imagined he wore a wrinkled suit with a black bow tie. To top it off, he would smoke a cigar, and the smell about his clothing would be nearly unbearable.

She contrasted the image she had of the vice president of the Texas and Pacific Railway with how she remembered its executive administrator. The picture she had of Gabriel Corrigan was as vivid as if she had seen him yesterday: dark hair against skin bronzed by the Texas sun, and black eyes that could pierce her very soul. His muscular body had been dressed in a crisp white shirt, and black pants were tucked into Hessian boots. She smiled as she tried to remember if they were well polished. So much for her article on finding a husband. No one pleased her, not Oscar Manning, not anyone else.

Gabe Corrigan, without even being aware of it, had doomed her to spinsterhood. He was the gold standard against whom all men were measured. And he was gone.

She looked over at Betty and Mary Ellen Courtright, who had fallen asleep on her mother's lap. A picture that she yearned to emulate, but it would never happen. She had told her father "The Empress will take care of Empress," and she vowed to herself that whatever it took, she would keep the hotel, her baby, open.

Dallas, Texas—November 1875

"Mr. Corrigan, we got a telegram from the colonel saying some folks are coming from Fort Worth any day now. He doesn't say it, but you know they're coming to gripe," the clerk said, laying the telegram on Gabe's desk. "Oh, and here's a dispatch that came in on the 602."

"If they do gripe, I can understand why," Gabe said as he read over the telegram. "They've watched Dallas turn into a boomtown even while the rest of the country is going bust."

After the London trip, the board of directors had appointed Gabe vice president of the Texas and Pacific Railway, and Colonel Scott had put him in Texas, moving Bond back to Philadelphia.

Gabe's promotion meant a huge increase in responsibility, but no increase in salary. And no increase in salary meant no salary at all, for he had been working for the past two years on a stipend that provided just enough money to stay alive.

But he had no need for money beyond his living expenses. Since he was not married—nor had he ever been, according to the annulment—he no longer felt the need to maintain a room. Instead, he had a cot in the office of the depot of the T&P, and that was where he lived. It had been almost two years since he'd last heard from Marthalee or her father. He barely gave either of them a thought now and had no idea whether Marthalee had remarried. Nor did he care.

He picked up the dispatch and began to read:

Dear Gabe:

The latest from Austin is as follows. It does not bode well for the T&P. We cannot get any more extensions. The land-grant agreement with the State of Texas is to be abrogated unless the railroad reaches Fort Worth by the adjournment date of the first legislative session following the constitutional convention. The tide has turned against us, and even our dear friend Governor Throckmorton cannot help us this time. Without more money, I do not see how we can possibly make that deadline. It may well be that our dream is about to come crashing down around us. I have not yet declared bankruptcy for the T&P, and for me, personally, because as you know, every penny I have is invested in this company. But unless something of a positive nature happens, and happens quickly, I may have to start the proceedings.

I am calling upon every moneyed friend that I know, even my old nemesis, Cornelius Vanderbilt, pleading with them to loan us enough money to keep the railroad afloat. In addition I am trying to call in favors from congressmen and senators, but the loss of

*Blaine as the Speaker is a serious obstacle.
We are so close, just twenty-three miles. If all
else fails, I will have to negotiate a sale with
that bloodsucking Jay Gould, who would like
nothing better than to see me fail.*

*Gabe, my friend, you have given up much
for me and for the railroad. For that, and for
what may lie ahead, I am truly sorry.*

Sincerely,

Thomas Scott

President, T&P and Pennsylvania Railroad

SIX

It took half a day to get to Dallas, including a stop at Eagle Ford, where Betty and Mary Ellen would leave them and catch the train to go on to Little Rock. When the coach got to the Trinity, Josie was impressed with the wire suspension bridge that spanned the river. The conversation Major Van Zandt and her father were having amused her.

"Can you believe this bridge was the brainchild of a woman? What makes a woman think she can enter a man's world like this?" Van Zandt asked.

"They say she had the good sense to put her oldest son in charge of the business end of the bridge. With the tolls she's charging on everything that crosses, she's making a lot of money," Henri added.

Josie couldn't resist. "And who would *she* be?"

"Sarah Cockrell, honey. It's just not right for a woman to be in a man's business like this."

"Is that the same Sarah Cockrell who has started the flour-milling company?" Josie asked.

"It is. And I'm thinking of building a flour mill in Fort Worth, as soon as the railroad gets there. I should look up this woman before we return. She may have some other ideas in the works," Van Zandt said.

"I may be interested in what she has to say, too," Henri said. "You wouldn't want to hear about men's business, Josie, so you can spend the time looking at all the new stores. You might get some ideas of things to add to Oscar's inventory."

"Yes, Papa."

When the coach stopped, Major Van Zandt hired a carriage to take them to the Texas and Pacific depot. Going inside, they saw a man on his hands and knees in the corner, his head covered with a gray knit cap. Spread around him on the floor were the grates of the big potbellied stove lying alongside the ash hopper. He was actively working with the shaker, trying to force an oversize clinker from its perch.

Another man, dressed in a wool coat and wearing gloves, came out of an adjoining room carrying some papers in his hand, then stopped with a start when he saw Josie, Henri, and Van Zandt standing there.

"May I help you?" The man had thinning blond hair and was wearing wire-rimmed glasses.

"Yes, we have come to speak with Mr. Bond," Van Zandt said.

"Oh, I'm sorry. Mr. Bond is no longer in Dallas."

"You mean he isn't the vice president?"

"No, sir. That's our vice president." He pointed to the man in the corner.

"He is?"

The man in the corner stood up, pulled off his cap, reached down to brush off his trousers, then turned toward the visitors.

"I'm sorry about the heat . . ." he said, stopping in midsentence.

"Captain Corrigan," Josie gasped.

A broad smile of recognition crossed his face. "Josie. Josie Laclede. How many times I have thought of you since I was last in Fort Worth!" Gabe stepped toward her, reaching for her hands.

Artfully deflecting his grasp, Josie turned her attention to her father and the major as a blush came to her cheeks. "Do you remember my father, Henri Laclede, and Major Khleber Van Zandt?"

"Of course I remember them." Gabe extended his hand to the gentlemen. "If you are the delegation from Fort Worth that Colonel Scott mentioned in his telegram, I am pleased to welcome you to the Dallas office of the Texas and Pacific Railway. What can I do for you?"

"It is more a question of what can we do for you," Van Zandt replied. "We have come with a proposal that we think may get the T&P to Fort Worth. We hope you find our plan worthy of your consideration."

"Gentlemen, Miss Laclede, you don't know how open I am to any suggestion you may put forward. Won't you please step into my office?"

Josie and the others followed Gabe into another room. A desk and two chairs were in the tiny room, as well as a trunk and a daybed sitting against the wall. Gabe picked up a shirt and stuffed it into the trunk.

"I'm afraid this is also my home right now," Gabe said with a chuckle. "The T&P spares no expense for its vice president."

He pulled one chair out from behind the desk and set it beside the other one.

"Gentlemen," he said, inviting Henri and Van Zandt to take the chairs.

Gabe then sat down on the daybed, indicating that Josie should join him there. When she sat, their combined weights made the bed sink in the middle, causing her to slide toward Gabe.

Her leg was touching his, and he made no attempt to move as she tried to wiggle away. Her moving around created more of a disturbance than if she had just tried to ignore the close contact.

Too close, Josie thought.

Gabe looked at her; then his gaze dropped from her eyes to her shoulders to her breasts. Josie remembered their first meeting, how the wet dress had exposed her breasts to him. That memory, and his bold stare, caused a tingling in the pit of her stomach, and she started to look away, but caught herself. No, she would not look away from him, she would not be intimidated.

His dark eyes twinkled, as if telling Josie that he, too, was remembering that moment. Josie had the idea that they were locked in a staring contest, and she wondered that her father and Major Van Zandt hadn't noticed. But when he turned toward Van Zandt, she realized that it had been only a brief moment.

"Now, Major Van Zandt, what is your proposal?" Gabe asked.

"It isn't *my* proposal, it is *our* proposal, that is to say, the proposal of the entire town of Fort Worth. Actually, to be accurate, it is Miss Laclede's proposal, since it was she who came up with the idea."

"Really?" Gabe looked at Josie again. "I would be very interested to hear what you've come up with."

"First let me ask you a question," Josie began. "Why is it that you have not brought the railroad on to Fort Worth? You have come so close."

"I can answer that question in one word. Money. We simply don't have the money to continue construction, though Colonel Scott is making a prodigious effort to raise the necessary capital."

"You need money for material and you need money for the actual construction, surveying, grading, and laying of the rails. Is that right?"

"Yes."

"Which requires the most capital?"

"The most immediate requirement would be the actual construction itself. We can get rails, I think; we can buy those on credit. But you can't pay workers on credit. You have to have the money to meet the payroll."

"You get the rails. We will do the rest," Josie said.

Gabe squinted his eyes in confusion. "What do you mean, you'll do the rest?"

"What she means is, we will take the contract for grading the road and accept a note due in a reasonable length of time," Van Zandt said.

"Who, exactly, is we?"

"The Tarrant County Construction Company," Van Zandt said. "We have already organized with a subscribed capital stock of twenty-five thousand dollars that has all come from citizens of Fort Worth. In these troubled times, you know what a commitment that really is. And now all we need from you is your authorization to allow us to undertake the project, and of course we need a supply of rails."

"Rails aren't enough. Do you understand what an endeavor you are undertaking?"

"Yes, we do," Henri answered, "but if we do not do this, our town will dwindle down to nothing. We have planted our roots in Fort Worth, and that's where we want to stay, and where we want to see our children and grandchildren prosper."

"You'll need ballast and crossties."

"We can pound the rocks to make ballast and we can cut the trees to make crossties. All that we can do," Van Zandt said. "It's up to you, Mr. Corrigan. We can't make rails. But if you can get the rails, and the rolling stock to transport them to us, we can get the railroad to Fort Worth."

An easy smile spread across Gabe's face. "I've no doubt if the whole town shares your attitude, this can be done. I will get the rails, if I have to beg, steal, or borrow them from someplace else. But I have one requirement. The train must enter Fort Worth by the end of this legislative session. Can you promise me that?"

"You get us the rails, and you have my word, the railroad will be built on time," Major Van Zandt said. He offered his hand to Gabe, and the deal was struck.

"This has been a most productive meeting," Josie said as she attempted to rise from her seat.

Gabe rose quickly and offered his hand to assist her. When she was on her feet, he continued to hold her hand, pulling her to his side.

"Will you be returning to Fort Worth this evening?" Gabe asked.

"No, we will be spending the night because Major Van Zandt and I want to call on Mrs. Cockrell. He is interested in building a flour mill in our city and we want to look over her operation," Henri said.

"Have you secured lodging for the evening?"

"We had thought to just get a room at a boardinghouse, but with your growth in population, I'm not sure we'll be able to find a vacancy," Van Zandt said.

"When you visit Mrs. Cockrell, check to see if she has a vacancy at the St. Charles. You may remember the hotel as The Dallas, but when she bought it she changed the name," Gabe said.

"Imagine that, a woman running a hotel. I like that," Josie said.

"Captain, may I beg of you to see to my daughter, that she reaches this hotel in safety?"

"Oh, Papa, I'm sure Captain Corrigan is much too busy to see to my needs. I'll find my way to the St. Charles."

"I would feel better, Josie, if—"

"Don't worry, Mr. Laclede. I would be happy to escort your daughter."

"Thank you," Henri said, and he and Major Van Zandt left the office.

"You don't have to do this, you know," Josie said.

"I know I don't have to. I want to."

"Besides, I can't go to the hotel yet. I promised Julius I would get him something while we were here and I can't let him down."

"Julius? My friend Julius? He hasn't run out in front of any more stampedes, has he?"

Josie chuckled. "No, I think he learned his lesson. He's ten years old now, and a big help around the hotel."

"The hotel?"

"The Empress."

"It's named for you."

"How did you know that? Very few people even in Fort Worth know it's named after me."

"You told me your name was Empress Josephine Laclede that night when you shared Uncle Willie's barbecue with me. I meant it when I said I've thought about you. I've thought about sitting on the rock on the bluff, and I've wondered how my life might have been different if you—"

"Where shall we go to get Julius a present?" Josie asked, her voice high and unnatural as she cut off any further talk about the past.

Gabe looked at Josie, his piercing black eyes never leaving hers. "What do you have in mind?" His voice was low and husky.

"I don't have anything specific in mind."

"Good. We'll just see what happens. You'd better wrap your cloak around you," Gabe said as he grabbed a jacket out of the trunk.

They took a horse-drawn trolley to the middle of town. But Josie, who was usually so observant, couldn't have told one thing that the trolley passed. She was only aware of Gabe's presence, not daring to enter into conversation lest she ramble on and say something totally incoherent. Where was the levelheaded woman who could always think on her feet? This man had a disquieting effect on her. Thank goodness she would be returning home tomorrow.

"I think this mercantile should be just the

ticket," Gabe said as they stepped off the trolley and headed toward a store.

Josie looked up to see a sign that said A STORE FOR ALL MANKIND. "There may be just a bit of false advertising here, but I'm sure I'll find something that will please Julius."

They had looked through several items when a clerk came toward them and asked, "Can I help you find something?"

"I'm looking for something for a young boy," Josie said.

"Would you want an item of clothing, or some amusement?"

"I'd like a toy, I think."

"How old is he?"

"He's ten."

The clerk led them over to a table with scores of children's toys, from dolls to tin soldiers to trains that could be pulled with a string. "As you can see, we have an entire table of the most delightful playthings."

"Thank you," Gabe said. "We'll look around."

"I'll be around. Call me if you need me."

Gabe started looking through the things on the table. "What about toy soldiers?" He held up a couple of soldiers, complete with painted uniforms and rifles.

"No, I'm not sure that's something he would like."

"What does he like?"

"You will never guess what he really likes best. It's money."

Gabe laughed. "Well, it's good to know that he's developing a sense of value at such an early age."

They continued looking through the table until Josie saw it: the perfect gift. "This!"

Josie picked up a little painted metal figure of Uncle Sam. Uncle Sam was standing on a box. Beside him was a satchel.

"Look." Josie took out a coin, put it in Uncle Sam's hand, then reached behind the little figure to operate a lever. As she did so, the hand lowered the coin toward the satchel, which opened to receive it. At the same time, Uncle Sam's beard twitched. "This he will love."

"Good selection," Gabe agreed. "Everybody needs to love Uncle Sam, especially next year when we all celebrate the centennial."

Josie made the purchase and had it wrapped, and then they stepped back out onto the street.

"Would you like a bite to eat?" Gabe asked. "When the fire went out this morning, Clinton and I didn't even get our coffee, and I'm starved."

"Oh, Mr. Corrigan, I would hate to take up any more of your time."

"Wait a minute. If I have to eat anyway, and you happen to be with me, how would that take up my time?" Gabe grabbed her arm and pulled Josie close to him as he started down the street with long strides. "We'll go to Myrtle McCoy's. I can say for certain that she sets a fine table."

When Josie and Gabe entered the establishment, Josie was struck by the clientele. From ten to fifteen men were seated at the two oilcloth-covered tables, with twelve chairs around each table. No women were to be seen.

"Should I be in here?" Josie asked as Gabe helped her remove her cloak.

"Of course. Why do you ask that?"

"Look around. There are no women."

Gabe laughed. "I hadn't even noticed. This place is not a restaurant or a boardinghouse the way you would normally think of it. I guess you would say it's for day boarders."

"That's a term I've not heard before."

"Since the T&P got here, Dallas has grown so quickly that there aren't enough places for people to live. And when you figure the population is about four-to-one men to women, there's a need for a place like this. Myrt serves two meals a day to anyone who pays a weekly fee, and her food is the best. The only thing is there is no choice. She just brings you what she made that day."

Just then a heavyset woman appeared from the kitchen.

"There's my angel," Myrtle McCoy said as she grabbed Gabe and kissed him on the cheek. "I can see why you're late, but you'd better keep this one in hiding. You know these galoots will steal your girl if you so much as take your eyes off this pretty little thing. I'll put you at Jesse's table."

"Thanks, Myrt. You take care of me."

When they were seated at a small table, Josie could see a garden through the window. From its size, she could imagine how productive the garden had been during the summer. But now, in November, only the tops of the turnip plants were still green.

Myrt returned with two plates that smelled delicious.

"What are you serving us today?" Gabe asked.

"Jesse went out at dawn this morning and got a good mess of quail, so that's what we're having. I hope you like it, missy," she said as she placed the plate in front of Josie.

"It looks and smells delicious," Josie said.

"Do you see why I come here?" Gabe asked with a smile.

"I do." Josie began eating the rice and stewed apricots that were on the plate with the quail, but neither she nor Gabe said anything.

Finally, after a long silence, Gabe put down his fork and looked directly across the table at her.

"Josie, it happened. And I for one am glad and I hope it happens again."

Josie looked at him with a question in her eyes.

"You know what I'm talking about. The kiss by the river. You felt something that night, and so did I. Can you deny that?"

Josie lowered her eyes before she spoke, almost in a whisper. "No, I can't deny it."

When she looked up, Gabe was smiling broadly. "Then, let's build on that one kiss. I am here, and if your crazy idea works and the railroad does make it to Fort Worth, we will have many opportunities to see one another. Will you allow us to be friends?"

"I would like that very much."

"Good. Let's start our friendship this very afternoon. I'll show you everything about Dallas before I take you to the hotel."

Gabe acted as the consummate tour guide, showing Josie all around Dallas—both the new parts and the old. The afternoon went quickly, and Josie could not remember a time when she had felt so exhilarated. The cool air, coupled with her joyous laughter, caused her cheeks to become rosy as her blond hair swirled around her face, becoming tangled and disheveled. She was truly enjoying her day in the company of this man.

Then, too soon it seemed, it was time for her to go to the St. Charles, and Gabe dutifully took her into the lobby. Her father had left word that she should go on to her room, that he and Major Van Zandt were being entertained by Sarah Cockrell and that they would meet her at six the next morning.

"I've had a wonderful day," Gabe said, taking both Josie's hands in his.

"And so have I."

Josie's blue eyes were reflecting the gaslights that flickered in the lobby, and Gabe thought he could never get enough of her. He wanted to take her in his arms and kiss her the way he knew she could be kissed. But he thought back to earlier in the day when he had sensed that she was filled with uneasiness. He desperately wanted her, but he did not want to rush her. In what was perhaps one of the most difficult things he had ever done, he lifted her hands to his lips and kissed each one gently.

"Good night, Josie."

Josie felt bereft and disappointed. She had thought he would kiss her.

"Good night." Josie turned and ran up the stairs that led to the upper floor.

When she reached her room, she unlocked the door and leaned against it, wondering what had just happened. She had wanted him to kiss her and he had not. He had said he wanted to be her friend, but he said nothing about when they might meet again. She was so confused. Why did she feel like this? She walked over to the window to look down, and she saw Gabe disappear around the corner of the building across the street. It was so hard to be a woman. Why couldn't she have just said, "Kiss me?" It wasn't fair.

Josie removed her cloak and looked around for her valise. She attended to her toilet and then undressed. Her whole body tingled with some feeling that she did not recognize. What was this feeling? It was delightful and at the same time tor-turous. What was she going to do? She got her brush and began getting the tangles out of her hair as she sat on the bed.

Just then she heard a faint knock on the door.

"Yes?" she said, thinking it must be her father checking to see if she had returned safely.

"Josie?"

She recognized the unmistakable voice of Gabe Corrigan, and she opened the door quickly—too quickly, because she forgot that she was wearing only her nightgown.

Gabe was standing at the door, and when he saw her, his eyes danced over her body, taking in the thin fabric of her gown, seeing the curve of her breasts.

His lips curved into a sensual smile; then, barely able to speak, he said, "You left this at Myrt's." He offered her the package that held Julius's Uncle Sam bank. "I knew you wouldn't want to leave without it."

Josie took the package, then stepped aside without closing the door. Had she done this unconsciously? Or was she hoping he would take that as an invitation to enter her room?

He stepped inside, then closed the door.

"You are beautiful." He took her into his arms and held her close to him as he kissed her, his kiss urgent and demanding. As his hard body pressed against hers, Josie felt herself spinning into a bottomless vortex.

"You don't know how much I've wanted to kiss you. This is what we were made for." Again he kissed her, and Josie wound her arms around his neck, feeling the texture of his hair as she ran her fingers through it. She returned the kiss with an urgency she could not define. As he held her in his embrace, he began to gather her nightgown, lifting it slowly.

Josie was aware, almost without being aware, of the feel of air against her legs, bare now, as more of the nightgown was bunched in his hand. Then she gasped as she felt his hand begin to knead the naked skin of her bottom. She felt a hardness pressing against her. Intuitively she knew she should resist, but she made no effort to do so.

A loud knock sounded at the door, and quickly Josie stepped out of Gabe's embrace, her nightgown falling to her ankles. The spell was broken.

"Josie, I'm just checking on you, honey. Are you here?" Henri said from the hallway.

"Yes, Papa. I'm here." A tremor of fear raced through Josie. What would happen now?

"Well, I hope you got my message. We'll meet in the lobby at six o'clock."

"Yes, Papa."

"Good night, sleep tight, my little girl."

"Good night."

Gabe and Josie stood immobilized as they heard Henri's door close behind him. Gabe put his head in his hands. What was he doing? What had he wanted to do to Josie? He had to get out of here. Was he any better than Sir Nigel Lancaster?

"I'm so sorry, Josie. I shouldn't be here. Had your father stepped into this room, your reputation would be ruined forever. Please forgive me."

Josie had no comment. She had wanted this as

much as he had. She took his head in her hands and looked into his eyes. With a calmness she didn't know she could gather, she pulled his head to her and placed a kiss on his lips that was the most exquisite feeling she had ever experienced.

Without saying a word, he backed toward the door and let himself out, never taking his eyes off her. When the door closed, Josie felt empty.

SEVEN

It was dark when the coach arrived to pick them up in front of the hotel. Josie, the major, and her father climbed in, and just as they were seated, a porter from the hotel handed each of them a small package.

"The staff of the St. Charles hopes you enjoyed your stay, and this is a small gift to make your travel more comfortable."

"Why, thank you," Josie said, accepting her gift. When she opened it, she found a hot biscuit with a piece of country ham. "Papa, this is a good idea. We should do this for our guests at The Empress."

"We'll remember it, dear, if we get any guests."

Josie scowled at her father, but she did not comment, for fear her contradiction of him would be embarrassing in front of Major Van Zandt. What did he mean *if*? There would be guests, she just knew it.

She sat in her corner of the coach and pretended to sleep, not wanting to participate in the conversation. She thought about Gabe Corrigan. *My angel,* Myrtle McCoy had called him. If he could get the railroad to Fort Worth, he really could be their angel.

When they reached Fort Worth, Dooley made a special stop in front of The Empress. The hotel was an impressive edifice, two stories high, with fresh whitewash contrasting with the weathered wood of most of the other buildings. Across the street was the city wagon yard, now almost empty. How different it had been in Dallas.

Willie and Julius were there to meet them as they climbed down from the coach. After Henri and Josie exchanged good-byes with Van Zandt, Dooley snapped his reins and the team pulled the coach away.

"I'm glad you're back, Mr. Henri, Miss Josie," Willie said. "I thought maybe you might stay another day."

"No, no. We got our business done and it's time to come home and get to work," Henri said.

A large grin crossed Willie's face. "Does that mean you got the railroad people to agree to your idea?"

"More than agree, Uncle Willie. They almost need us more than we need them. We were told we have to get the first train into town before the end of June, so that means we have no time to waste."

"Yes, ma'am. Lordy, let's hope we don't have a bad winter."

Just then Julius tugged at Josie's cloak. "Miss Josie, are you forgettin' somethin'?"

"What would I be forgetting?"

"You said you was goin' to bring me somethin' from Dallas."

"I did say that, didn't I?"

"Well, did you?"

"Julius. Mind your manners. You don't beg from anyone," Willie said.

"Yes, sir," Julius said contritely.

"Well, I did bring you something, and here it is." Josie handed a package to Julius and he ripped the paper off, then looked at the item, clearly not knowing what it was.

"Let me show you something." Josie took a penny from her reticule, put it in Uncle Sam's hand, and operated the lever, and the hand dropped the coin into the satchel as it opened. "It's a bank."

"Oh!" Julius said. "I can keep all my money in there."

For the next few weeks, the whole town was organizing the Tarrant County Construction Company. Walter Roche took charge of it and soon had men assigned, matching the strengths of each one to the best position. It seemed to be an almost insurmountable task.

Josie's first personal sacrifice was when Willie was drafted to be a teamster, running loads of provisions from the grocery store to the camps that were set up at Eagle Ford. Because everything was a donation, this took most of the incoming cash out of the coffer. Josie watched as Henri struggled to resupply the store from wherever he could forage, but the people, mainly women who were left behind, provided what they could. Some had eggs, others supplied butter and the resulting buttermilk, some baked countless loaves of bread, and others donated foodstuffs from their cellars.

Josie's beautiful dining room, meant for white tablecloths and fine dining, was turned into a collection point for vegetables. Rutabagas lay on one table, onions on another, and so on for cabbage, turnips, squash, sweet potatoes, and potatoes. Josie was busy putting the vegetables in crates, then packing them in sawdust that Julius brought from the mill. Julius's job was to sprinkle enough water on the crates to make them damp—but not wet, or the vegetables would spoil. While operating this production line, Josie heard a commotion in the lobby of the hotel.

"Go see who has wandered in. Everybody knows they're supposed to bring their food through the back door," Josie said to Julius.

Josie was so tired. She would have loved to sit down, but she couldn't. She still had comfrey poultices to make for the men, who invariably twisted an ankle or strained their backs, and calendula cream to rub on sore muscles. She could not complain, because everyone in town was doing their part.

As she lifted yet another crate of vegetables to her mounting pile, she stopped to ease her pain by rubbing the small of her back.

"I can do that for you," a man's voice said.

Josie turned quickly, her face brightening instantly. "Gabe! What are you doing here?"

"I've come to check on my crew—and to see you."

"Well, what you see is what you get." Josie looked down at her worn linsey dress. She tried to restore some of her fallen hair back into her topknot, and as she did so, a piece of sawdust fell into her eye. Instinctively, she started to rub it, and only made it much worse.

"Here, let me help you." Gabe took out a clean handkerchief from his back pocket and dipped it in the water Julius had been using to dampen the sawdust. He carefully wiped her eye as tears streamed down her face. "I didn't think it would be this bad when you saw me. Crying like this," Gabe said with a teasing chuckle.

"You should become a doctor."

"Well, in that case, I had better finish taking care of my patient." Gabe began pinning the errant strands of hair on top of her head; then he bent to place small, tender kisses on her cheeks where the tears had been. "Does that make it all better?"

"No, I need more," Josie said, her voice low and seductive.

Just then the back door opened and Hannah

Welch entered the dining room. "Do you think Willie will have room on his wagon for . . . oh, my goodness. Have I interrupted something?"

Josie's face turned crimson.

"I'll just set my smoked ham here on the table. I'm sure it will stay good and hot in this room," Hannah said as she made a quick exit.

"That was not good," Josie said as she moved away from Gabe. "Really. Why are you here?"

"I'm here to stay for a while. That is, if I can find a spare room at some hotel in this town."

Josie lowered her head. "There are rooms at Andrew's Tavern. I believe you stayed there when you were here before."

"I had thought I would stay in what the ad in the *Democrat* says is the finest hotel in Northwest Texas. Are there no rooms at The Empress?"

"There are rooms, but, Gabe, I don't think it would be good for you to be here."

"If I promise not to let what just happened happen again, will you let me stay?"

Josie shook her head. "That is your promise. I have not made a promise."

Gabe had a somber look on his face as he turned from her. When he reached the lobby, he picked up his bag and opened the door. Josie had followed and was standing in the arched entry to the dining room.

"I'm sorry, Gabe."

Just then Henri Laclede came up on the boardwalk in front of the hotel. "Captain Corrigan! It's good to see you again. What brings you to Fort Worth?"

"I'm going to be here for an extended period of time. Colonel Scott wants me to keep a close eye on the town's efforts and let him know if the T&P can be of any help."

Henri patted him on the back. "That is great news. And The Empress is happy to have you as our guest. Isn't that right, honey?" Henri turned toward Josie.

For a moment she hesitated. Then she walked to the desk and opened the check-in book. "Captain, you may have your pick. You will be our only guest."

Gabe smiled. "You choose."

"Then, it will be room 203." Josie got the key to the room while Julius went on ahead with the suitcase. Gabe waited until Josie had the key, then followed her up the stairs.

"Your suitcase is by the door," Julius said, holding his hand out, palm up.

"Oh, yes, the tip," Gabe said. "How much is proper?"

"I generally gets a dime," Julius said.

"Julius, you do not!" Josie scolded.

"I do, too. I got a dime from Mr. Cornett. And his suitcase wasn't near as heavy as this one was."

"This suitcase is quite heavy," Gabe agreed. "I think it is absolutely worth a dime."

He started to give the dime to Julius, but the boy held up his hand. "Wait, I'll be right back." He turned and ran back down the stairs.

"Where is he going?"

"I have no idea."

"Josie, about staying here. If it is going to make you uncomfortable, I mean, really uncomfortable, I will go. The last thing I want to do is make this difficult for you."

"It's not that, it's just—"

"Mr. Corrigan, you still there?" Julius called.

"I'm still here, Julius." Then to Josie: "You were saying?"

"Nothing. It will be fine having you here."

Julius returned with the Uncle Sam bank. He held it out toward Gabe. "Put it in his hand."

Gabe did as he was told, and with a big smile Julius pulled the lever. The satchel opened, the hand went down, and the coin disappeared.

"Well, now, isn't that a wonderful thing," Gabe said.

"I keep all my money in here now," Julius said, and he raced back down the stairs.

Gabe chuckled. "We chose his gift wisely."

Josie unlocked the door, then went inside and raised the window. A gentle breeze lifted the Battenberg curtains. "It might be good to get a little fresh air in here. It's been shut up for a while."

"Your ad in the *Democrat* is not an exaggeration. This is an elegant hotel."

Gabe looked around the room, which was larger than most he had stayed in. It was well furnished with an oversize, four-posted walnut bed with a down mattress, a chest of drawers, a tufted blue-and-gold brocade settee, and a chair with a blue velvet coil-spring seat. Off to the side was an alcove with a washstand and a chamber set, as well as a blanket chest and wooden hooks to hang clothing. Someone had clearly tried to provide anything a traveler could need.

"The fire is laid and there is a matchbox behind the mantel clock if you need some heat. You'll find a necessary and a bathing room at the end of the hall," Josie said as quickly as she could, and now she wanted to get out of this room. "If you need anything, just tell Julius and either Papa or I will try to find it for you." She turned to leave, and Gabe reached out to put his hand on hers.

Josie stopped and looked back at him. She was amazed at the impact that the touch of his hand had on her. Why, if he was just touching her hand, would she feel a tingling in the pit of her stomach?

"Josie?"

"What?"

"The key."

"The key?"

"You still have it."

"Oh! Oh, yes, I'm sorry." She handed him the key.

"Thank you."

They looked at each other for a long moment, their eyes speaking volumes, saying what their lips would not—could not.

Finally, Josie broke the silence. I must go."

"Yes."

Gabe watched as she stepped through the door and closed it behind her. Then he walked over to close the window. Gabe sensed a vulnerability about Josie that made him feel protective. He would do nothing to hurt her, either physically or emotionally.

If asked to describe her feelings right now, Josie would not have been able to put them into words. She felt a disquieting tension, a strange sense of incompleteness, as if a natural flow of events had been interrupted in midstream. Was there more to this situation than had so far been apparent?

She didn't know what love was, and she didn't know what sorts of feelings would emerge between a man and a woman at the beginning of a relationship. The beginning of a relationship? Was that what this was? She smiled as she contemplated the question. If being cold and hot and tingly and discombobulated all at the same time meant anything, then yes, this was definitely the beginning of a relationship.

She needed a little time to herself, time to think, to get control of her emotions before they got control of her. She should have gone back to her work in the dining room, but she went instead to the quarters where she and her father lived. The apartment was on the ground floor behind the lobby of the hotel. It had a keeping room, two bedrooms, and a kitchen of sorts. The kitchen had a cookstove, which had so far not been used to cook anything except the occasional medicinal teas or hot-oil infusions Josie concocted to be sent to the camp at End of Track.

Her own room was her sanctuary, her place to go when she needed to be alone with her thoughts. It was decorated differently from the rest of the hotel. Whereas the hotel had dark, heavy furniture with ornate carvings and rich fabrics, her own room was light and airy. Uncle Willie had built her furniture out of pine boards, then washed the wood with white milk paint. A watercolor of the riverfront in St. Louis hung above the bed with its quilt of many colors.

Ida had taught her to quilt, and together they had made her comforter from pieces of dresses she had worn as a child. It was as if she could look at a square in the quilt and recall the occasion upon which she first wore the dress. The white organdy had been worn at her First Communion at Christ Church; the blue gingham was her first day of school; the green stripe was an Easter Sunday excursion to Henry Shaw's Garden; and the blue chambray was when they'd left the riverboat in Shreveport and gotten into the wagon to come to Fort Worth. This quilt served as her scrapbook, her look back at the life she knew. Another dress was a part of her history, but it was a history she did not know.

Her christening gown. She kept it, as clean and fresh as the day it was made, wrapped in tissue paper in her trunk. Josie picked up the dress. She held it to her cheek, trying to visualize the mother who had put her in it before leaving her in Henri Laclede's carriage.

Though Henri had been unable to ever give her more than the bare details of how she was found, she knew that this dress was the key to her past. It was almost as if her mother, whoever she might be, was using that dress to reach out to her—to give her some connection, no matter how mysterious or tenuous—with her past. Holding the dress now, she marveled at the remarkable workmanship of the gown, the exquisite needlework that could reproduce, so accurately, the crests that encircled the hem. What were those crests? Were they merely decorations? Or did they have some significance?

She had held this dress many times, placing the soft material against her cheek as if she could somehow discover through touch the story of her past. Was her mother from some fine family?

Often, when she was younger, she would imagine that her mother was a princess from some European royalty, come to America to have her child in secret, away from the eyes of the court. At such times she wondered if Henri knew more than he'd told her. Was that why he had named her Empress?

But what terrible problem had her mother been facing that would have caused her to abandon her baby? No, that wasn't right. Josie had not been abandoned. The letter that was with her made it clear that Henri had specifically been chosen. That meant that her mother had to know Henri, had to know what a wonderful father he would be.

She had been right. Josie could not imagine a more loving father than Henri.

Josie assumed that her mother had gotten pregnant and did not want to shame her family with an unwed pregnancy. What kind of woman would get pregnant out of wedlock? A loose woman? What did that mean for her? Did she have those same tendencies? Could she get pregnant out of wedlock?

Gabe Corrigan.

Josie gasped. She was clearly attracted to him—aroused by him. Was that because she was her mother's child? Would she be capable of such a thing? Even as she thought about it, she knew that the answer was yes.

Carefully, she rewrapped the dress in the tissue paper and returned it to her trunk.

EIGHT

When Gabe awoke the next morning, he heard the ring of a blacksmith's hammer. In addition to the hammering, the storekeeper next door was sweeping his front porch and Gabe could hear the swish of the broom. As a countermelody, a hanging sign somewhere was squeaking in the morning breeze, while from the wagon yard, someone was using a sledgehammer to set a wheel. The result was a symphony of sound. *Ring, scratch, scratch—squeak—thump. Ring, scratch, scratch—squeak—thump.*

Gabe lay in bed for a full minute until the composition was broken when the blacksmith stopped hammering and the storekeeper stopped sweeping. Now all that could be heard was the squeak of the sign and the thump from the wagon yard. Gabe got up and dressed, then walked over to the window to look down upon the street.

Right across the street from the hotel was the city wagon yard, and next to it was a saloon advertised by uneven letters painted directly on the boards of the building. On the left side of the sign was painted a mug of golden beer, over which was a large FIVE CENTS. Across the center of the sign, in big white letters, was CLUB ROOM SALOON. Next door to the saloon was Young's Apothecary. Then there was the Occidental Saloon, and the Merchants' Café. Several boarded-up buildings stood as visual proof of the town's financial straits.

If Gabe was going to make this town his temporary headquarters—and if the town really was providing the labor to bring the track in—he knew he needed to mingle with as many people as he could.

Going outside, Gabe crossed over to Main Street and headed toward the courthouse to call on the town marshal and make his acquaintance. Fort Worth had the feel of a ghost town because for every occupied building he passed, at least three were unoccupied, most of them still sporting the signs that had been painted on the false fronts with such high expectations: BEEKER'S LEATHER GOODS, MCKINLEY HARDWARE AND FURNITURE, MISS EMMA'S DRESS EMPORIUM, GOODMAN LAW OFFICE, TARRANT LAND DEVELOPMENT. All of those buildings were boarded up.

Gabe thought back to three years ago, recalling the excitement and expectation the town had shown when he, Colonel Scott, John Forney, and

Governor Throckmorton had come bearing the promise of railroad prosperity.

He could compare his own life three years ago to that of the people of Fort Worth. Then, his life had been one of promise as well.

Buckley Paddock, in describing the plight of the town, had written: *From the highest point of expectancy, the people descended into the lowest depths of despondency.* That description could be used to perfectly define his own situation.

Gabe sometimes thought his life to be nothing but a series of failures. The collapse of Jay Cooke and the withdrawal of funding for the railroad was not Gabe's fault, but it set up the sequence of events that had brought him to Fort Worth, away from Philadelphia and New York. He had at one time envisioned himself being appointed the next president of the Texas and Pacific Railway, if not the Pennsylvania Railroad. He was sure Colonel Scott had been grooming him for one of those positions in the event that he retired.

Then there was his disastrous marriage. His wife had made a cuckold of him by dallying with a titled English fop, and Gabe had tried without success to get a divorce. The issue was settled when Marthalee, or, perhaps more accurately, General Galloway, arranged an annulment.

He had to question if this crazy scheme of Josie's would really work. Was it possible? Could this bunch of ragtag pioneers really grade the roadbed, put in ballast, bridge rivers and streams, cut ties, and lay the rail? In truth, Gabe didn't think they had the slightest chance of pulling it off. But Fort Worth needed the railroad to survive, and he needed the railroad to survive, so for better or worse, he and the town were in this together.

At six o'clock in the morning, in the dark, Josie knocked on the door to the Lane cabin. She pulled her shawl about her in the brisk air. A moment later the door opened and Ida looked out.

"Child, what are you doin' here so early in the mornin'? Is somethin' wrong with Mr. Henri?"

"No, no, I'm sorry I frightened you. It's just that, well, I was wondering if I could have some starter?"

"Starter? Gracious, you don't mean sourdough starter?"

"Yes, I do. I'm going to try those biscuits you always make."

A broad smile spread across Ida's face. "Well, bless your heart. Do you want me to come help you?"

"No, I want to try and do it myself."

"Good for you, that's the best way to learn. Come on in out of the cold, I'll get you a cup or two."

As Josie stood just inside the door, she saw Julius peering at her from behind the curtain that separated the sleeping room.

"Good morning, Julius."

Julius smiled.

"Here it is, honey, in this crock," Ida said. "It's all ready to use. Do you have any saleratus if you're goin' make biscuits?"

"I'm sure I do. Julius, in a little while, if you'll come over, I'll give you a biscuit that I made with my own hands."

"You ever made 'em before?"

"No."

"Then, how do I know they'll be fit to eat?"

"Julius!" Ida scolded.

Josie laughed. "Well, I guess we'll just have to find out, won't we?"

Returning to the small kitchen in the apartment, Josie found a large bowl and mixed the starter with flour, sugar, and salt. Then she remembered Ida's question.

"Thank you, Ida," she said aloud, as she added the baking powder. "These would have been a disaster if I had forgotten the saleratus."

After the concoction had risen, she pinched off small dough balls and placed them in an iron skillet that she had coated with butter and brown sugar.

After a while, the aroma of the baking biscuits filled the kitchen, and Josie was feeling pretty good about her effort. Then, when it was almost time to take them out, Hannah came in. Seeing Josie, she laughed out loud.

"What is so funny? Have you never seen anyone bake biscuits before?"

"Did you get enough flour in the bowl to even make biscuits?"

"What do you mean?"

"You've got flour from the tip of your nose to your elbows."

Josie walked quickly over to the hall tree and looked at herself in the mirror. "Oh, I look a mess!"

"It won't be that hard to clean you up. And I have to confess, the biscuits do smell heavenly."

"Thank you."

"Why did you suddenly decide you wanted to become a baker?"

"No reason."

"No reason, huh? Well, let me ask you this. Will Captain Corrigan be having breakfast?"

"I don't know. I suppose he will. He is a guest here, you know."

Hannah laughed again. "He is a guest here, he is going to have breakfast, but there is no reason why you suddenly decided to bake biscuits. I see."

"You see what isn't there to see."

"Is that what you're going to say about what I saw yesterday when I brought the ham?"

"Oh, I forgot to have Uncle Willie put it on the wagon. I'm so sorry."

"Aha, now she is so distracted, she can't remember the simplest things. Do I think someone is infatuated with somebody? Oh, no, that wouldn't be it," Hannah said as she burst out laughing.

"Stop it." Josie threw the cloth she had been

using to brush off the flour at Hannah. "But as long as you're here, you may as well join us for breakfast. Do I look halfway presentable now?"

"Yes."

"Good. I'm going to go up to room 203 now, knock on the door, and invite our guest down to breakfast, and I don't want to look like a tomfool."

"Then, maybe you should get the smudge off the end of your nose."

"What?" Josie began rubbing her nose, and Hannah laughed.

"I was teasing, there's no flour there. You look fine."

Josie opened the oven door and looked in at the biscuits. "Oh, I think they're just about ready."

"Go on up and get Captain Corrigan, I'll take them out of the pan. What else are you going to have?"

"Butter and honey. And coffee."

"I'll get that, too. Will we eat here or in the dining room?"

"I think the dining room. And get a tablecloth."

Josie felt proud of herself as she hurried up the stairs to the second floor. She stopped in front of the door to Gabe's room and knocked lightly.

"Captain Corrigan?"

There was no response, so she knocked again, louder this time.

"Captain Corrigan? Gabe?"

When he didn't respond to a third, very loud knock, she grew a little concerned and, looking up and down the hall, tried the door. It was unlocked, and she pushed it open.

"Captain Corrigan?" she called somewhat timidly.

Gabe wasn't there. She looked around the room and saw that his suitcase had been unpacked and his clothes hung neatly. A shaving cup, strop, and razor were on the washstand by the mirror.

The bed was unmade, and she walked over to it, put her hands on the sheet, and thought of his spending the night there. She almost thought she could smell him in the sheets . . . but knew it was nothing but the shaving lotion.

She sat down on the bed and pulled the comforter up over her chest. She felt a fluttering in the pit of her stomach, and a weakness in her knees, as she imagined herself lying in bed beside Gabe.

"My God, my God, what is wrong with me? Why am I doing this to myself?" She rose quickly and hurried out of the room. What if Gabe was just down the hall, and he returned to find her sitting on his bed, hugging the covers? If he was here, he would have to come down on his own. She vowed that she would never come up to get him again.

As Gabe passed by the office of the *Democrat*, he saw Buckley Paddock just beginning to lock his door.

Paddock flashed a broad smile when he saw Gabe and stuck out his hand. "Captain Corrigan, isn't it?"

"Yes, that's right, and you are the editor of the newspaper, Mr. Paddock, I believe." Gabe took Paddock's hand.

"I am, sir. And are you here to help us, or have you been sent by the railroad to get in our way?"

"Why would you think that?"

"You have to know that a lot of the bloom is off the rose where the Texas and Pacific is concerned. There are people who are hurting because of what you and that scoundrel Scott promised us. I'd watch my back if I were you."

"I understand, but I have to add that what the Texas and Pacific did was not intentional."

"I know, you had nothing to do with Jay Cooke's downfall, but everybody's a little hot under the collar about how the whole mess has played out. But, say, now that you're here, would you be willing to sit a spell with me? Just let me quiz you a mite about what you know. I'm sure my readers will be most interested in the details."

"I don't know that I can tell you anything you don't already know, but I'll certainly submit to an interview."

A delicious aroma assailed his nostrils, and Gabe realized that he was hungry. "Something sure smells good. Where's it coming from?"

"Tivoli's, next door. Herman Kussatz owns the place, and he makes a right good breakfast. Why don't you join me? We can talk as we eat."

"I can't turn that down."

Herman Kussatz was rotund and had a heavy

German accent, often dropping in German words as he spoke.

"Herman, you fat Dutchman, have you eaten all the biscuits and gravy this morning, or do you have some left for your customers?" Paddock teased.

Mr. Kussatz approached the table carrying two steins of beer and set them on the table in front of both Paddock and Gabe.

"Do you remember Captain Corrigan?"

"*Kapitän* Corrigan, this is the man with the railroad, *ja*?"

"This is the man with the railroad, *ja*."

"For you, *ein frei Bier*," Kussatz said. "Bring, please, the railroad."

"What about a free beer for me?"

"For you is not free. One nickel."

Paddock pushed the nickel over, and Kussatz went to get the breakfast.

"It seems a little early in the day for beer, isn't it?" Gabe asked.

"No, never too early for Herman's beer. He and another German saloonkeeper make their own brew. But that's not what makes it so special. Taste it."

Gabe took a swallow, not knowing what to expect. "It's cold."

Paddock had a big grin on his face. "It's always cold. Herman has one of those new Gurley patented refrigerators, and his beer is the same temperature year round."

Herman brought their breakfast of biscuits and sausage gravy and set it in front of them. In a minute he returned with two more beers.

"What is this?" Gabe asked.

"The Tivoli has all the free food you can eat, but you pay for your drinks, so Herman makes sure you drink a lot. You can bet this is one of the cowboys' favorite spots."

Throughout the meal, and for several minutes thereafter, Paddock interviewed Gabe, extracting as much information as he could regarding the railroad. He wrote the story at the very table where they had their breakfast, and when he was finished, he allowed Gabe to read it.

VICE PRESIDENT OF TEXAS AND PACIFIC MOVES OFFICE TO FORT WORTH

Captain Gabriel Corrigan, Vice President of the Texas and Pacific Railway Company, has relocated his office from Dallas to Fort Worth. This was done, he assures one and all, to make certain that the railroad reaches Fort Worth. Captain Corrigan afforded this editor a long and in-depth interview, during which the determination and honesty of the man could be adjudged.

It must be stated that in the last two years, railway construction in Texas has been practically suspended. A few short lines have been built from the main trunk to adjacent territory, but that is more for the purpose of controlling traffic than for the development of the country. Cities and towns that were built and boomed on the expectation of the arrival of the railroad have withered and gone away. Fort Worth is an example of such a town. It grew by leaps and bounds with the promise of the railroad. That promise is thus far unfulfilled as the rails of the Texas and Pacific have stopped many miles east of Fort Worth.

But if determination and grit are to account for anything, then the tracks for the Texas and Pacific Railway will surely reach the borders of our fair city. Captain Corrigan has assured this newspaper of his determination to work closely with the Tarrant County Construction Company, a corporation formed of local citizens for the specific chore of grading the roadbed, laying ballast, cutting and positioning crossties, and laying rails. I have taken measure of the man and believe him to be truthful in his assertions.

This newspaper now calls upon all our citizens to aid, in whatever way they can, the efforts that the Tarrant County Construction Company have thus far so nobly advanced.

"A good and fair article, Mr. Paddock. If, as you say, there are those who are upset over the railroad's progress, I think this will go a long way toward defusing any trouble."

"I'm glad you approve. It will be in this evening's edition. By the way, have you decided where you want to set up shop?"

"No, I haven't, but finding a place is on my agenda today. Do you have a suggestion?"

"I do. I can put a desk in my sanctum at the *Democrat,* if you'd like. And it would be good for both of us. You don't pay, and I get any news that comes in."

"That sounds like a workable solution, Mr. Paddock."

"Good. Oh, you can call me Buck. My friends all do."

"I'll be proud to call you Buck. And thanks for the beer."

Gabe left Paddock and continued on down the street to the courthouse and the jail. The jail was a log building on the corner of Rusk and Second Street. When Gabe entered, he was assailed with the scent of lye soap. A big man with hair down to his shoulders stood over another man on his hands and knees scrubbing the floor.

"That ought to do it, Elmer. Get yourself back to your cell, 'fore I put you in the dungeon," the big man said; then he turned toward Gabe. "And you must be Corrigan."

Gabe's eyebrows rose in surprise. "That's right."

"Jim Courtright." The man extended a slightly crippled right hand. "The whole town knows you're at The Empress. Now, what can I do for you?"

"Well, Marshal, I'm just getting a feel for the lay of the town right now. The Texas and Pacific is eternally grateful to the folks here, and we want to do what's right," Gabe said as he shook Jim's hand.

"Tom Redding is the marshal. I'm just the deputy and the jailer. Pinned my badge on two days ago. Can you shoot a gun?"

"I was at Antietam, if that tells you anything."

"A Yank, I'm guessing."

"That's right."

"I don't say it too loud around here, but so was I. People here don't pay much mind to which side you fought. They're all for Texas, and what you can do for her. But back to the gun. Get it strapped on your leg and keep it there."

"All right."

"When you do, come join me on my rounds tonight. That's how you'll meet the men you'll need to convince that they want to wield those pickaxes. The ones that are working out at Eagle Ford right now can't keep up the pace. They'll want to come home for Christmas, and I'll bet even money a lot of 'em won't go back."

"Thanks for the advice and the invitation. I'll join you this evening."

Gabe returned to the *Democrat* to set up his new office space and then went back to The Empress, hoping to see Josie.

He was not disappointed. When he entered the

hotel, he found her polishing the chimneys and trimming the wicks on the kerosene lamps.

"Do you just work all the time?" Gabe asked.

"Things have to be done, and with Willie gone most every day running back and forth to Eagle Ford, and Papa scouring the countryside for provisions, that leaves only Ida and me to take care of everything else."

"What about Julius?"

"Oh, yes, I forgot about my little helper. Oscar is teaching him his numbers and his reading, so he spends most of his day over at the store. He doesn't want to go because he's afraid someone will check into the hotel and he won't be here to carry their bags."

"Have I met Oscar?"

"Yes, when you were here before."

"And just who is he?"

"Oscar Manning is the man Papa wants me to marry." Josie looked directly at Gabe, with a smile that had a touch of sadness crossing her face.

"And you don't want to."

Josie looked down at her hands, running her thumb across her nails as she heaved a heavy sigh. When she looked up, her eyes were glistening with gathering tears.

Gabe caught her hands in his. "Josie, if you are not sure, absolutely sure, don't let anybody make that decision for you. It only brings heartache. I can tell you . . ." Gabe stopped in midsentence. This would be the perfect time to mention Marthalee, but he could not do it. He wasn't prepared to share this chapter in his life with anyone.

That evening Gabe did eat dinner with Josie and her father.

"Gabe, after meeting some of our people, do you really think they can do this? No one has any real experience with working on a railroad, you know," Henri said.

"Everyone I've talked to seems to have a lot of confidence," Gabe replied.

"The more I think about it, the more worried I get. What if we can't do it?" Josie asked.

"Look, it has everything going for it. Fort Worth wants the railroad, needs the railroad, so that is certainly enough incentive to generate the enthusiasm necessary to do the work. And, believe me, the railroad needs to come to Fort Worth—no, let's make that *must* come to Fort Worth if it is to survive."

"This whole thing was my idea, and so much is riding on the project. If we can't do it, then I'm afraid I will have just raised everyone's hopes only to see them dashed again."

"It has been my experience that anytime you have both partners in a relationship with an equal investment and incentive in its outcome, the chances for success are greatly improved."

"Ha!" Henri said. "You could say that about any kind of relationship—say a partner in a store or when a man chooses a wife."

Gabe chuckled. "I don't think marriage is quite

the same thing. There's more to it than just forging a partnership."

Josie laughed nervously. "Papa, why would you bring that up?"

"No reason. It just got me to thinking, is all. After all these years, I still miss Bridgette. She was a wonderful woman, and one of my greatest sorrows is that you never got to know her."

Josie got up from her chair and walked over to lean down and put her arms around Henri's neck. "I know I would have loved her as much as I have loved you."

Henri took Josie's hand and kissed it. "And she would have loved you, *ma chérie*."

Josie saw Gabe looking at them and knew that he must be curious. "Bridgette was not my mother." For now, Josie thought, that was explanation enough. "Would you like another glass of wine?"

Gabe held up his glass. "Yes, if you don't mind. The wine is delicious."

"What year is this?" Henri asked as he drank from his glass.

"It's the '68," Josie said.

Henri smiled. "You've chosen my finest year for our honored guest. This batch was the first wine that I made from Texas-grown elderberries."

"Hello! Anyone here?" The call came from the lobby, and Josie started toward the sound, but Henri interrupted her.

"No, no, you stay here and pour Captain Corrigan another glass of wine. I'll see who it is."

Gabe took the decanter from Josie. "Allow me. A lady should never have to pour her own wine."

He poured his own glass just as Henri came back in with Jim Courtright.

"I was going to introduce you," Henri said, "but Jim tells me you two have already met."

"We have indeed."

"Mr. Corrigan was just enjoying some of Papa's finest wine. Jim, would you like to join him?"

"Don't mind if I do." Henri pulled out a chair, and Courtright sat down. "So, Mr. Corrigan, are you ready to make the rounds with me tonight?"

"Please, call me Gabe. Yes, I said I would." He poured a glass of wine for the deputy.

"Make the rounds?" Josie asked.

"I've asked Gabe to go on watch with me tonight. There is no better way to get the feel of a town than to walk through it after dark when all of its denizens are out and about."

"Uhmm, very good, Henri," Courtright said after he took a swallow of the wine. He glanced toward Gabe. "Where's your pistol? If you're going with me, I want you armed."

"Oh!" Josie said. "Are you sure? Isn't that dangerous?"

"Just the opposite, my dear," Courtright said. "You know what it's like around here. A man would sooner go without his pants than without his gun, and if you don't carry, you're just asking for trouble."

"All right," Josie said. "But just bear in mind,

Deputy Courtright, if anything happens to Captain Corrigan that prevents the railroad from reaching this town, you'll have everyone down on you."

"Wait a minute. I thought for a minute there you were actually concerned about me, but now I hear you only care about the railroad."

"What?" Josie gasped. "Of course I'm concerned about you as well."

Gabe chuckled. "Good. I would hate to think that if something happened to me, I wouldn't have a soul to weep a few tears."

"Don't talk like that! Don't even joke about it," Josie said in a far too somber tone.

"I'm sorry. It wasn't a very good joke. Jim, my gun is upstairs, let me strap it on."

NINE

A few minutes after leaving The Empress, Gabe and Courtright were "making the rounds," which meant checking all the doors of all the shops and stores to make certain they were locked, that no windows were broken, that nobody was there who shouldn't be there. When they reached the White Elephant, Jim led the way inside.

"Set us up with a couple of Lemp's," Jim said to the bartender. When the two beers were poured, the deputy held his glass up and looked at it. "Yes, sir, the best brew around is made right here in Fort Worth. We take care of ourselves. We're a proud town, and don't you ever forget it."

"I'm beginning to see that."

Jim took a swallow of his beer, then wiped the suds from his mustache.

"So, what do you say, Gabe? Are you ready to

buck the tiger?" The two men moved to the green-baize-covered table that stood in the corner of the saloon.

The faro banker stood in the cutout of the oval table, and when the two men approached, he welcomed them to the game. "Move over, boys. Make room for the law and the railroad."

Once again, it amazed Gabe how with no introduction everyone in town seemed to know who he was. He took his place at the faro table between two portly gentlemen.

"This game is playing four-bit checks. How many will you have?"

Gabe took out $5 and was given ten chips, while he noticed Courtright put down $20 initially. As the game commenced, it occurred to him that the deputy must be a serious gambler.

They stayed at the White Elephant for at least a couple of hours. When they left, Gabe was exactly where he had started monetarily, but Jim was up by $20, and he was feeling pretty good. It wasn't just the winning hands that made him feel good, though; he had put away a prodigious amount of liquor, drinking at least three shots of whiskey for every one beer Gabe had drunk.

"Yahoo!" Courtright shouted after another winning hand. "Come on, railroad man, let's go down to the Club Room. I don't want to break the White Elephant in one night."

The others in the saloon laughed, and Courtright, in the mode of a hail–fellow-well-met, shook hands, slapped backs, and exchanged pleasantries with everyone as they left the saloon.

The Club Room Saloon was just down the street from the White Elephant, and a slight step down in its appointments. Whereas the White Elephant appealed to the business and professional men of the town, the Club Room Saloon catered more to the laborer and the cowboy, though it certainly had its share of businessmen as well.

Billy Nance and Bingham Feild were standing at the bar, and both were already intoxicated. The young men, both in their teens, were sons of prominent Fort Worth families.

"Boys, I'm sorry, but I think you've had about all you can handle," Lemuel Grisham said just after they had ordered another drink. "No more tonight."

"What do you mean no more? My daddy helped found this damned town, and no barkeep is going to stop me or my pal here from gettin' a drink when we want one," Bingham Feild demanded. "We got money. Now take it." He threw a handful of nickels at Grisham.

"Keep your money, boys, and take it someplace else, 'cause you'll not be gettin' any more liquor at the Club Room." Grisham pushed the coins back across the bar and turned back to his task of drying glasses.

Courtright stepped to the bar and ordered a whiskey for himself and a beer for Gabe.

"All right, fellas!" Courtright shouted. "My partner here and me, why, we just broke the bank down at the White Elephant, and we're fixin' to do the same thing here."

"You own the White Elephant now, do you, Deputy?" someone called.

"Nah, I decided to let Winsted hang on to it for one more night," Courtright quipped, to the laughter of the others in the saloon.

"Hey, Jim, where's your wife tonight? Does she know you're out this late?" another called.

"You know damn well she's still visitin' in Little Rock."

"Ha! I knowed she wasn't here. That woman can outshoot a good ten men. I seen her do it."

"There ain't no way our new deputy'd be out rousting the town if she was home."

There was boisterous laughter, and more barbs were thrown toward Courtright as he and Gabe found their way to the gaming table.

At the White Elephant the luck of the cards had been with Courtright, but here it was with Gabe. Of course, it could also have been that Courtright was close to being inebriated and wasn't paying that much attention to what he was doing, whereas Gabe was still sober.

"I tell you the truth," Jim bellowed after one hand, "if Captain Corrigan keeps on winnin' the way he is now, why, more'n likely he'll have enough money to buy the T&P, not just run it."

Nance and Feild, who were still chafing over

being refused another drink, had been watching the exchange with bemused interest until Courtright mentioned the Texas and Pacific.

"Wait a minute," Nance said to his friend, "is that the bastard that's runnin' the railroad?"

"That's what the deputy just said."

"I'll be damned." Nance turned his back to the bar, then leaned against it. "Hey, you!" he shouted loudly.

At first, neither Gabe nor Courtright looked around.

"You—you pig-faced son of a bitch! I'm talking to you!"

This time Gabe did look around, and he saw that one of the men had stepped away from the bar and was now pointing toward him. He was young, Gabe guessed no more than seventeen or eighteen, with a wild shock of ash-blond hair and gray eyes.

"Is that true? You're the railroad man?"

"I am."

"If you don't know it yet, I'm here to tell it to you. Folks in these parts don't much cotton to curs like you, Mr. Railroad Man."

Gabe tried to ignore the comment, perceiving that the young man had had too much to drink. He returned to the game.

"I'll copper my bet," Gabe said as he placed a token on the player's card.

"You, Railroad Man, my friend's talking to you," Feild said.

"I'm afraid I'm busy right now," Gabe said.

"You're goin' to think busy. I see that gun. Stand up and face me like a man." Billy Nance staggered as he stepped away from the bar. "Face me like a man so I can shoot you down like the dog you are."

"Now, why would you want to do that?"

"Look at this town. You see all the boarded-up buildings? That's 'cause your fancy railroad didn't get here. My pa and lots more like him are just hangin' on, and it's all your fault."

"I'm sorry," Gabe said, "but I think the town has figured out a solution. Your neighbors are out there working on the railroad every day, and I believe they can pull this off. The train will make it to Fort Worth."

"Yeah? Well, that's what you said three years ago, and my pa and me don't believe it'll ever happen."

"If we all pull together, I assure you it can happen."

"The only thing I'm going to pull is my gun, you son of a bitch!" Nance started for his pistol, but Gabe drew his gun before Billy could get his out of his holster.

Gabe didn't shoot; he didn't have to. When Billy saw how quickly Gabe had drawn, he jerked his hand away from his own pistol.

"No," Billy said. "No, I ain't goin' to draw against you."

"That's enough, Billy," Courtright said. "Bingham, get him out of here before I march you both down to the jail."

"Me? Why me? I didn't do anything," Feild said.

"You're with him, and that's enough to piss me off. Both of you get out of here now. And Billy, you better thank your lucky stars Captain Corrigan is a decent man. He could have shot you just now, and there wouldn't be a jury in Texas that would have found him guilty."

The two men left the saloon, but a moment later the sound of gunshots rang out.

"Damn fool kids," Courtright said with a sigh of frustration as he headed for the door. "They're goin' to make me throw 'em in jail."

"I've had enough entertainment for one night," Gabe said as he picked up his winnings. "I'm coming with you."

"I saw you draw that gun. If your railroad job falls through, you might be after mine. You don't have to come with me."

"I'm making the rounds with you, and wouldn't you say this is part of the rounds?"

Courtright laughed. "Yeah, I guess that's right. Come on."

The two went outside, but the boys weren't in the street anymore. Gabe thought maybe they had given up and gone home, but then they heard pistol shots coming from the alley. Courtright started between two buildings, going to the sound of the shooting. Gabe followed him.

"All right, Billy Nance, Bingham Feild," Courtright shouted. "You two are under arrest."

"You better stand back, Deputy, or you're goin'

to get shot," one of the boys shouted. Because they were back in the dark alley, Gabe couldn't tell which one of them had called out.

Courtright pulled his pistol, and so did Gabe. The two walked into the alley, the shadows of the buildings blocking out the moonlight.

"I said you're both under arrest. Now, give me your guns before someone gets hurt."

Nance dropped his gun and put up his hands. "We didn't mean nothin' by it."

"Corrigan, pick up Nance's gun, would you? All right, Bingham, let's go. You're under arrest."

"You just think you're the law. You're still the turnkey."

"I'm law enough to take you in."

Gabe heard the unmistakable sound of a pistol hammer being drawn back in the darkness. "Jim!" he shouted in warning.

Two shots were fired, the muzzle-blast flame pattern lighting up the rear of the buildings like two quick lightning flashes. Gabe felt Courtright fall against him as he tried to break his fall.

"Damn, Bingham! You shot the deputy!" Nance said.

"I—I didn't mean to."

By that time a dozen or more men had come swarming into the alley, not only from the Club Room Saloon, but from the White Elephant and the Red Light as well. Surrounded by that many men, the two boys stood there, with Bingham still holding his gun.

"Which one of you hotspurs did this?" one of the men asked.

"He did it," Billy said, pointing to Bingham. "He shot him in cold blood." Billy kept repeating this over and over.

"You again, Feild? This is the second time you've shot someone."

"It was an accident. I didn't mean it," Bingham said.

"Where are you hit, Deputy?"

"It's in my gut," Courtright said, his voice strained. Gabe was cradling him in his arms as he lay on the ground.

"Get the deputy over to the doc's office," someone shouted. "He's losing blood fast."

Four men lifted Courtright and ran down the street to the office of the two physicians in town, Dr. Burts and Dr. Feild, Bingham's brother.

"Come on, you two. You'll be spending the night in jail, and I expect, Bingham, you won't get away with saying this is an accident, like you did when you shot John Ogleby last year. You better hope your brother can pull Courtright through, or you'll be hanging from a rope this time."

"Captain, can you come with us down to the jail? I think Marshal Redding will want to hear what you have to say about this."

"I can go with you," Gabe said as he started to rise to his feet. At that moment he fell forward in a faint.

"Did anybody check Corrigan? Was he hit or is he just weak in the gizzard?"

A man knelt beside Gabe, rolling him over to check for a pulse.

"I can just barely feel his heartbeat, but it's goin' like a house afire. There's a big puddle of blood, so he was hit someplace. Give me a hand and let's get him out of here."

Two men, moving as quickly as possible, carried the limp man to the doctors' office.

"Who do we have?" Dr. Feild asked as the men burst through the door with Gabe.

"It's the railroad man. He was with Courtright when they met up with Billy and your little brother."

"Get him in here and let me take a look at him."

"Doc, how's the deputy? Is he still alive?" one of the men asked.

"Barely," the doctor said as he cut through Gabe's pants leg. "He may be better off than this man though, because at least he's awake."

"Doc, you can't let either one of 'em die. You know Billy Nance is saying over and over it was Bingham who did the shooting."

"So I've heard."

Josie awakened the next morning with a heavy heart. Even though she had no right to do so, she had kept an ear open for Gabe, and she could swear he had not come back to the hotel last night. And she knew that Betty Courtright was still with her family in Little Rock.

Where would Jim Courtright likely take Gabe?

He had said the White Elephant, but more than likely they had wound up at The Two Minnies, a saloon-bordello in Hell's Half Acre. The place had the reputation of being the classiest whorehouse in town, where she had heard respectable men say they went when they wanted to "get frolicky," whatever that meant. Rumor had it that the saloon had a glass ceiling, and when the patrons looked up, they could see the working girls playing tenpins, all of them naked.

Josie was disappointed. She liked Gabe Corrigan, and she thought he was an honorable man. She supposed that men had needs, but she had never really talked about such things with anyone, certainly not her father. She might have asked Ida, but when her menses had started, Josie had asked questions about it, and Ida had said, "Hush, child, you're going to bleed for the rest of your life. Now don't talk about it," and so Josie never did. She was a twenty-four-year-old girl—make that *woman*—and she was sure Julius knew more about the birds and the bees than she did.

Her father was probably right to push Oscar Manning on her. He was such a stick-in-the-mud, he would never guess what a ninny she was.

"I'm going to bake biscuits again this morning, not for you, Mr. High-and-Mighty, but for me. You missed them yesterday, and they were damn good." She put her fingers to her mouth, and then she laughed. She had never before cussed in her entire life.

"Damn good," she said again as she measured out the sourdough starter.

"Miss Josie, Miss Josie," Julius said as he ran into the private quarters. "It's Mr. Gabe. He got shot last night."

"No," Josie said as she dropped the crock with a clatter and grabbed hold of the edge of the butcher-block table. "Is he . . . is he dead?"

"Not yet, but they say he's bad, real bad."

Josie ran out through the hotel, grabbing a shawl as she passed the front desk. She had not waited to ask if Julius knew where Gabe was, but she ran to Dr. Burts and Dr. Feild's office.

Bursting in without knocking, she saw Marshal Redding sitting on a long wooden church-pew bench in an area that served as a waiting room.

"How is he?"

"Jim's still alive, but they don't expect him to pull through."

"Jim? What about Gabe? Gabe Corrigan?"

"The railroad man. Yeah, he was hit, too. But of the two, the deputy got the worst of it."

Josie wanted to ask what had happened, but just then Dr. Burts stepped into the waiting room.

"How is he, Doc?" the marshal asked.

"I'd say the chances are twenty to one that he won't make it. The justice of the peace thinks we should get a dying statement from Courtright."

"What about Captain Corrigan?" Josie asked, her voice anxious and agitated.

"Oh, well, he got hit in the leg, and it was a clean shot, but he lost a lot of blood, so he goes in and out of consciousness. I think he's awake right now. Do you know him?"

"Yes. He's a guest at The Empress."

"Well, if you want to step in to see him, come with me. Because Jim's wounds are so much worse, Corrigan's not getting much attention right now."

"Thank you, Doctor."

Josie followed Dr. Burts into an examining room so small that it barely had room for the bed and a table that contained a washbasin and some cloths. Gabe was lying on the bed, about three feet high, with wooden slats to prevent him from rolling off.

When Gabe saw Josie, he attempted to raise his hand, but he was so weak it fell immediately to the bed. Josie stepped forward and clasped it in her own hands. A wan smile crossed his face as his eyes closed.

"He'll probably be out for quite a while, so there's no need in your staying here," Dr. Burts said.

"I'll stay."

"Well, that's up to you. If he awakens and needs anything, I'll be down the hall."

Josie stood by Gabe's bed until her back began to ache, but she would not leave. Even though the room was cool, he seemed to be sweating profusely, and when she felt his forehead, it was hot. She dampened one of the cloths and began wiping his brow with water from the basin.

What a handsome man he was; even now he had strength in his face, a well-chiseled nose, a square jaw, and a strong, dimpled chin. His eyes were closed, but she knew they were deep and dark.

"Please, God, don't let him die."

The whispered prayer was enough to cause his eyes to slowly open. He focused on her face, and then in a voice so weak she could barely hear him, he uttered, "So pretty."

"Hi, Gabe." Tears glistened in her eyes. "How are you feeling?"

"My head. A pillow."

Josie noticed he was lying on a board, covered with a sheet. No mattress, no padding, nothing. Josie stepped into the hallway and went in search of a doctor. No one had so much as entered Gabe's room for the whole time she had been with him.

"Dr. Burts, I want Captain Corrigan moved to the hotel. I can do a . . ." She stopped in midsentence because what she wanted to say were not ladylike words. "I can do a hell of a lot better job taking care of him than you are doing. I know that Jim Courtright is near death, but that man is lying in there on a board with no one to even come in to wipe his brow."

"Josie, I can appreciate your anger, but Captain Corrigan was hit in the leg with a bullet last night. He has lost a lot of blood and he will need rest and proper nourishment to regain his strength."

"Do you think for one moment he is more comfortable lying on that board—without so much as a pillow? Is that how he will get rest?"

"He has an entry wound and an exit wound that will need attention. The dressing will have to be changed several times a day, and he needs to be watched that he doesn't get an infection."

"How many times have you changed the dressing thus far?"

"Jim's bullet hit near his stomach and we think it is now lodged in his right shoulder."

"Then you're telling me you haven't done anything for Captain Corrigan."

Dr. Burts did not answer, but looked at Josie with an unswerving glare.

"If someone will come and tend to his wounds now, I will learn what to do. I want this man brought to the hotel this morning."

"Josie, I know your intentions are well-meaning, but you don't know what you're getting yourself in for. He will need a lot of attention."

"Doctor, I am willing to accept the responsibility."

"All right, but if there is any change in his condition, he has to come back here. Once we get Jim stabilized, either Dr. Feild or I will call on our patient every day."

Gabe was wrapped in blankets and carefully loaded into Willie Lane's buckboard wagon. Josie climbed up on the seat beside Willie as they slowly traveled to The Empress.

"You look like you're a little green around the gills, Miss Josie. Are you all right?" Willie asked.

Josie was glad she had not eaten before she ran out to the doctors' office because if she had, her breakfast would be in her throat. Her stomach was churning with nausea after watching the treatment of Gabe's leg.

"Oh, Uncle Willie, what have I gotten myself into? But I couldn't just leave Gabe there."

"Don't you worry about it, Miss Josie. Ida will help you, 'cause she knows all about nursin'."

"I'm going to need her."

They pulled up in front of the hotel, and Julius came running out, his eyes wide with fear. Seeing Gabe in the back of the wagon wrapped in the blankets as he was, the boy asked, "Is Cap'n Corrigan dead?"

"No, Julius, Mr. Corrigan is alive, but he is very sick. Run and find Papa so he can help your dad get him inside."

Soon Julius, Henri, and Oscar Manning came hurrying up to the wagon.

"Josie, what have you done? Julius says Gabe is going to stay here," Henri said. "Shouldn't he be at the doctors' office?"

"I couldn't leave him, Papa. I think we should put him in a downstairs room where I can keep a closer watch on him. I'll go open the bed." Josie ran in ahead of the men, and as soon as she was out of their sight, she began to retch. She calmed herself, telling herself that there was much to be done and she had to be strong. By the time Gabe was put in the bed, Josie had her nausea under control.

"Dr. Burts sent some iodine and some carbolic acid for me to use to cleanse the wounds. He says I will need to apply a hot fomentation about every half hour to try to keep the infection away."

"Mr. Laclede, are you going to let Josie tend to this man? She is an unmarried woman. What will happen to her reputation when this gets out?" Oscar asked.

"Clara Barton's reputation didn't suffer when she was called to nurse men during the war," Josie said.

"Look at her now. She's going around the country advocating for this Swiss organization, the Red Cross, and every sane person knows there is no place for that in this country. But worst of all, Miss Barton is a follower of that Anthony woman. Do you want people to think of you like that?"

"Thank you, Oscar, for helping bring Captain Corrigan into the hotel. I believe you have a store to run," Josie said as she cut off the conversation and began to make Gabe as comfortable as she could. Once again he had fallen asleep.

Oscar stepped out of the room without saying anything else.

"You know he is right, honey. Willie said Gabe's

wound is on his upper thigh. It just wouldn't be right for you to tend to it."

"Ida will help me."

Gabe was at Gettysburg, and even though he was in the aid station behind the lines, he could hear the sounds of battle, the heavy thump of artillery, the rattle of musketry, the screams and yells of two hundred thousand men locked in deadly combat.

"Orderly! I'm going to have to amputate this leg. Get in here now so you can take the limb out!"

Gabe could feel the pain in his leg as the doctor started sawing on it. The pain was excruciating, and he groaned and bit his teeth against it.

Josie was scraping the wound with a sharp spoon and could feel Gabe writhing and moaning in pain. She wept silent tears as she realized that she was causing him such pain, but the doctor had told her this needed to be done to fight against the infection. Then, with the wound raw, she laid a layer of cloth over it and saturated the cloth with carbolic acid.

The doctor had removed Gabe's pants and his underwear so that, from the waist down, he was naked, covered only with a sheet. Josie had been careful to preserve as much modesty for him as she could, lifting the sheet only far enough for her to get to the wound, but not high enough to expose anything else.

> *Gabe wondered how long it would take before—wait, that wasn't a saw blade he felt. What he felt now was a burning sensation. The doctor was treating him with some sort of solution.*
>
> *Gabe opened his eyes to thank the doctor for not taking off his leg, but when he did so, he saw Josie Laclede. She was holding a cloth, soaked in some solution, and she was dabbing at the wound.*
>
> *Josie Laclede? How did she get here to Gettysburg?*
>
> *Gabe passed out again.*

"You're doin' a good job, honey," Ida said. "See how the wound is pussing up like that? That's good, that means all the poison is comin' out."

"How did the poison get in there in the first place?" Josie asked.

"I don't rightly know how it gets in there. Maybe it's somethin' that just gets inside whenever there's a hole put in a body. I just know if you don't get the poison out, sometimes you can get what they call the gang green. And that's somethin' for sure you don't want to have."

Throughout the rest of the day, Gabe drifted in and out of consciousness.

"He'll be needing something to help him build up all the blood he has lost," Dr. Burts had told Josie. "Make a rich beef broth, and get him to drink as much of it as you can."

That had proved to be easier said than done. Gabe had no appetite, and he resisted her attempts to feed him.

She stayed with him for the rest of the day, treating his wound first with the carbolic acid solution and then with a warm mustard poultice. When the fever began to shoot up, she bathed his head with cool water. Now, in the middle of the night, the banked wood in the fireplace was lighting the room in a soft golden glow. Josie dozed in a chair by his bed, praying for his safe recovery even in her dreams.

TEN

Gabe woke up, and for the first time his head was clear. Though he had a sense of a passage of time, he was unaware how long he had been in and out of consciousness. He did remember that he had been shot. As he glanced around the unfamiliar room, he wondered where the deputy was. He knew Courtright had been hit in the abdomen, and he remembered men running down the street carrying Jim. He knew he had then been asked to go talk to Marshal Redding. But from that moment on, everything was a blur.

Then he saw Josie sitting in a chair by the fireplace, her legs curled up under her. She was holding her head with her hand as her long blond hair partially hid her face. She looked so innocent, so childlike, so beautiful in that position. Even though he could not remember, he knew instinctively that she had been by his side through this whole ordeal.

"How long?" he asked.

"Gabe, you're awake!" Josie jumped up from the chair and went to his side.

"How long have I been out?"

"Three days."

"Three days? Have you been here the whole time?"

"Yes."

"Why?"

"The doctor said that someone needed to keep an eye on you."

"I've come to a few times, then I slip back again. Once I thought you were . . ." He paused in mid-sentence.

"You thought I was what?"

"An angel."

Josie smiled.

"Thanks for staying with me."

At present Gabe had a pressing problem. He urgently needed to use the necessary room, but he didn't know where it was. He sat up, being careful not to make any noise that would disturb Josie. When his feet touched the floor, a most excruciating pain shot through his left leg, and he could not control his anguished cry.

"Gabe! You can't get out of bed!" Josie was by his bed instantly. "You'll start bleeding again."

Gabe sat back on the bed, suddenly aware that he was naked under a nightshirt that someone had placed on him. "Did you get this for me?" He tugged at the shirt, trying to arrange it so that it covered his private parts.

"Ida brought it. It belongs to Uncle Willie."

"Do you think Uncle Willie could come and help me to the necessary room?"

"It's the middle of the night. I can help you. This room has a private chamber just a few steps away." Josie helped Gabe to his feet, and he leaned heavily upon her as they took the few steps to the chamber closet.

"Don't go too far," Gabe said as he stepped into the little room and closed the door.

When Josie got Gabe back in bed, he fell against the pillow, his eyes closing in exhaustion.

"Before you go back to sleep, let me change your dressing. Dr. Burts has been here every day since you were shot, and he says Ida is doing a good job caring for you."

"Then, Ida has been my nurse?"

"In the daytime, but I have been here at night." Josie gathered her tinctures and dressings and moved to the bed.

"Thank you."

Josie flashed a big smile as she moved his nightshirt to the side, making certain his modesty was protected. She carefully removed the old bandage.

"Dr. Burts says this is a new treatment, and he is very pleased with the results for both you and Jim Courtright. He calls it chloride of zinc, I think."

"Then, Jim is alive?"

"Yes."

"Good. I'm glad to hear it."

Josie began to pour the white liquid over Gabe's leg, working it into all the crevices and cavities of the wound. As it ran down his thigh, she rubbed it with her hand, massaging it into the muscles.

This time, however, something was different. Gabe was aware of what she was doing, aware, too, of how high up on his thigh she was. He could feel her hands, rubbing against him. As she worked on him, with her hands all over his inner thigh, he was no longer aware of any pain. He was aware of only one sensation, and his reaction to it. The nightshirt lifted.

Josie saw the cloth lift, and it both surprised and puzzled her. She stopped her massage and watched as the shirt moved higher.

"That has never happened before. Have I done something to you?" She had the most quizzical expression on her face.

Gabe laughed with a deep rumble. "Yes, you have done something to me."

"Oh, Gabe, I am so sorry. Does it hurt?"

"No, honey, it doesn't hurt." Gabe's eyes were closed, and his voice was raspy.

Curiosity got the better of Josie, and she brazenly lifted Gabe's nightshirt.

"Is that what it's supposed to do?" she asked when she saw the fully engorged organ.

"Yes. Yes, it is working very well."

Josie had a sudden urge to touch it, and at first she did so tentatively, as if exploring, feeling cautiously with her fingers. It had an intense heat. She had never experienced anything like this before—it was almost as if this thing that she was touching had a life of its own.

Even as she stood there, with her fingers on a sensuous path of discovery, she felt a weakness in her knees, and hesitantly she wrapped her hand around the shaft.

Josie began to move her hand slowly, sliding over the skin.

"Josie, do you know what you are doing to me?" Gabe asked, his voice strained, not with pain, but with something else, something she could sense, but not fully understand. She had never heard Gabe's voice sound the way it did, with some sort of pleading urgency, as if he wanted more, but she didn't know what that would be. Josie saw that his hands were balled tightly into fists by his side.

Then, as she slid the skin up and down over the shaft and felt the throbbing heat in her hand, that heat somehow seemed to transfer to her own body. She felt a stirring, first as a tingling in her stomach, then as a growing moistness in her private parts.

In the past, she had wondered what men and women did together, and she would sometimes feel a pleasurable but disquieting sensation of wonder, along with the awareness that there must be more. But never before had those feelings reached this level. As she continued to stroke him, she could sense a growing intensity within him, as if a spring were coiling up inside, ready to—to do what?

Somehow, though she didn't understand exactly how, she realized that she was experiencing the same sensations. All of this was happening just because she was holding—no, *stroking*—Gabe's shaft.

She continued the stroking, moving faster and faster, somehow knowing this was what he wanted, what he needed, even without being told. And then, with a gasp, Gabe suddenly thrust his hips upward. A milky liquid began erupting from the tip, and Josie, surprised and frightened by it, removed her hand quickly.

"Oh, Gabe, what have I done to you? Have I—have I hurt you?"

"No, little one. You have made me feel very good."

He rose from the pillow and wrapped his arms around her, kissing her with a tenderness she had never before experienced. When the kiss was over, he held her in his arms for a long time, not saying anything, but Josie sensed that he did not want to let her go. Then he kissed her again.

"I think Ida had better take over as my full-time nurse. We can't let this happen again," Gabe said.

"Why? Is it wrong?"

"No, my love, there is nothing wrong with what just happened. It's that I want so much more for both of us. Now, I want to go to sleep, and I want you to go back to your own room and have very pleasant dreams about me. Then in the morning bring me a biscuit."

Christmas Eve 1875

"'A Visit from St. Nicholas,' by Clement Clarke Moore," Henri said. Then he began to read:

> 'Twas the night before Christmas, when all
>   through the house
> Not a creature was stirring, not even a
>   mouse;
> The stockings were hung by the chimney
>   with care,
> In hopes that St. Nicholas soon would be
>   there.

Julius sat transfixed until Henri concluded the reading with the final lines of the poem.

> He sprung to his sleigh, to his team gave a
>   whistle,
> And away they all flew, like the down of a
>   thistle,
> But I heard him exclaim, ere he drove out
>   of sight,
> "Happy Christmas to all, and to all a good
>   night."

"If reindeer can fly, why don't the stagecoach people use reindeer instead of horses?" Julius asked. "They could hook them up to a coach and you could fly to places like Dallas and the moon, and maybe even as far away as St. Louis."

"Only Santa Claus's reindeer can fly," Henri said. "All the other reindeer must walk just like every other animal. And besides, they are too small to pull a heavy stagecoach."

"That would be good though, wouldn't it?" Julius asked. "I mean, if people could get into a stagecoach and fly somewhere."

"Don't be silly, Julius," Willie said. "That's impossible."

Henri laughed. "I'll tell you this, you've got to give Julius credit for having a vivid imagination."

Henri, Josie, Julius, Willie, and Ida were in the lobby of the hotel. Gabe was there, too, having hobbled in with the help of a cane Willie had carved for him. Earlier they had enjoyed a bowl of oyster stew, and now they were feasting on sweetmeats and ribbon candy that Ida had made. They were gathered around a five-foot-tall pine tree that Willie had brought when he had returned from his supply run to Eagle Ford. Gabe had arranged for the tree to be brought from Longview.

"You ladies did a wonderful job decorating the tree," Henri said.

"I helped," Julius said. "Don't forget, I helped."

"You certainly did, Julius, and I don't think we could have done it without you."

"Have you ever celebrated Christmas with a tree before, Gabe?" Henri asked.

"Yes. I grew up in Pennsylvania very near the German settlements where everybody had a yule tree. Even during the war, wherever we were, we had a Christmas tree." Gabe chuckled. "Once, we had to run from the Rebels—well, I believe General Rosecrans called it a repositioning of our troops—but it was running, pure and simple. And even then we had a little tree, and when we left, we took it with us."

"Sounds like a story," Henri said.

"Not one covered with glory, I hasten to add. It was Christmas of '62. I had about a hundred men in my company when the Rebs came after us with about four thousand. I ordered retreat. We abandoned the bridge we were supposed to be guarding, but we didn't abandon the Christmas tree."

"He had four thousand to your one hundred?" Henri asked.

"That was about the ratio."

"Then, General Rosecrans was right. That wasn't a retreat. That was just common sense," Willie said.

Gabe laughed. "Thanks, Willie. I appreciate your take on that."

"Oh, let's all tell stories about Christmas," Josie said.

"I remember my favorite Christmas," Willie said, "and it was because of you, Miss Josie. You and your papa."

"Do tell," Josie urged.

"It was in 1851, it was," Willie said. "I started that year as a slave, belongin' to Mr. Swayne Birdsong. Ida, she belonged to Mr. Thad Barnes. I went to Mr. Birdsong and I begged him, I said, 'I know Ida and I know she would make a good housekeeper for you, and she can cook and ever'thing. I want you to buy her so she can be my wife.'

"Mr. Birdsong talked to Mr. Barnes, but Mr. Barnes said that Ida was too good and he wanted too much money for her."

Willie reached over and took Ida's hand in his. "Ida birthed my baby, but the baby, a sweet little girl, died when she was only two days old. I thought maybe Ida was near 'bout goin' to die, too, 'cause her heart was plumb broke from losin' the baby and 'cause she couldn't be with me."

The sad expressions on both Ida's and Willie's faces revealed their sorrow. Then a big smile spread across Willie's face. "But then, along come Mr. Henri. There was a little baby got left with Mr. Henri, and 'cause that little baby didn't have a mama, he needed a wet nurse. So he bought Ida and then he bought me, and first thing he did after he bought both of us is, he give us our freedom.

"'All I want you to do is stay with me until the baby is weaned,' Mr. Henri said. 'And after that, you are free to go wherever you want. You can work for me, for good wages, or go off on your own.' We said we would stay, and here we are, twenty-four years later. And your first Christmas, Josie, well, that was the first Christmas Ida and me both were free."

"Oh, I am so happy for you," Josie said, with tears in her eyes, as she hugged both Willie and Ida.

"Honey, you drank my milk when you were nothin' but a baby. And in my mind, that makes you the same as my baby, though you are white and I am black."

"Then, that makes her my sister!" Julius said.

Josie laughed and hugged Julius as well. "But I'm your big sister, don't forget. And that means I can still order you around."

"That's quite a coincidence, that being your happiest Christmas," Henri said, "because it was my happiest as well. It was also my saddest."

"How can it be happy and sad at the same time?" Julius asked.

"It was happy because Empress Josephine came into my life that year. An infant who couldn't have been more than a month old when I found her in my carriage."

"You found Josie in your carriage?" Gabe asked, surprised by the announcement.

"That's right, Gabe," Josie said with a smile. "I'm really what you call a foundling." She hugged her father. "But I could not have been found by a more wonderful father in the entire world."

"You didn't say why you were sad," Julius said.

"I was sad because that was the first Christmas without my darling wife, Bridgette, who had died just a few months before I found Josie."

"What about you, Julius? What's your favorite Christmas?" Gabe asked.

"I'll answer that tomorrow when I see what presents I get," Julius replied, and the others laughed.

"Oh, listen!" Josie said.

From outside they could hear singing, and moving to the front door, they opened it, then stepped out onto the boardwalk. A group of carolers stopped out front and began to sing.

"You want to know my favorite Christmas?" Josie asked as the carolers moved on down the street.

"Which one?" Henri asked.

In the dark, and unnoticed by anyone else, Josie reached over and took Gabe's hand. "This one."

January 1876

"Captain Corrigan, here it is. I know you've been checking every day for this," Max Elser said as he entered the hotel lobby.

Gabe took the telegram and began to read. "Ha! This is wonderful! It's what I've been waiting for." He thumped on the telegram with his fingers and held it out toward Josie and Henri.

"What is it?" Henri asked, taking the proffered piece of paper.

"Our first load of rails has arrived, and they should be in Eagle Ford tomorrow. I have to be honest with you, even though when you came to Dallas, I promised you I could get the rails, it has been a bit of a challenge. Just before Christmas, Colonel Scott sent word saying he didn't think there was any way we could come up with enough to finish the road all the way to Fort Worth. I didn't have the heart to tell everyone after all the work the people have put in, but this takes care of it. At least for a little while."

"How many rails did you get?" Josie asked.

"This telegram says we are to get twenty flat-cars, and at the most there will only be about one hundred twenty-five rails on each one. That will get us seven miles closer, and then I'll have to come up with some more."

"That is good news," Henri said.

"Yes. I'll need to ride out to Eagle Ford tomorrow to take charge of the manifest, and quite honestly, I want to see the progress."

"Gabe, are you sure your leg is well enough to make the trip?" Josie asked.

"Nurse Ida is well pleased with my progress, and if she says I can ride, then I can do it."

"I was your nurse, too, and I don't think you should ride a horse for two hours when your wound is so fresh. Don't you agree with me, Papa?"

"She's right, you know. Why don't you go over to the wagon yard and get Judge Hendrick's closed carriage?"

"You don't think Eliza would mind?" Josie asked.

"I'm sure she wouldn't. Harrison was one of the original donors of the land that is set aside for the railroad depot, and if he were alive, he would be in the thick of this whole operation," Henri said.

"If you're going in a carriage, may I go with you?" Josie asked. "I'd like to see what's being done, too." Then, to her father: "Would it be all right?"

"I don't know, I . . ."

"She wouldn't be in the way, Mr. Laclede, and I know she would find it interesting," Gabe offered.

"And if Gabe's leg starts to bleed again, I know how to take care of it."

Henri stroked his chin for a moment, then nodded. "Very well, you may go, Josie." He pointed to Gabe. "But, young man, I am putting her safety in your hands."

"I understand."

"The widow Hendricks doesn't take this carriage out much in the winter, but I can lace these here leather curtains in place," Marion Thompson said as he pushed the dusty carriage out of the carriage house. "But you'll still be exposed in front, so you had best take this sheepskin to sit on and a buffalo robe to put over your laps."

"That's a good suggestion," Gabe said.

"Miss Josie, are you sure you want to be trotting off with this here fella in the middle of January? Why, the sun won't even be up for another hour or so."

"We're going to be fine, Mr. Thompson; just pick out a good horse for the trip."

"Now, Miss Josie, you know I'm giving you the best horse I've got."

"I never had any doubt."

Half an hour later, a big red horse, whose name appropriately was Red, was connected to the light carriage, and Gabe and Josie were seated on the box. On the floor was a covered basket that Ida had prepared for them, containing a couple of boiled-ham sandwiches wrapped in oiled paper, two tins of sardines, and some saltine crackers. Also, she had put in a half dozen sugar cookies and a canteen of fresh water that they would share.

It was quite cold outside, but the closed carriage kept the wind out, and the buffalo robe wrapped around their legs kept Josie warm.

Or was it the buffalo robe? Her leg was pressed tightly against Gabe's, and she could feel the warmth emanating from him. Or was the heat coming from her? Almost involuntarily, she pressed her leg more tightly against his, and he responded.

"How long will it take us to get there?" Josie asked.

"About three hours." Gabe took out his watch from a pocket in his vest. "My estimate is that we should be there before ten o'clock."

"Oh. That's a pretty long trip, isn't it?"

"Are you cold? Do you want me to turn back?"

"No, I'm fine. I'm not hurting your leg, am I?"

Gabe pressed his leg hard against hers.

"It's my other leg. You should remember that, because you dressed the wound often enough."

"Yes, of course I remember. I don't know what I was thinking."

That was a lie. Josie knew exactly what she was thinking. She was thinking about the last time she had tended his wound. True to his word, he had never let anybody but Ida or Dr. Burts change his bandages after the night she had, in his words, made him "feel very good." What did it feel like for him when he—when his—when whatever it was that happened, had happened? Did he feel the way she did that night?

She recalled her own feelings—the tingling in her legs and the hollow of her stomach, the moistness in her most private parts, and how delightful the sensation was. Yet, despite how wonderful that had felt, somehow she knew that was but a precursor to something else, something much more.

As she rode alongside him, her leg pressed tightly against his, she again began to feel that mysterious dampness and sweet aching desire for—for what? What was just on the other side of this mystery?

Josie wasn't the only one recalling that night of preliminary exploration, because Gabe was now thinking about that very incident. He should never have let her come with him, because this trip was certainly not a pleasure trip. He had to see for himself what kind of progress was being made and then convince Colonel Scott that these local men could successfully lay this track.

Gabe knew he should be staying at End of Track with Walter Roche. The engineer stayed in the supervisor's car, which moved with the boarding-house cars as the track was laid. But the gunshot wound had given him all the excuse he needed to stay in Fort Worth at The Empress with the Lacledes.

The feel of her leg against his, the memory of her hand on him, and the resultant relief her ministrations had given him were but an agonizing reminder of what could be. He felt a bulge in the front of his trousers. How easy it would be to reach over, take her hand, and put it in place to repeat the actions he was now recalling in such vivid detail.

For at least half an hour they drove without speaking, each lost in his or her own erotic thoughts. Only the steady and rhythmic clopping of the horse's hooves, plus the whisper of the narrow-rimmed wheels rolling through the hard-packed dirt of the road, invaded the silence.

Soon they were met by a number of empty supply wagons returning to Fort Worth, including Willie Lane's wagon. At first Willie did not recognize Josie, as her head was covered with a heavy woolen scarf.

"Miss Josie, does your papa know you're out here with the captain? Maybe you should hitch a ride back with me," Willie said.

"Papa knows. We'll be back before dark."

"Some of the rails were supposed to have arrived. Did you happen to see them?" Gabe asked.

"They're there. I'm mighty thankful that my job is driving this here wagon and not rustling those rails. They look powerful heavy."

"You're right about that. I think each rail weighs more than five hundred pounds, so I hope the crew doesn't try to get too much done all at once."

Another wagon came up behind Willie. "Are you sure you don't want to come back with me, Miss Josie?"

"I'll be just fine," Josie said as she heard Willie snap the reins to get the team moving.

"Your father, Willie, Ida—they all look out for you, don't they?"

"I suppose they do. But they always have. When Papa found me in the carriage, the note in my basket said that my mother had chosen Papa because she knew he was the kind of man who would take good care of me. Papa always says he thinks he is like pharaoh's daughter, and that I am like Moses in the bulrushes."

"But in the Bible story, the mother and the sister came to take care of Moses. Did anybody ever try to contact your father about you?"

"No. I've always wondered what would make someone do what my mother did, but now I don't suppose I'll ever know." Josie changed the subject. "Tell me something about you, Gabe. Where did you come from?"

"Well, my story is very ordinary. I was born in Philadelphia, and when I was a little boy, my family moved about thirteen miles away to a little place called Newtown Square."

"Why did you move there?"

"My father became a bone crusher."

"A bone crusher?"

"Yes, and he's still doing it. He has a small factory now, where he crushes bones and makes fertilizer for all the farmers in Delaware County."

"So that's where all those piles of buffalo bones go. To bone crushers, maybe as far away as Pennsylvania. Do you get to go home very often?"

"Not really. I haven't been there for about three years, but Katie, my little sister, says every red-blooded American has to come to Philadelphia for the centennial this year. If we get the T&P to Fort Worth in time, I'm going home for sure. Why don't you plan to come with me?"

"Oh, I don't know if I could do that. How would Papa manage without me?"

"Henri would want you to go, because how many times is the country going to reach a hundred years old? Colonel Scott tells me the new depot is almost finished, and that it's right across from the entrance to the exhibition. That means every visitor who comes by train will have to ride on the Pennsylvania Railroad."

Josie mulled over what Gabe had said. *Why don't you plan to come with me?* How easily he had said those words. Yet they had a greater implication if he was serious. An unmarried woman did not go traipsing off across the country with a man, especially one who could so arouse her inner feelings. But she could steel herself against his charms if she put her mind to it. Wasn't this very carriage ride proof of that?

When they reached Eagle Ford, Josie was amazed at the little town that had sprung up. End of Track, as it was called, had four boarding cars to serve the nearly two hundred men who just a short time ago were farmers or cowboys or draymen or sawyers or blacksmiths or any one of a number of such occupations. But now they were all railroad men working together for one common cause, to bring the railroad to Fort Worth, saving their town and their way of life.

One of the boarding cars was for eating, one for cooking, and two for sleeping. A much smaller car served as the T&P office and living quarters for the Roche brothers, who as the engineers were the only paid employees of the Tarrant County Construction Company.

"I don't know how long this will take me," Gabe said as he motioned toward the office car, "but I've got to meet with Walter and Leo. Why don't you just wander around wherever you want to go? I'm sure you know just about everyone who is working, but make sure you stay out of their way."

"Where shall I meet you?"

"How about in the dining car in a couple of hours?"

"That sounds very good, and I'll be careful."

Josie couldn't believe the amount of work that had already been done, just to get the roadbed prepared. Trees had been felled, stumps pulled, and boulders removed from the right-of-way. Now men were swinging pickaxes to get through the thick limestone and shale rock that lay only inches beneath the heavy clay soil. Other men were pounding the rocks into smaller pieces and replacing them in the dug-out roadbed so that the crossties could be put in place.

"Josie, Josie Laclede, is that you?" Big Bull Turner called out as he stopped to wipe his brow on his shirtsleeve. "Did you know what you was gettin' us into when you hatched this harebrained idea of yours?"

"To be honest, I didn't have any idea just how much work would be involved, but I can't tell you how proud I am of all of you. What you have accomplished in such a short time is amazing," Josie said.

"Well, all's I can say is it's a good thing them dad-blamed rails got here yesterday. It's hard to build a railroad with no rails."

"I think Captain Corrigan said you had enough for seven miles of track, so when they're used, that's only sixteen more miles to go."

"Sixteen more miles, huh?" Big Bull picked up his ax and started swinging again, breaking up more of the hard bedrock.

Josie turned to go back toward the boarding cars, even more amazed at all the activity. She watched as teams of horses pulled bundles of crossties into place, ready for men to put them onto the rock ballast that Big Bull's crew was crushing. Then a material car came up, again pulled by horses. Fishplates and kegs of nails, spikes, and bolts were thrown off on each side of the track, and one man's job was to burst open the kegs and cut the fastenings. Then men scrambled to fill buckets with the supplies and carry them up to be in place by the bundles of ties.

Finally the handcars loaded with rails were brought up and the rails were rolled off, one on each side, the sound as loud as what Josie imagined a military bombardment would be like. Ahead of the rails the crossties were set and spikes scattered alongside. A dozen tong men would grab a rail and run forward to drop it on the crossties. As many as forty men began putting the fishplates in place, then connecting the rails and driving the spikes. Finally more men tamped down the earth and ballast around it. Once those rails were in place, the empty handcar would be lifted off the track, and the next rail-laden car would be moved into place on the just-laid track. And so it went, over and over again.

Watching the whole operation, Josie had no doubt that these men were up to the job at hand. She could go back home and say with confidence that the railroad would get to Fort Worth—if they could get enough rails.

ELEVEN

From the *Fort Worth Democrat*:
The legislature assembled on the second Tuesday of this month, January 1876, our county being ably represented by the Honorable Nicholas Darnell. The current resolution in effect is that the railroad will be granted time until the adjournment of the first legislature held under the new constitution, and this is that legislature. Should the railroad not reach Fort Worth before that time, a date near to June 30, the state land-grant agreement with the Texas and Pacific shall be abrogated.

The news having gone forth of the organization of the Tarrant County Construction Company and their determination to resume work on the T&P has already produced a good effect on the business of our town. It has infused a new life and vigor into our people, which reacts on those coming here with good results. Stages and hacks come in well filled, and everything is beginning to assume the appearance of life, activity, and enterprise, which was shown here in the boom time of 1873.

But there is a sword of Damocles hanging over our fair city, that danger being the aforementioned resolution. The powers that be are not looking kindly upon the bigwigs of the Pennsylvania Railroad and its subsidiary, the Texas and Pacific. Our legislators read with interest of the expansion of the rails in the East, to include a terminal currently under construction, provided solely for the comfort of visitors to the great Centennial Exhibition in Philadelphia. We listen with understanding when we are told of the financial woes of the company, and how there is no money to complete our road. But this journalist fears patience has run out for our fellow Texans. Several in our legislative body have stated publicly that the allocated railroad land grants shall not continue beyond adjournment of this session. They are saying enough is enough, and perhaps with good reason.

Nevertheless, should the railroad not meet this time restraint and the land grants be withdrawn, all the valiant efforts of our hardworking neighbors will be for naught, and once again Fort Worth will lose ground, indeed perhaps to the point of ceasing to be a city.

*It is absolutely necessary that the railroad
reach Fort Worth by the time prescribed, or
that persuasion for an extension be lobbied
aggressively. Every citizen must realize that
this enterprise, bringing the T&P to our fair
city, is too rich a prize to be abandoned at this
late date.*

Gabe and Buckley Paddock were enjoying a
beer and breakfast at the Tivoli Hall.

"You didn't mince words in your editorial last
night," Gabe said as he placed the *Democrat* on
the table.

"I'm sorry, but it needs to be said. You can just
sense an air of anticipation, almost giddiness, in
the folks. Why, even you heard it from Josie the
other day when she came back from End of Track.
She's been tooting the horn for all the workers. It's
like in her mind and a lot of other people's, this
railroad getting to town is a fait accompli, and we
both know it's not."

"The men are doing a much better job than I
ever thought they could."

"Maybe so, but what's going to happen when
it's time for farmers to put in their crops, or when
it's time to trail cattle? Or when they just get tired
of working that hard for no money? They'll be
coming home, and then what?"

"I've talked to you enough, Buck, to know you're
getting at something. What's your suggestion?"

"I think it's time for a delegation to make a trip

to Austin and 'let the chips fall where they may,'" Paddock said, quoting the motto of the *Democrat*. "How many times has an extension been granted?"

"At least twice."

"That's my point, so what's one more? I think I'll talk to Major Van Zandt and see if he can go with me to see what we can get done. Can I count on you to go, too?"

"Of course. Fort Worth has a lot riding on this, but on a much lesser scale, so do I." Gabe was thinking of the sixteen sections of land that Colonel Scott had promised him if he brought in the railroad. He had always thought that he would sell the more than ten thousand acres he would receive, but the more time he spent in Texas, the more he liked the thought of staying here. Or was it someone who was in Texas that he liked more?

After leaving Tivoli's, Gabe stopped by Jim Courtright's house to check on the deputy marshal. Though his chances of survival had been grave, he had defied the odds and was recovering quite well.

"How's the leg?" Courtright asked.

"I can't complain."

"I should never have let you go into that alley with me. If you'd lost your leg, or worse . . ."

"To tell you the truth, I don't think I could have survived what you just came through. Are you about ready to get out of this law enforcement business?"

"No, I think I'm going to run for office come April, now that Redding has gone back to barbering."

"I heard he had left his position. That's too bad."

"Not really. You can't have cowboys going around drivin' the marshal into a saloon by twirlin' their ropes at him, and then shootin' under 'im. If you don't have these numskulls' respect, you don't have anything."

"Well, I think you have that in spades. I hear you told the judge not to prosecute the boys who shot us. Is that true?"

"Yeah, it's true. What would having two young kids locked up accomplish? They aren't bad boys; they were just drunk and foolish. And by lettin' 'em off, I may have gained a little of that respect I was talking about."

"I hope you're right."

"How goes the railroad?"

"I was out at End of Track a few days ago, and I was pleased with what I saw. But now I'm a little worried. Buck Paddock says the state legislature isn't too keen on giving us an extension beyond this session. I think we'll get here in time, but a lot can happen in four or five months."

"General Darnell is a good man," Courtright said, "and if anybody can get something done in Austin, it'll be him."

"I hope it's enough. I'd feel a lot better if James Throckmorton was still the governor, instead of Governor Coke."

"Captain Corrigan." Betty Courtright came into

the room. "Are you the man who almost got my husband killed while I was away?"

"I don't think it was quite like that," Jim Courtright said, taking his wife's hand. "Don't mind Betty. She's a little tired of all this nursing she's been doing, and I think she wants to shift the blame to anybody she can find."

"Well, Mrs. Courtright, I'd say you're a fine nurse to bring this man back from the dead, and I'm happy to make your acquaintance. But I'd best be going now."

"Perhaps we'll see you again soon, and next time you come, why don't you bring Josie with you? I've not had a good sit-down with her for a long time," Betty said.

"I'll do that," Gabe replied as he picked up his hat to leave.

As he was walking back to the hotel, he was thinking about Mrs. Courtright's comment. Why did she ask him to bring Josie with him? Had the townspeople begun to pair them together? Had it gotten around town that they had ridden out to End of Track alone? Gabe would have to be careful what they did together. He did not want her reputation to be damaged because of him.

Because he was their only hotel guest, Gabe took many of his meals with the Lacledes in their private quarters. He knew from overhearing comments from Henri and Ida that Josie was usually not the cook, but for some reason, she had suddenly taken an interest in cooking. A few of her offerings had been almost inedible, but both he and Henri had eaten everything she had put before them.

The meal that evening was green-pea soup and what Josie called beef hash cakes. The hash cakes were made from yesterday's corned beef, mixed with potatoes, then fried and put on a slice of buttered bread. It was not something he was familiar with, but it was quite good.

During the meal, Gabe shared his conversation with Buck Paddock about the goings-on in the legislature, then he told of his visit with Jim Courtright.

"Those two boys are walking the streets of Fort Worth today," Josie said. "They almost killed two people, and they should be locked in jail."

"We have to trust Courtright's judgment. If he thinks they'll be better off without incarceration, then, I have to agree with him," Henri said.

"I hope he's right," Gabe said as he unconsciously rubbed the site of his nearly healed wound.

"Oh, honey, I forgot to tell you," Henri said. "Willie has an extra big load of supplies tomorrow, so we're taking two wagons."

"Will Oscar be going with him?"

A big smile came across Henri's face. "Do you think you're the only one in this family who is curious about what's going on at End of Track? I want to see, too."

"Oh, Henri, I should have asked you to go with us when Josie and I went out," Gabe said. "I'm sorry I didn't think about it."

"Tell me, did you really want an old man like me tagging along with you young folks?"

"Oh, Papa," Josie said as she lowered her head, her cheeks flushing with embarrassment.

"I'm just joshing with you. Don't pay any mind to what I have to say. We couldn't have both gone anyway. We do have a hotel to run, and who knows when we might get a guest?"

"Wait a minute. No guests? What do you call me?" Gabe chimed in.

"You don't count. You're part of us," Josie said with a demure dip of her head.

Gabe just nodded as he gave her a warm smile.

Henri and Willie left just before sunup the next morning with wagons filled with dry beans, bacon, flour, cornmeal, coffee, eggs, and molasses. In addition to the food, they also had scores of gloves and socks, and woolen underwear. All the items came from Henri's store, all bought at a discount and on credit by the Tarrant County Construction Company for use by the men in the field. Oscar was constantly chiding Henri about the money that he was sure the store would lose if Henri continued to allow credit, but Henri insisted that when the railroad arrived, the lost money would be made up many times over.

Gabe came down about an hour later to see that Josie had already made coffee and was frying salt pork.

"Good morning," she said as Gabe went straight

for the coffeepot. "Biscuits are in the oven. How do you want your eggs?"

"However you fix them is how I want them, more than any other way."

Josie chuckled. "I'll try not to break the yellows."

"Did your pa and Willie get away this morning?"

"Yes, before daylight."

Gabe, with coffee cup in hand, stepped over to look out the window. "Hmm, hope they don't have any trouble."

"Why do you say that?"

"Those clouds. Looks to me like there's snow in them."

"Ahh, don't worry. We hardly ever get snow, and when we do, it never amounts to anything. Not like it was when we lived in St. Louis."

"We get a lot of it in Pennsylvania, and I sort of miss it. When I was a kid, we used to drag our sleds up Cemetery Hill and then come flying down, weaving in and out among the tombstones."

"Did you ever hit one?"

"Sure." He lifted his chin to show a scar that was tucked under it.

"I've never noticed that before."

"It's because you spend all your time looking away from me," Gabe said, his voice low and seductive.

As if taking a cue from him, she turned and removed her biscuits from the oven.

Gabe put his cup on the table and stepped over to Josie, turning her around so that she faced him.

"Josie, are you afraid of me?"

"No. No, I'm not afraid of you."

"Then, what is it? It's almost like you are avoiding me, even though we technically live in the same house."

"It was— I don't know how to talk about this, but it was after . . . after that night, the night when you . . . when you said only Ida could be your nurse. I thought you didn't want me to be around you anymore."

"My sweet, sweet innocent, I didn't send you away because I didn't want you. I sent you away for the exact opposite reason, because I wanted you too much."

"Gabe, you must think me a silly twit, but I am twenty-four years old, and except for watching animals mate, I know absolutely nothing about what men and women are supposed to do."

"Don't ever apologize for that. You are exactly what a man desires in a woman. He doesn't need a woman who is little better than a harlot, who will deceive him and lie with any man who will have her." Gabe's voice was edged with bitterness, and he was picturing Marthalee even as he spoke.

He ate his breakfast in silence, as Josie sat across from him. Before she was finished eating, Gabe rose and went out back, the door banging shut behind him.

What had she said or done? She was being truthful. She didn't know anything about men or how they worked. She had actually thought she was hurting Gabe the night she had made his manhood erupt, for want of a better word. He had said it made him feel good, and she could believe that, because her own body had reacted in a way that she had never experienced and she knew she liked the feeling.

Oh, how she wished she had a woman to talk to, a woman who was not afraid to talk about womanly things, as Ida was. How she longed for a mother, her very own mother. She had to wonder if her mother was alive or dead, and if she was alive, did she ever wonder what the daughter she had so unceremoniously given away looked like, or what had become of her? Josie thought her mother had to be dead, because she obviously had known who Henri Laclede was. They had not left St. Louis until Josie was sixteen years old. At some time her mother could have come forward and made herself known. What was so terrible about having a child that had made her mother abandon her?

The snow started midmorning, at first with flurries, then intensifying until it was falling quite heavily. Josie sat at the window as she watched big flakes join together to form even bigger flakes. Within what seemed like only moments, the ground was completely covered, but still it fell, unabated, as she was mesmerized by the beauty. The snowfall was so intense that Willie and Ida's house, no more than 150 feet behind the hotel, was barely visible.

"Where are you, Papa and Uncle Willie? Have you made it to Eagle Ford?" Josie asked aloud. "And where are you, Gabe Corrigan?"

Just then, like a snowman come to life, she saw Gabe stumbling toward the back door, his arms loaded with sticks of wood. Josie hurried to open the door for him.

"I should have thought of that," Josie said.

Gabe entered the kitchen, stamping the snow off his boots. "Put this in the woodbox, but be careful that we don't get the other wood wet. I'll get some more and pile it here by the door. Shall I bring up some food from the cellar?"

"I think we're fine on food."

Josie watched as Gabe tramped back and forth getting more wood than they could ever use. Then she watched as he disappeared in the snow, presumably carrying wood to Ida and Julius. She smiled when she realized what he was doing. He loved the snow and he was just making every excuse he could to stay out in it.

When he finally came in, his coat and pants were white with the stuff.

"Let me brush you off," Josie said as she started pushing the snow off his shoulders.

"I'm making a big mess for you."

"It's fine, but you need to get out of these wet clothes. If you like, I can run to your room and get you some dry things."

"All right, I'll stand right here and drip."

Josie stepped into Gabe's room. Ida had moved

all of his things downstairs, and it was the first
time she had been in his room since the night he
had sent her away. She looked toward the unmade
bed, the bed where he slept. She went to the chest
and opened a drawer. Everything was put away
carefully: his socks were all together, his underwear, his shirts and pants. They were all laid out
as neatly as if on display in a dry goods store. She
felt a touch of embarrassment as she handled his
undergarments. What was she doing here, in this
most private part of Gabe's life? It was as if she
were invading his privacy, though he had clearly
given her permission to do so.

As she looked at the shirt she had chosen, a
blue denim, she thought of the weather, and how
cold he must be for having been out in the snow,
and decided he should have a warmer one. She
returned the blue denim shirt to the drawer and
picked up a red flannel one in its stead.

That's when she saw the envelopes, two of them
lying there, but not bound together.

One had a postmark from England, but no
return address. It was addressed to Captain
Gabriel Corrigan, T&P Railroad, 21 First Street,
Shreveport, Louisiana. She thought that odd, that
someone would send a letter all the way from
England without putting a return address.

The other letter did have a return address, and
it invoked just as much curiosity as the first. The
return address on this envelope was preprinted:
Vernon R. DuPont, Judge, Caddo Parish, Shreve-

port, Louisiana. This letter was also addressed to Gabe, but at a different address in Shreveport. Written to one side of the envelope were the words *Official and Confidential.*

With all that was in her, Josie wanted to look inside the envelopes. She walked over to the door and looked outside to see if Gabe was anywhere close.

He wasn't.

Josie opened the flap of the envelope from England, pulled the contents halfway out, then stopped.

"No!" she said aloud. "Whatever this is, it is none of my business."

She put the two envelopes back in the drawer and covered them with the blue denim shirt. Then, proud of her restraint, though still burning with curiosity, she walked back into the small apartment kitchen, carrying the change of clothes.

"I got a warmer shirt for you. I thought you might want it."

"I'll appreciate it, thanks." Gabe shivered as he looked around the small kitchen. "Where should I go to change?"

"Do it here, by the cookstove. That's the warmest place in the house."

"Here?"

Josie smiled. "Don't worry, I'll step into the other room."

"All right." Gabe began unbuttoning his shirt.

Josie was a little surprised that he started

undressing right away, so she turned around quickly and hurried into the keeping room.

"I'll just drop my clothes right here on the floor if that's all right," Gabe called. "That way my mess will all be in one place."

"Don't worry about it. I'll take care of it."

As Josie listened to the sound of his clothing being removed, she thought again about the incident in his bedroom. She had only partially satisfied her curiosity then. She had seen the most private part of him, yes, but it was so isolated from the rest of his body that it was almost clinical. Now he was standing within six feet of her, and if not entirely nude yet, he soon would be. She visualized what his entire body would look like in the buff.

As he was undressing, Gabe draped his wet clothing onto a chair, and the weight caused the chair to tip over.

When Josie heard the loud crash, she instinctively rushed into the kitchen. What if he had fallen? When she entered the room, she found herself face-to-face with a totally nude Gabe Corrigan.

Enthralled, she stared for a long moment, from the broad shoulders across his muscled chest, down across his flat stomach, his muscled legs—and that part of him she had seen once before. Only this time there was nothing clinical about it. He looked like a chiseled statue.

Gabe was a little surprised by her unabashed gaze, but he made no effort to cover himself.

Josie stood still, watching as his anatomy changed before her very eyes. Gabe smiled at her.

"Oh!" she said, spinning around. "Oh, I'm sorry. I heard the noise, I just reacted. Please, forgive me."

"There is nothing to forgive, Josie. Like you said, you came when you heard the noise. It was a natural reaction." Gabe held the flannel shirt in front of him, in an effort to cover himself.

"I—I am so embarrassed."

Gabe chuckled softly. "Think nothing more of it."

Josie retreated back to the keeping room, then walked over to the window and grabbed on to the frame to steady herself as she looked outside.

She hadn't wanted to leave the kitchen. She had wanted to stay there with him, not just to see him, but to—to what? Josie's breath was coming in short gasps now, and she felt a churning in her stomach and a weakness in her knees. What was happening to her? What was this all about? And why was he changing like that? What made it grow so? She knew that, somehow, it had something to do with her and the things that happen between men and women.

"Thank you," Gabe said. "I'm much more comfortable now in dry clothes."

Gabe had come into the room with her, had spoken to her, but she didn't turn away from the window. She didn't know if she could face him now. She was sure that if she did, he would be able to read her face. He would know that she hadn't wanted to leave the room at all, that she had wanted to explore more fully these thoughts and feelings she was experiencing.

"It's still snowing outside," she said as she continued to stare out the window.

Gabe came up to stand behind her, so close that he was touching her. The strange tingling sensations in her body were intensified by his proximity.

"I thought you said it didn't snow in Fort Worth."

"I didn't say that it never snowed, I just said that we never had . . ."

"A snow like this?"

"Not since I've been here."

"You have to admit, it's pretty though, isn't it?"

As the two stood there, looking through the window, Gabe wrapped his arms around her waist and pulled her back against him. There was nothing forced about it—it seemed like a perfectly normal thing to do. And because he had done it easily, naturally, she didn't fight it. Instead she let him pull her closer to him. It seemed so right.

The snow fell all through the day without the slightest letup. Behind the Lane house was a forty-eight-inch board fence, and by dusk Josie couldn't see the tops of the fence posts. There was no thought of leaving the hotel, because the drifts were piled so high against the doors that they couldn't be pushed open. Even if they could be opened, where would anyone go?

"It looks like we're going to be here for a while," Gabe said.

"Yes, I can't get over how quiet, how peaceful, everything looks."

"I'm glad we're here and not out in one of the boarding cars where your father and Willie surely are."

"I hope they are there and that they didn't try to start back sometime today."

"You know they didn't, because this snow has not let up all day."

Josie heated some soup that Ida had made yesterday, and they ate while talking of inconsequential things. What hung over them, as obvious as the snow itself, yet unmentioned by either of them, was one indisputable fact. They were the only two people in the hotel, and with the blizzard, nobody could get in or out.

And night was falling.

TWELVE

The clock struck ten, the gongs reverberating through the lobby of The Empress. A fire burned in the fireplace in the keeping room, and though it had burned down and was not putting out a lot of heat, Josie and Gabe were sitting close enough to it to be comfortable. They were playing chess, the table and the board separating them. The flames found a gas pocket in one of the logs and it popped loudly, sending up a little shower of sparks.

"Should I throw another log on the fire?" Gabe asked.

Josie wanted to say yes—she wanted to build up a blazing fire so that they could spend the entire night right here in this isolated cocoon. Not so much because she was enjoying the chess game, though she was, but because she was enjoying being here, alone, with Gabe.

"I suppose you'd better bank the fire, and we

probably should think about going to bed. Papa always takes care of the heat so it's always warm and toasty when I get up in the morning."

"Why don't I spend the night in here, and then I can feed the fire all night long?"

"Oh, I wouldn't ask you to do that. You wouldn't be comfortable staying in here all night."

"Sure I would, I'll make a pallet right in front of the fire." Gabe moved the chess table and the two chairs out of the way, then went into his room. He returned a moment later carrying a comforter, blanket, and pillow. He spread the comforter and blanket out on the floor, then sat down on them. He held his hand up toward her.

"Come on down here. Let me show you."

Josie sat beside him.

"This sure beats camping out on the ground, with nothing but a poncho between you and the rocks."

Josie laughed. "You've done that, have you?"

"More times than I can count. Here, lie down. See how comfortable it is."

Josie lay down as he asked, her blond hair forming a corona around her face. "It's much better than I would have thought." Josie wriggled her body to make a nest in the feather comforter.

That simple action was much more erotic to Gabe than Josie realized. When she met his gaze, she saw in his dark eyes a look that caused her to tremble.

"Are you cold?" He brushed a strand of hair

away from her face and cupped her cheek, his hand against her skin feeling warm and tender.

"No," she said in a bare whisper. "I'm very warm."

Gabe chuckled softly. "I know. I should not be here."

"What about the fire?"

"That's not the fire I'm talking about," he said as a log shifted on the grate. "It's this one." Slowly he lowered himself to the pallet and, propping himself on his arm, he lay beside her, his hard body touching hers, his other hand coming to rest across her stomach.

The weight of his arm caused her to take a deep breath, and she watched a glimmer of a smile cross his face. Something inside her told her she should not be in this position with a man, with not a soul in the world within hearing distance should she need someone, but intuitively she knew Gabe would not hurt her. She had learned to trust him.

And so rather than seek a place of shelter, she moved closer to him.

"Do you know what you're doing?"

Josie had no answer. He knew that she was naive, but if she was going to learn, she wanted this man to be her teacher. With tentative fingers, she put her hand on his chest and clumsily began fiddling with the buttons on his shirt. Earlier, in the kitchen, she had seen his nude body, and that one look had shaken her to her core. She knew that something excited her when she looked upon him, and she wanted the opportunity to look at him at her leisure.

"Slow down, honey. We're not ready for that. Not yet."

He captured her hand in his and held it between them, intertwining their fingers as he bent down to kiss her. This was not the first kiss they had shared; she had thought the other kisses were sensuous and, dare she say it, loving, but this kiss was something to which she had nothing to compare.

It was slow, his lips moving over hers, his tongue forcing her lips apart, and his tongue then darting into her own mouth, only to be withdrawn to enter again and again. Shyly, she followed his tongue with her own, entering his mouth, only to feel his reaction as he smothered a chuckle. Then he kissed her hard and passionately as she pulled her hand free from his to pull him down upon her body. The move caused their lips to separate for the first time, and she regretted that this caused the pleasure to stop.

But she needn't have been concerned. He ran his lips down her throat, finding her pulse point, as she tipped her head back to allow him better access. By now, she thought her body could take no more, as she found herself raging in chaos. What was happening to her? She didn't know the answer, but she knew she didn't want it to stop.

There was more. Gabe pulled her to a sitting

position and began to unbutton the buttons that closed the back of her dress. She felt the cool air on her back as more of it was exposed to the draft caused by the pull of the air to the fireplace. When her dress was free, Gabe dropped it, taking her arms out of the sleeves as he did. The top of her dress was now bunched around her hips, with only her camisole covering her breasts.

"Shall I go on?" Gabe asked, a tortured look upon his face.

For an answer, Josie took his face between her hands and drew it to her, planting a kiss upon his lips that she hoped was all the answer he needed.

It was. Carefully he untied the ribbons on the camisole, and when it was free, he removed it and placed it beside them. He took her breasts in his hands and cupped them, looking at them with an intensity that caused Josie to shudder. She allowed her own gaze to fall on the motions as he then began to twirl his thumbs over her nipples, causing them to rise into hard little buds. The sensations that this sent through her body seemed unbearable, until she realized what he was going to do next. His head lowered, and the tongue that had so recently sent shock waves through her body when it explored the inner cavity of her mouth now began to stroke her nipple. It glistened in the glow of the firelight as he moistened it over and over. Then he drew it into his mouth and began to suck. Josie could take no more, and she fell back upon the pallet, her breath coming in jagged gasps. She lay there as a moan escaped her.

"Do you like that, my love?"

"Do you have to ask?" Her breathing became more and more ragged.

"There's more."

He lowered his head to her other breast and began the same ministration, going ever so slowly, the action causing her to writhe about as she thrust her breast farther up, begging him to take more of it into his mouth. He continued this, going from one breast to the other, never hurrying. Then he put his face between her breasts and shook his head, allowing the rough texture of his beard to rub gently against the soft skin. Like a million tiny pinpricks, this caused every fiber of her breasts to become enflamed.

Her private parts were now wet with a dampness that literally flowed from her body. "Gabe, I can't take any more," she gasped.

"Yes, yes, you can. Let me show you what it's really like when a man loves a woman. Lift your hips."

She did as she was told, and in an instant her dress and petticoat were removed from her body. As she lay there in her woolen socks and her underdrawers, Gabe took her leg and rolled off a sock, kissing the sole of her foot when it was free. Then he did the same to the other foot.

That left only her underdrawers in place. He

carefully untied the string, but he did not remove them. He placed his hand through the slit and began to knead his fingers through her mound of hair, his stroking increasing her flow of juices.

"Please," Josie begged.

"Please what?"

"Please take them off." She lifted her hips and struggled out of her underdrawers, allowing Gabe to guide them off her ankles.

Knowing that there was so much more, Josie began to strain and push upward, trying to get her body closer to his hand, and he did not disappoint her. He stroked her from her mound to that area where the juices were flowing, taunting her with a light touch. She grabbed his hand and pressed it harder against herself as she moved in concert with his motion.

"Just wait, my darling," he said as he unbuttoned his shirt and threw it aside. His torso was wet with perspiration and shone golden in the firelight. He moved between her legs as he sat on his haunches and went back to his stroking. When she was well lubricated, he eased a finger into her cavity, slowly, slowly, inching forward and upward, feeling her convulse around him. He could feel the tight membrane that was proof of her virginity. When his finger was sufficiently buried, he used his thumb to massage her nub, which was hard and erect. He felt her tense as he continued to stroke her, and he watched as her head fell back, her eyes closed. Faster and faster he began to rub, and she lifted her body off the pallet, wanting more.

"Let it happen," he soothed. "There is no feeling like it in all the world."

Then she knew what he was talking about. Eddies of pleasure began coursing through her body as wave after wave came over her, and she cried out in surprise and wonder. Then she lay back panting, and Gabe knew she had experienced her first orgasm.

He drew her into his arms and held her tight against him.

When Josie's breathing was back to normal, she asked, "Is this what happened to you that night?"

"Yes, my love. Now you know."

She drew back and looked up at him, a look of concern upon her face. "But this time, you didn't get anything."

Gabe laughed softly. "Oh, but I did. There is as much pleasure in giving as there is in getting. There will be many more times for us when it will be better than this, I promise you that, but for now, I think you've had enough. Come lie down beside me." He lay down and cradled her head against his shoulder, drawing the blanket around them. She was naked and he was shirtless, but his pants were still on. Out of curiosity, Josie lowered her hand to his abdomen.

"Don't do that, little one," he said.

When she felt the hard bulge, she was satisfied. "Do I make you do that?"

He let out a rumbling laugh. "Yes. Yes, you do."

"I'm glad," she said as she snuggled into the crook of his arm.

Gabe had no idea what time it was when he awoke the next morning, but the light streaming in through the keeping-room window was exceptionally bright. He wondered why it was so bright, then realized that the sun was reflecting off the snow.

Josie was still here! For a moment he was concerned, but that concern eased when he remembered that they were all alone in the hotel. He looked over at her. During the night she had moved off his shoulder to allow him to get up to tend the fire, and now she slept curled in a little ball, her head barely visible above the blankets. He reached over to smooth her hair, not wanting to disturb her.

What had he done last night? Had he violated his honor, doing such a thing under Henri Laclede's own roof? He felt guilt, though he believed that guilt was somewhat tempered because he had not compromised her virginity. Her maidenhead was still intact.

Gabe had no doubt that Josie had been a willing participant last night and would have gone further if it had been his desire. It had taken every ounce of willpower for him to stop when he did, and even now just thinking of her reaction to him caused a stirring in his pants.

He'd told her last night they would have many

more such experiences, and he sincerely meant that. He wanted this woman, not just for momentary pleasure but from now on. He knew that he wanted her to be his wife.

His wife. He had not said such a thing to her because until now, perhaps even until this moment when he had given birth to the thought, getting married again had been the furthest thing from his mind. He had been so badly burned by Marthalee that he was hesitant to ever think of it. Certainly, if he did marry, he wanted to make sure there was a mutual love.

Next marriage? No, it would be in his first marriage, for in the eyes of the law there had never been another marriage. He had a paper to prove that very thing.

The marriage between Gabriel Michael Corrigan and Marthalee Elizabeth Galloway does not exist, and is deemed not to have existed, the annulment had read.

Gabe felt sure he was in love with Josie Laclede, but he had to be careful before asking her to marry him.

He considered the marriage of Tom and Anna Scott. Time and again, Tom had been bested by Jay Gould and Cornelius Vanderbilt and had to struggle to hang on. All who knew the couple saw that Anna took a backseat to the railroad. Like Tom Scott, Gabe was committed to the railroad, and that meant he might have to follow it all the way to the West Coast.

The successful completion of the T&P would make Gabe rich. Cornelius Vanderbilt, Jay Gould, Leland Stanford, Thomas Scott, and, perhaps, Gabriel Corrigan? But did he have it in him to do the things these men had done to reach the pinnacle? Could he be so driven, so merciless in his dealings with others? Wasn't there more to life than money? Could he ask Josie to go with him, to leave her family and friends?

On the other hand, what could he offer her now? His personal fortunes were tied to the railroad. The Texas and Pacific was struggling and would not survive if it did not make it to Fort Worth in time to receive the Texas land grants.

As he contemplated all this, he knew one thing for certain. He was not going to complicate her life by having sex with her before he was sure of where this relationship was going.

He knew that he was setting an extremely hard task for himself. As he lay there propped on his elbow, looking down at her sleeping in such sweet innocence, he knew that he could take her, ravish her, and she would be more than willing.

Just then he was shaken out of his reverie by the sound of a shovel hitting the back door. Startled, he looked toward the door, wondering if Henri was about to come in on them.

"Josie," he called urgently. "Josie, wake up. Someone is coming in the back door."

"Oh, I don't want to get up, I'm too comfortable," Josie replied in a sleep-logged voice.

"But you have to," Gabe said as he threw back the covers. She was still nude, and even though he had seen her in all her glory last night, the impact she had upon him was breathtaking.

The cool morning air caused Josie to sit up instantly. "My clothes!" she said, grabbing for her dress and socks.

"Run to your room. I'll see who it is." Gabe hurriedly put on his shirt.

He had just finished buttoning his shirt and was walking to the back door when he heard it open. "Miss Josie, are you here? Mama told me to shovel you out and see if you're all right. We ain't seen no movement over here."

Gabe met Julius in the kitchen, intending to hold him up there long enough to give Josie time to get to her room.

"Cap'n Corrigan. What's you doin' here? Where's Miss Josie?"

"Oh, still in her room, I expect. Say, that was some snow we got yesterday, wasn't it? I sure hope your pa and Mr. Henri make it back home today."

"Mama says they will. She says the sun is bright today and a lot of this stuff will melt, but I don't know. I shoveled your snow."

"Did you, now? Well, thank you."

"Is that all? Just thank you? Where's Miss Josie? I need to tell her I shoveled her snow," Julius said as he headed for the keeping room. "Why is that there? Is this where you slept?" He pointed toward the pallet.

"Yes, it was warmer than staying in my room, and I had to keep the fire going."

"What's this?" Julius asked, picking up Josie's camisole.

"I don't know," Gabe lied. "It must be some girl thing that we men don't know anything about."

"I suppose so. Did you know I shoveled your snow?"

A smile crossed Gabe's face. "Why, something like that should be worth a dollar, don't you think?"

"A whole dollar? Yes, sir!"

Gabe gave Julius a dollar, and he ran toward the back door.

THIRTEEN

Josie marked off another day on the calendar. Today was Wednesday, March 22. The month was more than half-gone, and Gabe had been gone for all of it. The track laying had gone slowly through much of January and February. First there had been the snowstorm, which cost at least ten days before they could resume work. Cold rains had decimated February. Then when the weather got a little better, many of the men, good intentions to the contrary and realizing that their own livelihoods depended upon it, deserted to go home so they could tend to their spring crops.

When it became likely that the ragtag construction crew would not make the deadline in time to secure the Texas state land grants, credit became more difficult to obtain. It took more than three weeks to get more than the initial shipment of rails. Work was under way again, but they were still seventeen miles from Fort Worth. They had come only five and a quarter miles in the last eight weeks, with only fourteen weeks left. If this average of three-quarters of a mile per week was maintained, they would still be six and a half miles short of their goal when their allotted time ran out.

To cover that contingency, Van Zandt, Paddock, and Gabe had gone to Austin to plead the case, both for the railroad and for Fort Worth, that it was imperative that the time limit be extended until the railroad reached the city. Paddock wrote a column expressing the frustration of the citizens of Fort Worth at the intransigence of the legislature.

> *The people of Texas recognized the value of railways and made provisions for generous donations of land, money and bonds to hasten their construction. The state government appropriated sixteen sections (10,240 acres) of land for every mile of road thus far built, or slated to be built. Much of this land is rich and valuable, and all of it is useful to the railways in the financing of their projects. The total amount of land granted to railways thus far is 38,826,380 acres, or 22 percent of the total acreage of this fine state. That is an area that compares to that of the state of New York.*
>
> *Yet all of the investment in time and capital put forth by the railroad and the outlays of our citizens will be for naught if the legislature does not grant an extension beyond adjournment*

date of the current session. What exactly are we asking for? Not new land, for the land has already been granted and accounted for. Should the legislature, whose opposition seems to be mounting, turn down our earnest plea, it seems likely that Fort Worth will lose the railroad, and all the attendant opportunities that a thriving rail system has to offer.

We will have come to this sad situation for the lack of but six miles should our current construction schedule hold. What are six miles compared to a land grant the size of the state of New York? It is as a single bluebonnet to a one-acre lot. Major Van Zandt, your humble correspondent, and Captain Gabriel Corrigan of the T&P are carrying the fight to the halls of our state government with the able sponsorship of Representative Nicholas Darnell, even though he is suffering with untold infirmities. I wish I could give you a favorable report on our efforts, but, alas, I cannot, for the fight does not go well.

Ironically, the town's business had begun to pick up slightly. Some, upon hearing that the railroad construction had resumed, came to Fort Worth to buy property that had been abandoned after the last rush. That meant that the Lacledes' businesses were doing better, though only the store was showing a profit. And much of that profit was on paper, as the store continued to sell on credit the supplies needed by the Tarrant County Construction Company.

"I am telling you, Henri, your business practices are going to bankrupt the store," Oscar Manning insisted. "We cannot continue to furnish the work crew with food and provisions with the promise of payment that will never be received."

The conversation between Oscar and Henri, in the lobby of the hotel, was overheard by Josie. She was busy cleaning in the lobby, though in truth she was prolonging it so she could be a party to the conversation.

"Oscar, you do agree, don't you, that if the railroad reaches Fort Worth, all will prosper?" Henri asked.

"Ahh," Oscar said, holding his finger aloft, "you have just hit upon the operative word, and that is *if*. And I use the same word. *If* the railroad does not make it to Fort Worth, the promissory notes you have so freely accepted can never be redeemed. What will happen, then?"

"It won't matter."

"What do you mean, it won't matter?"

Josie could hold her tongue no longer. "What he means is, if the railroad doesn't make it to Fort Worth, the town won't make it. Then both the hotel and the store will go broke. We have no choice but to put everything we have into bringing in the railroad."

"Are you really concerned about the town? Or is it Captain Corrigan that you worry about?"

"What do you mean?"

"People talk. They come into the store. I hear things."

"Oscar," Henri said sharply, "if you have something specific to say, say it."

"No, I—that is, I don't have anything specific. It's just that you know well, Henri, that I care deeply for Josie, and I do not want to see her hurt, that's all."

"If you don't want to see me hurt, then don't insinuate such hateful things," Josie said as she turned and walked quickly from the lobby.

"I'm sorry, Henri. I meant nothing by it. Like I say, I'm just concerned, that's all."

"Maybe it would be best if you returned to your duties at the store."

"Yes, sir."

When Oscar left, Henri went into the dining room, where Josie was folding napkins.

"Are you all right?"

"I'm fine."

"Josie, if something is bothering you, I will be glad to listen. I know it has been difficult for you to grow into the fine woman that you are without the benefit of a mother's counsel. I accept that I am a poor substitute. But I want you to know that I will try to answer even the most delicate question as artfully as I can, within the confines of polite society, of course."

Josie put down the napkins, then walked over to embrace her father. "I know that, Papa."

Later that week, Max Elser, the town telegrapher, came into the hotel and, seeing Josie behind the desk, walked over to her. Josie smiled a greeting at him, but upon seeing the grim expression on Elser's face, her smile faded.

"Mr. Elser, what is it? Is something wrong?"

"I—uh, have a telegram for Captain Corrigan."

"But you must know he's in Austin. I think the delegation won't be back until early next week."

"Yes, I know. But the telegram . . ."

"What about it? You're frightening me."

"It's my job to read every telegram that is either sent or received, and I am bound by my own code of ethics that I not pass judgment on anybody's business. But sometimes for the greater good . . ."

"What is it?"

"I probably shouldn't do this. But in this case . . ."

"For heaven's sake, Max, what are you trying to say?"

Elser removed the telegram from the envelope and unfolded it as he laid it on the counter.

"I've delivered this to the recipient's proper address. Now, I can't control what happens to it after that, can I?"

Josie picked up the telegram and began to read:

TO G. CORRIGAN
YOUR SUGGESTION TO REDIRECT TRACKS
TO WACO BEING CONSIDERED. J. GOULD
PROMISES TO FUND. WILL CONNECT

WITH WACO AND NORTHWESTERN THEN
SOUTHERN PACIFIC. NEGOTIATIONS TO START
WHEN CURRENT LEGISLATIVE SESSION ENDS.
T. SCOTT

"He suggested . . ." Josie said in a weak voice.
"Gabe suggested that the tracks go to Waco instead
of coming here?"

"That's what it sounds like to me," Elser said.
"I know I shouldn't have shared this, but it affects
all of us. You can't keep The Empress going, and I
won't have enough business to keep the telegraph
office open. If the railroad doesn't come, that's it."

"Well, I'm glad you did. Let's not tell anyone
else about this right now. Give me a chance to find
out what the skunk has to say. I can't believe there
isn't some explanation, because Captain Corrigan
seemed so genuine."

"Believe me, that's the kind you can never trust.
Look at all the snake oil salesmen who come
through here. They're so nice, butter won't melt in
their mouths, and then they take your money and
run. I think the whole town has been hoodwinked."

"For all our sakes, let's hope you're wrong."

"Yes, ma'am. Oh, while I'm talking, I'll just tell
you the major sent Mrs. Van Zandt a telegram. He
said he expects they'll be home tomorrow."

After Elser left, with the telegram in hand, Josie
went into Gabe's room and sat down on his bed.
So much had happened between them. And this

one little yellow envelope took it all away. She sat
there visualizing the injured man who had lain in
this very bed with pain and fever as she sat in the
chair night after night, waiting for him to rally.
Then she remembered the night he had rallied
and what had happened.

Then there was the night of the snowstorm,
when she had trusted him completely. He had said
the words "when a man loves a woman," and she
had believed he was talking about him and her.
But now this small yellow envelope in her hands
made everything he said or did suspect.

Josie fought hard to hold back the tears. She
felt betrayed.

How could he have done this? How could he
have made the suggestion that the railroad bypass
Fort Worth? She could hold the tears back no longer as she placed the telegram on the bed. She ran
from his room to her own, where she fell upon the
bed with its quilt of memories and wept.

Gabe and the others had taken the Waco and
Northwestern from Austin, then transferred to a
stage at Waco to finish the trip to Fort Worth. Much
of the town had turned out to meet the stage, and
even though they weren't bringing good news,
Gabe was excited to be back. He had missed Josie
terribly, and he was disappointed when he didn't
see her in the crowd.

Major Van Zandt called for a town meeting the
next day, to be held at the courthouse, where he

promised that he, Paddock, and Captain Corrigan would give a full accounting of their trip. Following the announcement, Gabe took his grip from the boot of the coach and walked from the stage depot to the hotel. Josie wasn't there to greet him either, but Henri was.

"Welcome back, Gabe. We sure missed you while you were gone. And one person missed you more than anyone else."

"Really?"

Henri looked around the lobby. "I don't know where she's gotten off to. She was here just a short while ago."

"I'll check in the dining room. Oh, am I right? Did I hear that I am not your only guest now?"

"Yes, indeed, you heard right. I'll have you know that we have three guests now, and we've had guests almost every day since you've been gone. Folks are coming back to get in on the ground floor when the railroad does get here."

The smile left Gabe's face. "Yes, well, I wish we had better news to report from Austin."

"Don't lose hope, son," Henri said as he clasped Gabe's shoulder. "The people here are tough, and they won't give up. We're going to get this done. I just know we are. Oh, by the way, we've moved you back upstairs. I think the rooms are a little nicer up there."

A disheartened Gabe took his suitcase to his room, cleaned up from his trip, then went to the dining room for dinner. With other guests in the hotel, he surmised that his dining in the family quarters was over, and it was just as well. It would make it easier to stick to his vow to stay away from Josie until she was ready.

Gabe took a seat at one of the tables, and when he saw Josie, it was as if he had truly come home. He could not express how beautiful she was, and he smiled broadly, thinking she would come straight to his table. But she took the order of the other three diners first, then disappeared into the kitchen. It was several minutes before she came out again, this time carrying the orders of the other three guests. When she walked back by, Gabe called out to her.

"Hey, what does a man have to do to get service here?" He said it jokingly, but Josie didn't react to it. Her face was devoid of all expression when she stepped up to his table.

"What can I do for you?"

"Well, you could start by giving me a welcoming smile." Gabe flashed a big smile at her as he grabbed for her hand.

She deflected the move by purposefully arranging her hair. "I'm all out of smiles, at least for you."

The smile left Gabe's face, replaced by an expression of utter confusion. "What does that mean? I've been gone for more than a month, and this is my welcome home?"

"What do you want for dinner?"

"What do you suggest?"

"We have ham, fried potatoes, and black-eyed peas."

"Then, that's what I'll have."

Josie turned.

"Josie, wait. What's wrong? Have I done something I don't know about?"

"I think you can guess."

Josie walked away, leaving a puzzled Gabe. He had no idea what had caused this reaction.

Gabe had not seen the telegram when he went to his room to clean up, and when he turned the covers down to go to bed that night, he didn't see it slide off the bed and onto the floor. Neither did he see it the next morning when he was getting ready for the town meeting. He looked into the dining room and the lobby as he passed through, but Josie wasn't there.

So many townspeople had turned out for the meeting that even increasing the seating with boards between the chairs couldn't accommodate everyone. Those who couldn't find a place to sit stood, and those who couldn't find a place to stand inside, stood outside, even though a fine mist was falling.

Major Van Zandt opened the meeting. "I wish I had better news for you. But the plain truth is that there are more people in Austin opposed to granting the T&P an extension than there are in support. So it all boils down to this. Either we get the railroad to Fort Worth by the last day of the legislative session, or all support, which translates to money for the railroad, will be withdrawn."

"What do you say, Captain Corrigan?" Dr. Burts asked. "Will we get here on time?"

"The T&P is going to do everything it can to see that we do. I know that Colonel Scott is in Washington right now lobbying the Railway Commission for some federal money now that the State of Texas seems to be predisposed against us. And as some of you may know, the colonel was able to get an appointment for your old friend James Throckmorton on the commission. So perhaps he can shake some money loose for us."

"We do have one last card to play here at home, too," Paddock announced.

"What is it?" someone asked from the audience.

"It's what you might call an act of desperation, but it's worth trying," Paddock said. "If the legislature won't extend the time beyond adjournment, we will extend the adjournment."

"What? What are you talking about?"

"The reason we can't get an extension is because we don't have enough votes in the Senate. We do in the House, but of course both houses have to concur." Paddock paused for a moment, then smiled broadly. "And"—he held up a finger for emphasis—"both houses have to concur for adjournment. We have enough friends in the House—"

"By one vote," Van Zandt interjected.

"—by one vote," Paddock continued, "to delay adjournment beyond the last day of June."

"Well, how long can you keep delaying?" Tidball asked.

"Representative Darnell tells me we can delay indefinitely until the tracks reach Fort Worth."

"Yahoo!" someone shouted, and the others took up the yell. When everything had calmed down again, Gabe took the floor once more.

"It all depends now on the Tarrant County Construction Company. I know there have been delays that weren't the fault of the TCCC, but from now on, we have to do all we can to get the tracks here. Remember, we are all in this together."

Again, shouts, cheers, and applause erupted from the audience.

When Gabe returned to his room, his bed had been opened for him, and he saw, lying on his pillow, a small yellow envelope. When he opened it, he was surprised and confused. What did Tom Scott mean when he said that Gabe had recommended the tracks be diverted to Waco?

He had never suggested any such thing. At least, not recently. When he, Colonel Scott, John Forney, and Governor Throckmorton had made their initial trip across Texas, Gabe had suggested that there might be more population centers in West Texas if the track went farther south from Longview. He had suggested going through Waco, Brownwood, and then El Paso since the ultimate goal was to reach San Diego, but that was before the first rail had been laid, and it had been four years ago!

The other troubling thing about this message was the mention of Jay Gould. He was Colonel Scott's rival and had been doing everything he could to keep the T&P from reaching California. Gabe decided this could well be a hoax.

Now Gabe knew what was wrong with Josie. Somehow, she had seen this telegram and understandably had believed it. Stuffing the telegram in his pocket, he went looking for her. He found her in the dining room, changing the tablecloths.

"Josie."

"The dining room is closed."

"I don't want something to eat. I want to talk to you."

"I don't know that we have anything to talk about, Captain Corrigan."

"Waco?"

As Josie smoothed the tablecloth, she lowered her head, not wanting to look at Gabe. She didn't say anything for a long moment; then, quietly, she said, "How could you? And I don't mean how could you do something to me. I know it is the way of men to dominate women, and I believe I allowed you to do that. But I thought you were different, and I trusted you with my emotions."

"This conversation isn't about Waco, is it?"

"Yes and no. Gabe, it is one thing for you to make a fool of me, but you have betrayed the entire town."

"There is a simple answer."

"Simple? You set out to destroy a town, and you say the answer is simple?"

"Yes. The answer is simple, Josie, because I didn't do it."

"Are you telling me that you did not recommend that the tracks go through Waco instead of Fort Worth? I read the telegram."

"Yes, I did recommend that the tracks go through Waco."

"Thank you, at least, for not lying to me."

"Four years ago."

Josie looked confused. "Four years ago?"

"Yes, four years ago. When we first started planning the purposed route, before the first survey was done, before I had ever even come to Texas, I looked at a map and thought the best way to San Diego would be by a more southern route. That route would have taken the T&P through Waco. But after the people of Fort Worth were so accommodating, the decision was made to follow the thirty-second parallel, and to my knowledge it has never changed. I was happy with that decision then, and I am happy with it now."

"I—I thought you . . ."

"I know what you thought. You were wrong."

"I'm sorry, Gabe, I . . ."

Gabe put his arms around Josie, and they embraced.

"Now, that's the welcome home I wanted."

Gabe took the wadded-up telegram from his

pocket, smoothed it out, and showed it to Josie. "Look at this line." He pointed to the telegram. NEGOTIATIONS TO START WHEN CURRENT LEGISLA-TIVE SESSION ENDS.

"That means that as long as the current legislature is in session, the current construction will continue. You weren't at the meeting, but Buck Paddock said that Representative Darnell has promised to keep the legislature in session until we finish."

"But how long will he be able to do that?"

"Long enough, if we all keep the same goal in mind." Gabe kissed Josie on the forehead. "We're on the same side, my sweet. Don't ever forget that."

"Oh, Gabe, I'm sorry."

"It was understandable. You saw the telegram. And it is easy to be fooled, even by someone you've always trusted."

Though Gabe didn't say it, he was thinking of Colonel Scott.

FOURTEEN

For the next several days Gabe was back and forth from End of Track to Fort Worth, making sure the crews had all the materials they needed. He was pleased to learn that additional crossties were being sent from East Texas and that a shipment of rails was due within a week, which should take care of at least another five miles of construction.

One morning, after a particularly strong thunderstorm had passed through, Josie decided to ask Gabe to take a day to relax. It would be good for him to get away from all the problems that his position as the visible head of the Texas and Pacific created.

"Let's go for a ride out in the countryside today," Josie suggested.

Gabe shook his head. "You don't know how tempting that is to me, but I can't do it. Not now."

"What's going to be accomplished today? Will

they be digging grades? I don't think so. Will they be breaking up rocks to make ballast? Maybe. What about putting crossties in place? Probably not. About the only thing the workers can do in this muddy clay dirt is grub out stumps, and they don't need you to supervise."

Gabe laughed. "All right, Josie, you've made your point. I am not indispensable. What do you have in mind?"

"You'll see. I'll meet you right here in ten minutes. Oh, and, Gabe, dress like a Texan."

"What does that mean?"

"You decide."

Gabe went to his room and changed to denim jeans and boots. He strapped on his gun and put on a Stetson that Buck Paddock had given him. Then he reached for a denim shirt, but decided on the red flannel instead. He smiled when he remembered the last time he had worn, or rather *not* worn, this shirt. Would Josie remember?

He was waiting in the lobby when Josie appeared from her quarters. She was wearing a split leather riding skirt decorated with silver and turquoise medallions, and a white, fringed shirt. Her blond hair tumbled over her shoulders beneath a brown felt cowboy hat.

"Wow, if you don't look like a cowgirl," Gabe teased.

"I got this outfit from Betty Courtright. You know, before she and Jim came to Fort Worth, they were part of a Wild West show. She tried to teach me to shoot, but I never got the hang of it. I do know how to ride a horse, though—so are you ready?"

"If we're going to ride, I'll have to rent a horse from the livery."

"No, you won't. I've already asked Papa. You can ride Marengo, Papa's horse."

"All right," Gabe said. "Let's go."

Half an hour later, they were two miles south of Fort Worth when they saw a herd of cattle coming toward them. They could hear the drum of a thousand and more hoofbeats, the clattering sound of the long horns banging together, and the whistles and shouts of the cowboys as they raced to and fro alongside the herd, waving their hats or swinging ropes as they pulled in the wanderers, keeping the herd moving in the right direction.

Josie and Gabe reined up and watched as the herd rumbled past. A couple of the cowboys, recognizing Josie, galloped over to them.

"Howdy, Miss Josie," one of the cowboys said. "Don't reckon you remember me. I'm Clay Evanston from the Lazy R. We met a couple of years ago at a town picnic."

"Of course I remember you, Mr. Evanston," Josie said, though she had met so many cowboys over the last several years that she couldn't specifically place this one.

Clay waved his hat toward the herd. "We're takin' 'em to the railhead at Eagle Ford. Sure wish we were comin' to Fort Worth, though. Fort Worth was a lot more fun than Eagle Ford is. If you pardon me for sayin' it."

"We hope to get the railhead at Fort Worth by summer," Gabe said. "And when we do, you can start bringing your herds back again."

"Yes, sir, I hope so."

"Clay! Quit your palaverin' and get busy! You got some beeves stringin' out on you!"

Clay tipped his hat. "It was nice seein' you folks, but I got to get on."

Josie and Gabe stayed until the last of the cows had passed, then resumed their ride. A short time later, Josie's horse suddenly shied, then reared up on its hind legs. Only because Josie was a good rider was she able to stay in the saddle.

Gabe and Josie saw, at the same time, why her horse had reared. A rattlesnake was coiled in the path right in front of them. It was rattling, and it had its head lifted, ready to strike. Gabe pulled his pistol and fired, and a little spray of blood suddenly appeared where the snake's head had been. The snake, though headless, twitched for another moment before it was still.

"I had no idea you could shoot like that," Josie said.

"I graduated from West Point. We had marksmanship training."

"You learned well. I'm impressed."

"Not as impressed as I am by your horsemanship. Shall we continue our ride?"

"Yes," Josie said.

"Do we have a particular destination in mind? Or are we just riding?"

"Do you find riding with me to be unpleasant?"

Gabe laughed. "Josie, I could ride with you until this poor animal's legs are worn down to his knees."

"Good answer. But, yes, I do have a destination in mind."

"I'm glad you brought me out here. There's so much more to Texas than just the railroad. The longer I'm here, the more I like it."

"You could always stay. I could find a job for you at the hotel," Josie teased.

"If we get everything done on time, I won't need a job." Gabe was thinking of the sixteen sections that he would receive as compensation when the T&P reached Fort Worth. He started to tell Josie about it. He thought she would recognize that as incentive enough to reassure her, if his redoubled work efforts weren't sufficient, that he was committed to bringing the road to completion.

But then he held his tongue.

The telegram had planted a seed of doubt in Gabe's mind about his undying loyalty to Tom Scott. He knew that building the railroad to Fort Worth had only been a means to an end for Scott. If the T&P lost the Texas land grants, then Scott was perfectly willing to use Jay Gould, despite their enmity. The colonel often used his power and his money as a means of influence, and even now scandal swarmed around him. Scott's relationship with Speaker of the House James G. Blaine was already beginning to raise troubling questions, suggesting corruption among the nation's expanding railroads and favors granted to influential members of Congress.

At first, Gabe had resented being sent to Texas to oversee this phase of the project, but now, thanks in no small part to Josie, he was glad he had been spared all the controversy.

"Close your eyes," Josie said as she rode up beside him and grabbed Marengo's reins.

"Out here? What can possibly be a surprise?"

"You'll see." She prodded her horse and, leading his, started up a rise. When she reached the top, she stopped. "Now."

Gabe opened his eyes and gasped. Before him, as far as the eye could see, were waves of Texas bluebonnets. Everywhere he looked he saw blue.

Josie slid off her horse, walked out into the flowers, and sat down, the blossoms surrounding her. "Have you ever seen anything more beautiful?"

"Yes," Gabe said as he sat beside her, "and I'm looking at her right now."

"You don't really mean that. Look at me, all dressed up like some circus performer."

"It doesn't matter what you are wearing. In fact, if you remember, I've seen you without anything on, and I still think you are the most beautiful woman in the world."

"Gabe, what's going to happen when the railroad is finished?"

"Well, the town is going to grow, business is going to be bustling—"

Josie put her fingers to his mouth. "No. What's going to happen to us?"

"What do you want to happen?"

"I don't know. I'm a country girl and you are a city boy. As much as I might want to be a part of your life, I don't know that I would fit." She picked the stem of a flower. "We are sort of like this, you and I. The bluebonnets are beautiful and they give people great pleasure, but after a very short time, they are gone. Is that the way it is with us?"

"It doesn't have to be."

"What do you mean?"

Gabe put his fingers on her cheek, holding her face as securely as if he were using his hands.

Slightly, ever so slightly, Josie moved her face toward his.

Then he kissed her, his lips touching hers as gently as a soft summer breeze. There was no urgency, no raw hunger, no deepening of the kiss, and yet Josie had never felt more alive.

Then, as gently as the kiss began, it ended. He pulled back from her, and as she looked into his dark eyes, for just a moment she felt as if they were windows to his soul, and she lost herself in them until the windows seemed to close.

"Josie, you must know what you mean to me. I don't want to lose this."

Gabe knew that Josie wanted more from him now. But he couldn't commit, not until he felt

deserving of her love, not until his own situation
was resolved. As things stood now, he didn't know
whether he was going to be a man of means or a
pauper.

"Do you understand what I'm saying to you,
Josie?" Gabe asked, filling the protracted silence.

Come out and say it, Gabe, Josie thought. *How
hard is it for you to tell me that you love me?*
Josie smiled at him, then got to her feet and
offered her hand to Gabe. "Come on, I'll race you
back to town."

"That's not fair. You know the way."

"Then, that means you'll have to follow and I'll
win."

As Gabe trailed the galloping horse, he thought
about what Josie had said. She didn't know how
prophetic her words were. He was going to follow
her wherever she took him. If she loved him, he
would win, but if she did not, then what?

Gabe was glad Josie had suggested the trip away
from Fort Worth, and he looked upon the day as
sort of a watershed. They had thoroughly enjoyed
one another's company in a companionable way.
He knew had he wanted to, he could have kissed
her at any time and she would have reacted with
passion. But true love was more than that. True
love, everlasting love, meant cultivating a friendship as well as a marriage bed.

He was encouraged that she had asked what
would happen to them when the railroad was

finished. That question meant she had thought about some sort of relationship with him. It gave him hope, and with a jovial air the two ran into the hotel like schoolchildren, holding hands and laughing.

"Captain Corrigan," a man's voice bellowed from the lobby.

Gabe came to a complete stop, dropping Josie's hand as he did so. The voice belonged to General Grenville Dodge. Dodge had been chief engineer of, and the person most responsible for, the successful completion of the Union Pacific Railroad. Now he was chief engineer of the Pennsylvania Railroad—and by extension, the Texas and Pacific. His position of authority was superior to Gabe's own.

"General Dodge. I wasn't expecting you."

"I daresay that is an understatement. Are you not aware of the tremendous importance of getting this railroad to Fort Worth? It is the difference between enormous wealth and complete bankruptcy for the Texas and Pacific Railway as a company, as well as various individuals personally. And where do I find you? Dallying with a local showgirl, I daresay."

"General, I resent your reference to Miss Laclede as a showgirl."

"I beg your pardon," General Dodge said with a nod toward Josie. "Captain Corrigan, I would like a few words with you, if you don't mind."

"If you gentlemen would like, you may use our private quarters and have your conversation in the keeping room," Josie said. "I'll make certain no one disturbs you."

"Thank you, Miss Laclede," Dodge said.

"Would you like coffee?"

"That would be nice."

Gabe led the general into the keeping room, and they sat in cushioned chairs that were near the now cold fireplace. When Josie brought in the coffee, Gabe had a sudden flashback to the night he had spent with her before the fireplace.

"I visited End of Track," Dodge said. "You weren't there."

"No, sir, I wasn't."

"Have you an excuse for your absence?"

"I have no excuse, sir." Gabe could have added that he had a reason, but as a former military captain, he knew that excuses or reasons would sound weak.

"You are to be temporarily relieved by General John Brown, and you are being called to Washington."

"Washington? Why am I being called to Washington?"

"Colonel Scott's reputation and business practices are being impugned, and it has come to the attention of the House Judiciary Committee that perhaps your longtime association with him will shed some light on some of his activities."

"What do they want from me? You know I've been away for the last two years, and I'm not privy to anything going on outside of Texas."

"I believe the inquiry is based upon the colonel's relationship with Speaker Blaine and some bonds that were pledged as collateral for the Little Rock and Fort Smith Railroad. The Judiciary Committee seems to think these bonds were a bribe, and you're going to be asked what you know about them."

"What does that have to do with the T&P? All that was a long time ago, when Colonel Scott was president of the Union Pacific."

"Tell that to the committee. Here is your subpoena," General Dodge said as he handed an envelope to Gabe. "I suggest you take care of whatever loose ends you have pending here and be on your way to Washington as soon as possible."

"Yes, sir."

Gabe went to his room. He took off one boot and then the other, and in a fit of anger he flung them across the room and hit the fireplace.

"Damn," he swore. "Why now?"

He knew he had established a good working rapport with the Tarrant County crew. And he had promised Nicholas Darnell he would keep him informed on the progress of the road so that Darnell could find ways to keep the legislature from adjourning if that became necessary. Josie had accused him of trying to sabotage the railroad when she thought he wanted it to be diverted to Waco. What would she think now? Would she think this was some ruse to stop the progress?

In that moment he had an idea. Without putting

on his boots, he took the stairs two at a time on his way down. He looked into the dining room, where he saw Josie serving guests, including General Dodge and General Brown.

Good. Josie was busy.

Gabe went directly to the family quarters, where he entered without knocking. Henri was snoring loudly, his head thrown back as he sat in one of the chairs beside the fireplace. When Gabe saw him sitting there, he suddenly had second thoughts about his idea, and he turned to go. But Henri had now awakened.

"Gabe, I . . . I, uh, I'm awake. What do you need?"

Gabe took a deep breath, then plunged on. "I want to marry your daughter."

Henri's eyes opened wide as he jumped to his feet. "What? What did you say?"

"I said I want to marry your daughter, but she doesn't know it yet."

"Well, then, shouldn't you be talking to somebody besides me?"

"Henri, I love her with all my heart, but I don't know how she feels about me. She told me she doesn't think she would fit in my world, but that's because she's never seen any of my world. Today, I was told I have to go to Washington. I have been subpoenaed to appear before the House Judiciary Committee."

"My word, what for?"

"It's the James Blaine hearings. You may have

read about them in the paper. The investigation has to do with the connection between the railroads and Mr. Blaine and other members of the House."

"Are you in trouble?"

"I'm not in any trouble. They are questioning Colonel Scott, and I have been called to testify on his behalf."

"When are you leaving?"

"Right away. And I want your permission to ask her to go with me. After I'm finished in Washington, I want to take her to Pennsylvania. I've not been home for several years, and I have this need to see my family and let them see what a wonderful woman Josie is."

"Son, you've got it bad, don't you?"

"Yes, sir, I do."

"I'll give my permission, but I have one request. I'm going to speak frankly with you. To the best of your knowledge, is Josie a virgin?"

"Yes, sir, she is."

"Then, if she goes with you, I want your solemn vow that she'll return the same way. I'll not stand by and have her heart broken by any man, and if you do anything to her except honor and cherish her, I will personally shoot you. Do you understand me?"

"I do."

Henri extended his hand. "A gentleman's handshake will seal the promise you just made."

Gabe shook Henri's hand.

"When are you going to ask her?"

"To marry me? Not until we get back to Fort Worth."

"Get out of here," Henri said, laughing as Gabe turned to leave.

"Papa, Gabe has asked me to go to Washington with him."

"Has he, now?"

"Yes. And what's more, he said that he has already asked you, and that you gave him your approval."

"The final decision is up to you, child. Do you want to go?"

"Oh, yes! I very much want to go."

"Then, Gabe is right. I have given my permission."

"But, what will people say, Papa? I won't be chaperoned."

"Sweetheart, the people who know you know that you are like Caesar's wife. As long as your behavior is above reproach, and I know it will be, there will be nothing said. Go. How often will you get the chance to see our nation's capital?"

Josie hugged and kissed Henri. "Oh, Papa, you are the best father in the entire world!"

FIFTEEN

Josie and Gabe left Fort Worth before eight o'clock in the morning, and because the temperature was agreeable, and recent rains kept the dust down, the three-hour stagecoach ride was pleasant. They shared the ride with a whiskey drummer, a professional gambler, and an artist who was touring the West to "capture images for future generations."

The artist was skilled, and during the trip he sketched Gabe and Josie together. He showed the drawing to them just before they reached Dallas, and Josie was struck not only by the accuracy with which he portrayed them, but also by the expressions on their faces and the intensity in their eyes.

"Now, anyone who sees this will know what a loving couple this man and his wife are," he said.

"Oh, but we—" Josie started.

"Are very impressed with your talent," Gabe

finished. "Would you be willing to sell that drawing?"

"Oh, sir, I wouldn't want you to think that you have to buy this. I didn't draw it in hopes of turning a quick coin."

"I understand that, but I would still like to buy it. How much?"

"It's hard to put a price on a piece of your soul."

"Not really. People in Washington do it every day," Gabe replied. "Would you sell it for twenty dollars?"

The artist smiled. "Indeed I would, sir."

Gabe gave him a $20 gold piece, then took the drawing.

"Are you going to hang on to that all the way to Washington and back?" Josie asked.

"I thought maybe we could mail it to your father before we catch the train tomorrow."

Josie smiled. "Papa will like that. He will like it a lot."

After the coach reached Dallas, Gabe hailed a town wagon to take them to the St. Charles. At the hotel, a porter came out quickly to get their baggage.

"As soon as you secure your room, I'll take your belongings right up, sir."

"Rooms," Gabe corrected.

"Yes, sir, rooms."

In the lobby, Gabe stepped up to the check-in desk. The brass plate on the counter had two names. "Mr. Miner? Or is it Mr. Lloyd?" Gabe asked the man behind the counter.

"It's Miner. Norman Miner, and Mr. Lloyd and I are happy to have you as guests in our hotel. May I put you and your lady in one of our finest rooms?"

"Miss Laclede and I are traveling on business. I would like our rooms to be on separate floors, if that is possible."

"Indeed it is. I can give you a room on the second floor and another on the third."

"That will do nicely, and, Norman, may I ask a favor of you?" Gabe said as he was signing the guest register.

"Certainly, Mr. Corrigan," the hotel proprietor said as he read the name across the book.

"Will you see to it that this drawing is sent to The Empress Hotel in Fort Worth?"

"A lovely drawing, sir," Norman Miner said as he took the picture. "I can have it on the Butterfield stage tomorrow morning."

Gabe was just returning to Josie with the keys when an attractive woman, dressed all in black, came through the lobby.

"Gabriel Corrigan," the lady called out. "What a delightful surprise, seeing you here in the"— she made a show of looking around before she continued—"Wild West."

"Well, if it isn't Mrs. Woodhull," Gabe said as he opened his arms and the woman descended upon him. "How long has it been since I've seen you?"

"It's been a while."

"Miss Laclede," Gabe said, turning to Josie, "I would like you to meet one of the most—shall I say—*interesting* women I have ever known. This is Mrs. Woodhull, Victoria Woodhull."

Josie's mouth gaped on hearing the name. This was the woman who, in 1872, had run for president of the United States, and last year she had been a party to the scandal of the century. Mrs. Woodhull had printed an article in her magazine that had precipitated the trial of the great Brooklyn preacher Henry Ward Beecher. She had accused Beecher of committing adultery with Elizabeth Tilton, the wife of one of his associates.

"Mrs. Woodhull. I have read about you," Josie said, not knowing quite what to say. Normally she would have said *I am pleased to meet you,* but in this case, that might have been a lie.

"What brings you to Dallas?" Gabe asked.

"Let's be honest—money. My sister Tennie and I are on the lecture circuit, and surprisingly, my message is being well received across the South."

"Don't tell me, is your message still all about free love?"

"Oh my, Gabriel, did I detect a hint of cynicism in your voice?"

Gabe laughed. "Maybe a little."

"If you had practiced a little more free love, you could have saved yourself a lot of heartache."

"Say, could we get together sometime this evening? I would like to hear what's happened to you."

"I'm speaking at Field's Theater at seven. Why don't I send passes for both you and Miss Laclede to attend?"

"Oh, I don't think—" Gabe said.

"Thank you, Mrs. Woodhull. I would like that very much," Josie interrupted.

Victoria laughed. "A woman who speaks her mind. She could be one of my people. The tickets will be at the front desk." With that, she kissed Gabe on the mouth. Not a sensual kiss, just in parting.

This could be an interesting evening, Josie thought.

Once she was in her room, Josie wondered how Gabe had known Victoria Woodhull. She was truly one of the most controversial women in the country, and it only stood to underscore how little Josie knew about Gabe. When he'd first asked her to go with him on this trip, she'd turned him down out of hand. A lady did not travel across the country with a man who was not a relative, especially without a chaperone, or at the very least a traveling companion. Josie was sure her father would disapprove, and she had suggested that Hannah Welch accompany them, but his reaction was just the opposite. He not only approved of this trip, but when she had voiced her concern, he had insisted that she go.

And she was looking forward to it.

Hearing a light knock and thinking it must be

Gabe, Josie hurried to open the door. She was surprised, and frankly disappointed, to see that it was the desk clerk, Mr. Miner.

"Captain Corrigan has asked me to inform you that he is in the hotel lobby, Miss Laclede, and there he shall remain until you choose to join him."

"Thank you," Josie said as she withdrew into the room and closed the door. What was going on? Why had Gabe sent the desk clerk instead of one of the porters? For that matter, why had he not come to tell her that himself? It wasn't as if he hadn't been in a hotel room with her before, even a room in this very hotel.

Maybe he had been with Mrs. Woodhull this afternoon. Could it be that, in comparison, he didn't think Josie was sophisticated enough for him? She had seen some of the "sporting press" newspapers left by visitors to The Empress. The *Days' Doings* was the worst, and it frequently had woodcuts of Woodhull, often calling her a fast woman.

She was glad that the encounter with Mrs. Woodhull had taken place in Dallas. Gabe owed Josie nothing, but neither would she stand by and watch him become a philanderer with another woman, at least not while he was supposed to be her escort. They were only thirty miles from Fort Worth; it wasn't too late, and they hadn't come too far. If after tonight she had any reason to believe that her coming with him was a mistake, he would just get on the train by himself tomorrow. She could go back home, walking all the way if she had to.

"Oh my," Josie said as she clasped her face in her hands. "Have I just met the green-eyed monster?"

When Josie went down to the lobby a few minutes later, she caught her breath when she saw Gabe standing by a window looking out over the street, his black hair shining. She believed that he was the most handsome man she had ever seen. He was wearing a crisp white shirt under a brown jacket with dark velvet lapels. A patterned vest topped his trim-fitting dark brown trousers. Josie smiled when she saw his well-polished boots.

"Am I late?" she asked, as she approached him.

"No. Are you sure you want to go to this thing tonight?"

At first Josie was tempted to say she didn't want to go, but then she remembered her reaction back in the room. She needed to put jealousy behind her if she was going to be on this trip with Gabe. Anyway, she was curious to find out exactly what "free love" meant.

"I would like to go."

"All right, if you insist."

Three hansom cabs were standing in front of the hotel. Gabe hired one, then helped Josie in before walking around to the other side and getting in himself.

"Where to, sir?" the driver asked.

"Field's Theater," Gabe said.

The driver snapped the reins, and the horse moved out at a quick trot. As the cab made a turn, it caused Gabe to move closer to Josie. She felt his leg against hers, and her body immediately reacted.

"There it is, sir, just ahead," the driver called down.

Even if the driver hadn't pointed it out, Josie would have known what it was. At least a dozen carriages and hacks were discharging passengers, and scores of well-dressed people were gathered around the theater entrance.

"It looks like Victoria is drawing quite a crowd," Gabe said.

Josie couldn't help but notice that he had referred to her by her Christian name.

Josie saw that several of those gathered at the theater entrance carried placards saying such things as POTIPHAR'S WIFE, GO HOME or THE END OF CARNAL APPETITE or THE NEW EVE, A SECOND TEMPTATION.

"Maybe we shouldn't be here," Josie said, and she took Gabe's arm as they stepped out of the cab.

"You wanted to hear her, so let's go," Gabe said as he began steering her through the crowd.

Then Josie saw a full-size cutout of Victoria with a billboard announcing:

VICTORIA C. WOODHULL
FIELD'S THEATER
TUESDAY, APRIL 18, 1876
AT SEVEN P.M.
"THE PRINCIPLES OF SOCIAL FREEDOM"
INVOLVING THE QUESTION OF
FREE LOVE, MARRIAGE, DIVORCE, AND
PROSTITUTION

When they got their passes, they were escorted to a special box at the right of the stage. Already seated in the box was an attractive young woman.

"Victoria told me you were here," the woman said as she stood to embrace Gabe.

"Good evening, Tennie, I'd like you to meet a very special friend of mine. Josephine Laclede, this is Tennessee Claflin, Victoria's sister. They were the first women brokers on Wall Street, and the T&P did a lot of business with their firm."

At just that moment Victoria took the stage. She was conservatively dressed in a black skirt with a black, braided jacket fitted closely to her slender waist. Her only adornments were a watch-chain pendant hanging from her neck and a red silk rose at the collar of her jacket.

Just before she began to speak, a man stood in the audience and in a booming voice yelled, "Godspeed, Victoria!" She smiled graciously and mouthed a *Thank you*.

Victoria began, her voice rich and confident. "It has been said by a very wise person that there is a trinity in all things, the perfect unity of the trinity or a tri-unity being necessary to make a complete objective realization."

Josie listened intently to the speech as Victoria tied religion, politics, and social freedom together. Josie was amazed at the strength of the small, rather delicate-looking woman who took the derisive calls from several in the audience in stride.

"Harlot!"

"Whore!"

"Jezebel!"

These and even worse epithets were shouted at Victoria, and still she continued, her voice getting stronger and stronger.

Josie was not disturbed by her message at all. Many of the things she said made total sense. Her overriding theme was that there could be love without marriage, but there could not be marriage, a true marriage, without love.

Mrs. Woodhull said that women, no matter what level of society, freely accepted that it was a man's prerogative, whether married or unmarried, to dally with women, but a woman who did the same thing with a man was ostracized. She illustrated this point by saying that prostitutes were often prosecuted by the law—but the men who visited them were not.

She also said that a marriage contract between two people should be treated as any other legal contract; if things did not work out well, if a man and a woman found they were not compatible in either temperament or love, the contract could, and should, be broken by divorce. And divorce, she insisted, should not be a condition that forced a woman into poverty. That was too often the case, she pointed out, because in the marriage contract everything, including a woman's children, belonged to the man.

Her most controversial statement, though, and the one that brought the most catcalls, was "Yes, I am a free lover. I have an inalienable, constitutional, and natural right to love whom I may, to love as long or as short a period as I can; to change that love every day if I please, and with that right neither you nor any law you can frame have any right to interfere."

When Victoria said this, Gabe reached over and captured Josie's hand in his and gave it a gentle squeeze. He continued to hold her hand for the remainder of the speech.

Josie was confused by his action. Was he trying to tell her that he loved her, or was he telling her that he wanted to have free love—sexual relations during this trip, and at the end, each of them would be free to go his or her own way? Why, oh why, had she agreed to this? Her life in Fort Worth had been so uncomplicated until Gabe had come, and now her world was topsy-turvy.

She thought back to the night of the snowstorm. He had made her body react in ways that she had never imagined. Was she in love with him? She believed she was, but she had no way of measuring this because she had never been in love before. If she was in love with him, did he love her? He had not spoken the words, but he did say he wanted her to meet his family. He wouldn't want that if he didn't love her, would he? These thoughts raced through her mind as Victoria continued to speak.

Josie heard Victoria say something that spoke directly to her. She said she believed the offspring of love, free love, which was truly given, were the best and purest of children.

Could Josie accept that she was the offspring of love? Was that what had happened to her mother? Had there been a lover whom her mother loved beyond all else and, for whatever reason, that love had to be set aside? Had her mother been a mistress to a man of means? Or even a married man? Had her father been beneath her mother's position in society? All these questions plagued Josie, but until this very moment when this woman put it into words, Josie had always thought of her birth with nothing but shame. But now Victoria said a child conceived in love, no matter what the circumstances, should be thought of as the best and the purest.

Tears were streaming down Josie's face as she took to heart all that Victoria Woodhull was saying. Any twinge of jealousy Josie might have had was replaced by admiration for the woman, not only for her intellect, but for her personal courage. How brave she was to stand onstage and deliver an address even while being vilified in the strongest and most hateful language possible!

Gabe and Josie reached Washington, D.C., on the evening of the seventh day of travel. Josie looked out the window as they rolled into town, watching the carriage traffic on Sixth Street. Then she felt the train slowing, and even before they were stopped, the passengers began gathering their loose items, their hats, jackets, canes, and handbags.

"This is a new terminal," Gabe said.

Josie studied the depot as the train came to a stop. The impressive-looking brick building had cupolas and towers.

"Someday soon, we'll have a depot just like this in Fort Worth," Josie said.

"Maybe not quite as haughty as this one," Gabe said. "I see Washington as an old dowager. I see Fort Worth as . . ." He looked at Josie and smiled. "A beautiful young Empress."

Josie felt herself blushing.

They left the train and walked through the depot, which was thronged with people. She realized that if Gabe weren't with her right now, she wouldn't have the slightest idea what to do next. She followed him without question when he hired a cab.

"The Willard Hotel," he announced.

"Yes, sir."

When they reached the hotel, Josie waited in the public area as Gabe secured rooms for them.

The lobby was brightly lit with gaslights and had mosaic floors and a beautifully carved ceiling, which she was examining when Gabe returned with two sets of keys.

"You're on the sixth floor and I'm on the second," he said. "Colonel Scott and his wife are in parlor number six, which is on the second floor, too. I can't wait for you to meet Anna."

At that moment a man with golden hair and a Vandyke beard, wearing a US army uniform, came strolling through the lobby. Gabe glanced toward him; then a broad smile spread across his face.

"General George Armstrong Custer," Gabe said. "How are you, Autie?"

Custer looked at Gabe, and for just a moment his face registered confusion. Then there was recognition. "Cadet Corrigan, how is the cow?"

"Sir, she walks, she talks, she's full of chalk; the lacteal fluid extracted from the female of the bovine species is highly prolific to the nth degree."

"Very good." Laughing, Custer stuck his hand out. "How are you doing, Gabe? Still working for that belly robber Scott?"

"I am, and he's here in the Willard."

"You can do better than him." Custer looked over at Josie and made a slight bow. "And this lovely creature?"

"Josie Laclede, this is General Custer." Then to Custer, Gabe added, "Miss Laclede has been a very valuable part of our building the T&P into Fort Worth."

Custer took Josie's hand, raised it to his lips, and kissed it. "How delighted I am to meet you, Josie."

"What are you doing here in Washington? I thought you were out West with the Seventh Cavalry," Gabe said.

"I am indeed, but I've been summoned to Washington to testify before Congress in the Belknap case. What brings you here?"

"The same thing, in a manner of speaking. I am to testify in the Blaine hearings."

"Hah!" Custer said. "Leave it to honorable men such as we to hold to the fire the feet of such brigands as Secretary Belknap and Speaker Blaine. I've heard there have been a few fireworks in your hearing, but I'm sure the accusations against your august employer couldn't possibly be true."

"That's what my testimony is supposed to support," Gabe said as he grinned at Custer.

"We'll see about that. How long do you expect to be in the city?"

"I'd like to leave as soon as my testimony is over."

"You can't do that. Josie deserves to see our great capital. I've been told I had better have an audience with Grant, so no matter what happens with my hearing, I'll be here till next week. How would you like to have dinner with me Saturday evening?"

"Josie, could you stand to have dinner with the most egoistical officer in the US army?" Gabe asked.

"I'm not that bad. You're just jealous because you know there's nobody better than I am. She can't refuse my invitation." Custer winked at Josie in a flirtatious way.

"Sir, I accept," Josie said.

"Then, I'll have to tag along, just to protect her honor," Gabe teased.

"Good. I'll see you Saturday, and, Gabe, on a serious note, be careful how you answer every question tomorrow. These hearings can be treacherous."

"I know."

When Custer had walked away, Gabe and Josie entered the elevator and requested the sixth floor from the operator.

"How did you know General Custer?"

"First of all, he's not a general anymore. He's a lieutenant colonel, but because he was a brevet general during the war, he still has the right to be addressed as general. And the reason I know him is because we were at the Academy together."

"And what was that business about the cow?" she asked with a little laugh.

"Upperclassmen use questions like that as a way of demeaning plebes."

"That makes no sense."

"Tell that to the people at West Point."

The elevator stopped, and they walked down the plush-carpeted hallway to Josie's room. Gabe unlocked the door and placed her traveling valise inside.

"Gabe," Josie said as she placed a tentative hand on his arm. "What did General Custer mean when he told you to be careful how you answered every question tomorrow? Are you in some sort of trouble?"

"No, Josie, I am not, but Colonel Scott could be."

"What has he done? What is this hearing all about?"

"It's complicated. The House Judiciary Committee is accusing the former Speaker Blaine of conveying some of his bonds for the Little Rock and Fort Smith Railroad to Colonel Scott. They're saying the colonel paid eighty cents on the dollar when the market rate for the bonds was fifty cents on the dollar."

"Why would Colonel Scott do that?"

"Because there was a critical vote coming up that would benefit the railroad, and Colonel Scott needed Blaine's support. Blaine wound up with an extra sixty-four thousand dollars, and the committee is saying that's bribery, and they are blaming Colonel Scott."

"Did Colonel Scott really do that?"

Gabe smiled at Josie as he tipped her chin up and planted a gentle kiss upon her lips.

"More than likely we will be dining with the Scotts tonight. You are going to fall in love with Anna. I'll call for you at seven."

SIXTEEN

Josie and Gabe met for breakfast in the Willard Hotel coffee shop before leaving for Gabe's hearing.

"Josie, I've been thinking. Would you consider coming with me to Pennsylvania to visit my family?"

"Oh, Gabe, I don't know. I've been gone so long and Papa is all alone."

"He has Ida and Willie to help out, and don't forget Oscar Manning is there, too. While we are here in Washington for a few days, why don't you send him a telegram and ask if it would be all right to take a few more days? And I'd like a firsthand report on how the Tarrant County crew is getting along with General Brown anyway."

"All right, I'll do that."

Gabe took out his pocket watch.

"I'm not scheduled to testify before ten o'clock. Since it's such a beautiful day, would you care to walk to the Capitol building?"

"How far is it?"

"I'm sure it's less than two miles. We'll take our time and walk down Pennsylvania Avenue."

"I'd like that. It is beautiful here with all the spring flowers and the green grass. It makes me wonder why I love Fort Worth so much."

"What are you talking about? Did I not just see the most beautiful bluebonnets growing everywhere I looked? Here I'm falling in love with Texas and now you're looking to go someplace else." Gabe took her hand and placed it through his arm, drawing her close to him as they walked.

"Sometimes you say the most ridiculous things."

"I wouldn't say that was ridiculous. I do like Texas."

"Oh, look," Josie said. "Isn't that a Western Union office? I can send the telegram to Papa."

"I think you're right. Don't forget to tell Henri to send a return message in care of the Willard," Gabe said as they started across the street.

After sending the telegram, they continued walking in silence. Josie was looking forward to meeting Gabe's family. She had been concerned that if she came on this trip, she would have to fend off Gabe's advances, but she had to admit, she was a little disappointed. Not once since they had left Fort Worth had he even tried to kiss her, except for the chaste peck he had given her in order to avoid answering her question about Colonel Scott's activities. She thought that perhaps he was tense over his testimony. Josie would be as glad as Gabe was when this day was over.

When they arrived at the Capitol, Josie was awestruck by its sheer beauty. The rotunda was a circular, stone-paved room, directly in the middle of the building. Circles of gas jets marked every cornice and gallery, diminishing in diameter as they reached the apex of the rotunda, so that a thousand glittering lights illuminated the dome.

When Josie looked up, decorative frescoes abounded. The centerpiece was Brumidi's *The Apotheosis of Washington*, in which the first president looked more like a Turk in his seraglio than the *pater patriae* that he was. Washington was painted in the eye of the rotunda, directly overhead. On the walls below the dome were several large historical paintings by Trumbull, Vanderlyn, and Powell, among others. In addition to the beautiful paintings, over a thousand flags floated like rainbows, all the way up to the very summit of the dome.

"There you are, my dears," Anna Scott said as she walked across the rotunda, her heels clicking on the stone floor. "I'm glad you are early because I have so much to show you, Josie. We are going to have a fabulous girls' day out just sightseeing around Washington."

"I'm so looking forward to it," Josie said.

"We'd better get going because I don't want us to be mistaken for one of those dreadful wirepullers," Anna said.

Josie shot Gabe a questioning look.

"I don't think there is any possibility that our congressmen would mistake the two of you for female lobbyists, but just to be on the safe side, you'd better not go into the ladies' reception room," Gabe said as he smiled broadly.

"Believe me, we won't," Anna said. "Now, if Marthalee were here, that would be another story. Let's go, my dear."

Anna hugged Gabe for a long moment. "I'm worried about this one, Gabe. This isn't like all the other times."

"I know," Gabe said. "I will answer as truthfully as I can, but I will only answer the questions that are specifically asked of me."

"I'm counting on that. I know that Tom will have covered every base he can, but you know many of these people are so anti-railroad right now. How I do wish James Blaine was still the Speaker. I'd feel so much better."

"I know, but he's not. Our salvation lies with a group of determined farmers, ranchers, and tradesmen from Tarrant County, Texas. If they deliver, we are all going to be just fine."

"Can they do it?" Anna asked, her eyes clouding with tears.

"Yes. I guarantee it," Gabe said. "And so does Josie, so you're not to worry." He kissed Anna on the cheek. "Take my girl and have a good day."

Gabe turned and walked toward the House side of the Capitol, and as he reached the big wooden door, he turned and blew a kiss to Josie, who waved hesitantly.

Josie didn't understand a lot of Anna and Gabe's conversation, but she did understand that the railroad's making it to Fort Worth was a high priority for Colonel Scott, and that Gabe was determined to make it happen.

And she understood his comment "take my girl and have a good day." She knew she was the "girl" he meant, and she would take the moniker.

"I have been here many times," Anna said, "and I think Washington is more beautiful than London, or Paris, or even Vienna. But I do love Philadelphia, too, especially this year. Will you be coming to the Centennial Exhibition?"

"I would love to go, but I'm afraid I cannot stay away from my responsibilities at home for that long. I believe I have read that it doesn't open until the middle of May."

"That's right, but it's going to be all year. So maybe you both could come back and stay with Tom and me."

"Thank you." Josie was amused that the people they had met, from Victoria Woodhull to General Custer to Anna Scott, all assumed that there was more to the relationship that she had with Gabe. She had to admit that she rather enjoyed the pretense. But was it really a pretense? Gabe had left hint after hint that he wanted more. He had said he was beginning to come to love Texas; and then there was the "take my girl" comment. He wanted to take her to meet his family. Weren't all these the things that an affianced couple would do? Victoria Woodhull had given her the answer. You could have love without marriage, but you couldn't have a marriage without love. It seemed that Gabe was pushing her toward something, maybe even marriage, but never once had he said the word *love*. But then, neither had she. The word did not come easily to her.

". . . don't you think it is beautiful?" Anna Scott was saying.

Josie had no idea what the woman was talking about but she answered, "Oh, yes."

"It's just a shame he was a bastard."

"Who was a bastard?" Josie asked, trying to catch up with the conversation.

"Why, James Smithson. The man who gave us the money for the Smithsonian. He was the illegitimate son of a highly regarded English landowner and his mistress. And you know what happens in those cases."

"I've heard it said that children born of love, free love that was truly given, are the best and purest."

"Humph!" Anna snorted. "Don't believe that kind of talk. There's a strumpet who goes around the country giving speeches, and that's the kind of nonsense she preaches. You are fortunate you live on the frontier and you don't have to come in contact with that rubbish. Why, this woman even accused the greatest minister this country has ever had of committing adultery. Henry Ward Beecher. Can you believe that? Thank goodness a jury of his peers found him innocent."

Josie wanted to point out that there had been a hung jury, so no one would ever know the truth about Beecher, but she held her tongue.

"Would we be tainted if we entered the bastard's museum?" Josie asked with a smirk.

"Oh, no, it's a wonderful place," Anna said, missing the sarcasm completely, as she started up the steps of the Smithsonian. "I'm just glad he didn't keep the name he was born with. Jacques Louis Macie. Wouldn't that fancy dry goods store in New York City just love it if the greatest museum in the United States was called Macie's?"

Josie was bemused as she entered the museum. This woman, whom Gabe apparently respected— dare Josie say *loved*?—was a paragon of propriety. Did Anna know she was entertaining a bastard? And how would she feel about that if she found out?

The morning proved to Josie, more than ever, that no matter how much she might want to, she would never fit into Gabe's world. She was sorry she had already sent the telegram to her father asking for permission to visit Gabe's family. They were probably just like Anna Scott.

Josie decided right then to take every advantage of the rest of this trip because it would probably be her only opportunity to ever be in the nation's capital. When she got back to Fort Worth, she would ask Oscar Manning to marry her. Oscar would never think to question her parentage; he would say that if you worked, it didn't matter if you were a bastard. An ordinary life was what she wanted. To hell with the utopian idea that a marriage had to have love. Gabe Corrigan deserved someone with a pedigree, not a mongrel such as her.

Even if she did love him.

Josie and Anna had continued their tour of the city by riding the horse-drawn streetcars. They saw the President's House, Lafayette Square, the Corcoran Gallery, the unfinished Washington Monument, the Center Market, and a half dozen other places that were now a blur. For the rest of the day, Anna was gracious and generous, and Josie genuinely enjoyed the day.

Josie thought she might have judged Anna unfairly by reacting so strongly to her comments about the bastard. Anna was a lady who reflected the present moral attitudes, and it would take a lot to change them. This crusade had made Elizabeth Cady Stanton, Susan B. Anthony, and Victoria Woodhull causes célèbres.

When Josie returned to her room at the Willard, she removed the jacket of her day dress and hung it over a chair. Exhausted, she stretched out on the bed and was soon napping.

A light tap on the door awakened her.

"Yes?" she called.

"It's me," Gabe said. "Are you resting?"

Josie jumped from the bed, smoothing her hair as she went to answer the door. Gabe had his coat flung over one shoulder, his string tie hanging loose against his white shirt. His hair, usually perfectly combed, was mussed as if he had run his fingers through it over and over.

"May I come in?"

"Yes, of course."

He tossed his coat on the same chair where Josie had put her jacket, then took off his boots and climbed up on Josie's bed. "It's been a long day. I believe the first prerequisite for becoming a congressman is proving you're an imbecile."

"It was that bad?" Josie sat on the bed beside Gabe.

"Yes, it was that bad. First one man would ask a question, and I would answer, and then the next would ask the same damn question. Nobody listens to anything anybody says. Crawl up here and lie down beside me." Gabe closed his eyes as he patted the bed beside him.

More than anything, Josie wanted to do that. It was so tempting, but where would it lead?

Just then Gabe's eyes opened. "I mean it. I'd like more than anything to have you lie here beside me."

That was the only invitation Josie needed. She moved up beside him, placing her head on his shoulder as he cradled his arm around her.

It seemed like mere minutes until his breathing slowed and he was asleep.

Josie could think of no place she would rather be. She felt secure, she felt wanted, and she felt something else. She hoped it was love because she now knew that those were her feelings for Gabe. As she lay quietly, she wondered why he had not tried to kiss her. If a man and a woman were truly in love with one another, wasn't that what they wanted most to do? There was so much she did not understand.

When Gabe awakened, the gaslights on Pennsylvania Avenue had come on and were casting shadows into the room. He felt Josie's still body beside his, and he pulled her closer to him.

"I shouldn't be here," Gabe said as he kissed the top of her head.

"Who's to say that?" Josie asked as she tilted her head back.

A deep rumble started from Gabe. "My love, it would be so easy." He met her lips and started a long, slow, gentle kiss that ignited Josie. She moved to get into a better position to receive what she knew could be more, her hand roaming down Gabe's chest to rest upon his abdomen.

He caught her hand and moved it to his lips, kissing her fingertips.

"This can't be. I must go." Gabe sat up quickly, swinging his feet onto the floor.

"Why?" Josie's question was almost a whisper as she rose beside him.

Gabe shook his head as he grabbed her and pulled her to him. "I want you more than I can say." He dropped his arms and began putting on his boots. "The time will come, my love. I promise."

He picked up his coat and left the room.

Josie looked at the door after he left. She could not have given a clearer invitation than that, could she? What was wrong? Why was he hesitating?

Gabe didn't take the elevator; he walked down the six flights of stairs to regain control of himself. It had been all he could do to walk out of that room. He wanted her more than he had ever wanted any other woman—or anything. He recalled his conversation with Henri.

Then, if she goes with you, I want your solemn vow that she'll return the same way.

Gabe had made that vow, and he could not, and would not, violate it, for he held it as sacred as his love for her.

When he reached the bottom floor, he walked out into the lobby. Several people were there, many of whom he had seen in the halls of Congress earlier today. Some of the congressmen were being plied with drinks and promises of other rewards by advocates for one position or another.

Gabe stopped by the desk of the concierge and ordered a meal to be sent up to Josie's room. He had planned for them to enjoy a quiet evening dinner, then perhaps a stroll around the President's House, but that was not to be.

"With a vase of flowers," he added.

"But of course," the concierge replied conspiratorially. "I'm sure the young lady will be most pleased."

"I hope so."

Gabe said headed toward the Round Robin, the bar that was actually round because it was located in the hotel's corner tower. He took a seat at the bar and ordered a mint julep. When it arrived, he downed the signature drink in one gulp and quickly ordered another.

Damn the promise he had made. Had he known that his promise would not only deny him, but hurt Josie, he never would have made the damn thing.

A gentleman's handshake will seal the promise you just made.

So, if he was doing the gentlemanly thing, why did he now feel like such a heel?

The next morning, Gabe awakened with a headache, having drunk too much the evening before. He remembered getting into a heated discussion with some men at the bar, where he had wound up defending Colonel Scott for hiring men to grease the palms of congressmen. Gabe had never condoned this, but he did know that it happened, and he knew that the Willard was the place where most of the deals were made. The practice had become so pervasive that President Grant had started calling those who hung around the Willard Hotel *lobbyists*. After spending just one day before the House Judiciary Committee, Gabe had had enough. All he wanted to do was leave Washington and go back to Texas.

He stepped into a small cubicle in the bathroom, where he turned on a spigot that brought warm water cascading over his body. When the water finally turned cold, he still did not leave the little room. When his teeth began to chatter, he stepped out and grabbed a towel. His headache was cured.

After he was dressed, he looked at his watch: 10:15.

"Damn! Poor Josie." Gabe wanted to go directly to her room, but he decided he would go down to the desk. He prayed that she had not checked out, because after his behavior last evening, she had every right to do just that.

"Can you tell me if Miss Laclede is still in residence?" Gabe asked.

"Well, of course, Mr. Corrigan. A most delightful young woman. I had the privilege of delivering a Western Union message to her about an hour ago. Oh, and, sir, I have a post for you as well." The clerk retrieved a letter and handed it to Gabe.

He recognized Tom Scott's distinctive handwriting as he placed the envelope in his pocket.

Gabe stood in front of Josie's door with a sense of foreboding. He had felt less trepidation in the heat of battle than he did right now. How would she react when she saw him? Gabe realized that the answer to that question was extremely important for his future happiness.

He knocked on the door, so quietly that he barely heard it himself. The door opened, but he did not see Josie. What he did see was her open valise on the luggage rack, her clothes neatly packed. With his heart beating rapidly, Gabe stepped into the room. Josie moved out from beside the door.

"Captain Corrigan," she said, giving him a slight, and too formal, nod.

Gabe stood still. He was unsure whether he should continue into the room. "Josie—what? Are you leaving?"

"I think that would be best."

"I wish you wouldn't, Josie."

"I have no choice." Josie stepped over to the chest and picked up the telegram. "I suppose you know about this."

"About what?"

She tossed the envelope toward Gabe, where it fluttered to the floor in front of him. He bent over to pick it up and read:

GOOD IDEA. ENJOY GABE & FAMILY. BAD
NEWS HERE. COURTHOUSE BURNED. DODGE
STOPPED ALL TCCC CREW. ONLY T&P WORK
ON ROAD. LITTLE PROGRESS. PAPA

"I can't believe this," Gabe said.

"Are you saying that you didn't know that General Dodge has taken the building of the railroad away from us?"

"No, I had no idea. But it doesn't change anything."

"It changes everything. It means that General Dodge is not committed to bringing the railroad to Fort Worth."

"Dodge is not the Texas and Pacific, Colonel Scott is, and I know he is committed to getting the railroad into Fort Worth on time. So am I."

"Oh, Gabe, I so much want to believe you."

"Believe me. You have my solemn promise, Josie, the railroad will reach Fort Worth."

Josie smiled at him. "I do believe you."

"Good. Then, none of this business about your leaving today? I very much want you to meet my family."

"I'll stay."

"Oh, I just got a message from Colonel Scott. Maybe it has something to do with this."

Gabe took the envelope from his pocket and read:

> *Gabe, my boy,*
>
> *All my people on Capitol Hill tell me you handled yourself brilliantly before the Judiciary Committee. Chairman Knott is a hard man to face, but I hear you did so with dignity and aplomb. Even better, my sources at the Round Robin tell me you sparred with one of my most ardent detractors last evening. Bravo I say.*
>
> *Anna wishes you to pass on her best*

regards to your young lady. Miss Laclede meets with our heartfelt approval. Both Anna and I have observed what a different man you are in her presence. We sense that she is the one, and for that I am thankful, as I must admit to my part in your previous disaster.

As a small gift to you for your service and faithfulness, I would like to present you with four subscriptions of centennial stock. These will serve as invitations to the Centennial Ball to be held at the President's House this evening. I had planned that you and Miss Laclede should join Anna and me, but as always business calls me away. I must return to Philadelphia posthaste, regretting that I may not personally bid Miss Laclede adieu. But I trust I will meet her again.

    As ever,

    Tom

"Josie, if you had the opportunity to attend a ball at the President's House, what would you say?"

Josie had a perplexed look on her face. "A ball at the President's House? When?"

"Tonight."

Josie looked toward her open suitcase, then back to Gabe. "You make it very difficult, Captain Corrigan. What red-blooded American could say no to that invitation?"

A broad smile crossed Gabe's face. "That's

great," he said with a pump of his fist. "I don't suppose you have a suitable dress to wear, do you?"

"Oh, I hadn't thought of that."

"It doesn't matter. We'll find you the prettiest dress in Washington."

Josie and Gabe spent the day going from shop to shop looking for the perfect dress. She was amazed at his patience, never once having thought that a man would enjoy such an activity, but Gabe never complained. Finally, the dress was selected, and they returned to the Willard.

Upon entering, Josie remembered their previous engagement.

"Gabe, we have forgotten something. What about our plan to have dinner with General Custer?"

"You're right. I'll see him and ask if he would like to accompany us, since this is a subscription engagement and Colonel Scott bought four tickets. He may not be the most welcomed guest at the President's House, but if I know Autie, he'll enjoy sticking his finger in Grant's eye."

Josie furrowed her brow in question.

"Well, his hearing didn't go as well as mine did. It seems he implicated the president's brother in the sutler licensing and Indian agents' procurement scandal, and that didn't set too well with President Grant. It will be interesting to see his reaction to Custer."

"Fireworks, perhaps?"

"Oh, no, no. Everybody is much too civilized for that," Gabe said with a chuckle.

That evening a hired carriage deposited Josie, Gabe, and General Custer under the portico of the White House. Custer was in a full dress uniform, festooned with brass and gold braid, while Gabe was wearing an evening coat with tails. Josie noticed that both men were wearing identical gold rings engraved with the crest of the United States Military Academy.

Josie was attired in a sapphire-blue silk evening dress, with white silk roses catching eyelet panels on the skirt. She was unaccustomed to wearing an off-the-shoulder neckline with a fitted bodice, and at first she was reluctant to wear something that she thought was so risqué. But Gabe had convinced her that she looked beautiful, and when she saw herself in the mirror, she had to admit she liked the look.

A uniformed member of the president's staff stood at the door to the White House, checking to see that each person who entered had the centennial certificate that indicated he or she had contributed. The government had been reluctant to appropriate sufficient funds to manage the great Philadelphia Exhibition, so various methods of raising funds had been devised. This event was one of the last to be held before the opening of the Centennial Exhibition.

"General Custer," a distinguished gentleman said as he approached the doorman.

"Judge Christiancy," Custer said with a partial bow. "It is good to see a familiar face in Washington."

"From what I read, you need a few familiar faces. I ran into Judge Bacon only recently and he told me of your troubles."

"Yes. I stopped by Monroe on my way here, and had I known how long I was going to be away from Fort Lincoln, I would have brought Libbie to Michigan to visit her father," Custer said. "It is my hope that my travails with Washington politicos will soon be over. You may know I am to command the Seventh in the upcoming Indian campaigns, and I must get back quickly."

"Sounds like the gossip about you running for the presidency may be just a rumor, then."

Custer smiled. "We'll just see what happens on the Plains. Judge, I would like you to meet a West Point classmate of mine, Captain Gabriel Corrigan, and his lady friend, Miss Josie Laclede."

Both Josie and Gabe made their introductions to Judge Christiancy; then Josie turned to a beautiful young woman, standing beside the judge, who had been introduced as Lillie Christiancy.

"I would give anything if my own papa could be here with me, because I know he would be so excited to be a guest at the President's House. You're so lucky to enjoy this evening with your father," Josie said to the young woman.

"The judge is my husband," Lillie said rather smugly.

Josie was at a loss for words.

But General Custer was not. He immediately put his arm out for the young woman. "Madam, will you allow me to be your escort?"

Judge Christiancy fell in behind Josie, who was behind Gabe, following protocol that the man go first when meeting the president. Then came Lillie, followed by General Custer.

Josie was awed by the sense of history that she felt upon entering the Entrance Hall. All the portraits of the presidents from Washington to Lincoln hung on the wall protected behind a glass screen. President Grant stood next to a woman who was introduced as Elizabeth Duane Gillespie, the great-granddaughter of Benjamin Franklin, and then Mrs. Grant. The first lady, whom Josie was surprised to see had crossed eyes, was elegantly dressed, wearing a pearl-colored silk dress trimmed with pink silk and feathers. Josie thought her attire perfectly complemented the pink-and-white-marbled floor of the hall. Standing beside Mrs. Grant was her sister Ellen Dent Sharp. By the time Josie reached Mrs. Sharp in the receiving line, General Custer had reached President Grant. Josie watched as the president turned to his next guest, completely avoiding a handshake with General Custer.

The East Room in the White House was to be the scene of the Centennial Ball, but until it was time for the promenade, everyone gathered in the Cross Hall, the crowd making it impossible to move about. Finally the Marine Band started the music and the wide doors were opened. Gabe took Josie's arm and General Custer took Lillie's, while the elderly Judge Christaincy found a seat to become an onlooker.

The room was unlike any other Josie had ever seen. Two gold-decorated beams spanned the ceiling, which had been painted in soft pinks and blues to resemble the sky. Gold-and-white Doric columns supported the beams as they stood against gray-and-gold wallpaper. The windows were draped with heavy green-velvet curtains that complemented the gray carpet with rather large green medallions. But the most striking features were the huge chandeliers with three rows of white globes that covered gas jets. Josie had never seen a room more brilliantly illuminated.

"Gabe, thank you. Thank you for bringing me here. It is beautiful."

"I knew you would love it. Are you up for the German?" Gabe asked as the rather fast-paced music of the cotillion began.

Gabe and Josie had danced every dance and were just having a drink of Roman punch. Gabe had some of the meringue that floated on top of the champagne drink on his lip, and Josie reached over to carefully wipe it off with her finger. She then seductively put her finger in her mouth to clean off the egg white.

At just that moment Mrs. Gillespie stepped to a platform that had been erected and began to speak.

"Ladies and gentlemen, on behalf of the Women's Centennial Executive Committee, I would like to thank you for your generous support for the Centennial Exhibition to be held in Philadelphia, commencing May tenth. As a commemorative for this gala evening, the committee is making available a copy of the *National Cookery Book*, compiled with recipes gathered from women from every state and territory across this great land."

After a generous smattering of applause, Mrs. Gillespie continued, "In addition, each of you women at this special event will receive a carved tea box to remind us of those patriots who first threw the tea in the Boston harbor. And to make it even more special, Mrs. Grant has contributed handkerchiefs embroidered by her personal staff with the Great Seal of the United States. You will find them stored inside your tea boxes. The first lady and her sister Mrs. Sharp will personally hand them to you upon your departure. And now, let the dancing continue."

Gabe and Josie and Lillie and Custer stayed until only a couple of dozen people were left in the East Room. Only after the president retired did his son-in-law, Algernon Sartoris, began to sing. His wife, Nellie, had joined her mother, her aunt, and her sister-in-law at the table where the dispersal of the tea boxes was in progress.

Josie and Gabe expressed their gratitude to Mrs. Grant when she handed over the little box.

"This will become one of my most cherished mementos," Josie said as she accepted it from the first lady.

"Why, thank you, my child. I am so pleased that you could be here this evening," Julia Grant said.

"Wait a minute," Frederick Grant's wife, Ida, said. "You look so familiar. Would I have met you somewhere, maybe in Chicago, my home?"

"No, I've never been to Chicago. I am from Fort Worth, Texas, and until this trip to Washington, I have never done any traveling."

"But you were born in St. Louis," Gabe added.

"Yes, that's true. I left St. Louis when I was in my teens, but I have been in Texas ever since."

"I just can't place who you look like," Ida continued.

Just then the president's daughter stepped forward with the book Mrs. Gillespie was providing. "I almost forgot. Here's your cookery book," Nellie Sartoris said as she handed the book to Josie.

Mrs. Sharp began to chuckle. "There's your answer, Ida. Look at these two young women when they're standing next to each other. They could be sisters."

SEVENTEEN

On Sunday morning, Gabe and Josie took a horse-drawn streetcar to the Baltimore & Potomac Passenger Terminal located on the Mall. Josie looked up at the clock tower and saw that it was nearly 6:30 a.m. Their train would leave at seven. Last night, Custer had invited them to join him and Lillie Christiancy for a nightcap. Josie thought it a little unusual that Custer would be having a nightcap with a woman who wasn't his wife, especially a married woman. She was glad that Gabe had declined, suggesting instead that they meet for coffee in the lobby of the Willard this morning. But even that didn't happen.

Josie took one last look at the Capitol before getting on the train bound for Philadelphia.

"Are you excited about seeing your family?"

"I guess so. I was hoping we could stay longer and then go to the Centennial Exhibition, but now that General Dodge has stopped the Tarrant County folks from building the railroad, I feel like we have to get back to Fort Worth. As it stands now, it'll be almost the end of May before we get home anyway."

Josie was touched that Gabe had called Fort Worth "home." Could she dare believe that he really thought of Texas as home? Or was he referring only to her home?

"What can you possibly do?"

"I don't know. Probably the only thing I will be able to do for sure is see to it that I am an advocate for the people."

"Can Colonel Scott get something done if the railroad is close to being finished?"

"If it was just Washington he had to deal with, the answer would probably be yes, but the people in Austin don't seem to want to be bought off. Josie, I'm afraid if the road isn't done by the end of June, that's it for the Texas and Pacific."

"Would you be terribly disappointed?"

"For myself, my honest answer is no, but for the people of Fort Worth, it would be a disaster."

They were on the train for seven hours, which was but a short time compared to how long it had taken them when coming from Fort Worth. The depot in Philadelphia was right across from Machinery Hall and the main building of the not-yet-opened Centennial Exposition. Josie was impressed with the depot, a large, open, timbered Tudor-style edifice.

They didn't have long to enjoy it because they

took the Junction Railroad to the Media terminal, a trip of little more than half an hour. When they got off the train at the small building that served as a depot in Media, Josie saw, right across the road, a two-story building about forty feet wide and thirty feet deep. Smoke was coming from the chimney, and from inside the building came a loud banging sound. A lot of white dust also hung around the building.

But what caught Josie's attention first was the large sign that spread across the front of the building: CORRIGAN PHOSPHATE.

"Corrigan," Josie said, pointing to the sign.

"My father. Come, I'll introduce you."

Gabe led Josie across the road, through the cloud of dust, and into the building. A small space just inside the door had a huge window on the back wall that looked out over the mill floor. Two large vats were each underneath a great steam-powered stamping machine. The noise was horrendous.

"What are going into those vats could well be buffalo bones that came from Texas. When they come out, they look like this." Gabe picked up a bag on the floor in the corner and showed her a finely ground powder.

The door to the mill floor opened, and a white-haired, pleasant-faced, and relatively portly man entered.

"Yes, sir, and what can I be—" The man stopped in midsentence when he recognized Gabe, and a huge smile spread across his face. "Gabriel, my boy!" he said loudly. He spread his arms wide and the two men embraced.

"What a wonderful surprise! Oh, how happy your mother will be."

"Pa, I'd like you to meet Empress Josephine Laclede," Gabe said, as he began brushing away some of the dust he had gotten from his father. "Josie, this is Sean Corrigan, my pa."

"An empress, is she? Sure'n what a lovely lass you be," Sean said.

Gabe laughed. "*Empress* is her name, Pa."

"Well, it be a special name for a special lass."

"Everyone calls me Josie, Mr. Corrigan."

"Then, Josie it is. Are you home for a bit, Gabriel?"

"Not for long, Pa. I was in Washington, and since I was so close, I wanted you and Mother to meet Josie."

Sean Corrigan had a wide grin. "And would you be for telling me something that will make your mother's heart leap for joy?"

Gabe just shook his head, then looked at Josie. "Josie, are you sure you want to spend a few days here? There'll be more than a few of these comments."

"I'm ready," Josie said with a smile.

"Wait here for a moment. I'll have to tell Mr. Daniels that I'm leaving. What a grand surprise you'll be for your mother."

Josie didn't know how old Gabe's mother was, but she hoped that she would still be as attractive at that age. Morgana Corrigan was clear-skinned, with brown eyes and the same deep dimple that creased Gabe's chin. And though her hair was streaked with gray, it was still dark, giving evidence as to where her son had gotten his coloring.

Gabe's sister, Katie, was fifteen years younger than he was. She had beautiful auburn hair with bright blue eyes, and she obviously adored her older brother.

"You can't tell it by looking at me now," Sean said, "but sure'n my hair was once as red as Katie's. 'Twas what won their mother over to this Irish lad, Welsh though she be."

"You didn't know I'm a product of an Irish Catholic and a Welsh Quaker, did you?" Gabe asked.

"That's why you're so passionate and so patient," Josie said.

Sean's eyebrows suddenly rose.

"We know he's patient. We didn't know he was passionate," Katie said.

"I mean he is dedicated to his work," Josie said, her face flushing hotly.

"That is enough," Morgana said. "We are making Josie uncomfortable with all this tomfoolery. I am so glad you are here, my dear. Will you be staying for the celebration?"

"Celebration?" Josie asked.

"The Centennial."

"No, Mother, we won't be able to stay that long. We just came to see you."

"For that I am thankful, and we must cherish

every minute you are here," Morgana said. "Josie, you must be weary after your travels. Katie will show you to her room, and Gabriel will follow and pull out the truckle bed."

"Yes, Mother," the two Corrigans said in unison.

"I've been gone three years, but nothing changes," Gabe said with a smile as he took Josie's valise and started up the stairs.

The next morning, Josie awakened early, while Katie was still asleep. Josie went over to the window seat, which looked out over a pastoral scene with rolling hills and a bubbling stream. She saw Sean Corrigan herding three Guernsey cows into a stone barn, a collie walking obediently beside him. On the other side of the barn was a pigsty, where Morgana was tossing ears of corn out for the animals to eat. A separate frame building was set apart from the house as a summer kitchen. Next to the building was a lean-to, probably the woodshed. Everywhere the spring grass was green, the huge, spreading chestnut trees had new leaves, and purple irises bloomed next to the spirea with their cascading branches covered with white blossoms.

Gabe had grown up in this bucolic place. She could imagine him as a child running over the hills, standing knee-deep in the stream catching tadpoles, or climbing to the top of the chestnut tree. Then, even as she was thinking of him, she saw Gabe in the yard. He walked to the pigsty and helped his mother throw corn to the hogs. When they were finished, he and his mother, arm in arm, started back toward the house. A lump formed in Josie's throat as she watched. To most, she knew, this was an ordinary occurrence. But she had never experienced it.

"Good morning, Josie," Gabe said when Josie entered the cheery kitchen a bit later. The big, round table where Gabe was sitting was covered with a bright yellow oilcloth.

"I made some apple scones this morning, but Gabe insisted he wanted an Irish omelet," Morgana said, removing the hot, puffy mashed-potato-and-egg dish from the oven and setting it in front of Gabe. "Would you like one, too?"

"The scones smell wonderful." Josie took one and slathered it with butter.

"What would you like to do today?" Gabe asked. "Would you like to go back to Philadelphia and visit the Centennial grounds?"

"Would you be disappointed if I said no? I'd really like to stay right here. I was sitting in the window seat this morning, and it is so peaceful."

"That suits me. I'll show you all the places I used to explore when I was a boy."

After eating, and helping Morgana wash the dishes, Josie and Gabe left the house. They walked over the forty acres or so that made up the Corrigan farm, Gabe pointing out such things as where he had broken his arm by falling from a tree, where he had gathered nuts, and even where his favorite dog, Levi, was buried. Josie enjoyed the morning.

"Why did you ever leave?"

"I went to the military academy at West Point. Then came the war, where I met Colonel Scott. I guess I just wanted more from my life than being a farmer and a bone crusher."

"It seems like a pretty good life to me."

"It is for Pa and Mother, but I would have a hard time coming to live here again."

"Why do you say that?"

"Because what I want is in Texas."

Josie didn't answer. That statement had too many implications.

"There's one more place I want to show you," Gabe said. "It's where I used to go when I didn't want anyone to find me."

They walked a little way until they came to a small stone house no more than eight feet square. Gabe opened a door and walked in.

"This is our waterworks," Gabe said, looking over a low stone wall that housed a bubbling spring. "Pa has metal pipes that direct the flow of water to the cistern so we are never without water."

It was cool and dark in the springhouse, and she could hear the gurgling water.

"There is a bench here, and I would come and sit for the longest time. It was my own private domain, you see, and here I planned world voyages, great battles, my future. Come sit with me."

Gabe reached out to take Josie's hand to help her sit. It was an unhurried move, but at the touch of his hand Josie felt a charge of sexual excitation. She wasn't sure what brought it on—maybe the darkness of the springhouse, the musical bubbling sound, or, more likely, that they were alone in such a private place.

Josie leaned against him, shivering in the cool. She placed her head on his shoulder while he rested his cheek against the top of her head. Soon his hand moved to cup her neck and his fingers began gently massaging, while her heart beat more and more rapidly. He lowered his face to hers, brushing back her long blond hair. His lips came to within inches of hers. In those dark brown eyes she saw a smoldering fire, then he closed his eyes, resting his forehead against hers. His hand was clenched in a ball.

"Gabe, do you not want to kiss me?" Josie's voice was choked with emotion.

He kissed her hungrily, ravishing her mouth. His tongue met hers, the heat of it causing her mouth to burn as if it were on fire.

He withdrew his tongue and began showering her with tiny kisses, on her lips, her eyes, her neck.

"Don't ever think that again. Right now I want to make you purr like a kitten."

"Then, why don't you?" Josie asked in a bare whisper. She began to unbutton her dress while Gabe watched, his gaze riveted on her chest. When she had her dress unbuttoned, she slipped out of her sleeves and let the dress fall to her waist. Then she untied the strings on her camisole and freed her breasts for him to feast upon.

Josie felt his hands on her breasts, and she could feel him trembling with excitement. She thrust her chest toward him, allowing him better access. He trailed his thumbs over her nipples, causing the hard buds to strain with anticipation, waiting for his mouth to caress them. She wasn't disappointed. He lowered his head and laved her nipples with his tongue, first one and then the other, bringing waves of pleasure to her private place, creating an aching need.

She knew how that need could be satisfied. She reached for Gabe and felt his bulging manhood straining against his trousers. She began to stroke him with one hand while she struggled with his belt buckle with the other.

He grabbed her hands with his own and held them so tightly that she was sure there would be a bruise, all the while with a pained expression upon his face.

"Stop, Josie, please stop," he said with anguish.

"Why? Why should I stop? I have an inalienable, constitutional, and natural right to love whom I want, and I want to love you here, in your secret hiding place, so that every time you come back to this place, you will think of me."

"Don't do this to me, Josie. I can't resist you, and I must."

"What are you saying?"

"Honor. My honor. I made a vow to your father."

"My father?"

"Yes, your father. When I asked him if he would give his permission for you to come with me on this trip, he made me promise that you would return a virgin. As God is my witness, I wish I had never made that promise, but I did. If I took you back in any other condition, I could not face your father, and I could not live with myself."

For the first time in her life, she was annoyed with her father. Why would he extract such a promise from Gabe? Why was he interfering so? Then, as quickly as the irritation was born, it went away. She recognized it as the natural reaction of a father.

She also felt a sense of respect, and even more love, for Gabe because of his sense of honor.

"Oh, Gabe." Josie leaned into him, her nipples still taut as they came in contact with his shirt.

"Let me help you get yourself put back together." He slowly tied the strings of her camisole, then pulled up her dress. Before her dress was buttoned, he reached in and held her breasts one more time. "The time will come, my love, and I promise it won't be long." He kissed her, one long, slow, tender kiss, then bent over the stone wall to splash cold springwater on his face.

That night, as Josie lay in the truckle bed in Katie's room, she replayed the events of the day in her mind, particularly the episode in the springhouse. Gabe's disclosure that he had made a vow to her father answered a lot of questions for her.

In the bed above her, she heard Katie turning first to one side and then the other, causing Josie's bed to move with each turn. Then she heard a long sigh.

Finally, Katie spoke. "Josie, are you awake?"

"Yes."

"Do you love him?"

"What?"

"My brother, do you love him?"

"I . . . I don't know. To be truthful, it hasn't come up. He has never mentioned . . ."

"Do *you* love him?"

"Yes—that is, I think I do."

"Just thinking isn't enough. You have to be sure. If you love him, then you should marry him. But if you don't love him, and I mean really love him, then don't marry him. I do not want to see my brother hurt again."

Again? Josie wondered what Katie meant by *again*. But she was afraid to ask.

"It's not completely up to me. Doesn't Gabe have to want this, too?"

"You're saying that to me when Mother kept me away from the springhouse for over an hour today? Just let me think about that. What do I think my brother wants?"

Josie was glad she and Katie were having this conversation in a darkened room, because the very thought of Gabe's mother guarding their privacy while they were in the springhouse caused her face to glow.

"If I marry him, and bear in mind that the subject has never been broached, but if I do marry him, it will be because I love him, and because I know that he loves me, too."

"That's good to hear. Because if you hurt him, I will put a curse on you." Katie giggled. "I'm an Irish faerie, you know, and I can do such things."

"I'll not be hurting him, Katie Corrigan," Josie replied with a little laugh. "An Irish curse is the last thing I need."

You were gone for almost a month, and I certainly missed her, but I think the trip was very good for her," Henri told Gabe. "She seems happier than I have ever seen her. And to think she actually got to meet the president of the United States! What an experience that was for her."

"For both of us."

"And your parents? How did they like her?"

"They loved her, Henri. How could they not?"

"Indeed. How could anyone not? Have you asked her to marry you yet?"

"No, not yet. I think it's important that the railroad is finished on time, and I am determined to get it to Fort Worth if I have to go to hell and back."

"I understand. By the way, how did the hearings go?"

"Still unresolved. There are so many railroad

entanglements, I've no doubt the hearings will go on for years. You know how Congress works, especially when some of their own are involved."

"And Colonel Scott?"

"So far so good. Tom Scott did no more nor no less than any of the others. No doubt they'll be questioning Stanford or Gould or Vanderbilt next.

"Good for Scott. And, I don't want to sound self-serving here, but that is also good for you and the T&P, isn't it?"

"Yes. And speaking of the T&P, I feel I have to be at End of Track, so I'm moving out there as soon as possible, and that wouldn't be the best place for me to be if I want to court Josie."

"My prayers go with you, Gabe. You know I have great confidence in you."

"Thank you. I have a feeling we are going to need all the prayers you can muster."

From the *Democrat*—July 6, 1876:

> *We know of no term that expresses more fully the condition of affairs in Fort Worth at the present time than red-hot. In every line of business there is great activity, which increases day by day as the time when the steam whistle shall wake up the echoes in our city approaches. The population of the city may be said to be hourly increasing, so rapid is the influx of people who come to locate.*

With the influx of people came an increase in business, and every night now The Empress Hotel was filled. In addition, the dining room was crowded for every meal, not only by the hotel guests, but by citizens of the town. The railroad was now only a few miles short of the city limits, and the mood of all the citizens was upbeat.

Josie missed Gabe, but Willie reported that he was so busy, he barely had time to sleep. Josie and Ida were covered with work also, so much so that Henri hired Hannah Welch and her mother to help.

On one of their busiest days, Major Van Zandt came into the hotel. Josie was behind the check-in desk.

"Where is your father?" the major asked.

"He went with Willie out to End of Track. They needed two wagons to haul the supplies out this morning. Isn't it just wonderful to see what is happening to our town? Who would have thought we could have done this?"

The major took off his bowler and twirled it nervously in his hands.

"Oh, no, Major!" Josie exclaimed, her hand covering her mouth. "Has something bad happened? Has there been an accident? Is it Gabe?"

"It's bad, but it's nothing like that. We got a telegram from Austin saying the legislature is about to adjourn. We're so close, and Darnell can't get them to grant even a month's extension. We're so close."

"Is there anything that can be done? Does anyone know at End of Track?"

"Well, first thing, the town needs to have a meeting, and since the courthouse burned while you were out hobnobbing with the president—"

Josie smiled. "That's what I was doing."

"Anyway, I was going to ask your father if we could have the use of the dining room, but I see you are doing a brisk business. Maybe I can find someplace else. . . ."

"What time do you want the room? If the news gets out that the railroad may not get here, the people will leave as quickly as they have arrived."

"Thanks, Josie. I'll have our new marshal let everyone know it will be at five o'clock."

That evening, Marshal Jim Courtright, his new badge shining, stepped to the front of the dining room. He banged the butt of his gun on a table and began to speak when he had everyone's attention.

"Thank you all for coming on such short notice. I know everyone is busy, so I'm going to sit down and let Major Van Zandt tell you what has just happened."

"We have this telegram from Austin." Van Zandt held up the yellow envelope for all to see. "The Senate has passed an act of adjournment."

Groans and comments of regret came from the crowd.

"But, as we all know, it takes the vote from both houses to adjourn. Our valiant representative,

Nicholas Darnell, has put together a coalition of Texans who can see the future, who know what this railroad means not only to Fort Worth, but to all of Northwest Texas."

Boisterous cheers erupted over this news.

"There are those who, for whatever petty difference they may have with the Texas and Pacific, hope that this venture fails. Rumor has it that some may be in cahoots with Collis Huntington and Leland Stanford in their effort to have the Southern Pacific become the Southern Transcontinental Railroad.

"Nevertheless, Nicholas has one more vote than the opposition, so he can prevent the legislature from adjourning as long as he can keep every vote in line."

"Do you think he can do that?" someone called from the audience.

"It's his own vote that is in question."

"Not Darnell! He's one of us."

"Yes, Darnell. He is seriously ill, too sick to leave his bed."

"Did he cast a vote?"

A wide smile spread across Van Zandt's face. "He did. He was carried into the House chambers on a cot just so he could vote."

Now people cheered and applauded Darnell.

"How long can he keep that up?"

"He has sworn to keep it up as long as there is a breath in his body," Van Zandt said. "But that brings me to the next item. The Tarrant County Construction Company, led by Walter Roche and his people, did yeoman's duty last winter just to get the T&P to take notice of us. We proved that we want this railroad, and that we know how to work."

"Yeah! Yeah!"

"It is my proposal that we go back out to End of Track and show the T&P what we're made of. We did it once, and we can do it again. But this time, it's not going to be just a handful. All of us are going to get involved. Are you with me?"

"You tell 'em, Major. They'll hear the panther roar all the way to Austin!"

At End of Track, Gabe was sitting on a flatcar looking toward Fort Worth. He was tired, his clothes were dirty, and he couldn't remember the last bath he had taken. They had come so close. How could he tell Josie that the railroad had failed her? That he had failed her? How could he tell the town? But tell them he must, for not to face them would be the act of a coward.

With a sigh he hopped down from the flatcar, then walked back to his small office in the first boarding car. He was putting his paperwork and personal belongings in order when he heard a commotion outside. Stepping out of the car, he saw scores of wagons, carriages, buckboards, buggies, and horses coming toward him from Fort Worth. In the lead buckboard he saw Major Van Zandt, Buck Paddock, Henri, and the biggest surprise of all, Josie. He walked out to meet them.

"Can you use a little extra help?" Van Zandt asked.

"That's the understatement of the day. I know you've heard. There's been a call to adjourn the legislature. We're through."

"We did hear that, Captain Corrigan. But don't underestimate us. We are the people of Fort Worth. This railroad is going to make it into our town by the end of this legislative session or we're all going to die trying."

"I like your spirit, but there's no money. These men here working are preparing to strike camp and close up shop. Mr. Van Zandt, I wish I had the authority to hire you, but I don't."

"Hire us? Who said anything about hiring us?" Van Zandt asked. "My boy, what you see before you are three hundred volunteers. We've all but shut the town down, and just to show you how serious we really are, that even includes the saloons. All we need from you are the tools and the guidance. We'll double your work crew, put the tracks down, and take this railroad all the way to Fort Worth. That is unless Nicholas Darnell kicks the bucket—and every person who isn't out here is assigned the duty of praying that he doesn't."

Gabe ran his hand through his hair, smiling broadly at the prospect. "All right." He laughed, then pointed toward the flatcars that were loaded with material. "Let's get started. Major Washburn, Mr. Morgan!" Gabe shouted to the chief engineer and contractor.

"Yes, sir?" Washburn replied.

"Do you think you can find something for these men to do?"

Washburn nodded. "Yes, sir, I can!"

"Then, put them to work."

"This way, men!" Washburn shouted. "I've picks, shovels, hammers, spikes, rails, and crossties. You'll not be turned away!"

As the people of the town started toward the equipment car, Washburn looked over at Gabe.

"How do you propose to do this, Gabe? If we have to take time out to teach them what to do, we may never make it up again."

"Divide them up," Gabe suggested. "Put a new man with an old. That way we will increase our output, with no slowdown for learning, but remember, a lot of them are old hands at this. They worked last winter."

Gabe watched as the new crews went to work. Less than an hour after the townspeople arrived, End of Track was a beehive of activity.

Josie and the other women had brought food and extra water wagons, and Herman Kussatz had brought a beer wagon from Tivoli's. At first it was thought that they might have a break for a meal, but it was decided to feed the men as they worked. That way no time would be lost. Josie helped break the food down into servable portions, then went out with the other ladies to dispense the food. The men ate in place, gobbling down a cold piece of chicken or a ham sandwich and a quick beer before getting back to their labor.

When all had been fed, Josie looked around for Gabe and saw him standing by a flatcar, examining a paper he had spread out before him.

"Hello," she said as she approached.

Gabe turned toward her with a huge smile. "If I weren't so dirty and the fleas weren't so thick and there weren't six hundred men here, I'd give you the biggest kiss, right here and now."

"Have you missed me?"

"No, not much. Just with every breath I take."

Josie laughed, then she stepped in to him and kissed him, a chaste peck only, which she wished she could expand.

"Are we going to make it?" Josie asked.

"With all this extra manpower, we just might."

"Just might? That's the best you can give me?"

"We're going to make it, I promise you. Though . . ."

"Though what?"

"We've got Sycamore Creek to cross. Building a trestle is going to take a week, unless we can come up with some other idea."

"You will. And it's not going to take you a week, either."

EIGHTEEN

For the next week the railroad progressed at a mile a day, which was more rapidly than it had been built at any time since construction had begun. The residents of Fort Worth and the T&P employees worked around the clock, using torches at night both to provide light and to ward off mosquitoes. The women worked in shifts, preparing food and refreshments, sleeping when they could in makeshift tents or open wagon beds. Seeing the willingness of the people of Fort Worth to devote so much time and effort to the project seemed to energize the T&P crew, and they redoubled their efforts as well.

All the while, Buck Paddock brought daily telegraphic reports from Austin. Every day, Representative Darnell would be carried into the House chamber to vote nay on the resolution to adjourn sine die and aye on a motion to adjourn until the following day.

On one of his trips, Buck Paddock searched out Josie in particular.

"I think you will want to read this," he said, handing her a copy of the newspaper. "I believe Henri said you had the opportunity to meet the general. I'm sorry."

Josie wondered what Buck meant by saying he was sorry, and then she saw the headline:

A TERRIBLE SLAUGHTER OF SOLDIERS
Custer Attacks a Camp of Sioux
Custer, 15 Officers and 300 Soldiers Killed
The Greatest Massacre for Years

Mr. Taylor, bearer of dispatches from Little Big Horn to Fort Ellis, arrived this evening and reports the following: The battle was fought on June 25th, thirty or forty miles below the Little Big Horn. Custer attacked the Indians' village of from 2,500 to 4,000 warriors on one side and Col. Reno was to attack it on the other. Three companies were placed on a hill as a reserve. General Custer and fifteen officers and every man belonging to the five companies were killed. . . .

There was more, but Josie couldn't continue. She looked around for Gabe.

"Isn't it wonderful, Josie? The way everyone is—" Gabe saw the sorrow on her face. "Josie, what is it?" Gabe asked.

"It's General Custer," Josie said in a quiet, choked voice. "He's dead."

"Custer? Dead?"

Josie handed him the newspaper, and Gabe read the article quickly.

"Oh my God, Tom and Boston Custer were killed with him, and it says here his brother-in-law and his nephew were killed, too. What will Libbie do?" When he looked up, Gabe saw tears streaming down Josie's face.

"I think of him as we saw him at the ball in Washington, laughing, flirtatious, so—so alive."

Gabe opened his arms and drew her to him in an embrace.

Construction continued, with the men working day and night. Each day Buck Paddock would arrive at End of Track with the latest news from Austin.

"Yesterday marks the twelfth day in a row that Darnell was carried into the House chamber to vote no on adjournment."

"Hurrah!" the men and women shouted.

"We can't let this brave man down! He's doing his part," Van Zandt shouted. "Now it's up to us. We have to get these tracks through to Fort Worth!"

The men shouted their agreement, then went back to work.

Gabe stood with his hands on his hips, looking at the material that was to be used to build a trestle across Sycamore Creek. Washburn was standing beside him.

"That damn creek is going to determine whether we make it or not," Washburn said.

"We're going to make it."

"Yes, if Darnell stays alive long enough to keep the legislature from adjourning. But it's going to take a week to build that trestle."

"We're not going to build a trestle. With a trestle we will have to put in pilings and a superstructure. That will take too much time."

"What? What do you mean? You don't plan to run the tracks through the water, do you?"

"No. Look, I drew this out. What do you think?"

Gabe showed Washburn the paper he had been working on. Instead of a bridge crossing the creek, a series of squares were drawn. Gabe had drawn one of the squares larger so he could show what it was. The square was actually a box, a crib consisting of three frames on top of each other.

"I've measured the creek at its deepest point. I calculate we'll need eight of these. We can assemble them quickly, then put them in the water, and just run the tracks over them, sort of like stepping from one stone to another

"I see what you're getting at," Washburn said as he examined the drawings. "But where do we get the material to build these? It will take more than just ties."

"That's our supply, right there," Gabe said, pointing to the existing road bridge that crossed the creek.

"A good idea," Washburn said, "but how long do you think something like this will hold up?"

"Until one train rolls into Fort Worth."

The crib crossing took but six hours to construct, using ties and bridge timbers. Within half a day after the cribs were in place, the track had spanned the Sycamore. Once they crossed the creek, they were just a little over two miles from the Fort Worth city limits and were within sight of the steeple of the First Christian Church.

"Damn, wouldn't you know that the last two miles would have the worst terrain to go through?" Morgan said.

"We aren't going to follow the survey stakes," Gabe said. "We're going this way." He pointed to a dirt road that ran parallel to the right of way and was the main road to Dallas. "Lay the tracks on that road."

"We can't do that. The wagons and stagecoaches use that road."

"How many times will we be on the road at the same time? Use the road. That will save us a week."

"All right, if you are willing to take the blame for it."

"I am," Gabe said. Then, seeing Van Zandt, Gabe called out to him. "Khleber! Could you come here for a moment?"

When Van Zandt complied, Gabe told him of his idea to lay the last two miles of track on the roadbed itself.

"I think that would be a wonderful idea," Van Zandt said. "And you don't have to go two miles, only a mile and three-quarters." He smiled broadly. "This morning Mayor Day and the city council extended the city limits by a quarter of a mile. That's as far as we could go without legislative approval, and the way things are in Austin, you know damn well they wouldn't approve."

"We don't need them," Gabe said. "We're going to get this done."

From that point on, the ties were laid on the ground, supported at either end by rocks picked up from the right of way, and the rails were spiked to them. The route had several turns, some even saying it was as crooked as the proverbial ram's horn, but it bore up the rails. For the last two days of the construction, throngs of spectators went out to watch. Many of them had never seen a railroad or any of the equipment that was associated with it. Finally, the tracks reached Fort Worth.

Despite the great sense of satisfaction, the celebration was withheld as they waited for the first train to arrive. The entire city of Fort Worth and those who were within fifty miles were gathered at the track.

Buck Paddock had spread the word that there should be the biggest celebration the town had ever seen. He had asked for "boiled hams, light bread, cold chicken, salads, pickles, wines, anything, everything that is good," and the people had responded. The air was perfumed with the aroma of barbecued meat as Willie Lane and half a dozen other men had cooked as many cows to feed the thousands who were gathered. Beer and mint juleps were flowing freely.

Then, in the distance, they heard a sound that had never before been heard within the city limits of Fort Worth. They heard the whistle of a steam locomotive.

"I hear it!" someone shouted, though his shout wasn't necessary as everyone present had heard it.

Gabe, bathed and with clean clothes now for the first time in several days, was standing just inside a roped-off VIP area, with Josie at his side. Henri, Marshal Courtright, and the rest of the town dignitaries waited with them. Then, with its whistle blowing and steam gushing from its cylinders, Engine No. 20 arrived in Fort Worth, moving slowly over the hastily laid tracks.

"Lookie there, boys! Lookie who is blowin' the whistle. Why, it's ole Buck Paddock!"

Buck Paddock, leaning happily out the window, reached up to blow the whistle again.

"Welcome to Fort Worth, the Queen City of the Prairies," Major Van Zandt yelled, as he picked up a hammer and began beating on an anvil, while the crowd erupted with cheers.

The red engine had a diamond-shaped stack that poured thick black smoke into the air. Behind the engine were hitched flatcars loaded with the track workers.

Fireworks were set off and rockets blazed into

the sky. Men fired pistols into the air, and amid loud hurrahs people embraced each other. Gabe took Josie into his arms.

"You did it, you made it happen! Gabe, I am so happy," Josie said as she hugged him exuberantly. "I love you, I love you, I love you!"

"Will you marry me, Josie?"

"What did you say?"

"I said—"

"I know what you said! I just wanted to hear you say it again."

"Will you marry me?"

"Yes! Oh, yes!"

Their kiss was deep and passionate, but because of the celebration, only Henri saw it, and he beamed with approval.

The celebration continued for the rest of the day. The loud staccato of gunshots and fireworks kept up incessantly. The Fort Worth band played, the train whistle blew, church bells rang, blacksmiths beat upon their anvils, and men, women, and children shouted their huzzahs. Whiskey flowed freely throughout the town, and the bargirls and habitués of the saloons mingled with the solid citizens and wives united in celebration with not a thought or glimmer of separation between them.

Gabe and Josie walked through the town, exchanging greetings with the celebrants.

"We made it!"

"Watch us grow now!"

"The train is here, the train is here!"

One man stood in a horse trough, dripping wet, singing "Camptown Races" at the top of his lungs and off-key. *Doo-dah! Doo-dah! I bet my money on a bob-tailed nag, somebody bet on the gray.*

It was the same horse trough that Gabe had jumped into with Julius on that first day he had come to town. When they passed it, Gabe grabbed Josie's hand.

"Now I know what I did wrong. I should have been singing to you that day Julius and I were in that trough, and then you would have gone with me to California."

"That's all it would have taken," Josie said with a laugh.

Gabe and Josie continued down the street. Without commenting, they entered The Empress. For all the hoopla and clamor in the streets and saloons of the town, the hotel was quiet, save for the sounds drifting in from outside.

"Where is everyone?" Josie asked. "Ida? Julius?"

"No doubt they're still celebrating with everybody else. I don't expect many people will sleep tonight, just old fogies."

They walked through the empty lobby and into the deserted dining room.

"Josie, we need to talk about my—what I said."

Josie felt a quick stab of fear. Was he about to take his marriage proposal back? Was it something he had said in the throes of elation over bringing the train in and not something he had really meant to say?

"Yes?" she replied, her voice tentative.

"Did you mean it when you said yes? Or were you just caught up in the exuberance of the moment? Because I am serious. I want to marry you."

"Oh!" Josie laughed with relief, then threw her arms around his neck. "Oh, for a minute there . . ."

"For a minute what?"

"Nothing, my darling. Yes, I meant it. I meant it with all my heart! I will marry you!"

Gabe kissed her again, a long, deep, tongue-tangling kiss as body pressed against body. Finally, with both of them breathless from the kiss, they parted.

"We need to celebrate," Gabe said.

"Celebrate? What do you think is going on out-side? I doubt there has ever been a celebration anywhere in the country like this one."

"I'm not talking about the town celebrating, I mean us. We should drink to us. Do you have any more of your father's wine?"

"Yes. I just decanted a bottle this morning."

The wine and several stemmed glasses were sitting on a hutch against the wall of the dining room. Josie started toward it, but Gabe held out his hand. "No, you sit. Allow me."

Josie sat, and Gabe brought the wine and two glasses over to the table. He poured the wine for each of them, then set the decanter down and sat at the table across from her.

Gabe held his glass across the table and Josie brought hers up to it. Crystal rang on crystal. "Here is to the woman who has just made me the happiest man in the world."

"And here is to the man I love with all my heart."

Josie took a sip of her wine. Never had the taste been as smooth or as rich on her tongue. And never before had it made her feel so light-headed and giddy. Or, *was* it the wine?

Gabe lowered his glass and looked at her as if he could see into her mind and her heart. He drank her in with his eyes. "Josie, do you have any idea how you enflame my senses?"

"And do you know how much I wanted you to . . ." She didn't know how to finish.

"To do what?"

She searched for the right word, then came up with it. "Seduce me?"

Gabe smothered a laugh, causing him to spurt wine onto the tablecloth. "You wanted me to seduce you?"

"On the trip to Washington, and in the spring-house . . ." Her tongue seemed to grow thick and her voice weak. "I did everything I could to let you know that I wanted you."

"You have no idea how hard it was for me to hold back." Gabe reached across the table and took her hand in his. "My vow to your father haunted me for the entire time we were gone, but I could not break it, Josie. Had I done so, I would be unworthy of your love."

As they were talking, Josie could feel Gabe's thumb rubbing lightly on the back of her hand. With only that connection between them, she felt her insides beginning to melt.

"But you have fulfilled your promise to my father. Does the vow still hold sway?"

In answer, Gabe lifted her hand to his lips and kissed it lightly. Her hand had been kissed many times before, by gentlemen and men of consequence, but never before had it seemed more than a handshake. But this—this kiss from Gabe—filled her body with need, and chaos, and hunger, absolute hunger for more. It was almost more than she could stand. She wanted to say something, but she couldn't speak.

"My love, I am bound only by the limits you set."

Josie knew that she should not want him as badly as she did. On those earlier erotic excursions, he had set the limits, and that freed her of any personal responsibility. But now he was telling her that all restraints were gone.

Getting up, he walked around the table; then, leaning over her, he kissed her on the mouth, long, lingering, and so sweet that it was all she could do to keep from crying out. When at last the kiss ended, he stared at her with eyes so deep that she could look all the way into his soul.

Involuntarily it seemed, as if her finger had a mind of its own, she reached up to touch his mouth, those same lips that could generate such pleasure merely by their touch.

"I understand," she said.

Gabe took her face between his palms and said in a quiet voice that was soft, and oh so seductive, "Mere understanding isn't enough, my love. You must make a choice. Do we go on, or do we stop here and go no further?"

Josie stared at him, and for a moment the tumultuous thoughts spinning in her mind stabilized, and she saw things as clearly as if looking at them through a magnifying glass. From the first kiss on the rock, overlooking the Trinity so long ago, until now, it had all been building to this. The moment was at hand.

Lifting her chin, he looked deep into her eyes. "Now is the time, Josie. What do you want?"

"I want you, Gabe. I want everything that we have denied. I want everything there is. I want to be yours, totally, completely."

Gabe lifted her up from the chair and pulled her to him. She could feel the heat in his body, and she knew that hers was no less intense. He wrapped his arms around her and kissed her with fire on his lips, his tongue twining around hers. She returned the kiss in equal measure, pressing her body so tightly against his that it was as if she were trying to mold the two of them into one.

"Come," Gabe said, his voice husky with desire.

Strangely, until that invitation, Josie had almost forgotten that they were still in the dining room, that anyone could have come in at any time. Had he wanted to take her right here, right now, she would not have resisted.

A moment later, Gabe closed and locked his door behind him. Josie looked around, aware now that they were in his room, but she was almost unaware of having climbed the stairs to get here. It was as if they had somehow willed themselves here.

Once more Josie felt Gabe's lips against her own. Then his kiss left her mouth and moved to her throat. She could feel his breath against her skin, and as before, her body heated to his touch. But this was not like before. This time she knew that the great mystery would be revealed, that the ultimate pleasure that had so far been denied would, tonight, be achieved.

One hand went to her hair, and with it he held her head back as he continued to kiss her throat. The other hand began a teasing journey, down inside the top of her dress, inside the camisole, until he found one of her breasts.

"Wait," Josie said, the word almost an aching moan. Earlier, Gabe had asked her to make a choice, and Josie wanted him to know that the choice had been made. She was giving herself to him freely, so it was she who removed not only her dress, but her undergarments, presenting her naked body to him without shame or embarrassment.

Now she pressed her body against his, and though she knew that he would soon be as nude as she, she had the pleasure of feeling the rough texture of his clothes against her naked skin.

She kissed him again, and even as the hot seal of their lips remained unbroken, he shrugged out of his shirt, having some difficulty only because she would not let him break contact. Then, with a groan, he pulled away from her, and she felt herself being scooped up and carried in his strong arms the short distance to the bed, where he lowered her gently to the mattress.

"You are beautiful." Gabe's voice was thick with passion.

As she raised herself on an elbow, she watched him take off his boots, hopping around on one leg at a time as he did so. Under other circumstances, she might have laughed at the sight, but that laughter was quelled by the burning heat she was feeling.

The sounds of the celebration continued to drift in from the town, cheering whoops, the ringing of bells . . . or, were those sounds coming from the beat of her own heart, the drum of her pulse? She was staring up at him now, her eyes full of love and anticipation beneath half-lowered lashes. She enjoyed gazing at his body, a perfect sculpture of muscle and maleness, greatly intensifying the extreme sexual excitement she was feeling.

Now he took her hand and pressed her palm against his chest, then, slowly, moved her spread fingers down the length of his body in a soft, erotic slide. The fire inside her burned higher and hotter when her hand reached his erect shaft. She wrapped her hand around it, feeling its throbbing heat.

"This?"

"Yes," he said. "But wait, there is more, much more."

He raked his thumb across one of her nipples, and she shuddered. This was different from before because she knew there would be no abrupt end. This time she would not be left with that ache of being unfulfilled, and that knowledge made the sensations he elicited stronger, and sharper, more vivid, as he continued to roll the taut bud between his thumb and finger.

Her entire body was quivering, the throbbing ache between her legs a steady pulse that was mystifying and urgent. Part of her wanted him to hurry, to take that next, forbidden step. But a part of her also knew that this moment should not and could not be rushed. For the longer they delayed the conclusion, the more the enjoyment. The wait, the quest, was almost unbearable, yet the agony was so sweet that she wanted to prolong it for as long as she could.

Leaning over her now, he took her nipple into his mouth, suckling one, then the other, his mouth wet and hot, his lips tugging in a way that aroused the most exquisite sensations between her thighs. She closed her eyes as he continued, and the anticipation was almost more than she could bear. She heard a trembling moan vibrating through the room, and at first she didn't know where it was coming from, then she realized it was a moan of pleasure, coming from her own lips. She was lost, and she felt a swooping exhilaration in it.

"I want—I want . . ." Her words were a combination of moan and plea, but she didn't know how to say what she wanted.

"I know what you want, my darling," Gabe said.

Wet and wanting now, she allowed Gabe to spread her legs, then kneel between them. Grasping her thighs, he pulled her closer as he positioned his body into the welcoming vee. Josie felt the sensation of the first small penetration into her, and now, unable to wait any longer, anxious to have more, she opened her legs wide, rocking her hips to take him.

He thrust forward, pushing himself through the sweet, damp center of her. She felt a sharp pain, as if something had been torn, and she gasped in surprise.

"Don't worry, my love. It will last but a moment."

Even as Gabe soothed her with his reassuring words, the bliss returned, even greater than before.

"Are you all right? Shall I go on?" His voice was husky, and his lips brushed against hers.

"Yes, yes, please, don't stop!"

Josie wrapped her arms around his neck and pulled his mouth down to hers, and as his shaft plunged into her, she thrust her tongue into his mouth. She felt her inner muscles tighten against him, and moaning in complete ecstasy, she arched upward, meeting his strokes with her own, establishing a rhythm that sent exquisite pleasure through her. His movements grew faster and faster, and she knew that culmination was near. She heard herself gasping his name in throaty moans with every plunge as he slid deep into her, then pulled back, only to repeat the thrust into her wet cleft in erotic, seething strokes. She felt as if she were melting inside, a spring winding up, tighter and tighter. She wrapped her arms around his neck and held on tightly, those sensory-laden walls gripping the steel rod that was plunging and withdrawing, plunging and withdrawing. Then it happened.

It burst over her like a lightning bolt. Wave after wave of pleasure swept over her, and it was like her first time, but unlike it in that this was so much more than anything she had ever before experienced. She groaned with the pleasure of it, then realized by Gabe's own actions when she felt a shudder rack through him, then another, that he had found his release as well. He held her tightly in his embrace, burying his face into the curve of her cheek and shoulder, breathing in deep, contented gasps.

They lay there, male joined to female, as Josie drifted down in sensuous waves until the world returned, and she was once again aware of her surroundings.

The room was lit by the burst of an aerial rocket outside the window, and she could hear the sounds of continuing celebration. That was funny, she thought. For a while she had heard nothing, as her every sensory input had been diverted to her erotic quest for pleasure.

"If I had known it would be like this, I would never have allowed you to wait, vow or no vow," Josie said.

Gabe, who was still inside her, withdrew now, and leaned down to kiss her. It was not an erotic, eager kiss, but the kiss of lovers, and never before in her life had Josie felt so fulfilled.

"I love you, Josie. I love you more than words can express, more than life itself."

NINETEEN

Even though some said that the legislature had been kept in session by a ruse, a judge ruled that the railroad had fulfilled its commitment. Because of that, the state was required to grant the sixteen sections of land for every mile of track that had been laid.

Colonel Scott awarded Gabe his sixteen sections, and he intended to surprise Josie with this bit of information once they were married. His plans were to sell his property and use the money to build a track connecting Fort Worth with Waco.

For the next month, Gabe was busy supervising the rebuilding of the last miles of track, a building to be used as a depot, and a turning loop so that the trains that had arrived could turn around for the trip back. After that, trains began arriving twice a day, each filled with passengers—new immigrants to the now booming town of Fort Worth.

The hotel was doing more business than ever before. Josie was working behind the desk one morning when in came a portly man in a white suit, the stub of a cigar stuck his mouth. He was accompanied by a strikingly beautiful red-haired woman.

"Young lady, my name is Galloway, General Loomis Galloway. I've been told that this is the best hotel in town, and I do hope you can find accommodations for my daughter and me."

"I'm sure we can, General." Josie wrote the general's name in the register. "And what is your daughter's name?" she asked cheerfully.

"Marthalee."

"Marthalee Galloway," Josie said aloud as she continued to write in the register.

"Corrigan," Marthalee corrected.

Josie looked up in confusion and surprise. "Did you say Corrigan?"

"Yes. I am Mrs. Gabriel Corrigan. I was told my husband stays here."

Josie felt the breath leave her body. She dropped the pen and grabbed the edge of the desk. She felt as if she might faint . . . if she didn't throw up first.

"Young lady, are you all right?" Galloway asked.

"I—I," Josie stuttered, rendered speechless. "Please, you'll have to excuse me."

Josie stepped out from behind the counter and literally ran across the lobby, leaving General Galloway and his daughter standing at the desk.

It was all Josie could do to open the door to the

apartment and get to her room. There, she threw herself on her bed and wept loud, bitter tears.

She didn't know how long she had been there—the crying and hurt replaced now by a sense of numbness—when Ida opened her door and stepped into her room.

"Josie, child, what is it? What's wrong?" Ida sat on the bed beside her.

"Oh, Ida, I want to die, I absolutely want to die."

"Why, honey? Why would you say such a thing?"

"He's married, Ida. He proposed to me, he told me he loved me. We—we . . ." Josie stopped in midsentence. She was about to tell Ida that he had made love to her, but she held back. "I thought we were going to be married. He asked me to marry him and I said yes. But he is already married."

"You don't mean our Gabriel?"

"Yes, I do mean our Gabriel." Josie sobbed uncontrollably when she said his name.

"How do you know this?"

"His wife . . . she's in the lobby."

"Oh, Lordy." Ida wrapped Josie in her arms, holding her and rocking her, just as she had done many times when Josie was a child.

Gabe usually came back to the hotel at noon to have lunch with Josie. He saw Henri standing in the lobby when he returned.

"Now that the railroad is solvent again, and because we are no longer under any kind of time restraint, I've got a work crew working on the right of way that we bypassed. I also have some people building a legitimate trestle across Sycamore Creek." Gabe chuckled. "Before you know it, the Texas and Pacific will be a real railroad."

Gabe had expected Henri would laugh, or at least chuckle, at his reference to a *real* railroad. But Henri didn't even smile. Instead, he was staring at Gabe angrily. No, it was more than anger: it was hatred.

"Henri, what is it?"

"You dirty, rotten son of a bitch! How could you do that to her?"

"Henri, what are you talking about? I haven't done anything to Josie except tell her how much I love her and ask her to marry me."

"Don't lie, Gabe. Please don't lie. That only makes matters worse."

"Mr. Laclede." Although Gabe had been calling Henri by his first name for some time now, he sensed this wasn't a moment for congeniality. "I swear, I have done nothing to justi—" Gabe stopped in midsentence as he saw Marthalee coming toward him.

"Marthalee?"

Marthalee rushed toward him, then threw her arms around him and began kissing him.

"Oh, Gabe, the railroad made it to Fort Worth on time! Almost everybody said you wouldn't be able to do it, but I said, 'You all just don't know my husband. If he says he is going to do such a thing, he does it.'"

General Galloway was right behind Marthalee. He took the cigar from his mouth. "I have to hand it to you, Gabriel. I was one of those people Marthalee is talking about, but I was wrong. Just think about all those shares of railroad stock you have now. Why, you are a rich man, son."

"I'll leave you folks alone," Henri said as he glared at Gabe.

"Henri," Gabe entreated. "This isn't as it looks."

"I'm sure you have some story—just don't tell it to me."

"Well, who put a burr under his saddle?" Marthalee asked as she watched Henri walk off in a huff.

"You did, Marthalee. You did by coming here. What made you think I would ever want to see you again? What are you looking for?"

"Here, young man, don't you be talking to my daughter like that."

"You keep out of this, Galloway. Don't you say one more word to me, or so help me, I'll knock you right on your ass."

"Why, I'm not looking for anything, honey. Except to stand by your side and help you celebrate your great accomplishment, and to tell you the wonderful news I have to share."

"And what would that be?"

"We are still married, darlin'. Daddy got the annulment reversed. I am still your wife. Isn't that wonderful? And I have never been more proud of anything or anyone than I am of you."

She put her fingers on Gabe's cheek and smiled

at him. He was so angry that he wanted to hit her. As he looked at her, he wondered what in the world had ever made him think she was pretty. The conniving bitch.

"Did it not dawn on you, Marthalee, that perhaps I don't *want* the annulment reversed?"

"Oh, don't be silly, darling, that's just your pride talking. I know you were hurt when I got the annulment, so that's why I had Daddy get it reversed. You don't have to be hurt or upset or embarrassed anymore. I made a huge mistake, and I am the first to admit it. I'm just glad all this foolishness is behind us, and we can start over."

"It is not behind us, Marthalee. There is no way I am going to be married to you. Not now, not ever."

Gabe sat at a table in the dining room, watching Josie as she went from patron to patron, but not once did she pass by him. He stayed there until the dining room emptied and he was alone.

Finally, after he sat there for at least an hour, Ida came to his table. "Captain Corrigan, the dining room is closed."

"Ida, I have to talk to her," Gabe pleaded.

"I don't think she has anything to say."

"Ida, please, I'm begging you. Please, I must talk to her."

Ida went back into the kitchen, where Josie was busying herself with mundane tasks.

"He's still there?"

"Maybe you should talk to him, Miss Josie."

"No. There's nothing to be said."

"I've never seen a man, black or white, with such hurt in his eyes. What if he does have an explanation? Honey, two days ago you were the happiest woman on this earth. You loved Mr. Gabe with all your heart, and now you won't even let him tell you from his own mouth what this is all about. You owe him that much."

"All right. I will talk to him."

Trying to keep her face as expressionless as possible, Josie walked out into the dining room and over to his table.

"What do you want?" she asked in a flat voice.

"Josie, you've got this all wrong."

"Do I? Do you mean you aren't married to that woman?"

"We were married. That is, we were married, sort of."

"How can you be sort of married? Was it some temporary arrangement, just so you could sleep with her? God help me, that's what your engagement to me is all about, isn't it? It was just a way to get me to—to sleep with you."

"No, Josie, it wasn't like that. I promise you. I love you."

"Go away, Gabe. Please, just go away."

"Josie, I . . ."

Josie turned and walked away from the table. Gabe watched until the kitchen door closed behind her.

 ↶↷

Gabe and his "wife" had been gone for over a week. Josie felt betrayed and wondered if the pain would ever go away. She had thought that by staying busy she would gradually recover from her broken heart, but that wasn't the case.

She decided that the best way to get him out of her heart was to get him out of her mind. Anything that reminded her of him had to be removed. The first thing she saw was the drawing the artist had done of Gabe and her when they were in the coach on the way to Dallas. She looked at it for moment and tears began to stream.

"God, why couldn't he have been what I thought he was?" she asked prayerfully.

She recognized the naive expression the artist had caught in her face, naive because even then she was clearly in love with him. Then she saw the cookery book and the tea box she had gotten at the Centennial Ball at the President's House. She thought about General Custer and how she had been appalled that he, a married man, had been so attentive to Lillie Christiancy, and now she knew that Gabe had been doing the same thing. Only much worse.

Taking the book and the tea box, she held them in her hands. She wanted to throw them away, but she couldn't. After all, she had received them from the first lady of the United States. She would give them to Ida because someday, when Josie was old, she might want to try to relive that magical evening. Stepping out behind the hotel, Josie knocked on Ida's door.

"Miss Josie, come in," Ida said.

"I've been purging my room, and I want you to have some things." Josie held out the cookery book. "These are recipes collected from every state and territory in the entire United States. You might find something you will like in it."

"Well, I will treasure this, darlin', I swear I will."

"And this is a tea box. These things came from the President's House."

"Woowee. That's too precious for me to keep tea in."

"And this . . ." Josie held out the drawing.

"Oh." Ida looked at Josie with a wan smile. "What a beautiful drawing."

"I don't ever want to see it again. Tell Uncle Willie he can use it to get his next fire started."

"Oh, honey, no, I couldn't destroy that. I tell you what I'll do. Anytime I look at it, I'll just look at your picture, and not his."

Despite herself, Josie laughed.

Ida opened the tea box, then pulled out a small handkerchief. "Oh, honey, look at this. You might want to keep this. Somebody put in hours and hours of work on it."

Ida examined the handkerchief, which had the Great Seal of the United States government in the center beautifully embroidered in blue, white, and gold. Ida started to hand it to Josie, then stopped for a closer examination.

"Lord have mercy, child. Look at that." Ida pointed to the edging of the handkerchief—a series of crests of a white escutcheon with diagonal. Embroidered within the diagonal were three diamonds, each diamond with three fleurs-de-lis. "Isn't this the same pattern that's on your christening gown?"

Josie snatched the handkerchief. "It can't be. But it does look like it."

Josie and Ida went back to Josie's room, where Josie took the christening dress from her cedar-lined trunk and held next to the handkerchief.

"Look at that, child. It is exactly the same! Where did you get this?"

Josie's legs would no longer support her and she had to sit down. She held the dress in one hand and the handkerchief in the other as she compared the designs.

"I got it from the wife of the president of the United States."

Gabe had not gone back to Shreveport with Marthalee and General Galloway, though they had specifically come to Fort Worth to get him. Instead, with the annulment paper in his hand, Gabe went to Austin, where he met with the Texas State attorney general.

"That annulment certainly looks binding to me," William Walton said.

"Can the annulment be reversed?"

"Yes, I suppose it could be if both you and your wife . . ."

"Former wife."

"If you both agreed, you could petition to have the annulment reversed. Of course, it would be easier just to go ahead and get married again."

"I don't want to marry her again. I didn't want to marry her in the first place. And I had nothing to do with getting the annulment."

"You had to have been a party to it."

"No. I knew nothing about it until it was given to me. And now, General Galloway, the same man who had the power to declare the annulment, says that he has reversed it. Again, without my approval."

"I tell you what. You file that annulment with the State of Texas declaring that your marriage is now, and you wish it to continue to be, in a state of annulment. You do that and I can grant you a Texas document that will validate that condition. Then, there is nothing General Galloway, or the entire state of Louisiana for that matter, can do about it."

"How do I file it?"

"Give it to me, I'll take care of it," Walton said, "and I'll issue you a new one."

"Thank you, sir!" A wide smile spread across Gabe's face.

"No, sir, thank you. Who hasn't heard of your Herculean effort to bring the railroad to Fort Worth? That feat is not only going to benefit Fort Worth, it will benefit the whole state of Texas. This state owes you a debt of incalculable magnitude, and validating this annulment is the least I can do for you."

Gabe remained in Austin until the new document had been issued. He also had a certified copy made, and he mailed that copy, with a covering letter, to Marthalee.

> *Dear Miss Galloway:*
> *I address you as such because, as you can see by the document herein enclosed, the annulment secured by your father has been validated by the State of Texas. Without the consent of both parties, this annulment is irreversible. And I will never give my consent. You are forbidden, by law, from using my name. Do not attempt any further contact with me.*
> *Gabriel Michael Corrigan*

Almost at the same time Gabe was mailing his letter to Marthalee, Henri was mailing a letter to Mrs. Ulysses S. Grant, at the President's House in Washington, D.C.

> *The Empress Hotel*
> *Fort Worth, Texas*
> *August 20, 1876*

> *Dear Mrs. Grant:*
> *I beg, Madam, that you would forgive my intrusion into your privacy, but I take pen in*

hand to address you on a matter that may hold the answer to a mystery that has plagued my daughter for her entire life. I call her my daughter, but in truth she was left, a foundling, in my carriage, which was then parked in front of Boatman's Bank in St. Louis, Missouri. This event occurred on July 14th, 1851.

The circumstance of her birth, and the identity of the person who placed her in my carriage, has never been revealed to us. But recently my daughter had the high honor and privilege of meeting you at the Centennial Ball held at the President's House. All attendees were given favors of a cookery book and a small chest. Within that chest was a handkerchief bearing the Great Seal of the United States, surrounded by hand-worked edging of repeating crests. These crests, consisting of three diamonds, each diamond with three fleurs-de-lis, match exactly the crests that form the border of the christening gown my daughter, whom I named Empress Josephine Laclede, was wearing when I found her.

I cannot think but that there must be some connection between these patterns of crests, a connection that may bring an answer to my daughter's lifelong question. Please, madam, I know that a lady in your position must handle many letters from people petitioning your indulgence, and asking that you become an advocate for their cause.

> *My only cause is to find an answer. I would*
> *appreciate any enlightenment you may be*
> *able to provide.*
>
> > *Your obedient servant,*
> > *Henri Laclede*

Washington, D.C.

When Robert Douglas, private secretary to President Grant, knocked on the door of the president's quarters, the first lady's personal maid answered.

"Is Mrs. Grant in?"

"Yes, sir."

Robert handed a letter to the maid. "Would you see to it that she gets this, please?"

"Mr. Douglas, you know that Mrs. Grant won't be pestering her husband to do things for people, so there is no sense in givin' that letter to her."

"This is not that kind of letter. She may be interested in this one."

"All right."

The maid took the letter back to the sitting area where Mrs. Grant was reading the newspaper.

"What was it?" Mrs. Grant asked.

"It was Mr. Douglas, Mrs. Grant. He said you should read this letter."

"I told him, no more letters asking me to ask the president for favors."

"Yes, ma'am, and that's just what I told him, too. Only he said this wasn't that kind of letter."

Mrs. Grant took the letter with the irritation of one too often petitioned for aid. But, once she read its contents, the expression on her face changed to shock.

"Oh, my. Read this letter."

"Miss Julia, I don't have any right to read your personal mail."

"I beg of you to read this one," Mrs. Grant said, handing the letter to the maid.

"Yes, ma'am."

The maid began to read, and as she did, she began to cry, not aloud, but tears started rolling down her cheeks.

"What is it? Do you know anything about this letter?"

"Yes, ma'am. I know everything about this letter."

Fort Worth, Texas, September 1876

"What are you doing here?" Henri asked. "I wouldn't think you would have the nerve to show your face here, ever again."

"Look at this, Mr. Laclede," Gabe said, showing him a document. "This will prove that I am not married."

Henri took the proffered paper. "It's a little late to get a bill of divorcement after the fact, isn't it?"

"It isn't a bill of divorcement. It's an annulment. And please, look at the date."

CERTIFICATE OF ANNULMENT

Know Ye All by These Presents
That the marriage between Gabriel Michael Corrigan and Marthalee Elizabeth Galloway does not exist, and is deemed not to have existed. This union was declared void because there was no mutual consent of the parties. This annulment is final and uncontestable. Given this day, January 10, 1874, by my hand and seal.
Vernon R. DuPont
Judge, Caddo Parish, Louisiana

"Then, I don't understand," Henri said. "Why did that woman, and her father, say that you were married?"

"Because General Galloway is aware that by completing the railroad on time, I have come into a considerable amount of money. Galloway is not without some influence in Louisiana, and he attempted to have the annulment reversed so that his daughter might reap the benefits of my wealth. I have just returned from Austin, where I have met with the attorney general. I learned that once the document is filed in the state of Texas, it cannot be reversed without the consent of both parties. I am not married, Mr. Laclede, and in the eyes of the law, according to this document, I never have been."

"Did Josie know this?"

"No. This whole situation came as a surprise to me, too. I truly did not know that General Galloway had the power to pull me back into that loveless marriage against my will."

"She's in the kitchen. Go on in. No, wait, I should go before you." Henri smiled. "I will do what I can to smooth the waters."

Gabe paced nervously in the lobby.

Julius came in and, seeing Gabe, smiled. "Hello, Cap'n Gabe." Then the smile was replaced. "Wait a minute. I don't like you anymore. You did somethin' bad to Miss Josie."

"What did I do?"

"I don't know. But sometimes she cries when someone says your name. You did somethin' to make her feel bad, and I don't like that."

"You are a very good friend to her, Julius. I hope someday you and I can be friends again."

"Yes, sir, well, that won't happen till you an' Miss Josie are friends again."

Henri came back into the lobby. "Come on back, Gabe."

"How did she take it? Will she see me?"

Henri didn't answer, but he had called him Gabe, not Captain Corrigan. And the expression on Henre's face gave him some hope. Gabe moved quickly into the kitchen, where he saw both Josie and Ida standing.

"Is it true?" Josie asked. "You're not married?"

"Yes, that's what the document says."

"But, why didn't you tell me about this before?"

"Josie, do you remember what Victoria said in Dallas when we attended her talk? How you could have love without marriage, but you couldn't have a marriage without love? That's what I had with Marthalee. I had a marriage without love."

"Then, why did you marry her?"

"Because, God help me, I just didn't know how to get out of it."

"Do you really want to marry me, Gabe? Did you mean it when you asked?"

Gabe took a velvet pouch from his pocket. "I want to marry you more than I have ever wanted anything in my life." He withdrew a ring from the pouch. "I want you to wear this diamond ring as a symbol of my love and my commitment to you."

Gabe slipped the ring on her finger, and she held it up to look at its sparkle. But the sparkle in her eyes was even greater.

"Miss Josie, Mr. Henri says you better get out to the lobby," Julius said. "There's a lady who wants to see you, but I don't know how she can see anything. Her eyes are real funny. She's got lots of soldiers with her, too."

"What? What is it about?"

"I don't know. I just know Mr. Henri said to come get you, quick."

Curious as to the strange summons, Josie, Gabe, and Ida hurried out. There, standing in the lobby of Josie's father's own hotel, was the wife of the president of the United States.

"Mrs. Grant!" Josie said.

"Josie, this is my sister Ellen, whom you met at the Centennial Ball, and this is my old and dear friend Doaney Waters," Mrs. Grant said.

"Lord, child," Doaney said, tears streaming down her face. "The last time I held you, you were just a baby, a sweet, precious baby."

"The last time you held me?" Josie asked, now totally confused.

"I am the one who put you in Mr. Laclede's carriage."

Josie gasped. "Then, you know my mother. Where is she?"

"Your mother, our baby sister, is dead, Josie."

"Your sister?" Josie's voice was strained, and she felt a weakness in her knees. Her heart was pounding furiously, and Gabe steadied her as her face became pale.

"Yes. Your mother was our baby sister, little Mary. I am your aunt Julia, and this is your aunt Ellen."

Doaney told the story then, as all gathered around, listening to the voice that sometimes broke as she spoke.

"Mary was a good girl who fell in love with a good man. His name was Jean Marquette."

"Jean Marquette? I knew him!" Henri said. "The son of Judge Marquette. But he was killed, wasn't he? Jumping a horse?"

"Yes, sir, that was him," Doaney said. "And when he died, it broke Mary's heart. At the time, she didn't know she was with child. She came to me, afraid of what would happen if anybody found out. I helped her hide it. Then, when her time came"—Doaney looked over at Josie—"I delivered the child. Honey, my black face was the first thing you saw when you came into this world.

"I kept you in my cabin until the time came when Mary had to make a decision. It broke her heart to give you up, but we chose you, Mr. Laclede, even though you had lost your wife. Everybody knew what a good man you were, and we knew that if you took the baby, you would give her a good home and raise her proper."

"And he did." Josie looked over at Henri, her eyes glistening with tears. "I could not possibly have had a better home, or a more loving and caring father."

"Your mama had you christened at a little church that was just for slaves. Then, when it came time to put you in the carriage, it was Mary's idea to leave you in the christening gown. I think she wanted to give you a little something that would connect you to her."

"I knew it!" Josie said. "So many times over the years, I have held that gown close to me, knowing that it was somehow a tie to my mother."

"It was a family heirloom," Julia said. "All of us were christened in that gown, and we intended to christen all our children in it as well. But only Frederick was able to wear it. We couldn't find it for the other children, and nobody ever knew what happened to it."

"I'm sorry," Josie said.

"Don't be sorry, dear," Mrs. Grant said. "It is yours, it has been your only legacy. And, praise be, that dress brought you back to us, your family."

"Miss Mary took the cholera and died less than a year after you were born," Doaney said, continuing the story. "I kept up with you for a few years. Then, when Miss Julia moved to Galena, I left St. Louis. You were still but a child and I had no way of watching over you." Doaney looked over at Ida. "I knew that you were helping Mr. Laclede take care of her, but I couldn't say anything to you without giving away Miss Mary. And I know that my sweet little Mary and her Jean Marquette have gotten together in heaven, and they look down at the wonderful daughter they produced."

"Doaney, thank you for choosing me. You have no idea what a joy Josie has been. She has made my life complete." Henri took Doaney in his arms and held her tight. He was visibly shaken by the revelations that he had just heard. "And thank you, Mrs. Grant, for allowing my daughter to learn this beautiful story."

"Well, this, I would say, is a story with a happy ending," Mrs. Grant said.

EPILOGUE

Nobody in Fort Worth had ever seen such a train. The engine was shining red with brass trim, and in gold lettering just under the cab windows was the name of the engine, the TOM SCOTT. The tender was also red, but the gold lettering on it read TEXAS AND PACIFIC RAILWAY.

Behind the tender was a crew car, housing engineers, firemen, brakemen, and porters, as well as a complete kitchen staff. Next came three private cars, two consisting of eight bedrooms each, and the third car an elegant palace car with comfortable seats and a dining room. For two days, the train sat on a side track at the nearly completed depot, and almost everyone in town came to stare in awe at the shining marvel.

The special train had been sent by Colonel Thomas Scott to transport Gabe and Josie and their entourage to Washington, D.C, where they were to be married in the White House as special guests of President and Mrs. Grant. The wedding party consisted of Henri; Willie, Ida, and Julius; Major Van Zandt and his wife, Mattie; Hannah and her parents, Enoch and Jenny Welch; and Buckley Paddock.

Jenny, who made a brandy-soaked cake for every wedding that took place in Fort Worth, was taking a cake that would be used at Josie's reception.

"Just think," Jenny said. "My cake will be served at the President's House. Oh, do you think the president will eat any of it?"

"I'm sure he will, Mama," Hannah said.

"I can't believe it, the president of the United States—eating my cake."

The train had three complete crews, which enabled it to operate night and day. Because clearance had been arranged with every railroad they would encounter, the only stops the train would make would be for fuel and water. The trip from Fort Worth to Washington, which would take an ordinary passenger seven days to complete, was accomplished in but three and a half days.

Colonel Scott and Anna met the train at the depot in Washington. Sean and Morgana Corrigan and Katie were there, also.

"I am so happy I'm going to have a real sister," Josie said as she hugged Katie.

"I never once doubted this would happen. I knew you loved him even before you did," Katie said as she returned the embrace. "I worked on an Irish spell, but it's not a curse, it is a blessing."

The wedding was held in the most majestic setting any woman could ever have imagined—the Blue Room at the White House. President and Mrs. Grant were there with Josie's newly discovered aunts, uncles, and cousins.

Tom Scott was Gabe's best man, Hannah was the maid of honor, and Henri, looking striking in his black morning coat, gave the bride away.

As Josie stood there by Gabe's side, listening to the Reverend Byron Sunderland, the Senate chaplain, intoning the words that would make her Mrs. Gabriel Corrigan, she was almost overwhelmed by it all. She had been reunited with a family she had never known, she was in the bosom of the family she had always known, and she was about to become a part of a new family.

"I now pronounce you man and wife," the chaplain said. "The groom may kiss the bride."

When Gabe took Josie into his arms, it was much more than the perfunctory after-wedding kiss. The trappings of the White House, the family, friends, and dignitaries who were the guests, faded away. It was only Gabe and Josie, and a kiss that fulfilled every dream of her past and promised every hope for her future. She had no idea how long the kiss lasted; it was an eternity that was over too soon.

"Are you happy, my love?" Gabe asked, speaking so quietly that only she could hear him.

"I have never been happier in my entire life."

She fixed this moment in her mind as a memory she would treasure forever.

Look for the next Sara Luck Western romance

TALLIE'S HERO

Coming soon from Pocket Books

ONE

The reception didn't end until well past midnight. Then, when the last guest was gone and the Duke and Duchess had withdrawn to their own chambers, only Tallie and Arthur remained in the great Badminton Hall.

"I was beginning to think no one was going to retire until breakfast," Tallie said with a big smile. "I'll just go to our bridal chamber and prepare for you."

Arthur made no reply. Instead, he poured himself a drink, then looked at her over the glass when he lifted it to his lips.

Hurrying upstairs, Tallie found their rooms among the one hundred and sixteen in the house. Mrs. Ferguson, who had been Tallie's governess and caretaker since the death of her mother, was waiting for her when she entered the bedchamber.

"I'm so glad you're here," Tallie said as she embraced her friend.

"Let's get you out of your wedding dress and into some of these pretty things you've picked out." Mrs. Ferguson chose one of the most alluring nightgowns and held it up for Tallie. "I think Lord Arthur will really like this one."

When Tallie was dressed, she took a deep breath.

"Don't be afraid, little one. This is a rite that all women dream of, and your husband is a very gentle man. He will love and cherish you as only a husband can love a wife," Mrs. Ferguson said as she moved toward the door to let herself out.

"Mrs. Ferguson, thank you for taking such good care of me for the last ten years."

"I wouldn't have it any other way. Your parents would be proud of the woman their daughter has become, and I'm proud of you, too. Good night, my dear."

Mrs. Ferguson's words, *your parents would be proud of the woman their daughter has become*, played over in her mind. Would they be proud?

Here she was, married to a man whom she knew she didn't love. Perhaps that was the legacy she had been left by her parents. George and Millicent Cameron had been married for more than thirty years, and not once in the twelve years of her life before her mother died had Tallie ever seen an expression of love between the two of them.

Her father, a sea captain who had gone down with his ship when Tallie was a teen, was stern and stoic, unemotional, even at her mother's funeral, held at the parish church at Downe, Kent. When the young girl lost he mother, it was her neighbors Charles and Emma Darwin who had comforted her, it was not her father. The one positive thing he had done was hire Mrs. Ferguson.

It was she and the Darwins who helped to make Tallie the person she was, not her parents.

Every morning, once her lessons and chores were done, Mrs. Ferguson and Tallie would cross through the shaw of oak trees that separated the Cameron house from the Darwin house.

She still remembered the day Charles Darwin had given her a precious gift—one that had been her refuge since girlhood. Tallie had entered the drawing room, where the renowned author, with his flowing beard, gray-white and unkempt, was reclining on the sofa. An inviting platter of currant-filled pastries sat on a stool in front of him.

"Ah, Tallie, you are just in time. The plum-heavies are hot from the oven, and your Aunt Emma is just concluding her Bach fugue."

"My dear, did you practice your piano this morning?" Emma Darwin asked.

"Yes, ma'am," Tallie said as she took a seat on the floor in front of Uncle Charles, as he preferred to be called. "I loved the piece I played. I believe it is the most beautiful song Beethoven ever wrote."

"And what would that be?" Darwin asked.

"'Für Elise.'"

"I know that piece." Darwin began humming the familiar song so horribly off-key that one could not recognize the tune at all.

Emma shook her head at her tone-deaf husband's efforts, and Tallie hid her smile.

"I think we'd better start our new book."

"What did you choose, Uncle Charles?" Tallie asked as she moved to her favorite horsehair chair in the corner.

"I've chosen one I think you will enjoy. It's one of Jane Austen's books, *Lady Susan*."

"When Emma put the book down, it was well past six. Darwin rose from the sofa, and grabbing his cane to assist him, walked into the study.

"This is for you, my dear," he said, returning to the drawing room. He handed a red notebook to Tallie.

"Thank you." Tallie took the book and opened it to see blank pages. She looked back to Darwin with a quizzical look on her face.

"You study your lessons for Mrs. Ferguson, you practice the piano for your Aunt Emma, and I want you to do this for me. I want you to write something every day. Someday, I want you to write a story. And since you know how much I like happy endings, make sure your story has one."

Tallie was never without her red notebook. She had filled many pages, even writing a story about an orphan girl who had been adopted by a loving family. That story line had closely mirrored her relationship with the Darwins. And as she waited for her husband to come to their nuptial bed, she opened to a fresh page and began to write.

> *Helen waited expectantly for Lord Londonderry to come to their wedding bed. Lord Londonderry was a man who had proven his loyalty to the Queen by his exemplary military service. How lucky she was, a commoner, the daughter of a green grocer, to have won his love. And now, she was to share his bed, to be deflowered by . . .*

Smiling, Tallie laid the book aside. She wouldn't go any further until she had actually experienced this deflowering. In anticipation, she strategically placed a few drops of perfume on her body, one drop between her breasts and another drop on her stomach, just below her belly button. She laughed as she thought of Arthur's reaction when he discovered the scent of that drop. Then she lay back in bed, thinking of the great mystery that was about to be revealed to her, wondering what it would be like. She waited for Arthur to come to her.

When more than an hour had passed, she began to worry that something might be wrong, and putting on her dressing gown, Tallie left the room to search for her husband.

She found Arthur in the dressing room that joined the bedchamber to a small sitting room. He was fully clothed, sitting in a chair, staring into the flame of a single candle, a glass in one hand, and a half-empty bottle of whiskey in the other.

"Arthur?" she asked, the tone of her voice expressing her confusion and concern. "Arthur, is everything all right?"

Arthur looked over at her, and never had she seen such an expression of pain on anyone's face. He lifted the glass to his lips and took a swallow before he replied.

"No, my dear," he said. "Everything is not all right. I have made a huge mistake, and not for myself alone, but for you as well. I have forced you into a position where you must make a choice, and neither choice can be attractive for you."

"What are you talking about? What choice?"

"You must choose between a life of celibacy, or adultery. There is no third option."

"Oh, Arthur, what are you saying?"

"I'm sorry, Tallie." Arthur finished the whiskey that

was in his glass, then, taking the bottle, he rose and stumbled toward the door. "I can't tell you how sorry I am."

Texas Panhandle—Late summer, 1879

Jeb Tuhill, his brother, Jonas, and three other hands who worked for the Two Hills ranch, were separating out some imported shorthorn bulls that were going to stand as sire at El Camino Largo, a neighboring ranch.

"I don't agree with this," Jonas said. "Why can't Señor Falcon de la Garza buy his own bulls?"

"Pop wants all the herds to be stronger. He thinks these shorthorns have a better chance of beating Texas cattle fever, and the more there are on the range, the better we will all be," Jeb said.

"You could have talked him out of it—that is, if you'd wanted to."

At that moment, Travis Wellborn was prodding a bull, trying to force him into the chute, but the bull didn't want to go and, suddenly, without warning, the bull turned and charged the cowboy's horse. The frightened animal reared up and threw its rider to the ground. As the horse galloped away, the bull turned his attention toward the downed man.

Assessing the situation, Travis tried to reach the fence, but the bull was gaining on him. Seeing what was happening, Jeb urged his horse into a gallop. He grabbed his rope from the saddlebow and began whirling it around his head, making the loop larger and larger; then he threw the loop toward the bull.

The loop dropped around the bull's head and Jeb wrapped his end of the rope around the saddle horn.

"Dig in, Liberty!" Jeb called to his horse.

The horse, well trained for such things, held its legs out stiff, bracing against the pull of the bull. The bull was jerked up short before he could reach Travis.

By now, a couple of other riders were mounted and they, too, dropped a rope around the bull. Once stopped, they were able to lead him into the chute without any further difficulty.

"By golly, Travis! I thought you were a goner there!" Will Tate called.

"I sure would've been if Jeb didn't snare that bull," Travis said.

"My brother, the hero," Jonas teased, and the others laughed, though it was more a laugh of relief than of humor.

Jeb's rescue of Travis was the talk of the evening as the cowboys gathered around the embers of a low-burning fire, the smell of roasted meat permeating the air. The cook had barbecued a goat, and the men were well fed and satisfied.

"Yes, sir, ole' Travis's goose would've been cooked if Jeb hadn't roped that bull when he did," Will Tate was telling the others.

"You're a hero," Katarina Falcon de la Garza said as she approached the men. When she reached the fire, its glow reflected off her raven black hair and caused her flashing black eyes to sparkle.

"I'm not a hero," Jeb said as he took Katarina's hand and helped her sit beside him. "Anyone else would've done it. I was just in the right place at the right time."

Katarina, who was Felipe Falcon de la Garza's daughter, moved closer to Jeb and laid her head on his shoulder as his arm closed around her. He had met her when he first wintered a herd in the Palo Duro. The next year, when the Tuhills and Goodnights moved their operations from Colorado to Texas, the two had naturally fallen in together, and Jeb and Katarina developed a close friendship.

"That's my big brother," Jonas said, rather sarcastically, as he poured a drink from a jug of liquor that Señor Falcon de la Garza had brought for the cowboys. He took a swig of the tequila before he spoke again. "To the hero." Jonas raised his cup, and then threw its contents on the ground. "How is it that he's always in the right place at the right time? Can you answer that Katarina? What makes him so special?"

"Jonas, you ought to go easy on that stuff," Jeb said. He chuckled to ease the comment.

"You might get away with telling everybody else around here what to do, but you don't tell me," Jonas said. "I'm my own man. I don't need you for anything, and don't you forget it."

Just then, one of the cowboys jumped up.

"Dancers, form your squares!" he shouted.

"Come, Katarina," Jeb said, pulling her to her feet as he stood.

Katarina looked back at Jonas, who was once again filling his cup.

"Jonas, are you all right?" she asked in a concerned voice.

"I'm fine. Just fine," Jonas said. "Go on. Dance with the *hero*. You don't need me."

"I don't understand him, sometimes," Jeb said, as he watched Jonas head toward the bunkhouse. "It seems like no matter what I do, it gets under his skin."

"Jonas is jealous of you," Katarina said.

"Jealous of me? What have I done to make him jealous?"

"You really don't know, do you? Everything you do makes him jealous," Katarina said. "You're the only educated man in the canyon, and besides that you still do all the cowboy things better than almost anybody else. Every cowhand who is anywhere near the Palo Duro Canyon looks up to you. When there's a problem, who do they come to? It's not Jonas."

"That's because I'm older than he is."

"That's not a good enough reason. Your father is older than you, and yet you have the final say about everything. Papa knows that the bulls that are being put on El Camino Largo would not be coming if Jeb Tuhill didn't think it was the right thing to do."

Just then, the high skirling sound of a fiddle started the music, and the caller began to call a dance. He was clapping his hands and dancing around on the wooden floor, which had been put down on the ground, as if he were part of a square himself.

"Let's dance," Jeb said, glad for the diversion, because the direction of the conversation was making him uncomfortable.

There were only two women on the Two Hill ranch besides Jeb's mother. That was Edna, the cook, and Tess, the foreman's wife. Edna and Tess joined Katarina and an alternating cowboy to stand for the fourth women to complete one square for a dance.

Jeb and Katarina danced the first set. After that, he enjoyed watching her, her eyes flashing, her long hair swinging, and her colorful skirt swirling about her. She had to be exhausted, having ridden with her father and the men from El Camino Largo all day, but she danced with every cowboy who asked her. It seemed that she could make each man feel as if he were the most important person in her life. He admired that trait in her.

"Jeb," one of the men in the band called. "Why don't you come up here and play so Miss Katarina can dance for us?"

"Yeah, do it!" one of the cowboys called out, and the others mimicked the call.

"All right," Jeb said. "I'll have to go get my guitar."

"No you won't," Edna said. "I knew they'd ask you to play, so I brought it out for you."

Jeb looked over at Katarina. "It's up to you. Do you want to do this?" he asked.

"I love to dance," she said as she raised her hands over her head and struck a sultry pose.

Jeb removed his guitar from its red felt-lined case, handling it with care. After a bit of tuning he looked at Katarina, who took her position. He lifted his leg to put it on an overturned bucket, and resting his guitar against his knee, he began to play. His fingers were flying over the strings, the melody rising and falling as he thumped on the body of the guitar to keep the rhythm.

Katarina whirled and dipped as her boots made a staccato beat on the wooden floor. The strenuous performance of song and dance continued for more than three minutes, and then ended with a grand crescendo.

Their performance was met with loud cheers and applause. Just then, Jonas stumbled out of the bunkhouse in an obvious state of inebriation.

"You missed it, Jonas," Pete Nabro said.

"The hero again?" Jonas replied, slurring his words. "Nah, I didn't miss a damn thing."

Jonas went directly to Katarina and pushed aside the cowboys who were standing around her. He pulled Katarina to him and, in front of everyone, kissed her deeply, forcing her body back in a deep bend. Instinctively, she placed her arms around his neck.

Jonas pulled her up into an intimate embrace.

"You like that, don't you, Katarina?" He kissed her again with a crushing kiss.

Jeb stepped up to his brother and put his hand on his arm. "Back off, Jonas."

"Says who? Looks to me like the lady is likin' my attention. She's been waitin' aroun' for you to make a move, and where's it gotten her?" Jonas's words were slurred and indistinct. Once more he tried to kiss Katarina. This time, she turned her head to one side, but her arms were still wound around his neck, and Jeb noticed she was smiling.

"Come on, Katarina. I think it's time to call it a night," Jeb said, taking her by the hand and leading her away from Jonas.

"The boss man is telling us what to do, is he? Well, not this time, big brother. You're feedin' off your range. She's mine."

With that said, Jonas started swinging wildly. Jeb ducked under the swings, then picked Jonas up bodily and carried him, still flailing ineffectively, to the bunkhouse.

The next morning, Jeb headed toward the house for breakfast. He and Jonas had both slept in the bunkhouse, allowing Katarina and her father to use their rooms. When he went in, his father and Señor Falcon de la Garza were sitting at the table, where James

Tuhill was reading over some papers that Felipe had brought.

"Good morning, Jeb. Where's your brother?" Elizabeth Tuhill asked when he entered the kitchen. She was standing over the cook stove, watching bacon twitch in the pan.

"I expect he'll be along shortly."

"I understand things got a little rowdy last night," James said.

"It wasn't bad."

"Hmph. That isn't what Edna said when she came in this morning. She said Jonas got a bit out of hand."

"Really, it was nothing. He was just letting off a little steam. No harm was done."

Just then, Jonas came into the kitchen and went straight to the coffeepot.

"I don't need you to speak for me," Jonas said, and with trembling hands he poured himself a cup of coffee.

"Sit down, Jonas, and get that chip off your shoulder," James said.

"Where's Katarina?" Jonas asked as he took a drink of his coffee.

"She's still in bed," Señor Falcon de la Garza replied. "She was tired from the ride over and then the dance last night. I'm glad she'll have a few days to rest before we go home."

"Oh, then, we're not driving the bulls out today?" Jeb asked.

"No, take a look at this." James handed the paper he had been reading to Jeb, as Elizabeth set bacon, fried eggs, and hot biscuits in front of the men. Then, after filling their coffee cups, she joined them at the table.

The paper was an invitation to visit Charles Goodnight's ranch. With more capital from John Adair, the JA had grown to about one hundred thousand acres, making it the largest spread in the Palo Duro Canyon. Adair had tried to talk the Tuhills into expanding as rapidly as Charles had, but Jeb had thought it would be better to pay off their original note and own their land outright. As it stood, the JA and Two Hills were now the most efficient and prosperous ranches in the Texas Panhandle.

"Are we going?" Jeb asked.

"Of course we're going," Elizabeth answered. "How long has it been since I've seen Molly?"

Jeb chuckled at his mother's comment. "I guess that settles it. We're off to see the Goodnights."

"It's not just the Goodnights," James informed his son. "If you read on, John Adair will be there as well, and he's brought several of his English countrymen with him. It would be my guess that they know the kind of return John is making on his money, and they want to get in on this American cattle bonanza, too."

"It could be that, or maybe they're coming to us for investment capital," Jeb suggested.

"That's a possibility."

"When do we leave?"

"Will's loading the wagon now. Your mother wanted to ride, but Pattie's got a lame foot, so I think we'll leave her horse behind. You boys and Felipe will ride along beside us."

"Is Katarina going?" Jonas asked.

"No, I want her to stay here and rest. Anyway, she won't be up before noon, and when she does wake up, Edna can take care of her," Felipe said.

"I'll need to go over a couple of things with Travis,

and then I'll be ready to leave when you are," Jeb said as he finished his cup of coffee.

"I'm not going," Jonas said.

"The invitation was for all of us," James said. "I think you'd better come along."

"Pop, you know and I know that nobody will even know I'm there. Jeb's the only one Mr. Goodnight will listen to. He thinks Jeb knows everything there is to know about cows, and if he's trying to get money from some of these English dandies, you know how the conversation will go. 'Jeb, why don't you tell us a little bit about the profit and loss statements, if you don't mind,' and then my big brother will stand up and rattle off all the numbers. No, I'm not gonna go listen to all that bull. I'm stayin' right here."

"Who put the burr under your saddle?" Jeb asked.

"You did!" Jonas shouted. "Do you think I don't get sick and tired of it? 'Boy, ole Jeb sure got all the brains in that family. If you want somethin' done, and done right, don't bother goin' to Jonas. Jeb's the one you need to see.' Well, I've had enough. I don't plan to go over to the Goodnights and sit there and twiddle my thumbs while you play the big expert. And it's not just outsiders. Even you, Pop. You think I can't tell that Jeb's your favorite?"

"That's enough, Jonas!" James said sharply. "You're wrong. You're both our sons."

"I'm not going," Jonas said, folding his arms over his chest and slumping back in his chair.

"Well, then, suit yourself. It'll be your loss," James said as he rose from the table.